Death's Head

Hitler's Wolf Pack

Michael Alexander McCarthy

Rogue Maille
Publishing

Also by Michael Alexander McCarthy

The First War of Scottish Independence Series

KingMaker – Army of God

KingMaker – Traitor

KingMaker – Bannockburn

KingMaker – Death of Kings

Dedication

To Patsy – my number one fan!

'If the war should be lost, then the nation, too, will be lost. That would be the nation's unalterable fate. There is no need to consider the basic requirements that a people needs in order to continue to live a primitive life.

On the contrary, it is better ourselves to destroy such things, for this nation will have proved itself the weaker and the future will belong exclusively to the stronger Eastern nation. Those who remain alive after the battles are over are in any case only inferior persons, since the best have fallen.'

Adolph Hitler (March 1945)

'Every German is ordered to stand his ground and do or die against the Allied armies, who are preparing to enslave Germans. Every **Bolshevik**, every Englishman, every American on our soil must be a target for our movement. Any German, whatever his profession or class, who puts himself at the service of the enemy and collaborates with him will feel the effect of our avenging hand. A single motto remains for us: 'Conquer or die.''

Radio Werwolf Broadcast (1st April 1945)

1

It was like journeying backwards through time. David Strachan stretched back in his business class seat and gazed down at the familiar sight of the sun-baked Singapore skyline growing smaller below him as the British Airways Airbus A380 continued to climb and bank to the left above the glistening, shimmering waters of the Singapore Strait. He sighed subconsciously as he turned his thoughts to the journey ahead and the prospect of revisiting a place he had left behind almost twenty years before. He had taken the call in his office on the thirty-fourth floor the previous afternoon and had turned to stare out towards the Marina Bay Sands as his cousin tearfully informed him of his grandfather's death. His partners and staff in the private equity firm's offices would have been shocked if they had seen the extent to which the news rocked him back on his heels. Not a single one of them would have believed that the hard-bitten, mercenary and perpetually dour Scot had struggled to blink away his tears and had been forced to take a few moments to gather himself while his cousin chuntered on about the death of a frail, old man who was six months away from celebrating his hundredth birthday.

'Cancer?' He interrupted when he was certain that his voice would not waver and reveal his emotions. 'How did I not even know that he was ill, Irene?'

She did not miss the irritation in his tone and the accusation that it contained. In the short and awkward silence that followed, he caught the sound of a television in the background and heard enough to know that St Johnstone had just suffered a heavy defeat in a mid-week game against Celtic at McDiarmid Park. In spite of the great distance between them and the number of years he had spent away from his native country, he was still able to discern that the local news presenter was somewhat pleased with the result, even although he was attempting to appear completely professional and impartial. That brief snatch of banal, everyday life transported him back to a reality he had abandoned without a single backwards glance a lifetime ago. He pictured his cousin's house and knew that it would be unchanged from when he last visited it on rare trip home two years before. It would be as damp, rain-lashed and wind-blown as it had always been and the small garden would be as overgrown and unkempt as ever. It struck him as surreal that he would be leaving the heat, skyscrapers and steel and concrete order of Singapore to return to the cold, dreich disorder of rural Perthshire.

'He made me promise not to tell you, Davey.' She replied eventually, her voice both defensive and defiant. 'He made me swear. You know what he was like.'

Her use of the past tense caused his emotions to swell once again and he had to take a deep breath to steady himself before he spoke.

'Aye! It sounds like the old boy right enough!' He sighed as he scanned the paperwork strewn across his desk, his mind already turning to the priorities he would need to deal with to allow him to travel. 'I suppose I'll have to clear my schedule here, so if you can let me know the arrangements for the funeral and all that, I'll get my assistant to book my travel.'

Even although she was six and a half thousand miles away, the telephone connection did nothing to diminish the wry amusement and disapproval evident in her tone.

'You're not on, Davey boy! Not this time! I've been more than happy to keep an eye on him all these years, but you're no' delegating this to me. Not a chance! He was your Grandad, not mine! Get your arse on a plane over here and you sort things out!'

He could not recall the last time someone had slammed the phone down on him in anger. No partner, employee or even client would have dared to cut him off and risk his wrath, even although he knew well that he had given plenty of them good cause to do so. Neither could he recall the last time anyone had addressed him as Davey. He was strictly David to his peers and Mr Strachan to subordinates and those who sought to curry favour with him in the hope of capitalising on his talent for making money. He was Davey only to those immediate family members who had known him as a boy and that close, intimate and diminishing circle now contained only his sharp-tongued and spiky cousin.

He nodded his thanks to the smiling stewardess as she unfolded his table and placed a glass of champagne on a little paper coaster before him. He spent half of his life on planes travelling for business and his frequent flyer status entitled him to a privileged level of service. His beverage preferences were recorded on the airline's computer system and he was served before the other business class passengers without even having to request his drink. This helped him to ease into his habitual routine on long-haul flights. He would drink three flutes of champagne before dinner was served, have two glasses of Sauvignon Blanc with his meal and wash it down with a cold Heineken whilst watching one of the newly released films on the in-flight entertainment system. By the time the movie was nearing its end, the food and alcohol would have done its work and made him so sleepy that he would fall into a deep slumber that would last until the cabin lights were switched on for breakfast an hour and a half before the flight was due to touch down at Heathrow's Terminal 5.

With almost two hours to kill before his connecting flight to Edinburgh, he made his way to the British Airways First Class Lounge at the far end of the terminal. He was soon settled in an armchair at the window with a coffee and a bacon roll from the breakfast buffet. He scrolled through his e-mail messages as he ate. Nothing of any

4

great urgency had occurred while he was in the air and he was able to deal with the twenty or so messages by quickly scanning their contents and firing off curt and efficient replies to those that merited it and dismissively deleting those that did not.

He then turned his attention to the complimentary copy of the Financial Times and scanned its pages as he absent-mindedly wiped the tomato ketchup from his lips with a paper napkin. He found little that captured his attention. Most of the stories revealed only that the journalists concerned were not as well-informed as he was and only three articles covered deals he was directly involved in. He folded the paper, dropped it onto the table and turned to gaze idly across the airfield. The grey, overcast sky lent a bleakness to the scene that perfectly matched his mood. The news of his grandfather's death had left him weary with sadness and heavy with the guilt of having let contact between them unintentionally dwindle away to almost nothing over the past couple of years. He had never allowed himself to dwell on his emotions but was finding that he could not rationalise his regret away now that there would be no opportunity to atone for his neglect. His earnest intention of redeeming himself by making a big fuss of the old boy's centenary now seemed worthless and pathetic.

He cast his mind back to the day his parents and older brother were snatched from him with sudden, irreversible brutality by an eighteen-year-old with too little driving experience and one joint too many in his system to handle the power of his father's BMW. The old boy had been fit and well back then, even although he was already within a couple of years of retiring and picking up his bus pass. He had seemed to age twenty years that day and had appeared small and stooped as he wrung his hands at the side of the WPC who had accompanied him to deliver the news. He sighed as he remembered how the old man's eyes were so full of tears that they seemed to bulge from his head, but that he had held himself together through the sheer power of his will and had not let a single one escape and run down his cheeks. The old boy had choked back the misery and grief of losing his own daughter so cruelly and had instead focused on comforting his orphaned, teenage grandson and on providing him with a home and a family now that his own had been lost.

'Christ!' Strachan cursed under his breath as he wiped at his eyes with his fingers and glanced around the lounge to see if anyone was looking in his direction.

Like all teenagers, he had been too wrapped up in himself and his own misery to give a second thought to his grandparents and what they were going through. Only now, when it was too late, did he appreciate how much he owed them. Just when they should have been looking forward to all the joys of retirement, they were saddled with a moody, resentful and rebellious teenager. He cringed with embarrassment at the thought of the tantrums they had endured and the worry he had caused them with his defiant dalliances with drink, cigarettes, dope and motorbikes. He had eventually knuckled down to his schoolwork, but only because he recognised that academic success could win him a place at university and so enable him to escape what he saw as a disciplinarian and suffocating home environment. The regret and guilt threatened to overcome him again as he realised that his grandfather had never once uttered a single word of criticism despite all of his many provocations. He had taken great joy and pride in his grandson's every achievement and had been unfailingly helpful and generous in response to all requests for financial and practical assistance.

Strachan pushed himself to his feet and gathered his belongings with the intention of heading for the departure gate in order to break this unwelcome and uncomfortable train of thought. He knew that the coming days would be depressing and irksome enough without him sitting and dwelling on things best left alone. He strode towards the exit trailing his Rimowa aluminium suitcase behind him and checked the departure board for the gate for his flight to Scotland. He hissed angrily through clenched teeth when he saw that his flight was to be delayed by forty minutes but continued on towards the terminal and its many shops rather than return to his armchair and risk further needless brooding and self-examination.

His mood had soured still further by the time he arrived in Edinburgh. The plane had boarded an hour later than scheduled but had not actually pulled away from the gate for another hour and a half. He had eaten his third breakfast of the day on the flight, not because he was hungry, but merely in an attempt to alleviate his irritation and boredom. The greasy bacon and reconstituted egg lay heavily in his belly as he marched purposefully through the terminal building. With no baggage to collect, he was able to quickly make his way to the exit, slowing only to cut his way through groups of dawdling travellers and around bent-necked Asian students intent only on the screens of their phones. He cursed as he swept out through the automatic doors to be immediately assaulted by the biting, damp and frigid air of early winter in Edinburgh. He increased his pace and pulled his overcoat around him in a vain attempt to prevent the wind from chilling him to the bone. The brightly lit car hire centre seemed to offer the prospect of warmth and shelter but this proved to be illusory. The doors at either end of the building were held open to admit a constant stream of travellers and the resultant through-draught made it as glacial under the harsh, fluorescent tubes as it was outside.

Strachan joined the queue at the Avis desk and pulled his travel file from the brown, leather satchel that hung from his shoulder. The faintest trace of a smile played on his lips when he scanned the paperwork and saw that his Personal Assistant had reserved a prestige, executive vehicle for him. He had almost fired Yin Yin during her first three months in the role after a series of minor hotel and flight booking screw-ups. His partner at the time, Liliya, had persuaded him to give her another chance and it had paid off handsomely. The girl now knew his preferences better than he did himself. Any fleeting satisfaction from this thought was quickly replaced by growing irritation and impatience at the sole rental clerk's lack of urgency. He had dealt with the family at the head of the line quickly enough but was now engaging in unnecessary conversation with a middle-aged German couple. He restrained himself from tapping his foot in agitation while the spikey-haired youth provided amateur and inaccurate tourist information services but was visibly bristling with rage when he then moved on to flirt with his next customer, a thirty-something insurance agent eager for Edinburgh night-life recommendations.

Strachan slid his booking form onto the counter and tapped it with his index finger to distract the clerk from admiring the insurance agent's figure as she made for the exit.

'Nice, eh?' The clerk asked with laddish glee as he raised his eyebrows conspiratorially.

'I'm only interested in getting my car.' Strachan retorted icily.

'The XJ! Nice motor!' The clerk exclaimed in approval as he scanned the booking confirmation form. 'Let me just check that it's ready to go.'

Strachan watched impassively as the boy tapped away at his keyboard and gazed intently at his computer screen.

'The system's really slow the day.' The clerk commented without lifting his eyes from the screen.

Strachan briefly considered lacerating the irritating youth by questioning whether it was the system or the operator that was slow but decided against it for fear of prolonging their interaction.

Neil, as his name badge proclaimed him to be, then blew out his cheeks and slowly shook his head before announcing, 'It's no' here.'

'What?' Strachan snapped back.

'It was meant to be back in last night but it's no' been checked in.'

'Christ!' Strachan spat through gritted teeth. 'But the booking was confirmed!'

'Aye!' Neil replied with a nonchalant shrug of his shoulders. 'But what can you do if a customer's late? I can phone through to Glasgow to see if they have one, but it would be a couple of hours at least before we could get it here.'

'Just get me another car then!' Strachan demanded irritably. 'I don't want to be stuck here all bloody day!'

'Right!' Neil retorted, the smile melting from his face and his expression turning sulky in response to the harshness of the older man's tone. 'Let's see what we have available for you, sir.'

Strachan continued to glare at the top of the clerk's head as he tapped away at his keyboard pausing only to examine the computer screen and blow his cheeks out in exasperation before pecking away at the keys some more.

'I can do you a Ford Focus the now.' He finally declared. 'Or a Golf in about three-quarters of an hour.'

'A Focus?' Strachan asked incredulously. 'Are you serious? I booked a bloody Jaguar. If I'd wanted a bloody biscuit tin on wheels I would have asked for it!'

'I'm terribly sorry, sir.' Neil retorted in a tone that was devoid of any genuine hint of apology. 'It's been mad in here this morning. If you'd been even an hour earlier I could have done you a Merc or an Evoque. All I have now is the Focus.'

'That's not acceptable. I made my booking in advance and expect you to honour it. Get me the manager! Now!'

'Certainly, sir!' Neil replied solemnly before taking a step back from the counter. He paused momentarily, smiled his best customer service smile and then stepped forward again. 'Good morning sir!' He declared breezily. 'I'm Neil Drysdale, Centre Manager. How can I help you this morning?'

Strachan clenched his fists in response to the infuriating clerk's triumphant, shit-eating grin and felt himself tense in frustration. If he had not been so tired, cold and eager to be on his way, he would have gone toe-to-toe with the little shit. He took a deep breath instead.

'I'll take the bloody Focus.'

'Are you sure, sir?' Neil inquired gleefully. 'You should feel free to try your luck with one of our competitors if you are unhappy. One of them might just have a vehicle better suited to your needs.'

'Just give me the damned Focus!' Strachan ordered testily.

Less than twenty minutes later, he had his suitcase stowed on the Ford's back seat and the heating cranked up as far as it would go. He braked sharply as he drove towards the exit and swore in disbelief. The distinctive Jaguar XJ was parked in the car hire firm's bay with a sign hanging from the rear-view mirror. 'Drive me!' It stated in letters an inch high. 'I am checked and ready to go!'

Strachan seethed and cursed as he drove the Focus past Ingliston and out towards the M9 north.

2

The drive north did little to sweeten Strachan's mood and he found himself making constant unfavourable comparisons between the country of his birth and his adopted home. In addition to missing Singapore's superior climate and customer service ethos, he now had a new-found appreciation for the quality of its roads. The M9 motorway had been crowded and slow but it was a veritable joy compared to the winding minor road between Perth and Burrelton. Farm traffic had reduced the flow of traffic to a crawl for much of the journey, but even that frustratingly sedate pace had not saved his spine from being jarred by the impact of hitting some of the many potholes along the way. The side road towards Woodside had proven to be little more than a paved track and he counted himself lucky to have survived an encounter with a lorry on a bend just short of his cousin's cottage. His heart was still pounding as he pulled into the short, unpaved driveway and he could not quite believe that the Focus and the speeding lorry had been able to squeeze by one another on such a narrow lane.

He cast his eyes over Irene's little cottage as he pulled the keys from the ignition and released his seat-belt. It appeared completely unchanged from when she and Colin bought it almost seventeen years before. He remembered their joy at buying their first home and how their eyes had shone with excitement as they talked about their plans for renovating their little 'fixer-upper' and selling it for a profit that would swiftly propel them up the property ladder. He could see no signs of renovation. The wrought iron guttering looked rustier than ever and the orange staining on the harling around the ancient rone pipe looked ugly and permanent. Colin had upped and left within six months of baby Frazer's arrival and had disappeared to London leaving Irene to struggle on alone with both baby and 'fixer-upper' to contend with. Strachan had never liked the guy. He had thought him to be a weakling from the outset but had kept his own counsel as Irene lacked his ability to read people's characters and was smitten from her first sight of him. His lip curled into an unconscious snarl at the thought of the feckless bastard and the life of struggle he had condemned her and her son to.

He had offered financial help on a number of occasions but she was too proud and too stubborn to accept a single penny, preferring to instead eke out a living as a social worker with the council in Perth. This damp, little box had less square footage than the lounge of his apartment on Sentosa Island but he doubted that the mortgage payments left her with more than two pennies to rub together at the end of each month. She had driven the little Japanese car he was now parked behind for more than ten years and it had been old and second-hand when she bought it. He wondered how she would manage when it coughed its last as it must surely do in the not-too-distant future.

A muffled shout pulled him from this unhappy reverie and he turned to see her standing in the doorway wearing an expression that was half happy and half perplexed.

'I thought you were going to sit out there all day!' She chided him as he climbed from the car.

'I was reluctant to come away from my heater and venture out into the wind again.' He shouted back as he retrieved his satchel from the back of the car.

'Come and give me a hug.' She invited him as she came down the cracked and uneven concrete path towards him with her arms already spread wide.

He embraced her gladly and took comfort from the physical contact with the only living person who shared his grief.

'Come on inside!' She instructed him as she slipped her arm around his waist. 'The Singapore heat will have made you soft and I don't want you catching your death from cold from being out in this wind. I've got a pot of soup on for you.'

Strachan let her take the lead, a habit that came from their childhood when being a year older than him had lent her a natural authority.

'So, you're slumming it this trip?' She asked as she ushered him in through the door.

Strachan felt himself blush at the accusation, fearing that she had somehow read his distaste for her dilapidated, little cottage.

15

'I never thought I'd see the day when Davey Strachan lowered himself to driving a Ford Focus.' She continued, oblivious to his momentary discomfort. 'It must be a hell of a come-down from that Bentley you're driving in Singapore.'

Strachan muttered a non-committal reply and knew that his face had reddened further. He felt a pang of guilt at the realisation that the cost of his heavily personalised Bentley Continental GT could have paid off his cousin's mortgage ten times over. He had convinced himself that the extravagance was justified because he worked long and hard for his money but those arguments seemed thin and insubstantial here.

He watched her as she busied herself at the stove. She was still a handsome woman in spite of the new lines that had developed around her eyes and the few extra pounds that had crept onto her waist and thighs. They had been close at one time and, for him at least, there had been a spark between them in their teenage years. Nothing had come of it apart from a never repeated and never again mentioned semi-sexual encounter of the 'a look at yours for a look at mine' variety. He recalled that he had endured a thorough and somewhat painful intimate examination and received only a fleeting and unsatisfactory glimpse of downy pubic hair in return. A request for permission to examine the contents of her blouse had been firmly rebuffed and the episode brought to an abrupt close.

'This'll warm you up nicely.' She said as she placed a steaming bowl of chicken and vegetable broth before him on the rickety table wedged between the washing machine and the well-worn kitchen units.

He devoured the soup like a starving man. It settled a stomach so recently tortured by too much airline food and brought memories of childhood flooding back. Both his mother and his grandmother had made their broth this way with stock boiled from a chicken carcass and generous amounts of lentils, pearl barley, yellow splits peas, carrots, onions, potatoes and chicken pieces. He ate in silence and smacked his lips in satisfaction when the bowl was empty.

'You don't get broth as good as that anywhere else in the world!' He declared happily. 'Thank you for looking after me so well.'

'You're welcome Davey!' Irene replied with a smile before her expression turned more serious and her brow wrinkled in the way it always did when she was thinking. 'I suppose we had better sort out what needs to be done.'

'Presents first!' He replied airily as he reached for his satchel, relieved to have an excuse to put off the inevitable, depressing discussion for a few more minutes. 'I got this for wee Frazer.' He announced as he held a cellophane-wrapped box out towards her. 'A reward for doing so well in his exams earlier in the year.'

Her mouth dropped open in shock as she took the box in both her hands and gazed down at the brightly coloured image of the latest iPhone that adorned the front of the package. 'You didn't need to do that, Davey.' She admonished him. 'Take it back! It's too much!'

'No can do!' He replied with an emphatic shake of his head. 'I got it as a freebie through work. It'll just sit in a drawer if I take it back. I'm still stuck in the technology stone age and can't be parted from my Blackberry. At least it'll get some use if Frazer has it.'

'You're a bloody div and a liar, Davey Strachan!' She retorted with a mixture of annoyance and amusement. 'I know fine well that it was no freebie.'

Davey adopted an expression of feigned hurt and clasped at his chest as if he had been wounded by the accusation.

'The price tag's still on it, you moron! I can see that you bought it at the Dixons in Heathrow Airport.'

Davey held his hands up to defend himself. 'I did buy it at Dixons, but I used the loyalty points from my business credit card. I get them every time I pay for flights and hotels so I've got hundreds of thousands of them. The points are non-refundable so it would be a waste if I took it back. Let the boy have a wee treat, Irene. He deserves it.'

He saw immediately that the lie had worked. Her wrinkled brow told him that she was still wrestling with her pride but the glint in her eyes revealed that she was already imagining the look on her son's face on seeing his gift.

'It's very generous of you Davey. Thank you so much. His old phone is on its last legs and can scarcely keep its charge. He'll be absolutely delighted.' She laughed as she rose and turned to flick the kettle on and spoon instant coffee into two mismatched mugs. 'Bloody hell! He'll have a better phone than me now. The wee bugger will never let me here the end of it.'

'Well,' Davey began reluctantly, as he again reached into his satchel. 'That's no' strictly true. I got you one as well.'

'No!' She protested, putting her hands to her mouth and shaking her head. 'It's too much Davey! Far too much.'

'It cost me nothing.' He retorted. 'Throw it in the bin if you want, but I'm leaving it here. If I cannae treat my last living relatives then who can I treat?' He turned his head to the side and held his open palm towards her to show that he would brook no further argument on the subject.

'What about Svetlana?' She asked, raising her eyebrows as she spoke. 'Should you not be treating her?'

'Her name was Liliya.' He replied flatly. 'We went our separate ways at the beginning of the year.'

'Oh Davey!' She scolded him. 'Not another one? Was it the family thing again? Did she want kids?'

He nodded miserably in response, his sadness genuine in spite of the fact that he was deceiving her. It was true that Liliya was keen to start a family, but that maternal drive had not prompted her to clear her belongings from his apartment and shut him out of her life. Her sudden departure was more closely related to a gorgeous, twenty-eight-year-old, Indian content marketer he had met in the Citibank executive box at the Singapore Grand Prix. His drunken decision to accept her invitation to accompany her back to her suite at the Fullerton Hotel had been one that he had come to regret. Like Liliya, Vanni was intelligent and funny and boasted the face and body of a Victoria's Secret model. Unlike Liliya, she was married and had no interest in a relationship that extended beyond the end of the race weekend. It did not surprise him when news of his infidelity reached Liliya's ears. Singapore is a small place and its even smaller expatriate community positively thrives on gossip and tittle-tattle. The apartment seemed dull and empty without her, but it was also true that his heartbreak was tinged with relief. He knew that his reluctance to commit to a relationship was related to the loss of his parents and sibling at such a young age, but he never dwelled on that fact for long. He considered that such deep and painful matters were easier to bear if they were buried and left undisturbed.

'What about you?' He demanded, pulling himself up and away from his melancholy. 'Have you not found yourself a good man yet?' He smiled good-naturedly at the redness that sprung immediately to her cheeks and her neck in response to his teasing. 'I bet you spend half your time on Tinder swiping away in search of sordid wee hook-ups.'

'Away wi' you! She shrieked at him in mock horror. 'I'm no' on Tinder you cheeky bugger!' She fixed him with a disapproving glare before bursting into laughter. 'I have tried Plenty of Fish but I just seemed to attract the weirdos who still live with their mums or the married men just looking to have their ends away. I'm no' on it now. I might give it another try once Frazer's away to university. This place will seem very empty once he's flown the nest.'

Davey nodded sympathetically. 'You deserve someone decent, Irene.' He intoned softly. 'No' another prick like Colin. Someone who'll look after you.'

Her cheeks flushed even darker in the face of his concern and she jumped to her feet and set about changing the subject.

'Let me get that paperwork for you.' She announced as she left the kitchen and disappeared into the living room. When she returned, she solemnly laid a buff folder on the table in front of him and placed a comforting hand on his shoulder. 'The death certificate's in there along with contact details for the undertaker. The registrar's is just down from my work on the High Street, so I registered the death to save you the trouble. The hospital reckon that they'll release his body to the undertaker in the next couple of days. There'll be no need for a post-mortem given his age and the fact that he died in the hospital.'

Strachan's hand hovered above the folder for a moment as if he was afraid to touch it with his fingers. When he finally opened the thin, cardboard cover, the cause of his grief was laid out before him in harsh, bureaucratic black and white. He paused to gather himself before he spoke.

'All of this is a wee bit too real for me.' He croaked.

'Aye!' She replied in a tone that was defiant but also told him without looking that her eyes had filled with tears. 'Reality can be a right bastard sometimes.'

'What about the other stuff?' He enquired mournfully. 'I suppose that there'll be bills to pay, banks accounts to close and his will to sort out.'

'You'll probably find all of that at the house.' She replied flatly. 'I suppose you'll have to go through his things and find it all before you have the house cleared.'

'I was afraid that you might say that. I was rather hoping that I could avoid the place, coward that I am.'

'Then you'll just have to be brave, Davey. It's just one of things that you have to do in life. Just grit your teeth and get on with it. I'll be here if you need me.' She placed the flat of her hand between his shoulder blades and rubbed there to console him.

'I know you will.' He replied absently. 'I know you will.'

3

David reversed the Focus out of the drive and turned towards the A93, a winding, country road that would take him past the Meikleour Beech Hedge and through Blairgowrie and Rattray on his way to the house in New Alyth. He could have cut a couple of miles off his journey if he had taken the road to Coupar Angus instead, but he was keen to avoid having to lay his eyes upon the Grampian Country Foods chicken processing plant that lay on the outer edge of the town. The very sight of the place was enough to fill him with dread after long days of hard labour and excruciating, soul-sapping monotony suffered there during the endless summers of his university days. His uni pals had winced and recoiled when he told them what he did to earn the money to fund his studies. Most of them had parents with deep pockets and would never know what it was like to scrub dried blood from under their fingernails or wash the dust, feathers and shit from their faces at the end of a shift. He had no doubt that the experience had hardened him and contributed to his subsequent success, but even that knowledge left him with no desire to revisit the scene of his torture.

The short drive had a bleak and surreal quality about it that left Davey feeling that he was somehow detached from and set apart from the world. It seemed both wrong and absurd that the people of Blairgowrie were blithely going about their normal business completely unaware and unconcerned that life as he knew it was on the verge of unravelling. He found it hard to accept that their lives were unchanged when he was facing imminent confirmation that a permanent and ever-present foundation stone of his existence had been torn out from under him. He began to smoulder with irrational anger at the sight of two old biddies gossiping outside the supermarket and of three young bank clerks laughing and grinning at each other on their way to lunch at the Royal Hotel. The anger faded as he crossed the bridge over the Ericht and carefully navigated his way past the many cars parked along Rattray High Street. The sickening dread that lay in the pit of his stomach like a stone grew larger and colder the closer he drew to his destination. The distant Sidlaw Hills, once the sunny backdrop to his childhood, were now dark and foreboding beneath a grey and heavy sky as New Alyth came into view.

He exhaled sharply as he slowed to turn into the tiny village just short of the bus stop, the old red telephone box and the ramshackle building that had once, a long, long time ago, housed the village shop. He marvelled at how small it seemed now, the street barely wide enough for two cars and the slope far less steep than he remembered it from when he had propelled himself up it on his bike on a daily basis. He allowed himself a wry grin as he realised that he could name the occupants of each and every house, the Stantons, the Herons, the Grewars and the O'Malleys, though he doubted that any of them remained after the passage of two decades. He came to a stop at the junction and then edged out tentatively into Smith Lane, taking a wide arc to avoid scraping the hire car's paintwork against the corner of the Robertson house, which sat inconveniently and unapologetically tight against the road. He exhaled again and felt his stomach clench now that only a few short yards and a high, overgrown hedge stood between him and his cheerless objective. He crawled along in first gear until his Grandad's house came slowly into view.

The old place looked the way it had always done. His grandparents had bought the 1970s, two bedroomed, end of terrace villa during the first wave of Margaret Thatcher's sell-off of council houses in the early 1980s. They had immediately taken to home ownership with great enthusiasm and boundless energy and had happily devoted most of the next three decades of their lives to improving and upgrading the exterior, interior and the small garden. The old boy had always been good with his hands and, even after his retirement, was never out of his boiler suit as he set about painting, wallpapering, tiling, plumbing, roofing, insulating, planting and building. The fruits of his labours were still clear to see. Not a single slate was out of line, the pristine white walls were not besmirched by dirt or flaking paint and no weed had dared to sprout and make its home amongst the gravel on the drive or in the dark earth of his Gran's rose garden.

Nothing had changed and yet nothing was the same. For the first time in his life he was seeing the house as an empty shell, a soulless dwelling that no longer offered safety, comfort and warmth. What had once represented his permanent, ever-present sanctuary from the cruelties of the world was now little more than a collection of bricks and wood and slates. It had been reduced to an administrative footnote, a task to be performed and a duty to be executed. There was no-one to welcome him now and no-one to paint the shed in the spring or to tend to the vegetable patch and the short rows of raspberry canes and strawberry bushes.

Worse was to come when he retrieved the front door key from its hiding place beneath the terracotta flowerpot that had stood sentry on the front step for longer than Davey had been on this earth. He was assailed by memories before he had even set foot inside the little hall with its row of coat pegs. It was the doormat, of all things, that set him off. He was sixteen when he had arrived home from school in Blairgowrie just as his grandparents were unloading the shopping bags from the car after their fortnightly expedition to the Asda in Dundee.

'Look what I got, Davey!' His Gran had shouted when she saw him.

'It's a doormat.' He replied with a curled lip and a level of disdain that only a teenager can muster.

'I know!' She had replied happily, either ignoring his surliness or being oblivious to it due to the joy of her latest acquisition. 'Look at the thickness of it! It was four pounds!'

She went immediately to place it just inside the door, tapped at it with the toe of her shoe until she was happy with its position and then nodded her approval.

'It's meant to go outside ya daftie!' His Grandad had chided her as he squeezed past with three laden carrier bags grasped in each hand. 'You're meant to clean the dirt off your shoes before you come in the house, no' after!'

'Get away with you!' She had retorted dismissively. 'I'm no leaving it outside to get ruined in the rain! I paid fours pounds for that!'

'You paid for it?' His Grandad had quipped from the safety of the kitchen, his accent strong and unmistakably Scots, but still tinged with something foreign. 'I didnae see you reaching for your purse all afternoon.'

'Just ignore the old bugger, Davey.' She had instructed him with a smile as she reached for his shoulder and ushered him inside. 'Put your school bag in your room and I'll make us a cuppy tea. Then you can tell me all about your day.'

Davey pushed the memory aside, closed the door behind him and swore under his breath. 'Jesus! I'm no' even in the house and I'm close to bubbling!'

He shook his head in disbelief. He had been interrogated by the strictest banking regulators on the planet without so much as blinking. He had faced the RBI in Mumbai, the CBRC in Beijing, the FCA in London and a variety of hostile American attack dogs in Washington without breaking sweat. He had manfully stood his ground against belligerent CEOs, hard-as-nails board members and supremely arrogant billionaires but was reduced to jelly by a bloody doormat. He gave himself a mental shake and pushed on into the main body of the house.

The living room was exactly as it had been when he was a schoolboy. He had perched on that very sofa at his grandmother's side at the same time every evening to eat his dinner from a tray on his lap. The Grampian evening news had played on the same ancient television that now sat in the far corner of the room while they ate. The routine never changed. His grandfather would always sit in his armchair and provide a running commentary on the days main stories while they cleared their plates. He would disappear behind his newspaper the moment the meal was finished and would be fast asleep and snoring softly before Coronation Street was finished. The room was as scrupulously clean and tidy as it had always been, but he noticed a shabbiness about it, a hint of wear and tear that had not registered with him before. The indent in the cushion of the armchair created by years of the old man settling himself down caused Strachan to suddenly picture him there alone with only an empty sofa beside him and no ears to listen to his critique of the day's news reports. It was then that he realised why the place had that time-worn quality about it. Though he had cleaned and tidied and repaired, the old boy had not replaced or upgraded or improved a single thing since his wife had died. The cushions on the sofa and the coasters on the coffee table were the last ones she had chosen and the ornaments and photographs on the mantle occupied the exact same spots as they had ten or more years ago. A great wave of sadness threatened to overcome him as he pictured his grandfather seeing out his last years in what had become a lonely shrine to all that he had lost.

His eye fell on the sole item in the room that was out of place, the only object that his Gran would not have recognised if she was to walk through the door at that very moment. The small, garishly-coloured model of a Volkswagen Beetle sat on the sideboard between a framed photograph of his parents on their wedding day and a photograph of the whole family taken on the lawn in front of the Kings of Kinloch Hotel on the day his grandparents had celebrated their golden wedding anniversary. Strachan had been sent the little toy as a marketing gimmick by some car insurance company a little over three years before. It would have been unceremoniously tossed into the waste paper basket if it had not triggered a memory of the rust bucket his grandfather had bought and repaired for him when he was a student. His Gran had told him that the old boy spent weeks getting it running smoothly and readying it for its MOT. In a rare moment of uncharacteristic nostalgia and thoughtfulness, Strachan had popped the little car into a padded envelope along with a business card with, 'When I saw this – I thought of you!' scrawled on the back. He had forgotten all about it until this moment. A wave of sadness and guilt threatened to overcome him at the realisation that an almost inconsequential and instantly forgotten gesture on his part had been received with a far greater degree of significance by his Grandad. He let out a noise that was half sigh and half growl. He knew well that he had neglected the old boy but had no desire to wallow in that uncomfortable truth.

He turned for the doorway and made his way into the small kitchen to fortify himself with a strong coffee to combat the jet-lag. Here at least there must surely be fewer things to set him off and deepen his melancholy. The kitchen was uncluttered and almost clinical, a workspace rather than a living area. He subconsciously obeyed his grandmother's instruction from his youth by filling the kettle from the cold tap and not from the hot one. He opened the fridge with no real hope of finding any unspoilt milk there and was surprised to find that it was fully stocked. A litre of unopened milk and a carton of fresh orange juice sat in the door compartment and the shelves were filled with bread, pizza, cold meats, cheddar cheese, a family pack of Mars bars and a six-pack of Scotch eggs. He smiled at the sight of the last two items as their presence told him that Irene had been thoughtful enough to buy him a few of his favourite treats and had dropped by the house and left them for him. He laid the milk on the narrow counter and reached for the cupboard in search of a mug. The sight of the three mugs at the front of the shelf caused an involuntary sob to form in his throat. The first of these was a brown and white monstrosity bearing the legend, 'World's Greatest Grampy', a Father's Day gift Davey had bought for him out of his wages from his paper round. The chips and scratches in the enamel stood as testament to the fact that the old boy had used it daily for all these years. Next to it stood Gran's 'posh' Wedgwood mug, a rare extravagance purchased from Jenners on Princes Street just prior to the Millennium. His old mug was the last in line. It had come as part of a Cadbury Creme Egg Easter gift pack in the mid-1990s and had served as the vessel for every cuppy and hot beverage he had consumed at home from that day until the day he left for university. It choked him to see that his Grandad had it sitting there permanently ready for him on the off-chance that he might deign to visit and stay long enough to require refreshment.

It was then that he broke. He cried in a way he had not done since he was a boy. Safe from prying and judgemental eyes, he gave full vent to his grief, his loss and his guilt.

'Fucking hell!' He cursed when he was done, already beginning to despise himself for his weakness before the tears and snot were wiped from his face.

He was surprised to find that he felt better already. He knew that his well of sorrow had not yet run dry, but it no longer overflowed and he welcomed the return of his ability to exercise control over his emotions. He washed his face at the sink, reboiled the kettle and made himself a mug of strong coffee and accompanied it with a satisfyingly chilled Mars bar. Once he was restored and refreshed, he set about the task before him in his characteristically focused and methodical manner.

He had briefly considered employing the services of a house clearance firm to get the job done more quickly so he could return to Singapore with the minimum of delay. He had reluctantly rejected the idea as he knew that his grandparents would not have approved of strangers raking through their most private possessions. He instead planned to search the house from top to bottom to find any documents or items of value that would form part of the estate. He would then bag up clothing and linen to be donated to local charities and would give his cousin first refusal on the furniture and white goods before offering what was left to the Salvation Army.

He started upstairs with his grandparents' bedroom. He felt odd as he stepped inside this private space, the only room in the place that had been out of bounds to him as a child. The uncomfortable feeling that he was sneaking and snooping did not dissipate as he sifted through drawers and cupboards and he resisted the urge to hurry his task and instead proceeded carefully and respectfully. The old boy had kept all of Gran's clothes. Each item brought back memories of times she had worn it and he let them swirl around him, not brushing them away by hurrying his work but neither did he allow himself to dwell on them overlong. He folded them gently and placed them in the black bin bags before moving onto the next piece. His grandfather's things were both easier and more difficult to deal with. He owned less than a fifth of the clothes his wife had possessed, which made for less sorting and folding and provided fewer opportunities for memories and wallowing. The hard part was selecting and laying aside the clothes he was to be buried in. The suit and the shirt were easy enough as he had only one of each in a presentable condition. It was the tie that David agonised over. The black one was smart and formal but he decided that it was too dull and funereal. Most of the rest seemed to have been bought in the seventies and they were either too wide or too garish and he could not condemn the old boy to wearing any of them for all eternity. He decided on his Alyth Bowling Club tie in the end. It was smart in spite of its high polyester content and his grandfather had loved his bowling and the club's social life.

Darkness had fallen by the time he was done. Ten bags of clothes, sheets and blankets now stood on the stripped mattress. Another one sat at the foot of the bed half-filled with items that could not be donated such as combs, brushes, old socks and underwear and various toiletries and medications. David looked around the room and sighed to see that it was no longer his grandparents' bedroom. It was now merely a space filled with bags and furniture that would soon be whisked away by the charity collectors. He pulled the door closed behind him and laid his Gran's jewellery box and a shoe box filled with her keepsakes at the top of the stairs.

He pushed at the door opposite him and reached in with his hand to flick the light on. He was not surprised to see that the room had not been touched. It was just as it had been when he last left it with a train ticket for London in his pocket and the offer of a graduate traineeship with Standard Chartered Bank safely stowed in his suitcase. It now seemed almost fantastical to think that he had inhabited this tiny room for so many years. He shook his head in disbelief. It was barely large enough to accommodate a single bed, a wardrobe and a chest of drawers, but it had undeniably been his sanctuary when cruel fate ripped his life apart with sudden, brutal force. He had cried here and mourned his losses. He had healed and recovered and gone on to plot his escape. He had studied here and dreamed of a life less suffocating and dull.

His eyes fell on the worn, washed-out, pink bath towel that sat at the foot of his old bed. His eyes grew heavy with tears when he realised that it was his towel and that it must have been his Grandad who had folded it so neatly and laid it out for him. The towel had been bright red when they bought it for him the weekend after they took him in and it had remained exclusively his, even after several thousand washes had drained it of its colour. It humbled him to realise that the old boy had thought to make up his bed and lay out his towel because he knew that he was dying and that his passing would bring his Grandson home from the far side of the world.

'Christ Grandad!' He swore aloud as he sniffed and wiped the tears from his cheeks. 'It's almost as if you knew this would make me greet!'

He had reserved a room at the Lands of Loyal Hotel, an Edwardian country house hotel that lay just over a mile and a half away at the foot of the Alyth Hill, but he now decided that he would cancel the booking. If a dying man had gone to the effort of preparing his room, he could hardly ignore the gesture even for the comforts of four-star luxury. He was jerked from his thoughts by the ringing of the downstairs phone, the harsh and shrill intrusion into the house's hushed silence causing him to jump involuntarily. He thumped down the narrow staircase and snatched the receiver up.

'David Strachan!' He unthinkingly snapped out in the abruptly efficient greeting that had become a habit for him in answering the many business calls he received each day. He immediately realised that no hard-arsed brokers or corporate financiers would be calling for him on his grandparents' number and he tried to soften his tone. 'This is Peter Stachura's phone.'

'It's me.' The caller replied. 'I'm in Alyth and thought I might drop in and see you.'

Strachan's face creased in puzzlement. The caller's voice was one he thought he knew but he could not quite place it.

'It's Frazer!' The voice elaborated in the absence of any reply to his greeting.

'Christ, Frazer!' Strachan laughed. "I didn't recognise your voice. It's got so deep. It's no' as squeaky as it used to be.'

'Very funny Uncle Davey!' The boy retorted good-humouredly. 'I was in Alyth at a friend's and thought I might walk down and see you. If you're too busy then that's okay, but if you fancied some company?'

'That'd be great, Frazer!' Strachan replied enthusiastically, keen to grasp the offer of a very welcome distraction from his task. 'Why don't I drive up and get you? If we meet at the chippie I'll even treat you to a fish supper. I'm starving hungry and have a real notion for something that's been deep-fried to within an inch of its life.'

The three-minute drive to the fish and chip shop was like a trip down memory lane. The main street seemed narrower and shorter than he remembered it and the square, though undeniably picturesque, was nowhere near as extensive as he had thought it to be. Dimensions aside, much of the place was completely unchanged. David Sim's ironmonger's shop seemed to be frozen in time and he could see nothing that was different from when he had accompanied his Grandad there on his many trips to buy paint, varnish, nails, screws and a variety of other fixings and tools. The Royal Bank branch where he had opened his first ever account stood alongside it in apparent defiance of the trend for closures in small towns. The chip shop on the other side of the square was similarly unaltered, apart from the addition of some bright, new signage in the windows. He found Frazer already inside and joined him in the queue.

'I used to work in here.' He informed the lad once they had exchanged their greetings.

'Really?' Frazer responded incredulously. 'What did you do?'

'I was in the back room through there.' He replied with a flick of his head towards the door to the right of the counter. 'I peeled the tatties and cut them into chips.'

Frazer seemed to find this hugely amusing and he clutched at his ribs as he laughed. 'I'm just picturing you sat on a bucket flicking away with your peeler surrounded by a mountain of tatties.'

'Cheeky bugger!' Strachan retorted in feigned outrage. 'It wasnae the bloody stone age. There was a machine with an abrasive drum that rubbed the skin off the tatties and another one that cut them into chips. I just fed the tatties in and then collected the cut chips in buckets.'

'I preferred my version!' Frazer shot back with a grin.

Any opportunity for further cheek was cut off as they reached the head of the line.

Strachan gave his order to the red-faced girl behind the counter. 'Two fish suppers, a battered sausage, two pickled eggs and two cans of Coke please.' He then turned to Frazer and asked him if he wanted anything to drink.

'I'll have a Diet Coke if that's okay. Mum disnae like me drinking the full fat stuff.'

They took their food and drinks back to
Balgowan Terrace and ate it straight from the
paper as they sat side by side on the sofa. Neither
of them even considered settling down into
Grandad's armchair because it was inviolably his
even now that he was gone and would never
occupy it again.

Strachan belched loudly and rubbed at a
stomach swollen with fish, potato, sausage, salt
and vinegar and the best part of two cans of Coke.

'Christ! That was good!' He announced with
great relish. 'It'll have hardened my arteries and
taken years off my life, but it was definitely worth
it.'

Frazer smiled in response but did not speak as
he was still chewing and feeding the last of his
chips into his mouth.

'Your Mum tells me that you want to study
medicine.' Strachan continued. 'Have you
decided on a university yet?'

Frazer wiped at the grease and tomato sauce
around his mouth and swallowed the last mouthful
of his chips. 'Oxford if I can get a scholarship to
pay my fees. If I can't get any funding I'll try for
Dundee. I could get there by bus and keep my
living costs down so I don't need to take out such
a big student loan.'

'But Oxford would be the best?' Strachan
enquired, his eyes closely examining the boy's
face in order to assess his level of determination.

'Aye. It's ranked as the best medical school in
the world, but the living cost are crazy down there,
never mind the fees the English universities

charge now. I'm having to apply for scholarships, but the chances of getting one are pretty slim.'

'You know that I would pay?' He asked, watching Frazer intently to gauge his reaction.

'Aye!' The lad replied, his cheeks reddening as he did so. 'Mum told me you'd offered but she said no. She said it's a bad idea to borrow from friends or family. She reckons that it always ends badly.'

'But it wouldn't be a loan.' Strachan persisted gently. 'It would be a gift. I could probably write it off against my company's tax bill so it would cost me next to nothing.' This last part was a lie. If he paid it would come from his own pocket, though the cost of tuition and living costs for the whole degree would be unlikely to reduce his overall wealth by a single percentage point. A two-cent drop in the value of the dollar would cost him more.

'Mum wouldn't like it.' Frazer replied awkwardly. 'I mean, I'm really grateful for the offer, but you know what she's like.'

'Aye. I do that.' Strachan replied with a sigh. He did not vocalise it, but he thought that she was stupid to let her pride and stubbornness stand in the way of him smoothing her son's path with money he could well afford to part with. The lad had a big enough challenge in front of him without having money worries to contend with on top of the academic aspects. He let the subject drop and felt a pang of envy at the strong bond between Irene and her son. They were a tight unit and were close, loyal and devoted to each other. He was used to being alone but had not actually felt lonely until now.

He made coffee and he and Frazer chatted away for another hour and a half. They shared stories about Grandad, laughed at his foibles and eccentricities and, on more than one occasion, brought themselves uncomfortably close to tears. The young lad showed himself to have something of a talent for mimicry and he impersonated the old man with an accuracy that was imbued with both wickedness and fondness.

'If the rider is no good, it is the horse's fault.' Frazer intoned with mock solemnity, perfectly capturing Grandad's exaggerated Scottish accent with its subtle hints of the Polish of his youth.

Strachan smiled and shook his head. 'I can't remember how many times he said that to me. I've even used it myself!'

'He who rests grows rusty.' Frazer scolded whilst wagging his index finger in feigned disapproval.

Strachan laughed at the memory of being constantly on the receiving end of this rebuke. 'Jeez! It was impossible to have a single long lie in this house. If I hadn't surfaced by nine o'clock the old bugger would either come to wake me or would start hammering away at something outside my window. It was like being in the military at times!'

When it was time for him to go, Frazer declined the offer of a lift to Blairgowrie, where he was due to meet his mother, and Strachan had to satisfy himself with walking him to the bus stop and waving him off.

He had intended to continue with clearing the house after Frazer's departure but found that he could barely keep his eyes open due to the effects of jet-lag and the huge ball of fat and grease that now sat so heavily in the pit of his stomach. He finally admitted defeat and climbed beneath the fresh, crisp covers of the single bed. He was fast asleep within seconds of his head touching the pillow.

4

David Strachan could not remember the last time he had slept in until after ten o'clock. A habitual early riser, even on the weekends, it was unusual to find him in bed after six. He felt refreshed in spite of last night's unhealthy meal and had showered, dressed and nipped up to the bakers in Airlie Street to buy his breakfast within forty minutes of his feet hitting his bedroom carpet. The flaky croissants went down well with the coffee and fresh orange juice and he set about his house clearing duties with renewed energy.

He made such rapid progress during the course of the morning that he had to take a break and pay a visit to the Costcutter store on Airlie Street to buy more rubbish bags. It had been a Spar shop when he was younger and he had frequented the premises to exchange his pocket money for sweets and football cards and, when he was slightly older, to buy illicit beer and vodka from the assistant who was less fastidious about demanding proof of age from the town's spotty teenagers. He was standing at the counter paying for his black bags, a six-pack of Coke and a family size bag of Quavers when a voice called out to him.

'Davey! Davey Strachan!' The man said with a wide and expectant grin.

David felt his face redden and he cringed inwardly at the awful awkwardness of the situation. The man clearly knew him but he did not recognise him at all. He strained his memory and peered at the stranger in search of some clue to his identity. He reckoned that he was maybe ten years older than him and saw that he was balding and carrying around sixty kilograms more than was healthy for him.

'It's me!' The stranger declared, his smile slipping a little at the realisation that he was not recognised. 'Eric Bruce!'

Strachan knew the name and his mind raced as he tried to place it. He had gone to school with an Eric Bruce. They had sat together on the school bus each day until Eric, knowing that any level of exam success was wildly beyond his capabilities, had left at age fifteen to take up employment as a tractorman on a farm on the outskirts of New Alyth. That Eric Bruce had been tall and spindly with a full head of curly, blond hair. David frowned as he struggled to make the connection. It then hit him like a thunderbolt. Wee Eric Bruce's features were there in front of him but were stretched and hugely distorted by the man's excess weight.

'Eric!' Strachan finally greeted him as he continued to gape with horrible fascination at the change in him. 'It must be twenty years at least! How the hell are you?'

'I'm good, Davey.' Eric replied jovially, his grin now fully restored. 'I'm still at Moncur's.'

'Still driving tractors?' Strachan replied, trying hard to mask his surprise. He could not believe it was possible that the man had stayed in the same place, doing the same thing, for the same employer day in and day out for twenty years. He had not remained in the same job, company or continent for more than five years at a stretch and some of those spells had seemed interminably long and tedious. He could not comprehend how anyone could stand still for so long and still be content.

'Aye. I'm the head tractorman now.' Eric replied proudly. 'We just took delivery of a new one a couple of months back. State-of-the-art it is. John Deere 8R. Nothing like that auld Massey Ferguson I started with. I still won't let the young lads go near it! What about you? I heard you were out in Hong Kong or someplace like it.'

'Aye. I was there for a while but I moved to Singapore a few years ago. I'm just back for a visit. My Grandad died so I'm back for the funeral and to sort all his stuff out.'

'Oh, that's right!' Eric replied, his expression immediately changing to one of concern. 'Somebody told me that he'd died. He must have been some age though.'

'Aye! He was that.' Strachan replied, touched by Eric's evident sympathy and reminded of how quickly and efficiently news and gossip travels around small, rural towns. 'He would have celebrated his hundredth birthday come the summer.'

'That would have been something!' Eric exclaimed with a shake of his head. 'He cannae complain though. It was a good age right enough.'

Strachan took his leave and drove back to New Alyth. After a lunch of crisps and reheated pizza washed down with Coke, he set about the downstairs rooms with determination. The work did not require a great deal of close attention and he found that his thoughts wandered throughout the afternoon. The chance reunion with his old school friend had sparked a train of thought that was not entirely welcomed by a man who devoted little time to introspection and self-examination. It occurred to him that Eric, a man who had achieved and experienced so little since his schooldays, seemed entirely content with his lot in life while he, despite all of his successes and consequent financial rewards, remained unsettled and unsatisfied. He could not deny that he looked down on the tractorman for his lack of ambition, but he now wondered who was the happier of the two of them. Eric had only ever wanted to drive his beloved tractors and had achieved his ambition at fifteen years of age and had revelled in it ever since. He, in stark contrast, had yet to work out what he really wanted in life. It was a sobering thought and one that hung about him as the day wore on.

His sense of gloom was heightened by the nature of his task. The pile of rubbish bags stacked against the outside wall had grown steadily as he worked through one room after another. The worn and threadbare artefacts of his grandparent's existence seemed pathetic somehow. The coats, shoes, utensils, ornaments and other sundries they had deemed as essential to their daily lives now had little or no value and were fit only for the dump or charity shops. Apart from his Gran's jewellery box, three old mugs and a toy car, he had found nothing of any monetary or sentimental value worth setting aside. It seemed to render their lives pointless and inconsequential and their legacy hollow and non-existent. He paused when darkness fell and perched on the sofa to eat a makeshift meal of Scotch eggs and Quavers. He ignored the inner voicing chiding him for eating so much crap but promised himself that he would atone by hitting the gym when he returned to Singapore. He watched the national news as he ate, not out of any desire to catch up with current events, but merely so that the presenter's inane chatter would mask the unnerving silence emanating from the empty rooms that surrounded him.

He left the television playing in the background as he turned his attention to the last untouched part of the house. The small desk was jammed into the corner behind his grandfather's armchair. He knew that its three drawers would contain all of the paperwork and bills he would need to deal with. The top drawer contained stationery and the first of his grandfather's secrets.

'Naughty Grandad!' He said with a smile as he pulled the bottle of Johnnie Walker Black Label from the drawer.

It both amused and touched him to realise that his Grandad had felt the need to hide the evidence of his little vice. His Gran had been brought up with an alcoholic father and had never outgrown the discomfort she felt when in the company of even the most moderate of drinkers. It seemed that the old boy had remained discrete and considerate even when she was no longer there to disapprove. The cigarettes and disposable lighter were hidden at the very back of the drawer. Strachan pulled them out and shook his head. His grandfather had been a heavy smoker until just after his retirement and he had never ventured outside the house without tucking a golden Benson and Hedges pack into the top pocket of his overalls. His smoking days had ended the moment his heart murmur diagnosis was confirmed. Gran had made it her mission to police him during the withdrawal phase and would openly sniff at him in search of the slightest smell of smoke whenever he came indoors.

'I can't even sneak one on the fly.' He had complained to David on the day they had creosoted the fence together. 'She has the nose of a bloodhound and can tell if I have had so much as a single puff!'

It seemed that he had summoned the courage to defy her sometime after her death, but even then he had felt the need to indulge himself in secret. David placed the cigarettes on the desk beside the whisky and moved onto the second drawer. It was jammed so full of paper that the topmost sheets snagged as he pulled it open it and he had to reach in and push them down to unjam it. The bills had been filed methodically and it took him less than an hour to sort through them, pay the outstanding balances online or over the phone and transfer the services into his name until the house was sold. Only the council tax could not be resolved there and then as Perth and Kinross Council, unlike the utility companies, had not yet outsourced their customer service functions to a call centre in Mumbai or Pune.

The bottom drawer was filled with a bewildering array of tubes, packets, bottles and plastic tubs of medication. Even a cursory glance was enough to tell Strachan that these were the drugs his grandfather had relied on during his illness. There were painkillers, treatments for nausea, anti-heartburn medications and a range of other items he did not have the stomach to investigate further. Though he was not normally squeamish, he had no desire to dwell on what the old boy had gone through. He fetched the Costcutter carrier bag from the kitchen, hurriedly loaded the drugs into it and tied it shut. He deposited it in the hall with the intention of dropping it into the medical centre on the New Alyth road.

It was then that he noticed the notebook in the bottom of the drawer. It was a black, A4 size Moleskin notebook. He noticed that it looked brand new as he reached in and picked it up. This discovery unsettled him. He had been relieved to have cleared almost all of the house without coming across anything too personal. He had kept his emotions in check for most of the day and feared that this might represent a threat to his composure. His heart seemed to lurch in his chest when he opened the cover and saw the envelope carefully tucked inside. 'Davey' was written clearly in the centre of the envelope in his grandfather's unmistakable copperplate script. He stared at the envelope for long minutes before cursing under his breath. He dropped it onto the surface of the desk and turned for the kitchen with the intention of fortifying himself with coffee before facing whatever message his grandfather had decided to deliver from beyond the veil. He had filled the kettle from the cold tap and flicked it on when he decided that the occasion merited something significantly stronger than caffeine. He returned to the living room with a glass and poured himself a generous measure of Johnnie Walker. He swallowed half of it in a single gulp and closed his eyes to better savour the burning sensation as it ran down his throat and into his gullet. He then tore the envelope open with his forefinger, extracted the thin, lined notepaper and steeled himself to read it.

'Dear Davey

If you are reading this letter, then the cancer has finally beaten me. I have arranged my affairs as far as I could, so there should be little left for you to do. Any outstanding matters should be referred to my solicitor, Cameron Mackenzie. His office is on Airlie Street. He has my will and will inform you of my last wishes.

Please do not be angry with me for keeping my illness from you. You have suffered so much loss already in life and I wanted to spare you from the pain of witnessing my decline.

Do not be sad that I have gone. I have enjoyed a far better life than I ever deserved or dared to hope for. I count myself blessed to have won the love of a great woman and to have passed so many years of happiness and peace with her at my side. I pray that I will soon be reunited with her and with your mother and brother, for my heart has broken anew on each day spent apart from them. My family has been my greatest joy and you should know that my pride in you has long been a source of great satisfaction and comfort. I watched you grow from a frightened boy into a man of great ability and strength and have never been surprised by any of your many achievements.

It is your great strength of character that has convinced me that I should ask a last favour of you. While death no longer holds any fear for me, its imminent arrival has caused me to spend long hours thinking of the past. Old voices that I have ignored for years and years now ring in my ears and remind me of deeds I would rather deny and of debts I would have preferred to forget.

I am now too old and feeble to lay these ghosts to rest and must ask you, my little Davey, to act on my behalf. I know that you, as a banker, will understand the necessity of repaying what is owed.

I have laid it all out for you in this book and ask only that you read it and try to remember me as the man you knew. Once you know the truth you must decide on what course you take. If you decide to burn it and put it from your mind, I will not criticise you, for that is exactly what I did myself for so many years.

Always remember that we all love you, Davey. Not just Gran and I, but your Mum, Dad and little Petey too.

We're all so proud of you.

Love,

Grandad.

David wiped at his eyes and reached for his glass. The old boy certainly had a talent for making him cry. He downed the whisky and let the competing emotions swirl around inside him. The predominate feeling was one of sadness for the loss of his mother, father, brother, grandmother and grandfather, and it was rendered all the more poignant by the message being delivered from beyond the grave. In life, his grandfather had rarely expressed his emotions openly, preferring instead to hide them away beneath an impenetrable, stoic façade. Strachan could only recall one occasion when he had come close to cracking. It had been eighteen months or so after his Gran's death when he had returned home on one of his increasingly rare visits.

'Do you miss Gran?' He had asked while helping his Grandad to put in a new gatepost.

The directness of the question had taken the old man by surprise and he had jolted his head back almost as if he had been struck. His eyes had filled with tears and the thin and ragged smile he forced onto his face had failed to mask the depths of his misery.

'Only when I am awake, Davey boy.' He had replied in a whisper. 'For when I am asleep I dream that she is still here with me.'

He then turned for the shed muttering something about fetching a smaller spirit level. David had been taken aback by his grandfather's reaction to his question and so did not pursue the subject when he returned a few minutes later. When set against this single, isolated episode, his grandfather's letter was nothing less than an unfettered outpouring of emotion. In those two short sheets of paper, he had spoken about his love for his family and the impact of the loss of his daughter and grandson more than he had in the whole of David's life. He was struggling to process it all and was quite overwhelmed by it.

There was also the warm glow of pride at the rare praise from his grandfather. It surprised him that the old boy's approval still meant so much to him. Even the occasion of his graduation had succeeded in eliciting only faint, indirect praise from him. This was in spite of the fact that he was the first member of his family to ever earn a university degree.

'I think it is worth it.' He had said with a smile when David presented him with the invoices for the gown hire and graduation photographs and apologised for the exorbitant cost. That was the sole articulation of his pride and approval and Strachan had gobbled it down gratefully. Even now, the memory of it made him smile with real satisfaction. The words in the letter made his heart swell with pride.

Though it was perhaps somewhat shameful and distasteful to admit it, the swirling emotions of sorrow, grief, pride and gratitude were quickly replaced by something far less laudable. It was his curiosity that drove him to read the letter again. His forehead creased with consternation as he read. What were the debts that needed to be repaid? Why did his grandfather not deserve the life he had led so quietly and so blamelessly? He flicked through the notebook and saw that his grandfather had filled almost every page with his neat and graceful handwriting. He began to read and, although it was already late, he quickly realised that he would not see his bed until he had reached the very last page.

5

'Where to start? I have agonised over this blank page for weeks and can find no opening that is satisfactory. I have no doubt that I would have continued to hesitate indefinitely if the deterioration in my health was not so plainly visible. I have even thrown the notebook back in the drawer several times having decided that some things are best left buried where they fell. Only the withering of my flesh and the ticking of the clock have forced me back here to do the right thing at long, long last.

How to unravel a life that was built on lies? I suppose that I must begin with the biggest lie of all and toss it out from where it has long been hidden and cast it out into the light of day so that all the others might follow it. My hand trembles at the thought of revealing the great secret I have kept these last seventy-four years. I have tried whisky and cigarettes to settle my nerves but neither has had the desired effect. It seems that I must close my eyes and make the leap without dwelling on where I might land.

Piotr Stachura died in Poland in 1943. He was beaten until every bone in his body was broken and then he was executed in the marketplace of his home village. His friends and family were forced to watch him die. His corpse was left to blacken and rot for two weeks as a warning to the others of the penalty for resistance. I later took his identity and used it to win the life that was denied to him.'

'What the hell?' Strachan gasped in disbelief as he turned to the cover of the notebook in search of an answer that was not there. His face was creased in consternation as he tried to understand why his grandfather would write such a thing. He had been brought up with the story of how Piotr had fled his native Poland after fighting in the war and of how he had settled in Scotland, married his grandmother and built a life for himself. He shook his head in bewilderment and returned to where he had left off.

'I was born in June 1920, the only son of Helmut and Hanna Wolff. They named me Kurt in honour of my maternal grandfather who had passed away from pneumonia the previous winter. My father was a school teacher in a small village on the German-Polish border to the north of Breslau. I enjoyed an idyllic childhood there. We were insulated from the economic hardships and the unrest that plagued the rest of the country. The schoolmaster's house had a large walled garden and my parents grew fruit and vegetables and raised chickens and goats to ensure that we never went hungry. There was never any money for luxuries and I remember that I had to wear my shoes until they had holes in them and were so tight that they hurt my feet. I did not mind and simply threw them off and spent my summers running barefoot with my friends. Those friends were the best I ever had. Heinrich Mueller was the village doctor's son and I loved being his friend because he had the sunniest nature of anyone I have ever met. He talked constantly and made jokes that would make us laugh until our sides were sore. He could charm the birds from the trees and was never bullied by the other boys despite his short stature and lack of strength. Manfred Wissler was the local lawyer's son and was the leader of our little group from the time we were in short trousers. He was tall, handsome and utterly fearless and was always ready to fight the biggest of the older boys if they gave him or us any trouble. He stood up for us without flinching and we loved him for it. He was also generous to a fault and never failed to share the allowance his wealthy father bestowed on him.

It is always summer when I remember those happy days. The three of us would run for miles through the forests and hills and imagine that we were Teutonic Knights riding out to defend innocent peasants and fair damsels from bloodthirsty foreigners. Like all boys, we were drawn most to those places forbidden to us. This invariably led us to cross the river to venture into the Polish village on the other side. It excited us to think that we were crossing into a foreign land, though there was little difference between that village and our own. We would often play and sometimes fight with the local boys and, in later years, chase the local girls. We grew up speaking

Polish as fluently as our mother tongue and developed a liking for the hot racuchy bought from the Polish bakers with Manfred's pfennigs. My mouth still waters when I think of those thick pancakes filled with apple slices and dusted in powdered sugar.

We were too young and stupid to appreciate what we had. From the age of twelve we talked of nothing but our desire to escape the quiet tedium of village life. We thought that our parents were insufferably dull and considered them fools to have chosen to live in such a small and isolated backwater. It never occurred to us, in our arrogance, that they might have had good reason to choose such a sheltered and untroubled place to raise their families in. Manfred had visited Berlin on a number of occasion when he and his family visited his uncle there. We would listen with rapt attention as he described the bustling streets and avenues, the cafes and clubs, the constant stream of motorcars and the shops that sold a range of goods and luxuries that were almost beyond imagining. He made us daydream with his descriptions of the city at night, its streets ablaze with light and the pavements filled with the fine and smartly dressed ladies and gentlemen who strutted and promenaded on their way to attend the opera and the theatre and to stuff themselves with delicacies in the finest and most expensive of restaurants. We were particularly fascinated by his tales of the streets filled with noisy and brightly lit clubs and bars and the painted ladies who displayed themselves in the streets outside. If we had known better we would have clung onto our safe and boring existence for dear life. Instead, we dreamed of running from it with all haste and with no idea of what we were giving up or what we were hurrying towards.

Though the remote and rural nature of the village shielded us from much of what was going on in the rest of the country, we were not entirely immune to its effects. My father complained at great length about the enforced changes to the school curriculum and raged about the Nazis' obsession with physical education over academic achievement and with their insistence on infecting every subject with their ideology. We were taught that Germany had not been defeated in 1918 but had been betrayed and our army stabbed in the back by Jews and Marxists. I recall being bored to tears by interminable lessons on the importance of 'blood purity' and on the necessity of securing a suitable and appropriate mate. I was similarly unimpressed by biology lessons which primarily focused on criticising the Jews, their lifestyle, their looks and their essential untrustworthy and treacherous nature. Having never knowingly encountered a Jew at that stage in my life, it meant nothing to me and I concentrated only on the clock while I willed it to move round more quickly and bring my suffering to an end. Even mathematics was not exempt from Nazi meddling. Questions about the weight of apples were replaced with ones about the number of bombs a plane had dropped on Warsaw, the international centre for Jewry, or how many homes could be built for decent Germans if only the daily four-mark cost of caring for the country's four hundred thousand mentally retarded people was no longer necessary.

My father stubbornly resisted this unwelcome encroachment for several years. He refused to change parts of the curriculum and insisted on continuing with his classes in Latin and English. He finally relented just after my sixteenth birthday when he was ordered to attend a Nazi summer camp for teachers. He returned from it a different man. He seemed to have aged ten years, though he had been gone only a little more than three weeks. He walked with his shoulders slumped forward and his eyes cast down upon the ground. I scarcely noticed the change at the time but would later recognise it as the demeanour of a man who has been utterly defeated and has lost the will to fight. There were no deviations from the curriculum when the autumn term began and the 'Heil Hitler' greeting became an integral part of the school day.

I paid little attention to my father's struggles that summer because I was distracted by another much more exciting development in our little village. Helmut Fischer, a retired policeman from Breslau, had returned to see out his retirement in what had been his boyhood home and decided to occupy himself by establishing a branch of the Hitler Youth for the local boys. We joined the group immediately along with every other boy in the village. There were twelve of us in total and, in spite of our lack of uniforms, flags and equipment, we threw ourselves into the group's activities with great enthusiasm. We spent that entire summer boxing, wrestling, running, swimming, walking, fishing, camping and learning survival skills in the woods and hills of the surrounding area. Old Fischer possessed a huge amount of knowledge and we greedily drank it in as fast as he could dispense it. We learned how to build shelters, how to track and snare animals, how to tell the difference between plants that were edible and those that would poison us, how to light and cook over an open fire and how to navigate both with and without a map and compass.

What excited us most was Fischer's old bolt-action rifle. He told us that it was a Gewehr 88 and that he had carried it throughout the war of 1914 to 1918 and we accordingly treated it as a sacred relic, imagining that every score and scratch along its length had been inflicted in combat under heavy enemy fire. We normally had to content ourselves with watching the old man fire at some improvised target given that he could not afford to buy cartridges for the whole troop from his modest police pension. He would, on occasion, reward one of us older boys with a single shot if we had pleased him by correctly answering a question on some aspect of ideology, winning a boxing match or catching a rabbit or a squirrel. We competed fiercely for the honour of firing that gun. Manfred triumphed more often than the rest of us put together on account of his physical strength and aptitude for any form of fighting. Heinrich, who we called Maus or Mouse due to his short stature, and I had to battle for the scraps and satisfy ourselves with the occasional win when we answered a question correctly, won a race or showed some skill in woodcraft. It drove Manfred mad that I proved to be a better shot than him and earned warm praise from Fischer each time I was allowed to put the rifle to my shoulder. I don't believe that Maus ever hit the target, but he treated his lack of skill as some great joke and drove old Fischer to distraction.

It took almost a year of the old man writing letters before he finally persuaded some old comrade of his to provide us with uniforms. We did not care that they were second-hand and already faded from too many washes. We tore into the ragged pile in search of something that came close to fitting us and fought off the younger boys until we had the shorts, shirts, caps and neckerchiefs of our choice. Manfred, as always, came off best and looked as if the uniform had been specially tailored for him. My shirt was a little too tight around the chest and I had to constantly pull it down to prevent it from looking permanently wrinkled. Poor Maus came off worst as usual and ended up with a uniform that was far too big for him and we teased him and told him that he should not wear his father's clothes. Despite all of this, our chests were puffed out in pride when Fischer paraded us through the village that afternoon. Everyone stopped to watch us march by and some even clapped and cheered. It was by far the proudest day of my life.

The euphoria lasted until the moment I entered the house and presented myself to my parents. My father lowered his book and slowly examined me from head to foot while my mother stood in nervous silence.

'Take it off!' He instructed me abruptly, distaste dripping from his every word. 'You will not enter this house again while you are draped in those rags.'

I opened my mouth in outrage and was intent on challenging the unfairness of his judgement but the hardness and hostility of his expression caused me to simply close my mouth again without uttering a single word. I fled to my room to shed tears of frustration and swore that I would devote all of my energies to escaping the bounds of his authority at the earliest opportunity. I might have rebelled more violently if I had not been aware that I was entirely dependent on him for my chosen route away from home and village life. Manfred, Maus and I had set our hearts on going on to study in Berlin and we talked about it endlessly. There was an uncomfortable irony to the fact that I was reliant on my father's active support to make this happen. Things were different in those days. Admission into universities was based less on ability or academic merit and more on the connections your family had. It was to my father's great credit that he set aside the animosity that had grown up between us and worked tirelessly to secure me my desired place to study engineering at the Technical University of Berlin. He had hoped that I would follow him into the teaching profession but was fair and decent enough to give precedence to my wishes over his own. I look back now and wish that I had shown more gratitude for his unselfish attitude and for all the hours he had spent in writing letters and telegrams and for the two journeys he made to Berlin to renew old university friendships and acquaintances to enlist their support on my behalf.

My joy was complete when both Maus and Manfred received confirmation of their places to study medicine and law respectively. Neither of them had much genuine interest in their father's professions but they accepted the necessity of following in their footsteps as a small price to pay for the exciting prospect of city life and all the opportunities and temptations that it had to offer. That last summer seemed to last an age and we counted the days as it dragged past at an agonisingly slow pace. Our excitement was such that none of us cast a single backwards glance towards our boyhood village as we set off on that journey to Berlin. The whole thing passed by in a blur and I remember Father, who had borrowed a motorcar to transport us and our baggage on the first stage of the trip, repeatedly telling us to calm ourselves. I was surprised to see a tear in his eye when he dropped us at the railway station. I had rarely seen him display any emotion other than anger and it unsettled me to see him upset. I would only realise much later that he was afraid for me. He pushed an envelope into my hand.

'For emergencies.' He said and I nodded my thanks for the money.

He then embraced me before turning on his heel and walking quickly back to where he had left the car. If I had known that I would never see him again, I might have gone after him. I might have said something more meaningful, but I did not. Our train was waiting and my friends were calling for me.'

6

David Strachan laid the notebook down and rubbed at his eyes whilst stretching his aching back. The platinum Rolex Day-Date 36 given to him by his partners for bringing in the lucrative Indian payment processing deal told him that it was just after half past one in the morning. His grandfather's shocking revelations should have provided enough of a jolt to banish his fatigue but the jet-lag was making it difficult for him to keep his eyes open. His body was still stubbornly set on Singapore time and it was telling him that he should have enjoyed a full night's sleep by now. He was tempted by the thought of slipping into bed but knew that his mind would race too much to let him sleep. He decided that he needed a caffeine boost and padded through to the kitchen to boil the kettle for coffee. He leaned back against the kitchen unit while he waited and tried to get his head around all that his grandfather had revealed.

He now thought that he understood why the old boy had always been reluctant to discuss his experiences during the war. He had tried to get him to open up when he was studying the Second World War for his Highers. Each enquiry had been gently but firmly rebuffed. He had eventually stopped pestering him on the assumption that his reticence was a result of him having experienced events that were so traumatic that he could not bring himself to speak of them. Each new fact had caused him to shake his head in disbelief. The old boy was German and not Polish. He had studied engineering at university but had spent most of his adult life driving a lorry for a Scottish potato merchant. He sighed and swore under his breath as these facts sunk in. The engineering background now made sense. It explained why the old man was able to turn his hand to so many skilled tasks. He knew of no other lorry driver who was so competent with plumbing, electrics, carpentry, welding, soldering, roofing, car mechanics and a hundred other things. Even as this thought crossed his mind, his gaze fell upon the garden shed that sat in his eyeline through the window above the sink. The sight of it caused him to grimace. He poured the boiling water onto the instant coffee grounds and, stopping only to collect the cigarettes and lighter from the living room, made his way out into the night's chill, dark air.

He stopped on the front step and peered at the shed in the bright, orange light of the street lamp on the corner. He had never really examined it before but now saw that it was something other than the common shed he had always considered it to be. His grandfather has built it long before his birth but, in spite of more than thirty years of winters, gales and torrential Scottish rain, it bore no signs of weathering, warping or rot. He found the key in its hiding place on the ledge above the door and unlocked the padlock. He flicked the light switch on and looked around the familiar interior with new eyes. His suspicions were immediately confirmed. The structure was more solidly built than any other shed he had come across. The thick timbers were so expertly joined that there were no spaces between them. When he thumped his heel down against the floorboards he was rewarded with a solid 'thunk' unaccompanied by the hollow rattling and shaking he would have expected from any normal shed. He then examined the rows of chisels, screwdrivers, planes, hand drills, hammers, mallets and saws that were displayed upon the walls in their handmade holders, on their shelves, hanging on their hooks and stowed in their cubby holes. It occurred to him that it was all laid out with a neatness and precision that would not have looked out of place in a laboratory or an engineer's workshop.

'What other surprises do you have for me, you old bugger?' He asked, his voice thin and strained in the workshop's empty interior.

He found that he was not quite ready to delve back into the notebook after shutting the light off and locking the shed. He sat on the front step of the house and pulled a cigarette from the pack. He hesitated for a second, the memory of how hard it had been to give them up six years earlier causing him to pause, but he then shrugged to himself and sparked the lighter into life. That first drag was heaven and set the receptors in his brain jangling after such long abstinence and made him salivate at the familiar acrid taste. He smoked it down to the filter and drained the coffee from the mug before pushing himself stiffly to his feet and going back inside to discover what other lies his grandfather had told.

'I still smile whenever I recall that train journey. We thought that we were men at last and that we had thrown off the bonds of parental supervision. Manfred produced a small bottle of whisky and a pack of cigarettes 'liberated' from his father and we smoked and drank in celebration of our freedom. That happy illusion did not last much past our arrival in Berlin.

It had been agreed that we would lodge in Manfred's uncle's basement until Christmas, after which we were to find more permanent accommodation. I recognised him the moment I saw him waiting on the station platform, for the family resemblance was quite uncanny. If anything, he was taller, broader and even more handsome than our Manfred. It would be an understatement to describe him as dashing. Resplendent in his full-dress SS uniform, I was in awe of him from the beginning. He seemed to bask in our adoration and his every action served only to make us admire him more. Even then, I recognised his false modesty when he informed us that he had dismissed his driver for the night because he was keen to get behind the wheel of his newly delivered car. Our jaws fell open at the sight of the brand-new Mercedes-Benz 540 K. It was black with grey body sides and was polished to such a sheen that it glimmered in the lamplight. The black top was folded down and we squealed with delight when he roared off into the night with us holding on for dear life on the green leather seats with our luggage piled on our laps.

We struggled to hear him above the engine noise and the rushing wind but caught enough of his words to be in no doubt that he was a very important man. He casually informed us of his recent promotion to the rank of SS Hauptsturmfuhrer, or captain, as if it was no great achievement for a man still in his early thirties. He complained that his duties as liaison between the Reichsfuhrer SS, Heinrich Himmler, and the Reichsminister of Public Enlightenment and Propaganda, Joseph Goebbels, forced him to work long and unsociable hours and had him constantly flitting between their various offices in the Ordenspalais, Prinz-Albrecht-Strasse and the Reich Chancellery. He pretended to be unaware of our wide-eyed astonishment and set out to impress us further by bemoaning the fact that he was required to attend so many functions and soirees that he seldom crossed his own threshold before midnight. He reluctantly admitted that it was indeed a thrill and a privilege to spend evenings at film screenings, operatic and orchestral performances and mingling with great stars such as Lida Baarova and Leni Riefenstahl, but insisted that he would much prefer to be at home with his wife and young family.

If we were not already sufficiently in awe of him, he endeared himself to us even more as he helped us to carry our luggage into the cellar of his imposing three storey house on the edge of the Tiergarten.

'If you use the back entrance.' He said as he pointed towards a rough, wooden staircase. 'You can come and go as you please. I promised your parents that I would keep an eye on you while you find your way in the city, but that does not mean that I need to be aware of your every movement. Young men about town must have some freedom.' He winked at us as he spoke and was rewarded with three wide grins as our minds fairly reeled with thoughts of girls and drinking and dancing.

The reality of our first six months in Berlin fell far short of those early fantasies. Manfred's uncle was true to his word and left us to our own devices. We seldom saw him, although we often heard the roar of his car's engine when he returned home in the early hours of the morning. The same could not be said of his aged and infirm mother-in-law, Hildegard Winkler, who occupied the room directly above our basement. Though half-blind, nearly deaf and so unsteady on her feet that she could manage only a few short steps with the aid of her two canes, the old battle-axe made it her mission to squeeze all of the joy out of our lives. For someone who claimed that she was deaf, she had a remarkable ability to detect if we dared to speak in anything other than a whisper and would hammer at the floorboards with her stick with an impressive level of energy and fury. If we returned home any later than ten o'clock she would make her daughter aware of our transgression we would be treated to a dressing down by Frau Wissler the very next morning. She was a slight and softly spoken woman but was able to put the fear of God into us by merely asking us if we wanted her to inform her husband of our inconsiderate and discourteous behaviour. We were so eager to avoid incurring the displeasure of the man we so worshipped that we lived like mice and seldom dared to venture out to indulge in the delights of the city.

The sour and indomitable Frau Winkler was not the sole cause of our misery during those first few months. Though we were enrolled in different schools, our first experiences of academia were depressingly similar. We found our professors to be strict, unyielding, unsympathetic and harshly critical of anything that we said or wrote. If it was their intention to use our fear of discipline and ridicule to coerce us into applying ourselves to our studies, then they were successful. We would squint at our books in the flickering lamplight until the small hours of the morning, always careful to turn the pages with great care for fear of making a sound and provoking the fury of the ancient harridan above our heads. Money, or the lack of it, was another source of anxiety. Manfred's uncle's generous refusal to accept any rent for our basement accommodation made quite a difference, but our limited funds still disappeared at an alarming rate. Manfred and Maus were just about able to scrimp by on what their parents sent them, while I was forced to seek employment to earn enough coins to pay for tuition, books, food and other essentials.

I worked five nights per week, Friday to Tuesday, as assistant to the concierge at the Kaiserhof Hotel. I was expected to fetch and carry and run errands to procure whatever our well-heeled guests desired at all hours of the night. I was often run off my feet but always took the opportunity to read or doze in the quiet hours between two and five o'clock in the morning. I got to know every high-class prostitute in the city from showing them discretely to the rooms of respectable gentlemen and from escorting them out to their cars before the sun rose and the hotel came back to life. The pay was poor but the tips, especially those from guests who had spent the evening drinking heavily, were often generous and just about kept my head above the water. The lack of sleep took a heavy toll and I teetered constantly on the edge of exhaustion. Only my terror of my professors stopped me from falling asleep in class or from neglecting my studies in favour of a few hours of rest. I also worried about how I would cope when we were forced to find our own lodgings in the New Year. I did not have enough money to pay rent and was physically incapable of working any more hours. I feared that I would have to admit defeat and return to the village in shame and defeat.

As was so often the case, it was Manfred who came riding to my rescue.

'I have spoken to my uncle.' He informed me as we walked towards the house after class on a cold December evening. 'He has agreed to let us stay on in the basement.'

'My God!' I replied in genuine relief. 'That is good. How long for?'

'For as long as we like.' He grinned happily. 'I could not have you work yourself to death, could I? Even although I would like nothing better than to escape that old bitch! She has the ears of a cat! You see the sacrifices I make for you?'

I did and I thanked him profusely for being the true and loyal friend that he was. The situation had lain heavily on my mind and I felt giddy at having such a heavy burden taken from my shoulders. He waved my thanks away with an embarrassed shake of his hand.

'I have even better news for you.' He teased as we walked along. 'Something that will put a smile on even that pale and tired face of yours.'

He enjoyed the moment and would say no more until I had begged and pleaded sufficiently.

'We are to attend the Tenth Party Congress in September as my uncle's guests!' He announced, his voice high with the excitement of this revelation.

'My God! Is it true?' I gasped in disbelief with my eyes and mouth wide open. Attendance at the Nuremburg Rally was an honour that was highly prized. We had all listened to the Fuhrer's speeches on the radio but have never dared to dream of being present to witness it for ourselves.

Maus received the news with even more enthusiasm than I and marched around the basement playing an imaginary drum in celebration. Even the furious thumping on the boards above our heads could not dampen our elation. If we had known where the road to Nuremberg would lead us, we might have turned from it. As it was, we plunged on heedlessly, blissfully ignorant of what lay ahead.

With my financial worries much reduced and with our 'trip' to look forward to, the next nine months were a much happier time for me. I was still in a state of permanent exhaustion from studying and working at the same time but I found more enjoyment in both sides of my life. I took great satisfaction from making myself indispensable to my boss at the hotel and learned how to ingratiate myself with guests in a manner that made them more likely to be generous with their tips. I also went out of my way to cultivate relationships with our regular guests and made sure that they knew that they should come to me if they required something that was not strictly available from the hotel itself. Familiarity with the seedier side of Berlin could be quite lucrative at times. I also began to find academic life a little less grim and, although the professors remained as strict and intolerant as they had always been, I found it easy to immerse myself in both the practical and theoretical aspects of my studies.

Our little circle of friends also expanded during this time. We chanced upon one of Maus's fellow medical students during a rare night out at a bierkeller and liked him immediately. He introduced himself as Rudolph Stamm from Dresden but told us that his friends all knew him as 'Pferd' or 'Horse'. He reduced us to fits of hysterics when he insisted that the name was on account of the contents of his trousers when it was plain to see that it had been inspired by his front teeth, which were like huge, white slabs and were separated by a wide gap. He joined in with our laughter with good humour, called for more beer and was instantly accepted into the group. He slept on the battered sofa in our basement so often that I began to suspect that he had no accommodation of his own. The other new arrival was a native Berliner who studied alongside me. I confess that I initially gravitated towards him because he was academically gifted and was both willing and able to help me with the more complex problems I struggled to grapple with during the quiet hours at the hotel. It was he who saved me from professorial censure on more occasions than I can remember. Julius Kammler was quiet and studious but I came to appreciate his calm and methodical logic and to like him a great deal.

I have never seen a summer as glorious as that of 1938. Freedom from the demands of professors and their classes allowed me to work more nights and so enjoy long, lazy days with a little money in my pocket. We would take a picnic to the park, swim in the lake, doze in the warm sunshine and drink beer to cool us down. I counted myself lucky to have such good friends and could think of nothing I would like better than being in their company. Maus would always buy a newspaper after lunch and read it out to us as we lay sprawled out on the grass around him. We took great pride and satisfaction in the stories that celebrated our country's growing strength and lauded the Fuhrer's role in achieving it. His popularity had soared to new heights since March when he had courageously sent German troops into Austria to bring an end to the suppression of the ten million Germans who lived there. The fulfilment of his pledge to form a Greater German Reich in the face of opposition from those European powers who had so humiliated Germany after our defeat in the war of 1914 to 1918 was celebrated across the land and ushered in a period of great optimism and national pride. It seemed to us that nothing could stop us from marching on and claiming our rightful status in the world. The prospect of similar military intervention in Czechoslovakia hung in the air throughout the summer and our excitement and expectation were heightened by Manfred's uncle who would give us knowing looks and hint at greater things to come.

Momentous though they were, these events were not my primary concern during those hot and balmy months. I was much more enthralled by Julius Kammler's cousin, Erica. She had come with her younger sister, Heidi, to spend the summer in Berlin with the Kammler family. Their care was entrusted to Julius who would bring them with him to the park each day. I was fascinated with her from my first sight of her and could happily watch her for hours. I thought her to be the most beautiful creature in the world. Every part of her was utterly perfect in my eyes. I longed to run my fingers through her hair, to kiss her full lips, to feel the swell of her breast under my hand and to bury my nose into the soft, smooth skin of her delicate neck. Manfred and Maus made fun of me and mocked me for mooning after her like some poor, love-sick fool. I was immune to their teasing and ignored Julius and his gentle attempts to warn me off. I did everything I could think of to ingratiate myself with her, but she remained stubbornly resistant to my charms.

She finally relented two days before she was due to return home. I accompanied her to the park kiosk to buy drinks and took the opportunity to take hold of her hand and pull her towards me. She came willingly and let me kiss those cool, full lips, put my arms around her and push myself against her. I doubt if the encounter lasted more than two full minutes, but the experience left me floating on air. She kept hold of my hand until we were back in sight of our little group and left me bereft when she disentangled her little fingers from mine. I was heartbroken when neither she nor Julius appeared at the park the following day. I was devastated that she had left Berlin without saying goodbye to me and fell into such a state of misery that even my friends could not raise me from of it. They tried their best to cajole me into joining them on hikes and picnics but I preferred to wallow in my despair in the basement's dim interior, venturing out only to mope my way through my shifts at the hotel.

7

Manfred finally lost patience with me on the eve of our departure for the Party Congress in Nuremberg.

'Get up!' He snapped at me as I lay listlessly on my bed. 'My uncle has gone to a great deal of trouble for us. He will think you to be an ungrateful pig if he sees your sulky face.'

'Then you should just leave me here.' I replied miserably. 'I will only spoil it for the rest of you.'

'Up swine!' He roared at me before kicking the bed frame with enough force to rattle my head. 'Where is your self-respect? You look like a tramp. Get up, shave yourself, wash your stink away and dress in something that is not crumpled and dirty! Do it now or I will knock every last tooth out of your stupid head!'

The vehemence of his words and the violence of his temper shocked me into action. Manfred had never threatened me before and I was taken aback by the intensity of his attack. He stood glowering at me malevolently with his hands clenched into fists at his sides as I pushed myself up and set about cleaning myself.

'There will be plenty of girls for us in Nuremberg!' Maus informed me cheerily as I poured water into the washbowl. 'You will not even remember Erica a week from now!'

I could have punched Maus in that moment and only restrained myself out of fear of provoking Manfred further. At dawn the next morning I forced a smile onto my face and leapt into Hauptsturmfuhrer Wissler's Mercedes with sufficient pretended enthusiasm to earn a curt nod of approval from my oldest friend. I sent a silent prayer of thanks to God above for providing weather that was fine enough to persuade the Hauptsturmfuhrer to fold back the roof of his car for the journey south. The wind and engine noise made conversation impossible and I was able to continue with my brooding without challenge or interruption while I stared blankly out across the passing countryside. The chaos and excitement of Nuremberg provided so many things to distract my friends that they were completely oblivious to the continuing depths of my longing and unhappiness. I trailed along in their wake and let the endless parades, marching bands, singing and speeches pass me by. Maus was more excited than I had ever seen him and I was forced to respond with hollow smiles whenever he pointed out something that astonished or impressed him.

'Look there! Look there!' He squealed as we were propelled along the narrow street by the great throng of party members. 'It is Reichsfuhrer Himmler!'

'Where? Where?' Manfred replied while craning his neck around and straining his eyes to catch a glimpse of the great man.

'There! Look! In the steel helmet!' Maus replied as he jabbed his finger in the direction of a motorcar that had already passed us.

'No it wasn't!' Manfred retorted in a voice that revealed that he was excited but not wholly convinced. 'Did you see him Wolffie?'

'It was him!' I confirmed though I had only snatched a brief sighting of an unidentified man wearing a helmet and a uniform festooned with gold braid.

They chattered on about their brief brush with greatness and left me in peace to revel in my suffering and recall sweet Erica's beauty and the sensation of her lips upon mine.

In this way, I struggled through the week and counted the days until I could return to Berlin and seek refuge from the world beneath my blankets. I thought only of the day when Julius was finally due to return from his family's lake house in Grunewald. I planned to extract Erica's address from him so that I could send her the many letters I had already composed in my head. While my friends whooped with delight at the parades of tanks, mobile artillery, Hitler Youth, Wehrmacht, SS and members of the Women's League and stared upwards in awe as squadrons of warplanes flew overhead, I occupied myself with composing poems expressing my hopeless devotion to my Erica. That all changed when we made our way to the rally grounds on the last day of the congress.

No one could fail to be impressed by what awaited us there. The sheer scale of it had to be seen to be believed. The mere sight of half a million loyal party members arrayed in tight and ordered divisions was enough to stir the heart of any human being. There was a majesty and power about it and a strength that came not just from the numbers but also from the flags, banners and standards that stretched as far as the eye could see. Even my chest puffed out in pride in spite of the bruised and broken heart that was housed within it. In the end, even this proved to be only a temporary distraction. The discomfort of standing for so long and the interminable speeches caused my brief enthusiasm to wane and my thoughts soon turned back to melancholy. I paid little heed as all the major party figures and a host of lesser men took to the podium to praise the Fuhrer for reuniting our country and for defying our enemies.

'It will be the Fuhrer next!' Maus informed me in wide-eyed excitement when the day had already stretched on for an eternity.

I favoured him with a smile of genuine happiness, not because I shared his excitement, but because I was relieved that the rally was almost over and that I would soon be on my way back to Berlin.

A growing thunder and a shaking of the ground caused all three of us to look skywards in expectation of catching sight of yet another low-level fly-past by a squadron of our planes. It took us a few seconds to realise that the noise and the vibrations were coming from the crowd and not from the fast approach of roaring warplanes. It was the oddest of sensations. It was as if we were part of a huge and powerful engine that was being revved as hard as it would go. I felt the hairs on the back of my neck stand up and my face flushed red. The great roar that emanated from the crowd was deafening, frightening and exhilarating all at the same time. I glanced around myself and saw that everyone for as far as the eye could see was pumping their right arms into the air and shouting and screaming at the tops of their lungs. I was a little surprised to realise that I was doing the same thing, although I could not hear my own voice over the great din around us. We could see nothing of the platform through the impenetrable sea of arms that blocked our view entirely.

Manfred punched at my shoulder to get my attention and roared something at me with urgent excitement. I had no idea what he was trying to say and just grinned at him and continued to thrust my arm towards the sky.

The silence came slowly and seemed to creep over the crowd like a wave. Some sections were still in a frenzy, whilst others now stood stock still with their eyes set firmly to the front. The hush that fell over the whole parade ground was eerie and, in a strange way, was more oppressive than the previous tumult. The whole crowd seemed to hold its breath and men's arms fell back to their sides.

The view opened up in front of us and we saw him for the first time. Adolf Hitler stood silently on the podium dressed in a simple uniform that was bare of all the brocade, epaulettes and other adornments favoured by the senior men who filled the stands behind him. He wore only a simple belt, a shoulder strap and the Iron Cross he had been awarded for his courage under fire. His arms were crossed over his chest and he glowered at the crowd, his eyes travelling slowly from back to front and from one side to the other as if he was subjecting us to an exacting assessment. Though logic told me otherwise, I felt that his gaze fell upon me amongst the multitude and I straightened my back in a sudden desperation to not be found wanting. The tension built as the silence dragged on and, impossible though it may sound, I swear that the sound of a pin dropping would have been heard in that moment in spite of the presence of half a million people on that field. I was shocked to realise that I had not dared to breath since the Fuhrer's appearance and I exhaled slowly and quietly even although my lungs felt as if they would burst.

When he started to speak, he spoke so quietly that every man there leaned forward in order to better catch his words. It occurred to me then that he had us all in the palm of his hand. I realised that I was rapt and that I was happy to be so bewitched. The pace of his delivery quickened and the volume increased as his speech progressed. He wagged his finger furiously as he told us how our enemies had conspired to lay us low. He threw his arms wide and asked if he was to be expected to sit idly by while three and a half million of our fellow Germans were being brutally suppressed in Czechoslovakia. His voice grew more harsh and strident as he built himself into a fury over the historic and present injustices visited upon our

83

people. He reached such a crescendo when heralding the rejuvenation of our Volk and exhorting us to never again bow our heads to any alien will that his body almost seemed to convulse with the power of his passion and unshakeable determination. Five hundred thousand men responded in kind, each of us roaring our approval and hailing our leader to the heavens.

If he had ordered us there and then to march out to fight our enemies to the death, I do not doubt that every single person present would have done so with the greatest of enthusiasm. Even now, in spite of knowing what I know and having suffered what I have suffered, I do not doubt that I would answer his call again. The passage of more than eighty years has not dimmed my memory of that day and, though it fills me with shame, I cannot deny that it still sends a thrill through me that no other event in my life has come close to matching. They now paint him as a monster and claim that he was a hypnotist who mesmerised people against their will. That is a lie. Those of us who followed him did so willingly. He inspired in us an unbreakable loyalty and a burning desire to perform great deeds and so win his approval. The tragedy of it is that God decided to place so great a power in the hands of one flawed and fallible man. This is what led so many of us to death and ruin.

Our fates were set on that September evening as Hauptsturmfuhrer Wissler sped us back towards Berlin in his Mercedes and we chattered on as if intoxicated in voices that were ragged and hoarse from roaring out our approval of our Fuhrer.

'I will answer the Fuhrer's call!' Manfred announced solemnly with his right hand placed hard against his heart. 'I cannot indulge myself in study when my country has need of me. I will enlist in the Wehrmacht the moment I am back in Berlin. I will not shirk my duty.' He stuck his jaw out defiantly in anticipation of his uncle objecting to his plan.

Hauptsturmfuhrer Wissler glanced at his nephew and shook his head, though he was smiling as he did so. 'I admire your enthusiasm, Manfred.' He began. 'But would counsel you that enthusiasm without wisdom is nothing more than foolishness. You must be wise.'

Manfred crossed his arms tightly across his chest and glared out at the road ahead with his face set hard in determination. 'You will not dissuade me! My decision is made.'

'I do not seek to dissuade you from your course.' His uncle protested, momentarily taking his hands from the wheel so he could hold his arms apart to emphasise his point. 'I would merely point out that it is better to find the road that will bring you the greatest personal advantage whilst simultaneously serving the best interests of Volk, Reich and Fuhrer. You must surely see the sense in this?'

Manfred merely shrugged in response and continued to stare sulkily ahead.

'Alright! I will spell it out for you.' His uncle responded a little testily. 'I cannot say too much but I can tell you that a time of struggle is ahead of us and that the future will belong to those loyal party members who play a part in the winning of that struggle. It is the SS who will be instrumental in that great victory.' He turned in the driver's seat and looked at Maus and I before turning back towards the road. 'A wise man would lay his studies aside for now, play his part in what is to come and then take the rewards that will come following our triumph. Do not throw away your advantage by enlisting in the Wehrmacht like some common peasant. Submit yourselves to the SS selection process, complete your basic training, serve the required six months in the ranks and then attend officer training at the SS-Junkerschule in Bad Tolz. It is the SS officers who serve with distinction in what is to come who will become the next generation of leaders of the Reich. Choose wisely and your future prosperity will be assured.'

Manfred seemed to be partly swayed by this but turned to us for confirmation. 'What do you think?'

'I am for the SS!' Maus chuckled happily. 'The uniform is much better and will attract the girls!'

'What about you Wolffie?' Manfred asked me, though I could tell from his expression that he had already been fully persuaded.

'I want to be in the thick of it.' I replied gravely. 'And it seems that the SS will be at the centre of whatever is ahead of us.'

'Good! Good!' Hauptsturmfuhrer Wissler declared joyfully and he gunned the engine in celebration. 'Then we must hurry back to Berlin. I have calls to make and favours to call in!'

A brief shadow of concern then crossed Manfred's face. 'What about Mother and Father?' He asked somewhat sheepishly.

'You leave them to me!' His uncle replied. 'You know how persuasive I can be.'

David Strachan grimaced and thumped the mug back onto the table in disgust. The coffee had gone cold and bitter. He rubbed at his tired eyes but still struggled to focus on his grandfather's tight, neat script. He glanced at his watch and was surprised to see that it was already three forty. He groaned at the realisation that he was due to meet with the funeral director in Blairgowrie in just over five hours. He decided that his curiosity would have to keep until the morning and turned for the stairs and the prospect of a few hours sleep. He paused when his eyes fell upon his grandfather's illicit cigarettes. A short internal struggle ended with him snatching the packet up and venturing out into the night's chill air. He sat on the front step and stared up at the night sky while he smoked. He found himself shaking his head as he recalled all that the damned notebook had revealed to him. He asked himself if he should just burn the bloody thing and pretend that he had never seen it, but he already knew that he would not. The old man had him hooked and he just had to find out what had become of Kurt, Manfred and Maus.

8

The funeral director looked as if he had been born purely to take up his morbid trade. He reminded Strachan of the old, American cartoon dog, Droopy. He had the same mournful expression, the same long jowls and drooping lower eyelids and spoke in a similarly slow and lethargic manner. That is not to say that he was not good at his job. He exuded sympathy and gently guided Strachan through the sad and grisly process, taking great care to make each element as easy and untroubling as was possible in the circumstances. All Strachan had left to do was select the casket and its lining, confirm the details of his grandparents' plot, agree to the minister who was to hold the service and choose the gravestone and the inscription that was to be carved into it by the stonemason. Strachan had to admit that he was impressed by the end-to-end nature of the service on offer and found himself thinking that the financial services sector could learn a great deal from the funeral business. The undertaker was even able to arrange for a funeral notice to be placed in the local paper and to organise the wake in a local hotel of his choice. Once he handed over the suit that his grandfather was to be buried in, it seemed that all that was required of him was to attend the service and settle the invoice.

He had been about to take his leave when the funeral director surprised him with his question.

'Would you like to see him now? I have laid him out in the Chapel of Rest. He looks very peaceful.'

Strachan hesitated. He had assumed that he would not have to see his grandfather's body and his very strong preference would have been to avoid it and instead remember him as he had been when he was alive. He had begun to shake his head when his curiosity kicked in.

'Okay.' He replied uncertainly. 'Just for a minute.'

His grandfather did look peaceful but he also looked as if he had aged fifty years and lost half of his body weight since Strachan had seen him last. Tears jumped into his eyes and he instinctively reached out to touch the old boy's cheek. The skin was cold to the touch and felt dry and papery.

'Oh Grandad!' He sighed sadly. 'You should have told me. I would have come.' He then spoke to him softly for several minutes, aware that his old ears were now deaf but hopeful that he would somehow hear his words and know the contents of his heart.

When he had dried the tears shed for the man who had loved him and taken him in, his mind turned to the man he had not known, the man in the notebook. He remembered reading somewhere that members of the Waffen-SS had their blood group tattooed on the inside of their upper arm. His grandfather's body was still dressed in the short-sleeved, hospital gown he had been wearing when he died, which made it easy for Strachan to gently pull the sleeve up to reveal the flesh just below his armpit. He had no reason to doubt the veracity of the contents of the journal but some part of him still clung onto the faint hope that it was a fiction and that his grandfather was still the man he had thought him to be. At first, he could see nothing on the wrinkled and puckered skin and he felt a sense of relief wash over him. Then he saw it. The 'O' was rough and uneven and the ink had faded until it was almost invisible but its presence could not be denied or wished away.

'Christ Wolffie!' Strachan hissed. 'Why did you need to write your bloody journal? I'd have been none the wiser if you'd just kept it to yourself.'

He knew where the answer to that question lay and he left the undertakers intent on immediately driving the rented Focus back to New Alyth to find it.

'Manfred's uncle was true to his word. He worked his contacts and pulled in favours and secured us selection appointments at the SS-Junkerschule in Bad Tolz within three weeks of our return from Nuremberg. We had infected Julius and Horse with our new-found zeal and Manfred had pleaded with his uncle to include them in his requests. The five of us set off on the road for Munich in the Kammler family's brown Opel Olympia on the last Monday in October. The Opel did not have the space, style or power of the Wissler's Mercedes, but the slow, bumpy and cramped journey did nothing to dampen our spirits. We made frequent stops for food and refreshments, including at Leipzig, Bayreuth, Ingolstadt and, of course, Nuremberg by way of pilgrimage. We treated it as a great adventure and chattered constantly about the great things that lay ahead of us.

Any nervousness about the selection process itself evaporated upon our arrival at the officer training facility. Hauptsturmfuhrer Wissler's letter of introduction served to smooth our path and we were ushered past the other waiting applicants to complete our interviews, medicals and physical tests. We were then treated to a tour of the facilities and were impressed to see that no expense had been spared. A football stadium, athletics track, sauna, heated swimming pool and buildings dedicated to gymnastics, wrestling and boxing had been built for the use of the trainee officers. It was like a dream to us and we all agreed that we could picture ourselves there once we had completed our basic training and the mandatory six months of service in the ranks of the Waffen-SS.

We dawdled on our way home to Berlin, stopping off for two nights along the way, although only one was strictly necessary, as none of us wanted the adventure to end. Then began the agony of waiting. Manfred would pad softly upstairs each morning to enquire as to whether or not the postman had brought any letters for us and would then return glum-faced and shake his head in response to our expectant faces.

'How can it take them so long?' Manfred would demand angrily each morning. 'They must have made their decision while we were still there. How long does it take to write a letter and put it in a bloody envelope?'

The letters finally arrived in early December, bringing both triumph and despair. I tore my envelope open and nervously read the brief letter before reading it again to make sure that I had not misunderstood. I then leapt to my feet and cried out in ecstasy. Manfred jumped up to embrace me and we danced around the cellar in celebration, stopping only when Frau Winkler began to thump her stick violently against the floorboards above our heads. It was then that we caught sight of poor Maus, his face sour and his cheeks wet with tears. We went to him immediately and demanded to know what had so upset him. He could not even bring himself to meet our eyes and instead held his crumpled letter out to us. I took it from his hand, smoothed the paper and read it.

'What is it?' Manfred demanded impatiently. 'What is the matter?'

'He has been rejected.' I reported. 'They say that he does not meet the minimum height requirement and suggest that he joins the ranks.'

'Shit!' Manfred cursed. 'I cannot believe it. I will go and speak with my uncle immediately. He will sort this out!'

Julius and Horse arrived clutching their own letters before he returned and went through the same painful process of muting their celebrations when they caught sight of the dejected and distraught Maus.

When Manfred finally returned, his grim expression told us that our friend's fate was sealed.

'You will enlist with us as planned!' He ordered him in an attempt to resolve the problem. 'Once we have completed our officer training I will see to it that you are assigned to my section. We will have you promoted in the field at the first opportunity, won't we boys?'

Maus shook his head from side to side and stared sullenly at his feet. When he finally spoke, his voice was hard and edged with bitterness. 'If the bastards do not want me, then they can lick my arse! I will stay here and complete my studies.'

I was truly sorry for Maus but have to admit that it was a relief when he left for home at Christmas and announced that he would find his own lodgings when he returned. He had cast a dark shadow over the group and his absence allowed us to openly revel in our success and to look forward to the adventure ahead. With our training not due to start until February, we had a whole month in which to enjoy Berlin without having to worry about Maus or our studies. The four of us took full advantage of the opportunity and January flew past in a blur of beer and schnapps and as many women of dubious virtue as we could afford. It was not, with hindsight, the best preparation for basic training.

I do not remember quite what we had expected but the reality was a thousand times worse. For weeks and weeks on end we seemed to do nothing but run, march, parade, exercise, play sports and then repeat it all again while red-faced sergeants and corporals insulted and threatened us at the tops of their voices. Then, when we were far beyond the point of exhaustion, we were subjected to endless exacting inspections of our rooms, kit, uniforms, boots and all manner of other things. The most minor of infractions resulted in the imposition of harsh group punishments designed to turn your comrades against you. It is astonishing just how much hatred you can generate towards a person when their failure to remove a speck of dust from a shelf is the cause of you having to force your stiff and aching body out into the rain to complete a five-mile run in full pack. Frequent offenders were often dragged behind the barracks to receive punishment beatings at the hands of their comrades to encourage them to strive for higher standards. It was a miracle that we did not kill one another.

The political education was another form of torture altogether. The classes seemed to be deliberately scheduled to take place when we were so tired that it was a struggle to keep our eyes open. I can still remember my terror at jerking back into consciousness to be faced by a stern-faced instructor demanding an answer to a question on racial purity that I had not heard. I was often able to trot out some platitude that satisfied them, but more than once I had to suffer my comrades glaring at me in hostility while we stood to attention for hours on end in the pouring rain. The political instructor's role certainly seemed to attract the most sadistic zealots and we hated them almost as much as we feared them.

We thought that our luck had changed when we began our weapons training. Manfred and I could not stop ourselves from grinning when we were issued with our rifles. The Karabiner 98ks were handed to us straight out of their packing cases and we examined them with a level of awe normally reserved for sacred artefacts. We caressed the highly polished wood and unmarked metal with our fingertips and marvelled at the quality of their manufacture. They made old Helmut Fischer's ancient and scratched Gewehr 88 look like a remnant from a bygone age. We laughed to think that we had once salivated at the mere thought of holding it and that we had competed fiercely with one another in order to win the opportunity to fire a single bullet from it. We eagerly anticipated our sessions on the firing range and took great satisfaction from our improving accuracy. What spoiled it for us was the fact that shooting made up only a small part of our weapons training. Long hours were devoted to stripping the rifle down into its individual components and then reassembling it again. We grew heartily sick of it and resented the instructors with their stopwatches and their repeated instructions to do it again the moment we had finished.

'Christ!' Horse complained one afternoon a month into our training. 'What is the point of this? I know how to strip a rifle! I could do it in my sleep now!'

'That is the whole point of it, you lump of puke!' The instructor bellowed at him. 'If your rifle jams when bullets are flying around your head and the enemy is charging down at you, this might just save your miserable neck! Let's go again!'

We could not deny the truth of this, but we were still relieved when we entered the final phase of our training. These weeks focused on group, platoon and company tactics. Real explosives and live rounds were used to make these exercises as realistic as possible. There was a thrill to this at first, but, like all things in the military, repetition served to render commonplace and dull anything that was once shocking or the cause of excitement. Over one third of our intake was rooted out during this battlefield readiness stage as the weaklings, cowards and laggards were expelled to leave only the best of us. Manfred, Julius, Horse and I passed with flying colours and were able to celebrate our success and await our postings with great anticipation.

As much as it made us miserable, those long months of excruciating monotony made soldiers of us, or so we thought. Our bodies were lean and muscular, our shooting skills were of the highest calibre, we knew exactly what was expected of us on the battlefield and, in spite of the best efforts of those responsible for our political education, we remained loyal and dedicated to both party and country. We had yet to learn that we lacked that most essential element of any soldier's armoury, patience. We had fantasised about what life would be like once the monotony of our training was over with. We were dismayed to find that it was no better but began to understand that a soldier's life is largely one of crushing boredom, long inactivity and pointless routine punctuated by sudden, short, violent periods of great peril. We had cursed our luck at the beginning of our training when it was reported that German troops had swept across the border and occupied Czechoslovakia. The newspaper photographs of the Fuhrer entering Prague Castle made us proud but also left us fearing that we were missing out. That frustration paled into insignificance when we heard the radio broadcasts announcing that German forces had invaded Poland from the north, south and west in response to a cowardly Polish attack on a radio station in Upper Silesia. We were desperate to fight for our country, we were ready to fight and yet we were left in our barracks twiddling our thumbs. We genuinely feared that our opportunity for glory had passed us by.

Almost another month passed before we received the news that we so yearned for. We were informed in hushed tones that, along with a number of our instructors, we were being posted to the newly formed SS Totenkopf Division, the Death's Head Division, and that we would be immediately transported to a camp in Dachau for combat training. We could barely conceal our excitement but, as was so often the case, our expectations and reality proved to be very distant cousins. There was little sign of the oft-heralded ruthless efficiency of the SS on our arrival and chaos reigned for several weeks. It soon became apparent that the camp was not a military installation but had been used to imprison political prisoners, Jews and other undesirables until very recently. The stench of piss and shit persisted even on the windiest of days and the accommodation blocks were freezing and hardly fit for human habitation. Almost fifteen thousand men arrived there within a few short days and it was apparent that our commanders were struggling to cope with the sudden influx. Half the men were drawn from battalions that had worked together in the concentration camps and then fought together in Poland. The rest, like us, were new recruits and we naturally grouped together whilst keeping a wary eye on the battle-hardened veterans.

It was disconcerting to see our superiors struggle to implement even the most basic elements of military life. There were days when there was insufficient food to feed all the men and arms and equipment were in such short supply that our officers instructed us to sleep with our rifles to prevent them from being stolen. The poor state of our supply lines did have one happy effect in that it provided us with opportunities to escape the camp when we were sent out to forage for provisions or equipment. On one notable occasion, we were sent north to Oranienburg with orders to requisition thirty trucks and twenty motorcycles from a transport depot there. It is a miracle that we all made it back alive. I had never driven a truck before but, with only five minutes of basic tuition from Julius, I somehow managed to cover more than one thousand kilometres without incident. Manfred was even more fortunate. He flew past us on his motorcycle at such a speed and with such recklessness that I was certain that we would soon come upon his broken body strewn across the road.

Those early weeks were also characterised by a serious breakdown in discipline. Our close proximity to Munich did not help matters much and we all took the risk of venturing into the city in search of adventure, beer and girls. It could not last. The command structure began to solidify as November progressed and the subsequent crackdown was swiftly and harshly implemented. Officers were demoted, men were confined, all leave was cancelled and the issuing of three-day passes was forbidden. Manfred, Horse, Julius and I were fortunate indeed to avoid having our careers and lives ruined when our divisional commander, Gruppenfuhrer Theodor Eicke, furiously clamped down to bring the chaos to an end. We had joined with a dozen other men of the Fourteenth Company of the Second Infantry Regiment to steal two trucks and drive into Munich for an evening's drinking. By midnight we were so drunk that none of us was fit to drive. Manfred was undeterred by this and claimed that he drove better when he was inebriated. We set off for Dachau with the other truck in close pursuit and miraculously made it back to camp without killing ourselves or anyone else. We staggered to our beds oblivious to the fact that our comrades in the second truck had not returned. It was only in the morning that we learned that they had collided with a street-car on the Dachauerstrasse and had been apprehended by the police. We were told that it was a miracle that no-one had been killed or injured when both the truck and the street-car had been reduced to mangled scrap by the force of the impact. We speculated that it was the great volume of drink consumed that had saved them from harm as it was reported that the police found the driver merely dazed from the crash and his passengers still fast asleep in the back. We thought this to be the funniest of stories but our amusement quickly turned to horror when their punishment was announced. As an example to the rest of us, they were stripped of all rank, were summarily dismissed from the SS and were sentenced to imprisonment in the Buchenwald concentration camp. The brutality of the action had the desired effect and discipline was immediately restored.

The whole atmosphere around the camp changed almost overnight. The supply problems were addressed and our little excursions to requisition goods came to an abrupt end. Trucks began to line up at the gates to await their turn to unload food, ammunition, weapons, motorcycles, anti-tank guns, mortars, armoured cars, howitzers, whole field kitchens, halftracks, radio equipment, tents and every other type of military equipment one could imagine. The combat training then began in earnest. Endless formal lectures, combat exercises and weapons drills began at section level before being gradually scaled up to squad, platoon, company, battalion and finally regimental level. Every imaginable battlefield contingency was tested out in full-scale, mock assaults under live fire conditions with artillery support. The division gradually began to work like a well-oiled machine, with each of its parts working in concert with the others with the precise efficiency you would expect from such an elite division. Our collective pride and confidence grew with each passing day and our eagerness to enter the field of battle was fanned by reports of the defensive preparations being made by the French First Army and the British Expeditionary Force on the Belgian-French border and by persistent rumours of the imminent launch of the campaign against France. We knew that no enemy could hope to stand against a fully motorised division as well-equipped, well-drilled and as disciplined as ours and we itched to have the chance to show what we could do. The orders for the division to move to Ludwigsburg, just to the north of Stuttgart, were the cause of much cheering and celebration. Such a move towards the French border could only mean one thing and we packed up our kit knowing that we would be riding out against the Fatherland's foulest enemies within days if not hours.

In the face of such fevered expectation, the next five months and ten days were an agony of disappointment and frustration. Days and weeks passed and still our battle orders did not arrive. We grew disheartened as we suffered one misfortune after another. The winter weather made the exciting, large-scale assault exercises impractical, thus condemning us to weapons training, physical exercise and, to our horror, the resumption of political instruction. We had to watch on jealously as some of our comrades were sent for specialist training in the use of mortars, explosives, heavy machine guns, antitank weapons and river crossing techniques, while we humble riflemen were reduced to camouflage instruction sessions. This mainly involved lying in the undergrowth for hours while officers tried to spot us with their binoculars. We scarcely celebrated our hollow victories when we successfully hid ourselves away and forced them to admit defeat.

It was during one such exercise that I decided to unburden myself to our section leader. Rottenfuhrer Karl Lammert was not the kind of person I would normally choose to confide in. He was the most negative, irritable, foul-mouthed and sarcastic man I have ever known. We liked him because he was always fair to us, but we knew better than to expect warm words of comfort from him. I suppose that the combination of my frustration and the boredom of lying prone on the damp earth for hours must have eroded my usual caution and reserve.

'I am sick and tired of all this waiting.' I complained bitterly. 'Why do we not attack now? The longer we wait the better prepared they will be when we do come.'

'Hold on a second.' Lammert instructed me as he began to pat at his pockets as if he was searching for something. 'I have a memo from the Fuhrer right here! He has explained his strategy to me in great detail. Let me find it and I will read it to you!'

'Very funny!' I retorted. 'You might be happy hiding in bushes but I am not.'

'It would be funny if it was not so tragic,' He replied with a dismissive shake of his head. 'You are so desperate for glory but have yet to work out that you will never have the chance to win it.'

'What do you mean?' I snapped back at him. 'I have as much chance as you!'

'That is sadly true, young Wolff. Thanks to your boyfriend up there.' He jerked his thumb up the slope towards the place where Manfred had secreted himself. 'If this division ever gets to fight, we will always find ourselves far from the action. You wait and see! We will be forever condemned to sentry duty at the division's rear whilst others brave the bullets and the bayonets.'

'That's shit!' I retorted, though his words had worried me.

'You country boys are so slow on the uptake.' He shot back with an air of impatient weariness whilst keeping his eyes to the front. 'Let me lay it out for you in terms that you will understand.' He then continued in a sing-song voice that was a parody of how he might have read a fairy tale to a little child. 'Little Mani's uncle wants to ensure that his precious nephew comes to no harm. So, uncle SS-Hauptsturmfuhrer Wissler quietly telephones little Manfred's divisional commander, Gruppenfuhrer Eicke, and asks him to keep him safe. Gruppenfuhrer Eicke then tells little Manfred's company commander, SS-Obersturmfuhrer Fritz Knoechlein, that the nephew of such an important man must be properly looked after. The Obersturmfuhrer then delegates this heavy responsibility to Manfred's section leader and is careful to emphasise the dire punishment that will be suffered if a single hair on Manfred's precious little head should come to any harm.'

'You're lying.' I replied, though the bitterness in his tone told me that he was speaking the truth.

'I am not lying. I'm delegating the responsibility to you. You will guard the bastard with your life. If he should fall, I will face a firing squad.' He then turned his head and looked me directly in the eye. 'But I will have put a bullet in your head long before I am offered that final cigarette! Do you understand me?'

The following weeks brought me to new depths of despair. The first rumours began to circulate in early March but we dismissed them out of hand. We were convinced that the Death's Head Division would be at the forefront of the invasion of France and it was unthinkable that we would be relegated to the status of a reserve unit as part of the Second Army. Our worst fears were confirmed

104

at the beginning of April when we were subjected to a day-long inspection by Colonel General Weichs, Commander-in-Chief of the Second Army. I seethed and glowered at him from my hiding place in the bushes while he watched from an observation tower as we assaulted imaginary enemy positions. It stung to know that others would lead the line while we sat idly by. May brought fresh agonies as we listened to the reports of the astonishing gains being made by Guderian's Panzer Corps in southern Belgium and Luxembourg and of the fast progress of Gerd von Rundstedt's tanks towards the river Meuse. The tension was unbearable during those first days of the campaign and even our commanders were seen to place their heads in their hands when they heard how the weak French units were collapsing like wet cardboard under the weight of the attack. It seemed that the war would be fought and won in a matter of days while we sat on the sidelines in impotence.

It was seven long and tortuous days before despair turned into delight with the arrival of our orders to enter the fray in support of Rundstedt's Army Group A. At last we were going to war!'

9

'As boys we had galloped through the forests on the Polish border imaging that we were Teutonic Knights riding out to right wrongs and protect the innocent. Now we were doing it for real, Knights of the New Order rushing through the night in speeding trucks to restore our country's honour and punish our enemies for the injustices they had visited upon us. Armed to the teeth, dressed in the sacred uniform of the elite Death's Head and at the very peak of our physical fitness, we were invincible, unstoppable and yearning for battle. We sang as we went and thanked the stars that we had been born at such a time. The column stretched out for more than twenty miles as we hurtled into Holland, turning onto the highway south at Roermond on our way to Belgium via Maastricht. We sped by Liege, Huy and Dinant before halting to rest shortly after we crossed the border into northern France.

Our initial, headlong charge had been completed without sight or sound of enemy resistance. The only obstacles to our advance were the great traffic jams that occurred when we crossed paths with the rearmost units of Army Group B as they advanced northwest towards the front. We traded insults with the weary Wehrmacht soldiers telling them that they could rest easy now that the SS had arrived to show them how it was done. They in turn berated us for arriving when the worst of the fighting had already taken place. Their taunts bit much deeper than our empty boasting for it was clear from their tattered and dirty appearance that these units had already seen combat while our uniforms were still pristine and our boots free of French mud or dust.

Rottenfuhrer Lammert's prediction proved to be depressingly accurate. Just as he had said, Manfred and I were assigned to sentry duty at the rear of the camp. Though we had not caught sight of a single enemy soldier in Holland, Belgium or France, there was a real tension and excitement to that night's guard duty. We were deep in enemy territory and saw potential threats in every shadow and heard them in the creaking of every branch. We stood alert and ready to repulse any surprise attack. Adrenalin powered us through our tiredness after so many hours of being rattled and jolted on the hard, wooden benches in the back of the truck. We had slept for only a couple of hours after being relieved when Lammert awakened us by kicking our feet.

'Up ladies!' He barked. 'It seems that your dreams of combat are about to be realised. The French have counter-attacked to the west of us and have pinned Rommel's Seventh Panzer Division down at Le Cateau. We are to ride to his rescue!'

We were up in an instant and running for our truck. We heard the artillery and the tank fire even above the roar of our engines and the rattling and creaking of the truck's canopy within an hour of

107

setting off. Our noses soon detected smoke and the familiar, sharp odour of cordite as we advanced and the growing intensity of the machine gun and small arms fire told us that the battle was being fiercely contested over a wide area to our front. Our position at the rear reduced us to the role of spectators throughout the morning and afternoon. We advanced from one small village to the next and witnessed the aftermath of the vicious house-to-house, hand-to-hand fighting that had taken place as our comrades cleared the enemy from our path. I had seen my first dead body by 9 a.m. and my two hundredth by noon. Julius puked into his hand at the sight of one man whose face had been reduced to bloody ruin to such an extent that his eyes, nose and mouth formed a single ragged hole. Manfred and I might have berated him for his weakness if we had not been struggling to keep the contents of our own stomachs inside our bodies. Our role was to gather up all of the weapons and supplies the French had abandoned as they were beaten back. We piled them in the centre of the burning villages and then guarded them until trucks came up to take them to the rear. Our own packs were soon bulging as we helped ourselves to French chocolates, wine, cigarettes and coffee.

We watched with contempt as the first French prisoners were escorted away from the front. They were dirty, many of them were wounded and the air of defeat hung about them as thickly as the acrid smoke that billowed up into the sky. That first trickle of prisoners grew into a deluge as the afternoon wore on. Hundreds of them trudged by us dejectedly until we scarcely paid them any heed as we went about our business. The only ones that really caught our attention were the few wiry, brown-skinned men amongst their numbers.

'They must be Moroccans.' Lammert informed us sagely. 'Drawn from the French colony.' He then shook his head as he watched one of them limp past us with a leg wound that was still bleeding profusely. 'You can say what you like about them, but they can't half fight!'

'What makes you say that?' Manfred demanded, his face twisted in puzzlement at Lammert's apparent admiration for the coloured men.

'How many brown faces do you see amongst the prisoners?' Lammert asked as he drew on his cigarette. 'Only a handful. Most of those we see are corpses. They fight to the death while their French masters surrender in their droves. It is not hard to work out who are the better soldiers.'

The debate was cut short by the arrival of a motorcycle courier. Lammert went to briefly confer with him and returned with a rare smile on his face.

'No more labouring for us today.' He announced happily. 'The French have broken and are in full retreat. We are to advance on Arras, scouring the countryside for any French stragglers as we go.'

'Ach!' Manfred spat in displeasure. 'You mean that we are to follow on behind the division and sweep up whatever they have left?'

'Exactly so, little Mani.' Lammert teased. 'We wouldn't want to risk you getting your precious head shot off, would we now? We'll stay safely at the rear and keep you safe from any nasty Frenchmen.'

Manfred cursed at this but not as viciously as I wanted to curse him and his uncle for keeping me from the fight. The dead bodies and the destructive power of the French artillery shells had given me pause for thought but had not dampened my hunger for action. I resented them both for keeping me from the fray.

We blundered upon the machine-gun nest less than an hour later. Lammert had ordered us up the wooded slope to search for any French soldiers who had run when our comrades broke their lines. I was so intent on sweeping the trees and bushes as I advanced that I stepped out into the clearing on the brow of the hill without realising that the forest ended there. I dropped my rifle to my side and gazed down the slope at the narrow, winding road at its bottom. I recognised immediately that the column of trucks and staff cars speeding along it were those of my own 14th Company of the Death's Head Division. I watched for a moment, marvelling at the huge cloud of dust that they threw up in their wake. I suppose that I thought it to be an impressive sight. It was only when I glanced to my left that I saw the Frenchmen. They had dug a shallow trench into the crest of the hill and had set up their two heavy machine guns to cover the road below. My heart shot into my mouth in horror as I realised that they were about to fire into the column beneath us. Lammert, Julius, Horse and Manfred emerged from the treeline at that moment and froze at the sight that greeted them.

My eyes met with Manfred's and he simply nodded in response to my unspoken question. We raised our rifles and started to sprint across the clearing with Julius, Lammert and Horse following on behind. I doubt that we had taken more than a dozen steps before the Frenchmen opened up and began to pour bullets down into the German trucks. None of the two machine-gunners, the two loaders and the two accompanying riflemen turned as we raced towards them. With their eyes fixed on their targets and their ears deafened by the din of their weapons, they were oblivious to our approach even as the first of our bullets tore into them. My first shot took one of the riflemen in the side of the head and he fell backwards and away from his comrades who remained oblivious and intent on wreaking havoc amongst the German convoy at the foot of the hill. My second hit the nearest loader in the chest and he slumped forward, causing the soldier manning the machine-gun to catch sight of us and begin to turn his weapon in our direction. If his comrade's twitching corpse had not been in the way, he would have torn us to shreds with a single squeeze of his finger. Despite viciously wrenching his gun against the dead weight of the cadaver, he only managed to turn the barrel through sixty or seventy of the ninety degrees required to bring us into his sights. He fired uselessly across the slope just to the right of us until my bullet caught him just below the chin and threw him backwards like a rag-doll. I was barely conscious of the bullets fizzing through the air around me as my comrades emptied their clips into the French soldiers. The last of the riflemen turned his gun on me just as I reached the lip of the trench. He pulled the trigger at point blank range and then went down as I hammered at his skull with the butt of my rifle. I stopped only when Julius had put two bullets into him.

'Are you hit?' Manfred demanded as he ran his hands over my body in search of holes.

'I don't know.' I replied shakily from the shock of the assault.

'Christ Wolffie!' Lammert exclaimed. 'You have the devil's own luck. I thought we were dead for sure when that bastard turned his gun on us.'

'How can he have missed you?' Horse demanded, his voice shrill with excitement. 'The barrel of his rifle was practically pressed into your chest.'

I could not answer him. I saw the Frenchman pull the trigger and heard the bang but had not suffered so much as a graze or a scratch. I found myself saying a silent prayer of thanks to God above even although such superstitions were forbidden for us men of the SS. I had enjoyed more good fortune in those few short minutes than most men do in the whole of their lives, but that was not the full extent of my luck that day. Amongst the smoking ruins of the trucks down below us sat the staff car of Gruppenfuhrer

Theodor Eicke, commander of the SS-Totenkopf. He had watched on as the five of us sprinted out from the trees and charged at the machine-gun nest with what he perceived to be suicidal bravery. He could not have known that the machine-gunner had fired well wide of us and instead thought that we had unselfishly and courageously endured a hail of bullets and risked certain death to save our SS comrades from the ambush. He called us down from the hill, saluted us, shook us all by the hand and had his adjutant take our names. He then commanded our comrades to cheer us and told them that we were the very embodiment of the values that were at the heart of the SS in general and the Death's Head Division in particular. I would have burst with pride if I had not still been worried that there was a French bullet secretly lodged somewhere in my body.

Wiser men might have reacted to this brush with death by yearning for a return to sentry duty far from the dangers of combat. Unfortunately for us, we were too full of the arrogance and the false sense of immortality that come with youth and instead itched for further contact with the enemy. Our wishes were realised in spades as we advanced north over the next few days. The British Fifth and Thirtieth Divisions smashed into us the following afternoon. The battle was a confusing mess of tanks, armoured cars and infantry and the Death's Head Division faced its first serious reverses during the course of that afternoon. A few companies broke at the sight of the monstrous, thirty-ton, British Matilda tanks and those that stood their ground suffered heavy casualties when our anti-tank shells bounced harmlessly off their thick armour. We would have been pushed back if it had not been for our artillery battalions firing directly at the British tanks over open sights and for the arrival of the Luftwaffe in the form of Stuka bomber squadrons. We counted ourselves lucky that we had not been directly in the path of the tanks and we emerged unscathed from our defensive positions having exchanged heavy fire with British infantrymen who retreated the moment the Luftwaffe put in its belated appearance.

We expected the British to crumble as we advanced because it was clear that they lacked the support required to mount a sustained defence. It puzzled us that they continued to harass us at every turn and to resist us more stubbornly with each passing day. Every hilltop, farmstead, riverbank and bridge was defended to the last and they pounded us with mortars and artillery in a bid to halt us on the bank of La Bassee Canal. There is nothing as dispiriting as a sustained artillery barrage and many brave men were reduced to quivering wrecks as we huddled in our trenches and prayed that the next shell would land elsewhere. A trench to our front took a direct hit and we ran through the mud and pouring rain in search of casualties. We found no sign of the dozen men who had sheltered there apart from a single pair of boots. They sat one beside the other with both sets of laces still neatly and tightly tied. That image stayed with me for a long, long time and I often wondered how an explosion could be powerful enough to blow a man clean out of his boots and leave no trace of him behind. It was somehow more horrific and sinister than the bloodier and gorier injuries more commonly caused by artillery fire.

'Why do these Britischer bastards fight so hard?' Julius demanded bitterly in the midst of a particularly intense mortar attack. 'They must know that they are beaten now that they are surrounded on all sides. Why prolong the agony?'

Lammert laughed and shook his head as if he could not believe the stupidity of the question. 'They sacrifice themselves to buy their comrades the time to escape the trap we have sprung on them. Each day that they hold us here allows more of them to reach the coast and sail for England so that they might live to fight another day.'

We knew immediately that he was correct and it seemed to make the task ahead more daunting for we knew how hard we would fight to save our own friends.'

10

'By the time the order finally came to cross the canal, we were tired of hiding away in fear from the British shells. We tore across the water like snarling, rabid hounds intent on tearing into our enemies in revenge for the grave injuries inflicted upon our comrades and the indignity and terror that they had subjected us to. Any normal, rational men would have folded in the face of the intensity and fury of our attack but the British were neither normal nor rational. They fought on stubbornly against overwhelming odds, withdrawing or surrendering only when their last bullets had been fired. They called us the unhinged fanatics but we were nothing compared to these soldiers. A handful of Royal Scots barricaded themselves inside a pigsty and kept our entire section pinned down for a day and a half. Their piper played the entire time we were exchanging fire and taunted us by saving his jauntiest tunes for when our attacks had been repulsed. It took a direct hit with a mortar to bring their resistance to an end. We found them in a sorry state when we burst in. Four were dead, one was bleeding from a wound to his chest and the last man was merely stunned. All of them were soaked in the pig shit they had lain in for the past two days. They had four bullets between them. I could not help but laugh when the wounded man addressed me.

'Sorry about the mess.' He apologised with the most serious of expressions upon his face. 'We would have cleaned up if we had known that you intended to call upon us.'

'You should have surrendered before we brought the mortar up.' I scolded him. 'What could you have hoped to achieve with only four bullets?'

'We had rather hoped to keep you pinned down until tea-time.' The uninjured man replied with a grin that did not quite mask the pain he was suffering. 'Then we could have scarpered in the dark.'

'Take these stinking bastards to company headquarters.' Lammert ordered us, his face crumpled in distaste. 'The smell of piss and shit makes me want to vomit.'

'But it's almost time for dinner and I'm starving.' Manfred complained. 'Let us take them in the morning.'

Lammert shook his head as he gagged. 'No! I could not stand to have them around. If you go through the woods you could get there, dump the prisoners and be back in an hour. Go now!'

'Christ! The buggers do stink!' Manfred exclaimed as we tramped through the woods behind them. 'It's almost as if they bathed in pig's shit.'

'You should just let us go!' The uninjured man shouted at us over his shoulder. 'Save yourselves the trouble.'

'Keep walking.' I replied. 'Your fighting days are at an end!' I smiled in spite of myself. I found that I enjoyed the man's easy humour and admired his calm demeanour in the face of the disaster that had befallen him. I tried to engage him in conversation about the strength and numbers of the British forces as we walked, but he limited himself to name, rank and serial number and to teasing us and encouraging us to set him free. The only things I learned about Kenneth McLelland were his name, that he was a private and that he had been brought up on a farm in Stirlingshire.

'Look there!' Manfred cried as we exited the woodland and came out into a meadow. 'See what has become of your mighty English army!'

McLelland and his comrade did indeed look glum at the sight of so many of their countrymen being herded into a paddock on the far side of the clearing. Even at such a distance it was clear that these men had been defeated. Their heads hung low and they had been stripped of their arms, helmets and equipment.

'You will be joining them there in a few moments, my friends.' Manfred announced cheerily. 'Then we will be rid of your stink and can go and have our supper.'

The sudden, violent burst of machine-gun fire caused us to flinch and duck down as we searched for the source of the attack. The mass of English prisoners on the far side of the meadow seemed to cry out in fright and throw themselves to the ground in panic and disorder. I opened my mouth to berate them for their cowardice but was stopped from uttering a sound by McLelland dropping to his knees in front of me.

'They have slaughtered them!' He gasped, his voice reduced to a bare whisper by the shock of what he had seen.

I turned to Manfred and saw that all colour had drained from his face. He stood stock still with his mouth agape in disbelief. Despite witnessing it with my own eyes, my brain could not seem to accept that the hundred or so unarmed prisoners had been cut down by my SS comrades. My frantic search for a rational explanation came to an end when the distant German soldiers responded to a shouted order, fixed their bayonets and advanced towards the stricken British soldiers. The sight of them stabbing down at the mass of wounded men caused hot bile to rise quickly in my throat and I vomited the sour, acidic liquid onto the grass at my feet.

'Dirty German bastards!' McLelland snarled up at me from where he still kneeled upon the ground. 'Even animals would not slaughter unarmed men!'

'It must be a mistake!' I stammered uselessly, though I knew that he was right. There was no excuse or justification that could wash this horror away. I was so stupefied that I did not realise that tears were running down my cheeks until McLelland growled at me again.

'Cry all you like!' He snapped. 'You will all be damned for this! Damned!'

'What do we do with these bastards now?' Manfred demanded, his voice high-pitched and trembling. 'If we hand them over here they will be executed.'

'We must release them.' I replied as I dried my cheeks. 'No man deserves to be slaughtered like a beast. Let them find their way back to their own lines.'

'Are you insane?' Manfred screeched. 'They'll shoot us for letting prisoners escape. Is that what you want?'

His panic threw me off balance and made me doubt myself momentarily. I did not think that they would shoot us but knew for certain that they would have us dismissed from the SS in disgrace and then confined to a concentration camp for a time.

'It's a simple choice, Manfred.' I replied, trying to keep my voice even in a bid to calm his state of near hysteria. 'We either let them go or we hand them over and watch them being killed in cold blood. Do you want to take them in?'

Manfred glared at me as if I was an idiot before finally shaking his head. 'They'll fucking shoot us for this!'

'Get up!' I ordered McLelland in English. 'You must go now!'

'You are letting us go?' He asked incredulously when he tore his gaze away from the atrocious scene on the far side of the field. 'How do I know that you won't just shoot us in the back?'

'If I wanted you dead I need only march you over there. It seems that there are Germans there who do not share my squeamishness. You should go northwest. Even if you do not reach your own lines, there are Wehrmacht units there. They will treat you humanely.'

'Will they?' He retorted as he got to his feet and began to nervously help his comrade away. He glanced back at us several times before they disappeared into the trees.

'I don't know.' I finally answered him when he was out of sight, for I was no longer sure of anything.

We had little time to dwell on the outrage at the farm at Le Paradis for we were ordered forward against the British at dawn the very next day. The advance followed the same pattern as before. They held us up with stiff and stubborn resistance and so forced us to clear out villages one house at a time, the struggle often reduced to hand-to-hand fighting and to hacking at one another with entrenching tools. They then retreated to the next defensive line and again forced us to cower beneath fierce, sustained and accurate artillery bombardments. By the time they had repeated this cycle a second time, the bulk of their forces and a large part of the French First Army had withdrawn into the Dunkirk perimeter. The Death's Head Division had suffered such great losses of men and equipment during this battle that we were immediately assigned to a peaceful area around Boulogne to refit, recruit, repair and recover. It was then that the rumours began to circulate.

Lammert made the connection immediately and questioned us about what had happened when we took our prisoners to Le Paradis. We told him that we had marched them to the farm and left them there. He dismissed the claims as salacious gossip at first but became less and less convinced as the chatter continued with increasing intensity. We heard that several SS officers had challenged Hauptsturmfuhrer Knoechlein, the commander of the execution squad, to a duel in disgust at the savagery of his actions. We were told that Himmler himself had berated the Divisional Commander for the incident when he came forward on his personal train to Bailleul to review the division's combat performance. We also heard word of a number of senior officers being despatched from Berlin to investigate the accusations. Manfred and I kept quiet and did not even confide in Julius and Horse because we feared for our reputations and our careers if it became known that we had released our prisoners. Some might call us cowards for not speaking out but we knew that it would make no difference. We were soon proven to be correct when the rumours died away without any duels being fought, any investigations being conducted or any changes being made to the division's command structure. We did not enjoy our rest period in Boulogne due to the constant, gut-wrenching fear of discovery. I seldom slept without suffering a nightmare in which Private McLelland was captured and pointed me out as the man who had set him free.

Our state of mind was not helped by our duties during those early weeks of June. We were ordered south to defeat the remaining French forces but soon discovered that all meaningful resistance had already collapsed. Our section saw no further action and was fully occupied with clearing refugees from the roads to allow our troops to pass and with processing the French soldiers who were surrendering in their droves. A single day saw us take more than one thousand three hundred prisoners. Manfred and I lived in fear of seeing McLelland and his comrade amongst the faces on the road and tried to find comfort by convincing ourselves that they had surely been killed if they had not made it to the British lines and been evacuated from the Dunkirk pocket. Our worst fears seemed to have been realised when Lammert informed us that we had been summoned to Paris by a command that came directly from the Divisional Commander.

'What for?' Manfred demanded. 'What do they want of us in Paris?'

'How would I know, you little shit?' Lammert retorted in irritation. 'Do you think that Gruppenfuhrer Eicke confides in me? Do you think that he likes to spend his evenings sipping cognac and sharing his innermost thoughts with me? Idiot! All I know is what is in the order. Paris, two days from now, full dress uniform, truck leaves first thing tomorrow!'

'Full dress uniform?' Manfred hissed to me in an urgent whisper. 'We are to be court martialled! They must have captured those two English bastards and made them talk.'

'But how could they have identified us?' I protested weakly, not entirely convinced that Manfred was wrong about the court martial.

'Because of you!' He retorted, jabbing his finger at me aggressively. 'Did you not chatter away to them like a nervous girl as we traipsed behind them through the wood? You told them our names, our regiment and where we are from! You gave them all they needed to fuck us, you fool!'

The journey north was nothing short of torture. I felt sick with fear and had to contend with Manfred sulking with me while Lammert, Horse and Julius jabbered away in excitement like children on a trip to the beach.

'Cheer up, you miserable swine!' Lammert scolded me as we drew closer to Paris. 'Would you rather still be herding sullen Frenchmen into their pens?'

He sighed at my weak attempt at a smile and left me to stew in peace. I closed my eyes, not because I thought I could sleep, but merely to discourage the others from speaking to me. I was eventually jolted back into consciousness by the truck shuddering to a halt and by the sound of orders being barked out with urgency.

'Out!' Lammert commanded us. 'It seems that we have arrived later than expected.'

I jumped down from the truck, my eyes blinking in the sudden sunlight and my limbs stiff from so many hours of sitting hunched on the truck's hard bench. My heart hammered in my chest at the sight of ranks of soldiers standing to attention in the forest clearing. I was puzzled to see that a variety of regiments and divisions were represented there. I recognised the uniforms and insignia of the Wehrmacht, the Luftwaffe, the SS

Panzer Division Das Reich and the Leibstandarte Adolf Hitler. Manfred shot a look at me and I knew that he too was wondering if this was some kind of mass punishment parade. A captain I recognised as being from Gruppenfuhrer Eicke's staff came and hurried us along, leading us to the far side of the clearing where around one hundred of our divisional comrades were arrayed. He directed each of us to our allotted places in the front rank and wished us good luck.

Long minutes passed in which nothing happened, no-one spoke and no man moved a muscle. Then, out of the far corner of my eye, I saw a group of officers emerge from an avenue in the trees and begin walking towards us. Even at such a distance and even although I was standing to attention and had to rely on my peripheral vision, I recognised the figure at the centre of this group immediately. A sharp intake of breadth from Julius on my left told me that I was not mistaken. The mere sight of him struck me rigid with awe just as it had when I had gazed at him across the field at Nuremberg. My fears evaporated and were replaced with elation at the prospect of falling within the Fuhrer's sight. The same desperate need to impress that I had experienced at Nuremberg returned and I stood to attention so rigidly that a muscle in my shoulder cramped painfully in protest. I now recognised the men accompanying Adolf Hitler as they made their way towards us. Herman Goering walked on his left clutching his Field Marshall's baton in his hand and Deputy Fuhrer Hess was on his right with our Divisional Commander, Gruppenführer Eicke, in close attendance. Reichsminister Ribbentrop, Field Marshall Keitel, Grand Admiral Raeder and Field Marshall von Brauchitsch followed on behind. I drank this all in whilst keeping my eyes resolutely to the front. My mind already reeled with fantasies of how impressed and envious my friends and comrades would be when I told them that I had been within touching distance of the most powerful men in the Reich. My blood turned to ice when Eicke leaned in towards the Führer and held his hand out towards us.

'These are the men, mein Führer.' He announced, before gesturing at his adjutant to come to him.

Adolf Hitler turned his head and looked directly into my eyes. The world seemed to swim around me and I became conscious that my legs were shaking so uncontrollably that my knees were in danger of knocking against each other. A sheen of sweat instantly bathed my face and rivulets ran down my back. The Führer seemed to frown at me for a second before he broke into a smile.

'Ah! Of course! The Wolves of Le Cateau! Reichsführer Himmler brought your report to me personally when the battle was at its fiercest. The moment he told me of the brave German soldiers willing to run into heavy machine-gun fire to save their comrades, I knew for certain that we would prevail. How could the French hope to stand against men of such courage and determination? I told all my generals the story of my SS Wolf Pack to keep their spirits high and to turn them away from caution when they became nervous at the speed of our advance. The French would not now grovel at our feet and would not be surrendering to us here if I had not persuaded them to display the same courage as our soldiers. Now! Tell me which man led the charge and I will reward him first!'

Gruppenfuhrer Eicke pointed his gloved finger directly at me. 'This is Rifleman Wolff. I saw him run directly at the machine gun nest with my own eyes. He did not falter despite the hail of fire.' He then turned to his adjutant, took something from his hand and passed it to the Fuhrer.

'These are awarded to only the most courageous of us.' He told me as he hung the Iron Cross around my neck and adjusted it so that it sat squarely in the centre of my chest. He then looked me directly in the eye with such intensity that I honestly feared that he could see into my soul. He then smiled again and patted me on the left shoulder with his right hand. 'Wolff by name and wolf by nature. Do not lose your instincts Rifleman Wolff. We will have great need of your fangs and claws before much more time has passed.' He patted me once more and then turned to repeat the process with Lammert, Manfred, Julius and Horse.

The place where he had laid his hand upon me burned with a heat that seemed to sink into my bones. I know that it sounds fantastical, but that heat stayed with me for weeks after that momentous day in the forest at Compiegne. Even now, when I cast my mind back, I can feel it radiate out from my left shoulder. I cannot explain it but know in my heart that it was not imagined.

The whole thing left us dazed, delirious and so filled with pride that we feared that our chests would burst. I can remember little else of what happened in the clearing except that a band began to play the national anthem and the Fuhrer and his party saluted the troops before taking their leave. Even when we were ordered to fall out there was little chance to celebrate. We had just begun to embrace and congratulate one another when Eicke's adjutant appeared at our side.

'I have a car for you!' He announced as he pointed towards a large, open-topped Mercedes that made Hauptsturmfuhrer Wissler's car look like a toy.

'Where to?' Julius demanded, though he still seemed more interested in examining his Iron Cross.

'The Fuhrer is to tour Paris.' He informed us, a subconscious twitch of his nose betraying the fact that it pained him to be delivering this news. I would encounter this reaction a thousand times in the years to come when men's eyes reflected the jealousy they felt at seeing the medal at my neck. 'He has commanded that you are to accompany him to the city as part of his bodyguard.'

We could not believe our luck. We would have counted ourselves fortunate just to have been in his presence. To be honoured by him and then be invited to accompany him as he toured the capital of the defeated French was beyond our wildest imaginings. As it turned out, we did not encounter him again directly but formed part of his retinue as he visited the Paris Opera, the Champs-Elysees, the Arc de Triomphe and the Eiffel Tower. I fell into polite conversation with a man as we waited outside Napoleon's tomb while the Fuhrer paid his respects. He took quite an interest in my engineering studies and advised me to return to university when the final peace was achieved. I would later learn that he was Albert Speer, Hitler's architect, and our paths would across again in a very different capital.'

David Strachan dropped the notebook onto the sofa cushion next to him and rubbed at his tired eyes with the heels of his hands. He had been so engrossed in his grandfather's journal that he had read on into the late afternoon without stopping to eat or to make himself a drink. He searched the fridge while the kettle boiled and found a clear plastic package containing four Asda iced ring donuts. His cousin's thoughtfulness made him smile. She had remembered his passion for the donuts from his student days. He tested one of them with his fingers and, though it was a little hard, he decided it was still edible. He reasoned that they could not go off given that they were ninety percent sugar. He returned to the sofa with the donuts and a strong, black coffee.

He pulled his laptop from his satchel and switched it on as he ate. When it had booted up, he sucked the icing from his fingers and typed

'Hitler Paris' into the search engine. The screen was immediately filled with an assortment of black and white pictures of the Fuhrer's victory tour of Paris. He ignored the first three as they showed only Hitler and Speer with the Eiffel Tower in the background. The fourth image showed a similar image but with an entourage of about twenty Nazis following in the Fuhrer's wake. He increased the magnification and began to examine each face in turn. He let out a long whistle when he found it.

'Bloody hell, Grandad!' He muttered under his breath in astonishment.

Only the top half of his face was visible behind the shoulder of some nameless, forgotten, Nazi general but the eyes were unmistakably, undeniably those of his grandfather. Any lingering doubts about the truth of the journal were blown away. His grandfather might have lived a lie for almost all of his adult life but it seemed that he had not lied in his final testament. Strachan took a bite out of the third donut and lifted the journal back onto his knees.

11

'The next twelve months were the happiest of my life. The Division was posted south to police the demarcation line between the occupied zone and Vichy France. We were mainly quartered in Bordeaux with short amounts of time spent in Avallon and Biarritz. Our mood was one of elation and, having proved ourselves in battle, we were able to relax and fully enjoy this extended period of military inactivity. We spent our days swimming in the clear waters of the Bay of Biscay, basking in the summer sun upon the beaches and lounging in the pavement cafes drinking endless cups of coffee and smoking endless cigarettes. Fraternising with the civilian population was forbidden, but that did not stop us from admiring the French womenfolk or from enjoying the lingering glances we enjoyed whilst dressed in our uniforms with our medals on show. What we looked forward to most of all were our evening excursions into Bordeaux. The wine was cheap, the people were welcoming and we were often so drunk that we danced until our officers or the military police dragged us from the dancefloor and herded us back onto the trucks. We made these excursions even more frequently after Gruppenfuhrer Eicke was thoughtful and considerate enough to have seven Bordeaux brothels reserved solely for the use of the men and officers of the Totenkopf Division.

It was in one of these, a former guest house just off the Rue Sainte-Catherine, that I first saw and fell in love with her. The moment I caught sight of her across the crowded bar, I was completely enthralled. She had a look about her that reminded me of Julius Kammler's cousin, Erica, the girl I had been briefly besotted with back in Berlin. She had curves that Erica did not and an air of world-weariness that I found utterly irresistible. Manfred, in an uncharacteristic moment of insight, saw it immediately and shook his head at me.

'Not again, Wolffie! Just find another girl to fuck. I could not stand to have you mooning around like some love-sick fool again. You were insufferable!'

It was already too late. I was hooked before I had exchanged a single word with her. The moment I worked up sufficient courage to approach her, I was immediately convinced that we had been fated to meet. Her heavily accented French told me that she was Polish and her eyes widened in surprise when I addressed her in her native tongue. This broke the ice between us and I quickly learned that she was called Ania Stachura and that she had been brought up less than ten miles from my boyhood home. She smiled as we talked and no longer looked at me with an expression of haughty disapproval on her face. She laughed when I told her of my love for racuchy and she reached out and laid her fingers on my forearm. I went upstairs with her that evening, I paid her for her services and then did nothing more than talk with her.

'You're not right in the head!' Horse opined when I told them this in the truck on our way back to our quarters. 'Who on earth pays for a whore and then does not stick it in her?'

Manfred just rolled his eyes and shrugged his shoulders. 'Here we go again!' He sighed wearily. 'At least it is not a relative of yours this time, Julius.'

They continued to tease and mock me but it made no difference. I saw Ania every chance I got. I spent all of my pay on her and did nothing more than peck her on the cheek on meeting her and again on taking my leave. I did not see her as a whore as I knew that she, like many of the women in the SS brothels, had been pressed into service against her will. I worshipped her when I was awake and dreamed of kissing and caressing her when I was asleep. My friends warned me that she was taking me for a ride but I was deaf to any words of criticism of my Ania. When my duties took me into Bordeaux more often during the winter and early spring, I seized every opportunity to see her, even to the point of borrowing sizeable sums of money from my comrades. The end, when it came, was sudden, unexpected and would bring disaster crashing down upon me.

If her bottom lip had not been so swollen, I might never have learned the truth. It was only when I pressed her about this injury that she burst into tears and reluctantly pulled her dress down from her shoulders. Of the dozen bite marks across her chest, at least half of them had broken the skin and two of them had left ragged holes where the flesh had been torn away. The rage that overcame me at that moment was so intense that I genuinely feared that I was on the verge of having a seizure.

'Tell me who did this!' I snarled. 'I will slice the bastard open from crotch to throat!'

She refused to name him for fear of what he would do to me if I challenged him and what punishment he would inflict on her for speaking out.

'Then I must get you away from here, Ania.' I declared solemnly. 'I will not leave you to the mercy of such animals.'

'How?' She snorted in derision. 'How will you get me out of here? Will you marry me? How can you when the SS do not allow their men to marry Polish whores?'

The truth of it was that I had no idea how I would help her, but I knew that I would find a way. It was Lammert who reluctantly provided the solution in the end. In return for only two bottles of cognac, his cousin, a clerk at regimental H.Q., drafted the travel papers, added the official stamp and expertly forged the signature of SS Obersturmbannfuhrer Heinz Lammerding. I saw her off at the train station two days later, exchanging the papers for the name of the man who had so violated her. We kissed on the platform and her scent and the feel of her tongue on mine made our parting even more bitter-sweet.

I was happy that she was returning home to Poland and the safety of her family home but knew that I would miss her so much that it would break my heart. We promised to write to one another each and every day and I watched her train until after it was out of my sight. The rage that I felt at that bleak moment was far worse than anything I had felt before. It was as cold as ice, as hard as steel and totally devoid of mercy or decency.

We found Unterscharfuhrer Brandt drinking wine at a table outside a café on the left bank of the Garonne river. He smiled and rose to his feet as he saw me coming.

'How's your little whore, Wolff?' He asked with a grin that revealed his little, rat-like teeth. He then nodded to his friends. 'Perhaps we will all go to see her now and take it in turns. It's what she likes the best!'

I drove my fist into the side of his jaw with such force that it knocked him off his feet and sent him sprawling across the table. As his comrades staggered back and wiped at the red wine that now soaked their trousers, I grabbed the bastard by the throat with my left hand and pummelled at him with my right fist. One of Brandt's friends made a move towards me but was halted by Manfred smashing his elbow into the centre of his face.

'Leave it!' He barked at the others. 'It's between the two of them!'

It was Julius who pulled me off him to stop me from killing him. 'That's enough!' He insisted as he dragged me back. 'I doubt that he'll be biting any more whores.'

I felt not an ounce of pity for that odious man even although I had battered his face to a bloody pulp and left a dozen of his teeth scattered across the pavement. If I had beaten him to death I would have regretted whatever punishment I received but not the act itself. It was no more than he deserved.

It was Lammert who brought the full scale of the disaster home to us when we returned to our quarters.

'You're screwed!' He raged at me as I washed the blood from my knuckles and pulled the ragged skin away from where it had split on Brandt's teeth. 'Little Mani here is not the only one with powerful relatives. Brandt is a distant cousin of our own commanding officer, Obersturmfuhrer Fritz Knoechlein. Who do you think he will favour in a court martial? Brandt was there at the massacre of the English troops at Le Paradis! Knoechlein will move heaven and earth to look after him so that he will keep his mouth shut about what happened that day. Your tale of the mistreatment of some Polish bitch will not sway him for a second.'

'So, how bad is it really?' Manfred demanded. 'Setting aside your great love for drama, exactly how fucked do you think we are?'

Lammert rubbed at his chin as he considered his response. 'I think you're dead if you stay here. Brandt is a vicious little bastard and will never let this lie. I doubt if you'd last a week in Knoechlein's custody.'

Manfred groaned and dropped his head into his hands. 'My uncle will be furious with me. I will send a telegram in the morning.'

'Then it will already be too late for him to help you.' Lammert retorted 'If you are to live, you must keep yourself out of their hands. If you want to stay out of their reach, you must leave now. I would not delay for even another hour if I was you.'

We stopped off at the telegraph office on our way to the station so that Manfred could call his uncle. His face was pale and drawn when he emerged.

'I have never known him to be this angry.' He told me when we had taken our seats and the train had pulled out of Bordeaux. 'He agreed to issue orders recalling us to Berlin but he was not at all happy about it.'

It was some comfort to know that we would not be pursued as deserters but the journey to Paris and then onto Berlin was a miserable affair. We both feared that we had thrown our careers away and I knew that Manfred was beginning to resent me for getting him into this predicament.

'I hope she was worth it!' He muttered as we left the lights of Paris behind. He did not speak another word to me all the way to Berlin.

Hauptsturmfuhrer Wissler was similarly taciturn when he met us at the Anhalter Bahnhof and drove us back towards his house. He did not remain mute for long once we arrived and he let rip at us the moment his study door was closed.

'You have placed me in an intolerable position!' He raged, his every red-faced utterance sending flecks of spittle arcing through the air towards us. 'The Reichsfuhrer is already embroiled in a struggle with Gruppenfuhrer Eicke over the recruitment and supply arrangements for the Death's Head Division and Eicke will no doubt use your recall as a stick to beat Himmler with. I will be forced to use up all of my political capital to keep you two imbeciles out of the grips of that psychopath Knoechlein. And for what? A Polish whore! What the hell were you thinking?'

He continued in this vein for some time, alternating between fury and disbelief at the depths of our stupidity. I could have wept with shame for I worshipped the Hauptsturmfuhrer and was devastated at being responsible for bringing so much trouble to his door. I was also wracked with guilt for having dragged Manfred down along with me. It was not his fight and he had, as the most loyal and true friend a man could wish for, only become involved to protect me from harm.

'I will turn myself in.' I announced when Hauptsturmfuhrer Wissler had paused for breath and to re-moisten his mouth. 'Manfred should not suffer for my mistake. I will take full responsibility for all of it.'

Manfred's uncle stared at me for a moment, his expression aghast and his lips twitching as if he wanted to speak but was struggling to select the right words to use. 'Are you a blithering cretin?' He exploded when he had recovered the power of speech. 'Manfred broke the bastard's nose and stopped the others from coming to their superior's rescue. Has that little whore caused your brain to turn to shit? Do you honestly believe that they will let him be simply because you have put yourself at their mercy?' He shook his head at me dismissively. 'No! They will not. Now I will be forced to call in more favours and find a place for you that it is far beyond their reach.'

'What about Bad Tolz?' Manfred asked tentatively. 'Perhaps now would be a good time to go there.'

The Hauptsturmfuhrer laughed wryly and shook his head again. 'You can forget about officer training after all this shit.' He spat bitterly. 'I doubt if I will be able to find you anything better than washing pots in a field kitchen in some shitty corner of Poland.'

The extent of my infatuation with Ania was clear from my internal reaction to the Hauptsturmfuhrer's words. Rather than feeling dismayed by the prospect of such a poor assignment, I was actually pleased by the thought of being posted somewhere close to her. I wrote to her that night to tell her that we would soon be re-united. Manfred spoiled my mood somewhat by sourly asking if I thought she would charge me the same price as she had in France. I could have quite happily punched him in the mouth for this insult but decided against it on account of having ruined his career and having diminished him in the eyes of his beloved uncle. We moped quietly around the house for several days and tried our best to

139

stay out of the Hauptsturmfuhrer's way. When he finally brought us news of our new posting it was only his sombre and reproachful glare that stopped us from celebrating openly. We had been certain that our SS days were over and were consequently delighted to hear that we were to be assigned to a SS unit in Posen in central Poland. We even dared to hope that the recent disastrous turn of events might yet prove to have been a mere bump in the road and not the end of our careers as we had feared. I was also delighted that I would soon be separated from my love by only a three or four-hour drive in a truck.

'You have got off lightly this time.' The Hauptsturmfuhrer admonished us, though I could tell that he was secretly pleased with the arrangements he had made for us. 'But it is the last time! I will not put my neck on the line for you again.'

We thanked him profusely, promised that we would not screw up again and went off to pack our kit and prepare for our departure. Neither of us wanted to leave Berlin without catching up with poor old Maus, so we arranged to have dinner with him at a place we knew just off Franzosische Strasse. I was surprised to see that he had not changed at all since I last laid my eyes upon him. I was certain that he was even wearing the same jacket and trousers that he had worn when we bunked together in the Wisslers' basement. I was pleased to find that he had come to terms with his rejection by the SS and had thrown himself enthusiastically into his studies. When I told him that I thought he would make a fine doctor, I meant every word. I was equally happy that I detected not even the smallest trace of envy or bitterness on his part. When we told him the details of our service in France and the award of our medals by the Fuhrer himself, I found his congratulations to be entirely warm and genuine. The cause of his current state of contentment was only revealed when we had cleared our plates and called for cognac. Her name was Clara, her father was a professor of literature and Maus was hoping that they would become engaged within the year. He blushed like a beetroot when we teased him about his beloved Clara but we were happy for him. I was happy for all of us because, although we were to be spread across Poland, Germany and France, life seemed to be going in a positive direction for Manfred, Maus, Horse, Julius, Lammert and I.

The first weeks in Posen were almost like a continuation of the life we had left behind in Bordeaux. With the occupation already established, our duties were light and we were left with plenty of time for recreation. There was little prospect of being granted a three-day pass so soon after our arrival so I was forced to bide my time and content myself with writing letters in the hope that Ania would eventually reply. We heard the rumours of an imminent invasion of Russia but dismissed them as we had lived with similar talk of an invasion of Great Britain the whole time we were stationed in France and the gossip there had come to nothing. I noticed the change towards the end of April 1941. There had always been a constant flow of men through the SS due to promotion, reassignment, illness and training, but I observed a discernible increase in the pace of arrivals and departures from the middle of that month. It grew more frenzied as the month progressed and even Manfred became convinced that something was afoot. The prospect of a war against the hated communists filled us with excitement and we even counted ourselves fortunate to have been placed closer to the action than the friends we had left behind in France to continue with their pointless border patrols.

We received our orders the following week and they served to wipe the smug smiles of self-congratulation from our faces. There was to be no front-line role for us and no opportunity to add honours to those we had already won.

'I don't know what you did to deserve this.' Our squad leader intoned when he gave us the bad news. 'But you've either pissed someone off really badly or they think that you're cold-blooded enough to fit in with that shower of sadistic bastards. Whichever one it is, I wouldn't wish it on my worst enemy.'

'What's so bad about it?' Manfred demanded sourly. 'We hunted stragglers, partisans and saboteurs in France. I cannot see why it would be so much worse here.'

The Scharfuhrer leaned back in his chair and regarded us both for a long moment, his eyes flicking constantly between us as if in search of some sign of impertinence. He eventually seemed to conclude that we were dense rather than impudent and he shook his head sadly.

'It is true that Einsatzgruppe B is to have responsibility for combating partisan groups in occupied territory, but that is neither their main function nor their main area of expertise.'

'Then what is their main function?' I asked fearfully, for I detected something in the hardness of the man's expression that greatly unsettled me.

He leaned forward across his desk and dropped his voice so that it was little more than a whisper. 'These men are not fit to wear the SS uniform. They are the lowest of the low. They are nothing more than scum. They are criminals, murderers, psychopaths and sadists who delight in hunting and killing cripples, Jews, Gypsies, intellectuals, communists and homosexuals. They are the kind of men who avoid fighting for their country so that they can delight in the torture and murder of defenceless women and children. I would put a bullet through my own foot before I would serve with them. I would advise you to do the same.'

12

'Our worst fears were realised and then exceeded when we arrived at Einsatzgruppe B headquarters in Posen to report for duty. The staff sergeant who took our papers, Oberscharfuhrer Sauer, made our skin crawl from simply being in his presence. The sour tang of body odour, the greasy skin and the matted hair told us that he was a stranger to soap and water. His tunic was spotted with food stains and was so crumpled and dirty that it seemed likely that he slept in it. This initial impression was not improved when he opened his mouth and enveloped us in the stench of the previous night's garlic and schnapps. When his beady eyes fell upon the Iron Crosses at our necks, his thick lips peeled back in a sneer to reveal a mouth filled with brown, uneven teeth.

'I heard that they were handing out medals like sweets in France.' He snorted, his jealousy writ large upon his face. 'They say that they were handed out to men who did nothing more than direct the traffic.'

'These were presented to us by the Fuhrer himself.' Manfred shot back, his eyes burning with anger. 'For extreme valour under enemy fire. There was no traffic for us to direct when the French opened up with their heavy machine guns!'

Sauer glared back at him whilst digging a dirty thumb nail in between two of his upper molars in a bid to dislodge some stubborn morsel from his breakfast. 'Good!' He said finally, when the silence had dragged on uncomfortably. 'You will need all of your courage where we are going.' He then tapped his index finger against the side of his hooked and bulbous nose with the smug gravitas of a man who is in possession of some great secret not yet entrusted to lesser men. 'But I can say no more about it for now.'

I have never felt a greater degree of contempt for any man than that I felt for Oberscharfuhrer Sauer at that moment. It amazed me that he was stupid or deluded enough to believe that the imminent invasion of Russia was anything other than common knowledge. Only a fool would have failed to reach that conclusion when the last few days had seen the roads suddenly fill with supply trucks, fuel wagons, troop carriers and enough tanks to shake the foundations of the buildings as they passed. I would later read that Stalin had been surprised when the first reports of the invasion reached him. I was mystified by this failure of Soviet intelligence as the clouds of dust raised by the massing troops were so huge that they could be seen clearly from thirty miles away.

'Ah! I see that you were part of Knoechlein's company.' Sauer declared enthusiastically as he examined our papers, the mere mention of the name causing both Manfred and I to stiffen in dread. 'I knew old Fritz back in Munich! I will let

145

him know that you are with me now and will ask him to dish the dirt on you!'

He grinned up at us as if he expected us to share in his joy at this revelation. He shook his head in irritation when we did not respond in kind.

'I will assign you to Gruppenfuhrer Nebe's bodyguard. He likes to surround himself with the finest specimens of German manhood. I have no doubt that it will please him to have two such heroes to protect him and make him look good when the Reichsfuhrer comes to check up on him.'

'Reichsfuhrer Himmler?' I asked with some excitement. I still recalled our brief sighting of him in the street in Nuremberg.

'Yes, yes!' Sauer replied, waving my question away with his hand. 'We have been told to expect an inspection at some point but that is no concern of yours. Go and find your quarters!'

'Christ!' Manfred exploded once we were outside. 'We might as well have stayed in France. Knoechlein will know where we are in a matter of days!'

The next few days did nothing to improve our mood. We found our new comrades to be even more loathsome than we had been led to believe.

'I do not think I will be able to sleep here.' I whispered to Manfred as we made up our bunks in the barracks. 'It is as if we have been thrown into an institution for the criminally insane.'

'It is worse than that Wolffie.' Manfred replied, his shoulders hunched as if to shield himself from the unwavering and malevolent gazes of the slack-jawed half-wits who lay upon the bunks behind us. 'Remember the political instruction we received at the training camp at Dachau? Remember how the tutors raged and ranted about the Untermenschen, the genetically inferior, subhuman parasites who are morally and spiritually incapable of resisting their most basic urges? They told us that we would find them to the east, but they were wrong. We are amongst them now and they are wearing the uniform of the SS.'

Our spirits sank still lower when the sudden movement of men and materiel told us that the invasion of Russia had begun. It was bad enough to be forced to sit on the sidelines while there was glory to be won, but it was intolerable to have to do so in the company of the type of despicable rats we would have avoided like the plague in our previous lives. It was something of a relief when we were ordered forward in the wake of the armies of Field Marshals von Leeb, von Bock and von Rundstedt. The armies advanced with such speed that they drew so far ahead of us within a couple of days that we could no longer see columns of battle smoke on the horizon or hear the thunder of the artillery as they smashed the Russians to pieces. The early days of the invasion saw Einsatzgruppe B involved in genuine combat operations against stragglers from the overwhelmed and shattered Russian armies. This, along with the fact that our roles within Gruppenfuhrer Nebe's bodyguard kept us at a distance from day-to-day operations, allowed us to bury our heads in the sand and ignore the true

147

purpose of our task force. It became harder to sustain this state of blissful ignorance as we approached Minsk and began to make preparations for the establishment of Nebe's headquarters in the Belorussian capital

Our experiences in France had hardened us to the realities of war and we were not fazed by the sight of the burnt villages by the roadside or by the bodies of partisans hanging from the trees in village squares. The scene that we briefly glimpsed as we sped through the little lakeside hamlet to the northwest of Minsk was very different and brought the reality of our situation crashing home to us. The truck was moving at speed to keep up with Nebe's staff car and we passed by so quickly that we did not have time to count the bodies our comrades had strung up from the branches of the ancient tree at the hamlet's centre. It was not just the sheer number of bodies that filled us with horror, though it was unusual to see so many in a single place. It was not even the fact that at least half of them were women, though it sickened me to know that men of the SS had thought it acceptable to summarily execute them despite their gender. What made the bile rise to my throat and burn there was the sight of the little bodies hanging limp and lifeless alongside their families. The smallest was little more than a toddler and the eldest cannot have been much older than nine or ten.

'What madness is this?' Manfred hissed at me, his face ashen. 'Are we murdering children now?'

148

'It is for the best.' The man on the bench opposite me interjected. 'If we do not kill the children now, they will grow up and our own children will be forced to fight them. It is best to grasp the nettle and be done with it once and for all.' He shrugged and drew on his cigarette when we glared back at him. 'Just be thankful that you do not have to do the dirty work. I have heard that Gruppenfuhrer Nebe wants five hundred Jews killed every day once we are in Minsk.'

'I will telephone my uncle.' Manfred promised me when we had found our quarters for the night. 'He will get us out of here.'

Manfred spoke with Hauptsturmfuhrer Wissler three times during the following month but was never able to raise the subject of us being assigned to another unit because the orderly in the communications room refused to leave him to speak privately.

'Did you offer him cigarettes as I suggested?' I asked him after his third attempt.

'The bastard neither smokes nor drinks.' Manfred snapped back. 'I dare not speak in front of him as I am certain that Sauer would hear every word within minutes of the connection being cut.'

Though still somewhat insulated from the horrific reality of our situation by our bodyguard duties, we were not altogether immune. We heard the rumours of the executions that were taking place and of the daily orders exhorting the killing squads to greater efforts. Even in this endless morass of depravity, we learned of things that sickened us and took us to new depths of disbelief and despair. It was Sauer himself who gleefully told us about the fate of twenty-four mental patients from a psychiatric hospital on the outskirts of Minsk. He told us that it had been decided to use explosives rather than bullets to bring their suffering to an end. He detailed the laborious process of digging a bunker and then forcing the poor, frightened and reluctant souls down into it. I will never forget his sadistic glee when he described how the explosion had killed only half of the patients and how the others had scrambled out of the smoking bunker screaming, horribly injured and soaked in blood and gore. He shook his head sadly at the thought of how much time and explosives had been wasted and rued the fact that it had taken more bullets to cut the terrified and fleeing patients down than it would have done to just shoot them in the first place. Sauer was so caught up in the telling of his tale that he did not notice Manfred reaching for his pistol or me laying my hand on his to restrain him.

'I cannot stay here, Wolffie.' Manfred informed me later that evening, his voice breaking with emotion. 'I am close to losing my sanity. I swear that I will put a bullet into that twisted bastard's brain and then turn the gun on myself!'

'It is the Reichsfuhrer's inspection tomorrow.' I replied, patting his shoulder to calm him. 'Perhaps there will be an opportunity to telephone your uncle during the dinner that is planned for the evening. Stay calm! We will find a way out of this. I promise you!'

I had always harboured a naive belief that our leaders knew nothing of the outrages that were being committed in their names. Reichsfuhrer-SS Heinrich Himmler's visit to Minsk tore that comfortable delusion away from me. I saw him at close quarters when he inspected the ranks on his arrival at Nebe's headquarters and I found nothing that impressed me. When I was young and before it became dangerous to utter a word of criticism of the Nazis, my father would deride Himmler as a jumped-up chicken farmer. My first sight of the Reichsfuhrer in the flesh brought my father's words back to me. It was hard to believe that this man was one of the most powerful and most feared men in the Reich when, stripped of his uniform, you would have thought him to be a tax inspector, a customs officer or some other sort of petty functionary. The man who followed behind him was a different proposition altogether. SS Gruppenfuhrer Reinhard Heydrich was a tall, impressive figure with an overly large forehead, wide, full lips and the small, cruel eyes of a fox. His eyes passed over me for only a second but his gaze bore into me with such intensity that it caused the hairs on the back of my neck to stand up and my scrotum to contract involuntarily and pull my balls hard up against my groin. He spoke to Himmler once they had passed me in the line and his voice was strangely high-pitched and his speech staccato. My every instinct told me that I was in the presence of a malign and bestial creature and I felt waves of malice and spite radiate out from him like the heat from a fire. It

151

was only when he had passed out of my sight that I realised that I had been holding my breath out of some visceral fear the whole time he had been close to me. I knew in that moment that my days in the SS were almost at an end, for I did not want to be part of an organisation that was led by men such as these. My pride in the uniform had been based on an illusion and had now degenerated into shame and disgust.

The events of that afternoon reinforced my decision to the point that it was irreversible. We accompanied Nebe and Himmler's inspection party to a clearing where a large pit had been dug in the ground. A line of prisoners stood along its edge. I knew immediately what was about to happen and turned to glance at Manfred. His expression was as grim as my own and I saw that his hands were trembling at his sides. They shot them ten at a time, pausing only to cover the first group in a thin layer of dirt before bringing up the next ten for execution. In the course of this demonstration of the Einsatzgruppe's skill and efficiency, they murdered ninety-eight Jewish men and two Jewish women. I initially thought that the Reichsfuhrer was enjoying the spectacle for he stood on the very edge of the pit to watch the killings at the closest of quarters. It was only when the inspection party came back towards us as they returned to their cars that I realised that the horror he had just witnessed had brought him close to fainting and vomiting in front of the killing squad. His face was waxy and deathly pale as he passed us and one of the senior officers had taken his arm to keep him from collapsing. I heard him speak just before he climbed into his car and caught his words even although his voice was low and shaky.

'We must find alternative methods.' He told Nebe. 'We must think of the welfare of our men.'

Any lingering vestiges of respect I had for the man or for his rank evaporated in that moment. It seemed despicable to me that the man responsible for so much slaughter and death was so weak that he became nauseous and squeamish when faced with the reality of his own policy.

'You must make that call tonight!' I told Manfred once we were seated in the truck. 'I will come with you and pull that bastard orderly away from his radios and telephones if I have to!'

We were fortunate to find the communications room empty and Manfred wasted no time in calling Hauptsturmfuhrer Wissler. I nodded encouragement as Manfred outlined our situation to his uncle and then grimaced in despair when it became increasingly evident that his pleas were falling on deaf ears.

Manfred swore as he slammed the telephone back into its cradle. 'He will not help us. We are on our own!'

My heart sank at these words, though they merely confirmed what I had already gleaned from Manfred's side of the conversation and from the indistinct and angry buzzing that had reverberated down the line from Berlin.

'He offers us nothing but metaphors.' Manfred complained bitterly, his shoulders hunched and his expression pained. 'He says that we pissed in our own soup and so have no right to complain about the taste. He also advises us against shitting in our own nest and made it plain that he feels that, as we made our bed, we should now lie in it.'

'But what about the executions?' I demanded. 'What did he say when you told him about that?'

'He already knew.' Manfred replied, his eyes filling with tears. 'He said that the work is unpalatable but necessary if the lands to the east are to be successfully settled by the German people. Unpalatable? He would not say that if he had seen those little children hanging from the trees! He would think of his own girls and be filled with revulsion.'

My mind was racing at the sight of my friend unravelling before my eyes. I fought to regain control of myself for I genuinely feared that he might do something stupid before taking his own life. He had always looked after me and I was determined to do the same for him.

'Then we must extricate ourselves from this nightmare!' I declared with more confidence than I felt. 'We will go to Sauer and request a transfer in the morning!'

We disturbed Oberscharfuhrer Sauer in the midst of mining the inside of his left nostril with the nail of his filthy, ragged index finger. He was so intent on his task that he did not register our presence until he had located a tasty nugget and pulled it out for closer examination. Most people would be mortified to be caught in such an act but

Sauer was unabashed and waved us forward as he consumed what he had caught.

'Ah!' He declared sarcastically. 'If it is not the Fuhrer's little heroes. Tell me, what is it that you can do for me today!'

I ignored this puerile and well-worn attempt at humour and got straight to the business in hand. 'We wish to submit a request to be transferred to a front-line unit at the earliest opportunity. We feel that the skills we gained in the battle for France would best serve the Reich at the front rather than far behind the lines.'

Sauer raised his eyebrows in an expression of disbelief and gazed at each of us in turn. 'You know that the Ruskies are different to the French?' He leaned forward as he spoke and waved us in towards him as if he was about to share a confidence with us. 'They do not throw down their arms and surrender at the first sight of our Panzers. They send men charging at our guns all day long and then pummel them with their artillery all through the night so that there is not a moment's rest from one day to the next. I have it on good authority that our glorious advance has been halted in its tracks and our casualty rates are the highest in recorded history. You would be leaving all of this to jump into a mincing machine.'

'Nevertheless.' I replied with calm determination. 'We would like to be transferred.'

Sauer's face creased in puzzlement and he gnawed on his fingernail as he examined us. His eyes flicked constantly between us as he tried to work out what trick we were trying to pull on him. He then grinned horribly and tapped at the side of his head with his finger.

'I see what you two are up to!' He then pointed at Manfred and wagged his finger at him. 'I saw you at the execution yesterday. You were the only man there who was paler than the Reichsfuhrer. Christ! I should have known it! Your little hands were trembling and jerking like a pervert's cock at an orgy.' He shook his head in disapproval, but his facial expression revealed just how much he was relishing the moment. 'It's typical of you mummy's boys! You strut around with your medals on show but do not have the guts or the balls for the work we are doing here. You make me sick! Don't think for a second that I don't see you looking down your noses at us! It's us who should look down on you! Bloody cowards!'

'Cowards?' Manfred challenged him, his face reddening in the face of his insults. 'Then why are we asking to go to the front while you are happy to stay here to murder defenceless women and children miles from any enemy soldiers?'

'Then you shall have your wish!' Sauer spat back furiously. 'We don't want any spineless bastards here. We need real men with the guts to do what is necessary. You'll go to the front to be torn apart by the communists but you won't disgrace that uniform while you do it. I'll have you discharged from the SS with immediate effect and you'll be transferred to the first Wehrmacht regiment desperate enough take you! Now get out! You will have your papers by the morning!'

156

There was a time when the prospect of being drummed out of the SS would have filled me with dread. Now that it had happened, I felt as if a great weight had been lifted from my shoulders and I was light-headed with elation.

'Your uncle will be furious when he hears of this.' I teased Manfred in my joy as we walked towards the barracks. 'He will think that it reflects badly on him.'

'Fuck him!' He retorted sourly. 'He was happy to leave me to rot with these sick, sadistic bastards. I owe him nothing now!'

We received our papers at dawn the next day and were on a truck heading east before the sun had reached its highest point in the sky. Neither of us cast a single glance back towards Minsk even when the distant thunder of artillery fire reached our ears.'

13

The shrill ringing of the telephone jolted David Strachan back into the real world and he dropped his grandfather's journal onto the sofa on his way to answer it. It surprised him to see that the sky was darkening outside as he had been unaware of the passing hours as he read. He smiled at the sound of his cousin's voice and blinked in an effort to soothe his tired eyes.

'What are you up to?' She asked, the long-established familiarity between them negating the need for any level of formality.

'Just going through grandad's stuff.' He replied evasively, as he had not yet decided whether or not he would be sharing the contents of the journal with anyone. 'I should be done by the end of the weekend, I reckon. It's just his shed left to do but its crammed with stuff and it might take a wee while to sort it.'

'That'll leave you a few days before the funeral then. Do you fancy doing something tomorrow?'

'What like?' He asked, his gaze falling on the journal where it lay on the sofa, much of it still tantalisingly unread.

'Spot of lunch in Perth, maybe see a film and then finish with some retail therapy.'

'How about Monday instead? That way I can get finished up here and really enjoy it.'

'That would work for me.' She replied happily. 'I can nip into the office for a couple of hours in the morning and then use some of that flexi-time I've been building up!'

Strachan felt a little guilty for putting her off but he was dying to finish the journal. He now had the whole weekend to devote to it without fear of interruption. He boiled the kettle and spooned three measures of Nescafe into his Crème Egg mug.

'Right Grampy!' He drawled to himself as he ripped the Mars Bar wrapper open with his teeth. 'Let's see what the hell you got up to next!' He washed the chocolate and caramel down with a mouthful of the hot, bitter coffee and began to read.

'Sauer's description of the Russians was intended to frighten us but it also turned out to be completely accurate. They fought like cornered beasts and resisted us fiercely in spite of our great superiority in weaponry and leadership. Manfred and I were assigned to a Sixth Army infantry battalion that was part of Field Marshal von Rundstedt's Army Group South. We joined them as they pushed towards Kiev and found morale amongst the troops to be high after weeks of heavy fighting which had seen them advance hundreds of miles into enemy territory and defeat all who stood in their path. Our officers shared in this elation and took great joy in telling us that more than three million German and allied troops had been committed to what was the greatest military offensive in history. They detailed the territory gained, the numbers of Russians killed and taken prisoner and the great volume of supplies and armaments seized from our defeated enemy and hailed them as irrefutable evidence of our superiority. It was accepted as a fact that we would prevail and be in Moscow by Christmas.

We found it very easy to get caught up in the triumphal atmosphere as the buccaneering Panzer Groups of Field Marshals Kleist and Guderian smashed through the Russian lines before turning back to fall upon their stricken armies while we infantrymen came up to encircle them. It brought to mind our early days in France with Lammert, Julius and Horse when we imagined ourselves to be the dashing Knights of the New Order as our trucks flew through the French countryside and rushed us towards our enemy. It was similar but not the same. We had changed since then and had lost the naivety and certainty of righteousness that came with youth and blissful ignorance. We no longer thought that our cause was just while that of the Russians was purely evil. We now recognised the shades of grey and accepted that none of us was free of sin. The nature of the struggle was also different. We had not come here to fight the Russians until they surrendered honourably and signed a peace like that concluded in the forest at Compiegne. It was not enough for us to face them in battle and force them to submit. We had not come to defeat them, we had come to annihilate them totally. That savage strategy forced the Russians to conduct themselves very differently to the French and British troops in France prior to their defeat. They did not throw down their arms and surrender once their last bullets had been fired. Soldiers and civilians alike fought on with blade and bludgeon and with tooth and claw. The struggle brought out the worst in men and plumbed new depths in brutality, savagery and depravity.

The battle for Kiev was like a slow descent into the very depths of hell. It lasted only a little over a month but I remember it as an eternity of smoke, dirt, thunder and an ever-present fear of death that haunted even those few fitful dreams I had when rare, truncated opportunities for sleep arose. We were told that five Soviet armies were trapped in the pocket created when the pincers of our advance closed around them. It is beyond me how a single man survived the onslaught when our tanks, artillery and aircraft bombarded them mercilessly from one dawn until the next. Even the civilians resisted us when all sense dictated that they should yield. Old men and young boys took up arms and fought alongside the military while their womenfolk picked up shovels to dig trenches to halt our tanks and buried thousands of mines to impede the advance of infantry and mobile units. It is difficult to contemplate the level of determination and hatred required for them to stand their ground in the face of such force. We were clearing houses on the outskirts of the city when I saw an old man charge at a platoon of infantry wearing only his underclothes and brandishing a cooking pot as a weapon. They shouted warnings at him but he kept on coming, his face twisted in fury and a low growl coming from deep in his throat. The first bullet slowed him but did not put him down. The second almost took his leg off at the knee but it did not stop him from cursing at them as he writhed and bled out in the dirt.

'We have made animals of them.' I said to Manfred as we watched him breath his last.

Manfred nodded, his face grave beneath the layers of soot and dirt that masked his features. 'Then it would be best for us to finish them here. Can you imagine what they would do to us if the shoe was ever on the other foot?'

I shivered at the thought and then went to fetch the old grandfather's cooking pot. Manfred had found a fish and some potatoes in one of the houses and we would have need of it if we were to have them for our supper.

Our meal was simmering away above a fire made from the slats of a broken garden fence when our Section Leader, Unterfeldwebel Backe, came with the news that the Russians had finally surrendered.

'Somebody should tell these bastards then!' Manfred declared sourly as he pulled his stirring stick out of the pot and pointed it towards the sound of gunfire coming from only a few streets away.

Backe shrugged and might have grimaced though it was difficult to tell when his face was as dirty as our own. We called him 'Smiler' behind his back on account of him being the most

162

miserable bastard either of us had ever met. He had an expression of extreme discontent permanently etched onto his face and I could not remember having ever seen him laugh or even smile. He was the kind of man who was incapable of enjoying a celebration and would instead fret about who was going to clear up afterwards. His attitude to the news of the surrender of the encircled Soviet armies was typical of him.

'Now we will have the job of escorting the prisoners to the rear.' He complained. 'They say that there are more than three hundred thousand of them.'

'Christ!' Manfred exclaimed with a whistle. 'The bastards will clean out our stores if we are to feed them!' He then shook his head and returned to his stirring. 'Cheer up!' He chided Backe. 'At least we will not have to fight them now. That's a good thing!'

Backe glared back at him, the corners of his mouth turned down even further than was usual. I suppose that he must have grown sick of being told to cheer up so many times over the years. Then, before my very eyes, a remarkable thing occurred. A grin started to form on Smiler's face. It was small and weak and looked out of place in such alien territory, but it was an unmistakable sign of genuine amusement. I watched as he reached into his pocket with his long, thin fingers and extracted a ragged scrap of cloth.

'Congratulations Wolff!' He announced cheerily. 'You are promoted to Squad Leader.' He then tossed the patch towards me.

'Christ's sake!' Manfred exploded. 'Why him? I have more leadership skills in my little finger than he has in the whole of his body!'

'I did think of you when Greiser stepped on that mine and got his foot blown off.' Backe replied, his grin now wider and even less in keeping with the rest of his face. 'But then you told me to cheer up! Giving it to Wolff and pissing you off has cheered me up no end!'

Manfred was still muttering to himself as we scraped the last of our meal from the bottom of the pot and watched as the first of the prisoners were escorted past us on their way west. It was not the number of them that disturbed me most, though there must have been three whole armies' worth of them in the endless, ragged procession that continued to trudge past us long into the night. It was not their wretched condition that troubled me, though more than half of them were wounded and all of them marched forward with their shoulders hunched and their gazes fixed upon the ground. It was their eyes that made my stomach churn and brought the sour taste of acid and half-digested fish to the back of my throat. It was as if the great trauma of their defeat had torn their souls away from them, leaving them as ghosts of their former selves with their blank and empty eyes reflecting their essential hollowness.

'Christ!' I exclaimed as we sat and smoked while the remnants of the defeated Soviet armies tramped dejectedly past us. 'I hope that we are never defeated Manfred. Look at what it has done to these poor bastards. It's like the march of the damned.'

Manfred shook his head and took a long drag before exhaling. 'I doubt that it will happen to us, my friend. How can they continue to fight when they have lost so many of their men already? You cannot just conjure up armies from nothing. The Russians are all but finished. You can take my word on that.'

'Sir!' I replied, forcing myself to keep my face straight and my eyes to the front.

'What?' Manfred demanded, his face creased in confusion.

'You should have said, 'You can take my word for that, sir.' I'm your superior now so you should address me accordingly.'

'Get fucked!' He shouted at me in disgust. 'I'll address you accordingly by shoving the toe of my boot up your arse!'

'Up my arse, sir!' I teased and then ducked to avoid the cooking pot as it whistled over my head. It clattered and banged as it rolled across the road towards the marching prisoners but not one of them looked up in response to the din it made. They just traipsed on, oblivious to everything except their own purgatory of loss and hopelessness.

There was no rest for us in the days following the surrender of the Soviet troops. We were ordered into the countryside to the east of the city to hunt for stragglers and partisans. We found thousands of them, some cowering in the undergrowth in the hope of evading us and some sitting in the open as if they had resigned themselves to being captured. The vast majority of them threw their arms into the air at our approach and came without a struggle. The reason for this was clear when we searched them, for we found no man with more than a handful of bullets in his possession and most had none at all. A few brave souls did attempt to resist but none of them lasted for very long. If the machine gunner could not move them with his MG 34, we would try to blast them out with a few well-placed grenades. There was only one occasion when we were forced to call for mortar support and those men had thrown their weapons down before the second shell had even hit the ground.

Manfred had always been ruled by his stomach and had a reputation for being able to sniff out food no matter what situation he found himself in. It was towards the end of the second day of the clearing out operation that he suddenly appeared with a dead goat across his shoulders.

'Is it fresh?' I asked him suspiciously, my nose wrinkling as I tried to detect any hint of corruption. 'It looks as if it was hit by machine gun fire.'

'Would I be blooding carting it around on my shoulders if it was rotten?' He retorted. 'Now, you go and fetch some firewood while I gut it. We'll have it roasting nicely before the sun goes down!'

The aroma of roasting meat soon filled the air and it brought Backe and a few other members of our section to the fireside. Manfred waved them in as there was more than enough for all of us.

166

'Have you heard the rumours?' Backe asked us as he tucked into a slab of hot, greasy meat.

'Yes.' I nodded. 'We heard the explosions in the city and saw the fires burn long into the night. They say that it was the work of Russian spies.'

'Not that.' Backe replied brusquely. 'I was told that your old friends have been busy.'

'What friends of ours?' I demanded, for I could tell from his expression that his news was unlikely to be to my liking.

Backe finished chewing what was in his mouth and wiped the grease from his lips without taking his gaze from mine. 'An officer from an anti-tank battalion told me that your old SS comrades are here. He said that they plastered the city in posters ordering the Jews to report to them for resettlement. He reckoned that thousands and thousands of them reported at the time and place they had been instructed to, but that the men of the Sonderkommando and Einsatzgruppe C did not load them onto transports. He told me that they forced them into a ravine, stripped them of their clothes and valuables and then shot them ten at a time. Not a single one of them was spared, not even women and babies. Can it be true? Would they have done such a thing, your old Einsatzgruppe comrades?'

I found that my appetite had suddenly vanished and I dropped my eyes to the ground to avoid the question. Manfred had no such compunction and answered without hesitation.

'It is their function.' He said simply with a shrug of his shoulders. 'They come along behind

167

us and liquidate the undesirables in the conquered territories.'

'That's shit!' Snapped one of the riflemen who had come with Backe. 'You are fools if you swallow such Russian propaganda. They spread these lies to damage our morale. You cannot believe that such outrages would be allowed. The Fuhrer would not let it go unpunished!'

'I have seen them do it whilst Himmler watched on and applauded them for their work.' Manfred replied. 'I saw nothing of what happened in the city, I but believe it to be true.'

'I could report you and have you shot for spreading these lies.' The young man retorted angrily. 'It is forbidden to say such things about the Fuhrer.'

'How can it be lies when the Fuhrer has laid out all his plans for those of us not too blind to see? I know that you carry a copy of Mein Kampf in your pack. I suggest that you read it. He said that he would punish the French for the humiliation of Versailles and he has done so. He said that he would conquer the lands to our east to create living space for the Reich and here we are winning those lands for him. He also committed himself to the bloody process of eliminating the Jews and this too is being done in his name. Read it! Open your eyes and see what we have become!'

'Arsehole!' The rifleman snapped, his face crimson with rage as he tossed his cut of meat at Manfred's feet. 'Keep your shitty goat! I would rather starve than take a single morsel from your hand!'

168

Backe watched him go with a sardonic expression on his face. 'Goodness me! I am glad that I did not mention the Russian prisoners. It would have given him a seizure!'

'What about the Russian prisoners?' Manfred enquired as he continued to chew, his appetite unaffected by the subject and intensity of his exchange with the rifleman.

'Let's just say that we do not have to worry about feeding them. I am told that they are to be marched all the way back to Germany. I doubt that many of them will make it now that winter is almost here.'

'There must be more Russian soldiers behind us now than there are to the front.' Manfred replied thoughtfully. 'They will collapse soon enough and we will be in Moscow for Christmas.'

We all nodded and continued with our meal, not yet aware that the Russians had no qualms about sending untrained civilians into battle and so could indeed conjure up whole divisions from thin air.'

14

'It seemed that Manfred's prediction of Christmas in Moscow was not so far-fetched when we received our new orders the next morning. The Sixth Army was to be detached from Army Group South to join Army Group Centre in an all-out drive for Moscow. Our spirits were high as we climbed into our trucks and set off across the wide expanses of conquered territory. The first days of the offensive were reminiscent of our early days in France. Guderian's Panzer Group raced ahead to break through the Russian lines and we followed in their wake to mop up whatever was left behind. The resistance was so light and ineffectual that we believed our own stories and theories about the inevitable, imminent collapse of the whole Soviet military. We covered several hundred miles within the first six days of the advance, half the distance between us and Moscow, and succeeded in encircling the strategic city of Bryansk. We then set ourselves to the familiar task of neutralising the Russian troops we had surrounded. We found them to be in a sorry state, short of weapons and ammunition, dressed in uniforms that were threadbare and mismatched and dazed by the speed with which they had been overtaken. They surrendered in their droves and we marched them west in columns that seemed to stretch as far as those that had made their way out of Kiev.

It was while we were conducting these clear-up operations that I won my Iron Cross First Class and my second promotion. I had assumed that the men we were tracking through the forest were merely another group of dispirited, demoralised stragglers who would likely give themselves up the moment they caught sight of us. I only realised my mistake when they opened up on us with their heavy machine-gun, badly wounding two of my six-man squad in the process. It was this that caused me to lose my head, for I took my leadership position seriously and believed that it was my responsibility to keep my men safe from harm. I did not hear or see the bullets as I ran at them and was only aware that they were firing at me because of the splinters that exploded from the trees to either side of me. It was an unseen tree root that saved me. My foot slipped on it as I brought my heel down and it sent me sprawling across the damp earth before coming to rest against a thick, rotten, moss-covered tree trunk. It jumped with a hollow thud with every bullet that they poured into it. Manfred came scrambling and sliding to my side.

'Have you lost your mind!' He snapped at me, ducking down to avoid a shower of dirt and rotten bark thrown up by the bullets crashing into the damp, soft wood. 'There's about ten of the bastards there! I saw two machine-guns and some kind of mortar before you decided to rush out and get your arse blown off!'

'Shit!' I cursed, now realising that I had made the situation worse rather than better. I looked back towards our original position and grimaced at the lack of any cover to protect us if we decided to retrace our steps. My stomach lurched when the firing stopped and an eerie silence fell upon the forest.

'Mortar!' Manfred hissed in a whisper. "They mean to blast us out!' He then jerked his thumb towards the tree trunk and mimed an explosion with his hands to indicate that it would provide us with no real protection.

I knew immediately that there was only one possible course of action open to us that had some small chance of success. Manfred nodded his agreement when I signalled this to him and we pulled the grenades from our belts. We counted to three and threw the grenades as hard and as fast as we could before ducking back under cover. The fuses were set to five seconds but it seemed to take an age before they detonated with a bang that caused my ears to ring. A second, louder explosion sounded immediately after the first and showered us with dirt and splinters as we vaulted over the rotten log and charged at our enemies. Whatever Russian ordinance had been detonated by our grenades had wreaked havoc amongst them. Six men lay dead in the smoking crater and three writhed upon the ground in agony from their terrible injuries. Only one man fired at us with his rifle and his face was so torn from shrapnel that his own blood poured into his eyes and prevented him from shooting with any accuracy. I paused on

172

the edge of the crater and emptied my clip into his chest. I then stood in shock and gazed at the carnage we had caused. One of the Russians had lost his arm at the shoulder but just sat in the dirt wide-eyed and blinking. He was so dazed that he did need seem to have noticed his loss or the fact that his lifeblood was pumping out of him in great crimson spurts. Another was trying to crawl away from us with one hand while using the other to stop any more of his guts from sliding out of the ragged hole in his abdomen. I knew immediately that we could do nothing for them. The few bandages we had between us would have been insufficient to stem the flow of blood from a single one of their wounds. I resigned myself to having to watch them die as I did not have the stomach required to put them out of their misery.

It was then that I turned my head to the left and looked out across the clearing below us. I jerked in fright at the sight of a section of men staring up at us and then relaxed when I realised that it was Backe and the rest of his men. His eyes were as wide as saucers and his face as white as milk.

'Jesus Christ!' He declared as he approached me. 'The bastards would have had us if you had not run at them. Look! Two heavy machine-guns! They would have ambushed us and slaughtered every last one of us!'

I saw immediately that he was right. The Russian machine-guns had not been pointed at us but had been set up to cut down any Germans who emerged into the clearing below.

'I owe you my life, Wolff!' Backe announced solemnly as he reached out and grasped my shoulder, his eyes still wide from the shock of coming so close to death. 'I would be lying dead now if it were not for you. I owe you a great debt.'

'Then build us a fire!' Manfred shouted up at him from where he had been foraging in the bottom of the crater. 'This bastard had two rabbits in his pack! Look! He has already skinned them for us!'

My stomach gurgled and grumbled at the thought of hot meat despite the carnage at my feet and the horrible groaning of the dying Soviets.

It was two weeks later when we received the summons to present ourselves at headquarters. We were not actually told why our presence was required but Backe had informed us that he had submitted a report on our actions along with a recommendation that our courage under fire be recognised. This prospect cheered us greatly and we welcomed the opportunity to escape the daily grind of our duties for the duration of the two days the round-trip would take. It was Field Marshal von Reichenau himself who pinned the medals on our chests. He was what I would describe as an old-style Prussian General, tall, aristocratic, with steel-grey hair and a monocle jammed between his brow and the top of his cheek bone. I noticed his nose wrinkle as he presented Manfred with his medal. We had made an effort with our appearance but, without access to a bath and laundry facilities, we were less than fragrant and the dirt ingrained into our trousers and tunics had

174

resisted all of our efforts to brush it out and wipe it away.

'Sort these men out with new kit!' He ordered his adjutant as he came to stand before me. 'It is the least they deserve for taking out an enemy machine gun post!' He then reached behind him for the Iron Cross and went to pin it on my tunic. 'You will tell your grandchildren about the day a Field Marshall awarded you this medal.'

'I was awarded the first by the Fuhrer himself, Herr Field Marshal.' I replied a little nervously.

'Did he now?' The Field Marshal replied, a slight smile playing upon his lips. 'Then you shall just have to make do with me this time, I suppose.' He paused for a second and looked me directly in the eye before winking at me. 'Just remember that it was I who awarded you the Iron Cross, First Class. He did not stretch beyond the Second Class award! Neither did he promote you as I am about to do.'

We were happy men when we climbed into our truck and left the headquarters behind. Our new medals were pinned on crisp, new uniforms. Our worn and battered kit had been taken from us and replaced with fresh, new items, from boots, to belts, to rifles, to underpants. We had even found the time to sew our new patches onto the shoulders of our uniforms so that our comrades would see that Manfred and I were now Squad and Section Leaders respectively. Life was good, Moscow lay at our mercy and victory would be won by Christmas. We shared a bottle of schnapps as the truck bumped and lurched its way back towards

175

the front and the warm buzz from the strong alcohol perfectly matched our sense of contentment and fulfilment. The first snow of the winter began to fall as our lorry pulled into camp and those few flurries marked the point at which everything began to turn to shit.

The snow continued to fall for days. It did not lie but melted as soon as it hit the ground. The earth grew saturated and degenerated into thick, cloying, sticky mud wherever men drove or walked upon it. The roads and tracks were transformed into quagmires and brought our trucks and tanks to a juddering, sliding standstill. We advanced, as that is what we had been ordered to do, but could only creep forward at a snail's pace. We spent long days shivering in the knee-deep mud heaving at the backs of our trucks in a bid to keep them moving. We would break our backs freeing them from the morass only to watch them become bogged down again within a few short minutes. We pushed on with increasing desperation, for we knew that every moment we were delayed was a minute in which the Russians could regroup, re-equip and fall back to new defensive positions. Our only comfort during that long, miserable month was the sight and sound of the Luftwaffe squadrons passing high above our heads on their way to pummel the Russians and impede their defensive preparations.

Even this small improvement in our morale was short-lived. A palpable sense of despondency enveloped us as our daily struggles on the road left us exhausted with precious little to show for all of our efforts. The strain of battling through the mud took its toll on our vehicles and the rate of mechanical breakdowns increased just as our ability to repair them diminished due to the difficulty of procuring spare parts. The same logistical difficulties prevented fresh troops from reaching the front and we struggled on with our numbers still depleted from the weeks of heavy fighting. The persistent rumours also took their toll. We heard that the Fourth Panzer Division had suffered a serious defeat at the hands of the Russians. It was said that they had deployed a new tank that was impervious to the guns of our own Panzers. Given our complete reliance on the Panzer Groups to break through the Russian defences, this sent a shiver down all of our spines. If the Panzers were neutralised, we knew that we would be expected to break the lines with our own soft, vulnerable bodies. We also listened with dread to the gossip about the new Russian armies that had suddenly appeared and had begun to dig themselves into in three defensive rings around Moscow. It seemed to us that the fight ahead was to be more brutally and viciously contested than we had hoped.

It seemed that our fears were shared by the Army High Command because the moment the ground began to freeze in the middle of November we were ordered forward with all urgency. There was no pause for supply lines to be restored now that the roads were rock hard and passable. No time was taken to ensure that vehicles were repaired or holes in our ranks filled with new recruits. We were to advance in our present, lamentable condition in a bid to seize the initiative and regain our previous momentum. We were to gain ground by any means necessary and this meant mounting daily frontal assaults with no thought for the number of casualties we were taking. The change in the weather might have made the roads usable once again but it hampered us in every other way. The temperature dropped to minus forty-five degrees centigrade by the end of November and wreaked havoc on an army clothed and equipped for a summer campaign. Cases of severe frostbite became so commonplace that the loss of a finger or the tip of a nose was scarcely a matter for anything other than a passing comment amongst the men of my section. If a man died, we would fight over his clothes before we stopped to say a prayer for his soul. We left our trucks running day and night for they were almost impossible to start once the engines grew cold. If we ran out of fuel it was often necessary to light a fire under the lorry's sump and leave it burning for an hour or more to heat it sufficiently to coax the engine back into life. I even saw an artillery man sitting with a shell between his legs and banging at it with a hammer and chisel to chip away at the packing grease that had frozen around it.

The Russians had made good use of the temporary reprieve won for them by the wet weather. They now awaited us in much larger numbers than before and in much stronger defensive positions. What had once been a headlong advance towards Moscow was reduced to a bloody, grinding war of attrition. Then, in early December, the Russians threw their reserve divisions into a counteroffensive and we became the defenders fighting desperately to avoid being encircled and annihilated as we had so often done to the Russians before. There was no rest for us as their infantry attacked us throughout the day and they then bombarded our trenches with artillery throughout the night. It was not even possible to stand up straight and stretch one's back because they had marksmen constantly alert and capable of putting a bullet into the head of any man careless enough to provide them with a target to hit. Neither was there comfort, for the earth of the shallow trenches we huddled in was frozen so hard that even hunching close to the fire was not enough to drive the chill from our bones.

We prayed for relief but our commanders seemed blind to the obvious fact that the front could not be held. They ordered us to defend every miserable patch of ground with our lives and told us that any man who turned coward and ran would be running straight towards a firing squad. The Luftwaffe disappeared from the skies in the weeks prior to Christmas and left the Russian bombers free to add to our misery. We knew that the offensive had failed and that there would be no Christmas celebrations in Moscow when our commanders began to fall. Our Commander-in-Chief, Field Marshal von Brauchitsch, went first, the whispered rumours of his dismissal reaching our ears just before Christmas. We celebrated this news and convinced ourselves that it was his incompetence that had caused our present predicament. Our hopes for a radical change in strategy faded in the days before New Year in the face of persistent reports that the Panzer Generals Guderian, Hoepner and Strauss had been removed from their commands. Most of us admired Guderian in particular and we hoped that the rumours would be proved to be false. When no such repudiation was forthcoming, we reluctantly and gloomily accepted it as confirmation that the invasion had failed and failed totally. News of the death of Field Marshal von Reichenau in late January brought Manfred and I to our lowest point. We felt some connection to him from when he had awarded us our Iron Crosses and his loss seemed to us to mark the end of our hopes for a positive outcome to the war with Russia.

Our despondency reached new depths when we received word of who was to replace the Field Marshall as commander of the Sixth Army.

'Paulus?' Manfred asked with a shake of his head as he stamped his feet in a bid to restore feeling back into his extremities. 'Never heard of him!'

'That is because he is not a fighting general.' Backe replied sourly. 'He is a bureaucrat who has risen to the rank of Lieutenant General by carrying the bags of men like von Reichenau and Guderian. He is a planner, not a soldier. I have heard that he has never commanded a unit larger than a battalion before.'

'That cannot be true!' I protested, though the knot that had formed in my stomach told me otherwise.

'It is true, Wolffie.' Backe replied, his face made more grim by the frost and icicles that clung to the stubble on his chin and cheeks. 'We needed a Rommel, a Guderian or a von Manstein to get us out of the shit and they have sent us an unproven novice instead! We're screwed, my friend! Completely screwed!'

15

'It is amazing how much your opinion of a person can change when you just happen to have benefitted from some arbitrary decision they have made. This was certainly the case for us with General Paulus. We spent the harsh winter months cursing him as we shivered in our trenches and suffered the constant grind of the Russian attempts to wear us down with their sporadic headlong assaults, their unending bomber and artillery attacks and their damnable, ever-present snipers. Our view of him brightened immensely the moment we received our orders to withdraw from the front and leave our Army Group Centre comrades to take our places in the shallow trenches we had scraped into the frozen earth. We accorded him further esteem when we rejoined Army Group South and were immediately re-equipped and presented with fresh recruits to fill the holes in our ranks left by the many men killed and injured during the disastrous advance on Moscow. I was delighted to have a full section for the first time since my first promotion. We would soon have much more substantial cause to laud General Paulus as he was about to prove his detractors wrong in spectacular fashion. We watched him soar as 1942 progressed and did not have the sense to realise how catastrophic the crash would be when he fell from the heights he had so quickly scaled.

We counted ourselves lucky to have been allocated a place on the front south of Izium. We faced the Russians across a wide river and, apart from the occasional artillery barrage, we were largely untroubled from one day to the next. There was heavy fighting to the north of us during March of 1942 but the thunder of battle was so distant that it scarcely disturbed our peace. I had grown to hate the long night watches by that point, as the quiet and solitude gave me too much time to dwell on matters that were best left alone. The atrocities in Minsk and elsewhere hung heavily on my mind and no amount of thinking could cast them in a light that was in any way palatable. There was no comfort to be found in matters of the heart, for my Ania had not replied to a single one of my letters and I had given up writing to her each day and now only did so when driven to it by boredom or despair. I was mentally composing a desperate plea for a response from her when my ears picked up a faint but familiar sound carried on the breeze in the stillness of the night. I held my breath and strained my ears and then my blood ran cold in my veins. I called out in the darkness and bade Manfred to come to me.

'What?' He demanded in a voice that was surly and thick with tiredness. I suspected that he had been on the verge of falling asleep while he was supposed to be on watch.

'Listen!' I ordered him tersely. 'Can you hear that?'

'Hear what?' He retorted testily before tilting his head to one side in the manner of a dog that has heard some distant barking. He stayed like that for several seconds before his eyes suddenly grew wide and he held his hand out to stop me from speaking. 'Jesus!' He exclaimed in shock. 'It is those damned English tanks. The same ones that bombarded us as we huddled along the banks of that shitty French canal. The ones with armour so thick our Panzer shells just bounced off them and left them unharmed!'

'Are you certain?' I asked, eager for confirmation that my own ears had not deceived me.

'I am certain!' He replied, no trace of doubt evident in his voice. 'I remember shitting myself whenever I heard the sound of their engines in France. A man does not forget something that has the power to make him soil himself in fear. You must report this!'

'But what would English tanks be doing here in Russia?' I demanded. 'It is not possible!'

Manfred waved me to silence and listened once again. 'Possible or not!' He declared after a few long seconds. 'There are English tanks here and lots of them. You must report it.'

I quickly made my way back towards the communications tent with some nervousness because I feared that I was about to make a fool of myself. I might not have gone at all if I had not run out of cigarettes and needed to go to the rear of our lines to buy or barter for another pack. The bored and heavy-eyed radio operator took my

184

verbal report down with a pencil and barely-disguised disinterest and relayed it to headquarters while I stood before him. I then left him and went in search of someone with cigarettes to sell. I had just made a bargain for two crumpled packs of cigarettes and a few squares of chocolate when the radio operator appeared and brusquely ordered me to return to the tent immediately. I took issue with the tone he used to address someone of a senior rank and so told him to go and fuck himself.

'Suit yourself!' He replied as he turned away. 'I will tell the General that you were unwilling to obey his order.'

I had to grit my teeth and follow him back to the tent. He spoke into the microphone and then held the headphones out towards me.

'Wolff!' A voice barked in my ears, the clipped tone of a member of the officer class clearly evident despite the tinny speakers and the whistle of interference. 'You have reported hearing the sound of English tanks on the far bank of the Donets. How can you be certain that this is what you heard?'

'I would recognise the sound of Matilda tank engines anywhere, Herr General.' I replied, subconsciously standing to attention now that I was addressing Paulus directly. 'I spent long hours listening to them when they held us up at La Bassee Canal during the Battle for France. The sound is quite distinctive.'

'We knew that the British were providing the Russians with weaponry through Archangel and Murmansk.' Paulus replied, though I suspected

185

that he was thinking aloud rather than consciously addressing me. 'They would surely have sent such superior weaponry to Moscow if their intention was to mount a counteroffensive there. The presence of these tanks so far south must surely indicate that they intend to attack here rather than against Army Group Centre.' He paused for so long that I was on the verge of asking if he was still there. 'You are certain of the numbers?' He demanded suddenly.

'Yes. Herr General!' I snapped back immediately. 'No less than ten and no more than twenty is my estimate.'

'Thank you, Unterfeldwebel Wolff.' He replied. 'Keep your eyes peeled and report any other enemy activity that comes to your attention.'

The exchange left me feeling sick with anxiety and I feared for the consequences if it was to transpire that I had been mistaken. This sense of unease was to grow worse within two hours of this conversation when the alert was raised and we were all ordered to battle-readiness. Manfred and I scanned the horizon nervously as dawn began to break and grimaced at one another at the sight of artillery platoons and reserve infantry battalions moving up closer to our lines.

'You know that this is all because of your damned report.' Manfred told me with an eyebrow raised in mock admonishment. 'If you are wrong, they will kick your arse from here to Moscow and back again!'

'But you heard it too!' I protested. 'If I was wrong, then so were you!'

'That is true.' He replied, managing to keep his face almost completely straight. 'But I did not submit a report or tell general Paulus what I thought I'd heard. I think I will get off lightly in comparison to you.'

'It was you who insisted I make the report!' I growled back at him, distinctly unamused even as he giggled away like a naughty schoolboy.

My stomach cramps increased as morning turned into afternoon and then evening with the horizon remaining stubbornly empty.

'Christ, Wolffie!' Manfred teased as he pointed towards where the artillery units were digging in behind us and where half the Italian army seemed to be setting up their camp. 'Those guys are going to be really pissed off when they find out that they have done all this work for nothing because of your phantom tank attack. I would be very worried if I was you. These Italians are very fiery when they're roused!'

If my punch had landed it would have left him with quite a bruise. As it was, he ducked away from me and I had to satisfy myself with cursing him as vilely as I knew how.

The artillery bombardment started just as the first light of dawn began to creep onto the far horizon. The German lines to the north of us took the brunt of it and we watched on grimly as clouds of dust and great columns of smoke began to rise into the sky. The ground under our feet shook so hard with the force of the explosions that we could not believe that any of our poor comrades directly below the bombardment could have survived it.

187

The big guns began to fall silent after an hour of thunder and the air was filled with the angry drone of the Russian bombers and the buzzing of the fighters escorting them. The Luftwaffe arrived almost immediately but we groaned when we saw how heavily outnumbered they were. It seemed inevitable that they would be quickly overcome by the superior Soviet numbers. Our despair turned to cheering within a matter of minutes as our brave fighters tore into the Russian planes with both great skill and great courage and sent large numbers of fighters and bombers hurtling towards the earth in flames with smoke trailing behind them as they plummeted down.

The elation lasted only until we tore our eyes from the skies and glanced towards the horizon. It was if the devil himself had thrown open the gates of hell and was now leading his legions against us in an avalanche of dust and fury. The visible masses of tanks, the thick columns of artillery, the endless infantry divisions and the huge cavalry regiments poured across the plain as far as the eye could see even with the aid of binoculars. It seemed to us that the whole Soviet army was attacking us in a massive counteroffensive that would surely sweep us back to our own border. We watched in horror as the Russians hit the German lines to our north with such speed and ferocity that, in spite of a murderous rate of defensive fire, the line bent, buckled and then broke altogether. The Russian attack came within range of our machine guns for a time and the artillery units to our rear fired into their flanks over open sights and tore great holes in their armoured brigades. To our great shock and relief, they returned fire only briefly, seemingly willing to soak up the casualties we inflicted on them in order to continue their push to the west. The reserve divisions were immediately ordered to contain the great bulge in the front and we were instructed to hold our position on the riverbank at all costs.

In the course of a morning, the battleground had been transformed beyond all recognition. We now faced the Russians on two fronts, the existing one to the east and the newly opened front to the north. The Soviet infantry now arrived in great numbers and dug in while we harassed them with artillery, mortars, machine guns and rifles. The thunder of artillery and the columns of smoke to our west told us that the real battle still raged there. We learned later that they had advanced five miles to the west before their offensive ran out of steam. We were reduced to little more than spectators over the next four or five days. Ferocious artillery, tank and small arms fire thundered in the middle distance without pause, shaking the earth and lighting the night sky with the power of a great, rumbling lightning storm. We watched on grimly as the Russians poured their reserve infantry divisions and tank brigades into the newly formed salient and were cheered by the sight of the shredded, depleted Soviet battalions limping back from the meat-grinder the front had become.

Every man who witnessed the power and scale of that offensive knew in their hearts that Army Group South could not hope to contain it. Only an act of God could have stopped them from smashing through the front and setting us to panicked, disordered retreat. It was the weather that halted their advance, just as it had brought us to a standstill when we were closing in on Moscow. The skies opened and the rain fell in torrents, turning the earth into a thick mud that clung to boots and wheels and robbed the Russians of all momentum. Immobile and weakened from the casualties incurred during their frenzied and suicidal onslaught, the Russians were sitting ducks when the Luftwaffe swept in to save us. It seemed to us that every fighter and bomber in Germany had been sent to our aid for the sky was filled with Messerschmitts, Junkers and Heinkels from one dawn until the next. The stricken Russian units were pounded by our artillery on the ground while the bombers shredded their ranks from above with a continuous shower of cluster bombs. The long columns of trucks, tanks and assault vehicles stranded on the water-logged roads were torn apart by machine gun fire as our fighter planes tore along their lines until every last bullet had been expended. We cheered the pilots as they did their bloody work and blessed them for their tirelessness and courage as they flew sortie after sortie, pausing only to refuel and re-arm before taking to the air once again. They flew missions of mercy as well as ones of death with squadrons of bombers devoted to dropping supplies to us so that we could fight on and hold the front.

We knew that the Soviet offensive had failed when the Third Panzer Corps rumbled past our positions on their way north and the Luftwaffe began destroying the bridges over the Donets River.

'We will be moving soon.' Backe informed us sagely. 'They have bombed the bridges to stop the Russians from escaping and Kleist's Panzers have been sent to encircle the poor bastards.'

He was right. We were ordered forward that afternoon to begin the familiar, bloody work of destroying the armies trapped by our Panzer Divisions. It is amazing just how hardened you can become to death and destruction when you are immersed in it. I hardly blinked at the sight of the thousands of broken and burning vehicles or the hundreds of shattered tanks, though I do remember thinking that it was such a terrible waste. I scarcely shed a tear when thousands of retreating Russians linked arms and charged at our machine guns without guns or ammunition only to be cut down with a few short bursts. I suppose that I must have admired their courage but I could not fathom what sense or purpose they saw in sacrificing themselves so needlessly when the battle was already lost. I was sickened by the sight of anti-personnel cluster bombs raining down on a mass of thousands of infantrymen, leaving only churned earth and smouldering rags in their place when the smoke cleared. Even so, I did not dwell on it for long because I knew that they would have done the same to us if only they had been presented with the opportunity.

The losses in the Kharkov salient were staggering. The Soviets lost three armies with twenty rifle divisions, seven cavalry divisions and fourteen armoured brigades along with more than a thousand tanks and hundreds of artillery pieces, mortars and aircraft. We marched a quarter of a million prisoners through the streets of Kharkov after the battle, a third of whom were carrying wounds. The sheer scale of the carnage should have staggered and disgusted me but I was somehow able to let it wash over me. Strange though it may seem, it was only the horses that moved me to tears. The battlefield was littered with the corpses of these gentle, blameless creatures who were ripped open by bullets and shells whilst struggling to pull field guns, ammunition and supplies through the thick, sticky mud. Men have some small say in their destiny but these poor, innocent beasts had none and it sickened me that men had caused them to suffer and perish in such great numbers.

I found that I could not celebrate our victory along with my men and even the prospect of a twenty-four hour pass and a trip into Kharkov could not jolt me from the black mood that had descended upon me during the weeks spent clearing the salient. I only agreed to accompany Manfred to stop him from nagging me and chattering excitedly about what delights the city would offer us.

'Christ, Wolffie!' He chided me as we joined the throng of soldiers in search of beer and entertainment. 'Cheer up! Milk would turn sour at the sight of your face!'

He shook his head in exasperation when I could manage only the weakest of smiles in response.

'Come!' He ordered me. 'Let's go in here. The sooner we get some beer inside you the better it will be for both of us.'

I followed him into the crowded bar as he pushed and shoved his way towards its centre. It was the cap sitting on a table at the far side of the room that first caught my eye. I had not seen the Deaths Head symbol of the Totenkopf Division since Manfred and I had made our hasty departure from Bordeaux. I then froze in shock and blinked my eyes in disbelief at what I was seeing. The SS officer was holding court with five or six of his men who were seated around a table covered in empty glasses. Rottenfuhrer Karl Lammert looked no different from the last time I had set my eyes upon him apart from the fact that he was dressed in the uniform of a Sturmfuhrer or Second Lieutenant. He glanced in my direction as he spoke and looked directly at me before turning back to his men and raising a glass to his lips. The glass stopped just short of his mouth and he froze before slowly swivelling his head back towards me. His eyes then widened in recognition and he leapt to his feet, spilling beer over the table as he jumped up.

'Wolffie!' He cried across the bar in delight. 'What the hell are you doing here?'

It was as I was embracing him that I caught sight of Julius and Horse coming to greet us. My spirits were transformed by this unexpected surprise and were raised to ever higher heights as we talked and drank late into the night. My old friends looked well, though Horse had suffered a wound when a Russian bullet struck a wall he was leaning on to steady his aim and sent fragments of broken stone flying into his mouth. His top lip was now mashed and puckered and one of his front teeth had been shattered completely. The loss of a front tooth never improves a man's appearance but it was especially bad for Horse given the hugeness of his teeth. All three of them had Iron Crosses, First Class at their throats and Manfred and I demanded to know how they had won them and how Lammert had managed to be elevated to such a senior rank.

They told us that they had not languished in France for long after our departure before being ordered east to join Army Group North in the push for Leningrad. Like us, they had suffered in the mud caused by the autumn rains before being smashed back from their objective when the Soviets launched their great winter counter-offensive. Unlike us, they were overtaken by the speed and fury of the Russian advance and found themselves completely encircled.

'The Fuhrer ordered that we were to hold our positions at all costs!' Lammert declared proudly. 'And that is what we did for two and a half months

194

despite the Russians bombarding us with bombs and shells and sending division after division to break our lines.'

I nodded in genuine admiration of their achievement given my own experience of the punishment suffered by armies when they are encircled. I had witnessed at first hand at Kiev, Bryansk and Kharkov the carnage that artillery and bombers can inflict on an army that is surrounded.

'We have the Luftwaffe to thank for our survival!' Lammert announced in a voice that was only very slightly slurred. 'We would have been overrun and slaughtered if it was not for the supplies, ammunition and men that they delivered to us. Did you know that the Totenkopf suffered such heavy casualties that it is no longer a division?'

'It is true!' Julius confirmed with an emphatic nod of his head. 'They have reduced it to the status of a brigade given its diminished strength.'

'That is why Lammert here has risen through the ranks!' Horse offered with a mischievous, gap-toothed grin. 'So many of our officers were killed or wounded that he was given one field promotion after another. Sometimes more than one in a single week!'

'That is how these two idiots got their medals.' Lammert retaliated sardonically. 'Only two men out of every ten survived the whole ordeal so there were few men to reward when the victory was won. The generals were so keen to celebrate the occasion that they gave them out to any fool who had managed to avoid getting his head shot off!'

'So, why are you here now?' Manfred enquired, asking the question that was on the tip of my tongue.

'The Totenkopf Division is so completely devastated that it will be returned to France to be fully refitted and for new recruits to be trained. The need for manpower here is such that we are to be reassigned to the Sixth Army. We were told that Paulus is keen to replace his losses with experienced men.'

Manfred and I grinned at each other as Lammert spoke, delighted at the prospect of being permanently reunited with our old friends. I did not think that I could be happier than I was at that moment but Julius quickly proved me wrong.

'Your old friend did not fare so well during our struggles in the Demyansk Pocket.' He declared solemnly as if he was about to impart some grave news. He paused for effect but could not keep himself from smiling at our concerned and puzzled expressions. 'Unterscharfuhrer Brandt sadly disgraced himself when he lost courage in the face of an enemy infantry attack. He turned and ran, leaving his comrades to fend the Soviets off at close quarters. He was shot as a deserter when they captured him cowering in a ditch two days later.'

I cannot say that I had lost much sleep over Brandt since joining the Sixth Army, but the fear of being called to account for my assault on him must have been at the back of my mind because I felt a huge sense of relief at this news. I was pleased that I would no longer have to keep looking over my shoulder and felt a grim satisfaction that a man who took pleasure from torturing women had met an end that seemed appropriately shameful.'

16

'My happiness was fully restored during the early part of the summer of 1942. We had survived another major Russian offensive and won another victory against them, I had been reunited with my oldest and dearest friends and the build-up of men and materiel on the west bank of the Donets told us that we would soon be pushing eastwards again to put an end to the Soviets once and for all. The order to advance came at the end of June and we tore across the Donets behind the Panzer Corps intent on encircling and destroying what would surely be the last of the great Soviet armies. We streamed eastward across the vast, empty steppes, our tanks, armoured vehicles, half-tracks and trucks charging across the immense fields of corn and sunflowers that stretched as far as the eye could see. We charged ahead exultantly, enjoying each glorious day and revelling in our power as was evidenced by the huge clouds of dust thrown up by our passing. We were halted more often by our own success and rapid progress than we were by any resistance from our enemy. Our supply lines were so far extended that we were often forced to halt to allow the fuel tenders to catch us up and refill our tanks. Traffic jams built up as vehicles ground to a halt and they delayed us by several days at a time.

The lack of any organised Soviet defence meant that we covered hundreds of miles in the first ten days without having to fire more than a shot or two. We were then ordered to support clearing operations around Millerovo where Russian troops had been cut off and surrounded by XL Panzer Corps. The encirclement was much smaller than those we had executed before and the trapped armies were destroyed by our artillery fire and aerial assaults in less than three days. When we had bombed them into submission, we were sent in to sweep the area for stragglers and to herd the eighteen thousand prisoners into makeshift, barbed wire enclosures. The numbers seemed paltry in comparison to the hundreds of thousands who surrendered to us at Kharkov and we abandoned them as quickly as we were able so that we could rejoin the headlong charge to the east.

If we had not been so blinded by our arrogance, our premature triumphalism and our belief in our essential superiority, we might have seen the clear signs that the Russians had abandoned their old tactics and adopted the new ones that would sow the seeds of our destruction. The portents were there to see but we were all so intent on the rush for glory that we did not recognise their importance or interpret them correctly. By letting us gleefully gallop across the steppes, they stretched our supply and communications lines to the point that they broke down with increasing frequency. By retreating before us, they denied us the opportunity to destroy their ill-equipped and ill-trained armies and so built up reserves that could be unleashed upon us when we inevitably became isolated and unsupported. There was even a subtle but fundamental change in the character of the light resistance we faced as we advanced towards Stalingrad. The stragglers and partisans we encountered surrendered themselves less often than before and would fight to the last in a bid to inflict the maximum number of casualties on us before they fell. Many of the villages we passed through had been abandoned, their buildings burnt to the ground, their crops destroyed and their livestock driven off to deny us both shelter and sustenance. There was a bitterness and a steely, determined hatred amongst the peasantry that we overlooked because of the joy we took in the stunning gains we had made. Julius told us how his unit had lost a captain, a sergeant and two enlisted men when they had set off in pursuit of three Russian soldiers who had been lurking at the edge of a small wood. They had dropped down dead when they were fired upon, only to jump back to their feet and fire into their pursuers when they came close enough to examine their bodies. There were also tales of old hags and young girls who watched sullenly as our troops marched by only to pull out pistols and rifles and pour fire into their backs once they had passed. It shocked us to hear of these murderous and suicidal women and of these dishonourable, duplicitous men, but we failed to register that the struggle had entered a phase that would be marked by the depths of its brutality and depravity. We were unsettled but we pushed on through the heat and dust still drunk on the certainty of glory and victory.

Units competed with one another to cover the most miles in their desperation to win the race for the river Don. We might not have been so eager if we had known what awaited us there. The Russians had finally found a line that they could defend and they set about reminding us just how determined they were to stop our advance. They brought the whole of the Sixth Army to a shuddering halt as we approached the Kalach bridgehead and then threatened to throw it back with the suddenness and ferocity of their attack. We were forced to dig trenches and cling on for dear life in the stifling heat as they sent wave after wave of infantry against our defences. We would have perished there if it had not been for the Luftwaffe. The fighter pilots blew the Russian planes out of the sky and cleared the way for our bombers to destroy tanks, defensive fortifications, ammunition dumps and infantry formations. We worshipped those airmen and cheered them as they tore over our heads during the opening days of the battle, for we knew that we did not have enough men or ammunition to repel an all-out assault. The tide turned in our favour only when the quartermasters caught up with us and we were resupplied. The willingness of the Russians to sacrifice themselves in large numbers shocked us to the core. They threw themselves at our lines with suicidal courage in the vain hope of overwhelming our much superior fire-power with the sheer dead weight of their bodies. Their most determined assaults ended with heaps of their twitching corpses piled only yards from our trenches. The sight of it was so hellish that it drove more than one man in my section to madness and men would moan and cry out in their sleep as these visions of hell haunted their dreams.

Just when we though that it could get no worse, the Soviets showed us that there were further depths to be plumbed. We were roused in the cool, early morning air of the last day of July by the familiar roaring of the Russians as two battalions of infantry poured out of their trenches and charged towards us. We fired into their ranks until the barrels of our rifles became too hot to touch and those of our heavy machine guns glowed bright red. Not one of them made it to within ten paces of our trench before they were cut down.

'Jesus!' Manfred exclaimed in shock in the deathly silence that followed the order to cease fire. He then scrambled up and crawled forward towards the bodies of the men who had fallen closest to our position. 'They have no rifles!' He called back to me, his face pale and his voice shaky. 'They tried to charge us down with only the weight of their own flesh and bones! My God! What would make men do such a thing?'

We did not have to wait long for an answer to that question. Another all-out assault came at us later that afternoon. It was an altogether more serious effort preceded by an hour-long heavy artillery bombardment and was accompanied by supporting machine gun and mortar fire. The Soviets would undoubtedly have broken our lines

202

if it had not been for the 91st Motorised Flak Regiment. They had set up their anti-aircraft guns just to the rear of our position and, in the absence of any aerial threat from the Russians, had prepared them for ground combat operations. They deafened us as they fired over our heads and tore great, bloody holes in the advancing Soviet ranks. I watched with a horrible fascination as whole rows of men were snatched suddenly and violently from the line leaving little or no trace of them behind. The sight of their surviving comrades turning and running for cover filled me with relief at the prospect of the attack being brought to an end. That relief turned to horror when those men began to fall and some turned and ran back towards us. It took me a few seconds to realise that they were not being cut down by German fire but by Russian machine gunners positioned behind them. In spite of all that I had seen and experienced, this was a new and terrible low. It seemed barbaric to me to shoot your own men for retreating in the face of insurmountable force and inevitable slaughter.

'It is just as they say.' Manfred opined that evening while we tucked into the chocolate that had been distributed as a reward for holding our ground. 'These Untermenschen are not the same as us. They may look and sound human, but they lack the basic morals and decency that set us apart from them. Today was a good day because it reminded us of that. We must remember it if we are to have the strength to prevail!'

We all nodded our agreement and steeled ourselves for the horrors we were only now beginning to realise lay ahead of us.

The grinding battle was brought to an end after two weeks when the armoured spearheads of the Fourteenth and Twenty-Fourth Panzer Corps smashed through the Russian lines from the north and the south and linked up to the west of the town. All eight rifle divisions of the Soviet 62nd Army were encircled and we were ordered forward to join with the Panzer Divisions and the Luftwaffe in destroying the surrounded Russian forces. The resistance was fiercer than ever before. I witnessed more than one Soviet officer use his last bullet to shoot himself as we closed in on him. We were also told of numerous instances of surrendering soldiers being shot by their own comrades. We were forced to smoke the last of them out by setting fire to the woods in which they had hidden themselves. This drastic tactic brought them out in their droves with their hands held high and those few that continued to resist screamed horribly when the flames consumed them. By dusk of that day we were exhausted and covered in soot but were able to report that the area had been cleansed of all enemy personnel. We sent more than forty thousand prisoners west before we moved forward to cross the Don. The devastation around the town of Kalach convinced us that the Russian army was on the brink of collapse for we believed that no nation could suffer such losses and still fight on. Our bombs and shells had left great smoking craters in the earth and the landscape was littered with the blackened and twisted metal of the hundreds of tanks, trucks and guns that we had destroyed and with the ragged corpses of the tens of thousands of Russian soldiers who had sacrificed themselves in their futile bid to defeat us. We marched for Stalingrad and talked of the quarters we would find there for the winter and of the possibility of leave when the city fell.

My first sight of Stalingrad should have filled me with dread, but I felt only joy. We had left the Don in the morning and were within reach of the Volga before darkness fell. The Luftwaffe bombers had filled the sky above us as our trucks sped through the great clouds of dust thrown up by the Panzers as they rumbled their way across the hard-packed, sun-baked earth. The city stretched for many miles along the western bank of the Volga and was in flames by the time we reached it. We had seen the thick columns of smoke from more than twenty miles away and, as darkness fell, the fires lit up the night and we wondered how anyone could survive such an inferno. Our tank regiments were already engaged in the battle and exchanged fire with the city's anti-aircraft batteries, which had depressed their barrels to an elevation of zero and now fired indiscriminately in a bid to halt the advance.

There was a strange, almost celebratory atmosphere as we made camp in an area of parkland that was bordered by allotments. We picked fruit and nuts from the trees as the Luftwaffe attacks continued to roll in and rain incendiary bombs down on the city like some immense, macabre firework display. Even the river itself was aflame as burning fuel from some ruptured fuel store floated out of the city and off into the distance.

'That's Asia over there!' Lammert informed us as he pointed towards the far bank of the Volga. We all nodded happily at this information. We were relieved to have reached what was surely our final destination and were certain that both the city and all of Russia were teetering precariously on the edge of collapse. It seemed that one final push was all that was required to bring the whole conflict to a victorious conclusion.

The surreal atmosphere was heightened by some of the bizarre sights that greeted us as the evening progressed. Julius pointed out the first of these as he gazed towards the city through his binoculars.

'What is it?' Manfred demanded, too lazy to rouse himself from where he lay feeding berries into his mouth from the pile he had collected in his helmet.

'You would not believe it!' Julius replied. 'There! At the base of that ant-aircraft battery! There are schoolgirls in their uniforms digging a trench while our Panzers fire over their heads!'

I took the binoculars and shook my head in astonishment. I did not think that any of them were older than ten or twelve but they continued to excavate the tank-trap even as the shells exploded around them and showered them with earth.

'You would not catch Berlin schoolgirls doing such a thing!' Horse commented when he took his turn to watch them. 'A car backfiring would be enough to send them scuttling for their mothers' skirts!'

'Like I have said before.' Manfred chimed in from where he still reclined on the grass. 'They are Untermenschen! Only the worst barbarians would put such young girls in harm's way. They should have evacuated them long before our Panzers reached them!'

We were still watching the girls when a group of men came marching out in loose formation from the streets behind them. They began to advance towards the firing Panzers. I assumed that they were fleeing workers because they were dressed in dirty tunics and overalls. It was Lammert who spotted that about half of them were carrying ancient rifles.

'They are going to attack our tanks!' Lammert announced in disbelief.

'That's shit!' Manfred retorted, finally forcing himself to his feet and demanding the binoculars. 'Christ! You are right! The fools have only one rifle between every two men but mean to defeat armour plate and shells with their muskets!'

It was like watching lambs gambol towards the abattoir. The Panzer turrets turned slowly towards them as their bullets began to ricochet around the ears of the tank crews. The hail of fire that engulfed them cut more than half of them down immediately. We thought that the survivors would turn and flee but they stopped only to take the weapons from their dead comrades' hands before continuing to creep forwards. The rest were cut down quickly and so forty men were lost in a matter of moments without causing a single German casualty. One of them screamed on in his agony for an hour or more after the Panzers had turned their sights back towards the anti-aircraft batteries.

'We should go and help him.' Julius suggested uncertainly when the anguished cries had gone on for longer than we could stand.

'No!' Lammert ordered. 'You know how these bastards fight. The moment we reach him he will stop his screeching and shoot any of us he can hit. Leave him where he lies.'

We were all relieved when he finally died or fell into unconsciousness for his howls of agony distressed us and quite spoiled our enjoyment of our dinner.

The following days were an orgy of destruction on a scale I had never witnessed before. Nothing I had seen in France, Kiev, Kharkov or Kalach came close to it. The Panzers fired into the city night and day, pausing only to allow the barrels of their guns to cool or when they had exhausted their shells. Artillery regiments dug in to our rear and sent a barrage of high explosives whistling over our heads and into the heart of the poor, beleaguered city. All the while, wave after wave of aircraft rained a hail of bombs down onto suburbs and industrial sectors alike, sending great plumes of smoke into the air and setting off a whole series of firestorms that left the city permanently obscured by a thick fog of soot and ash. One landmark after another disappeared under this onslaught and we watched on in awe as the power of our guns turned the sprawling city into a sea of rubble and ruins. The Russian artillery was not idle during this time and we were forced to dig trenches into the rock-hard soil and huddle there while their shells turned the parkland and the allotments into a mess of craters and scattered earth.

'They cannot survive this!' Lammert announced with full confidence as we surveyed the wreckage before us. 'They will have collapsed before September is out and we will occupy the city.'

'There will be nothing left to occupy.' Manfred retorted. 'Their city will be obliterated because of their idiotic refusal to see that they are already defeated. We will dance on the ruins and then leave it to return to dust.'

We all nodded our agreement for any fool could see that the end was near.'

17

'It was the change in the weather that first began to eat away at my confidence. The heavy rain came down in a deluge and filled our trench until the water ran into our boots. We all remembered how the autumn rains had halted our advance on Moscow and impeded our supply lines so badly that there were occasions when we fended off Soviet attacks with so little ammunition that we were forced to rifle through the pockets of the dead in search of a bullet or two. It is hard to believe now, but we were actually cheered when the first frosts arrived in September. Horse was grinning from ear to ear when he showed us the thin skin of ice on our water bucket and we returned his smile from the relief of knowing that the roads would now be hard enough to guarantee that fuel, food and ammunition would continue to reach us.

Our officers were bullish and full of certainty when they finally ordered us into the city in mid-September. The accepted wisdom was that the Luftwaffe and the artillery battalions had done our work for us and that we would be unlikely to find a single living creature that had survived the firestorm. We were to push through the city as hard and as fast as we could in order to reach the Volga and so bring the city under our control. It was like descending into hell itself. No street was undamaged, no road or alley was clear of rubble and the many fires still burning seemed to suck the oxygen from the air and replace it with smoke, soot and dust. My throat burned and my eyes watered as I moved forward. It took only moments for our illusions of a quick and easy victory to be blown away. We had foolishly believed that the destruction of so many buildings had robbed the Russians of defensive positions from which they could hold us back. We even joked that our clearing operations would be less arduous than those we had conducted in France as we would be spared the trouble of going from house to house in search of enemy combatants. Rather than clearing our path, the long bombardment had created a field of rubble, shell craters and churned up earth that slowed us to a crawl and provided the Russians with an infinite number of places in which they could secrete themselves and then attack us at close quarters.

The haste with which we advanced and the great multitude of hiding places around us conspired to put us in a situation where we soon found ourselves being fired upon from all directions. Some of them had buried themselves in the dust and dirt and would raise their heads and fire a couple of shots before ducking back down before we had spotted them. Precious time was lost as we were forced to send men crawling out in search of those who attacked us. The few buildings that were still standing were even harder to clear. The Soviets had nailed boards across the windows to force us to stumble from room to room in complete darkness, leaving us vulnerable to attack from fighters whose eyes had long grown accustomed to the lack of light. Even those who had run out of ammunition would crouch in the dark and fall upon us with knives, clubs or entrenching tools. This brutal, close quarters fighting was somehow worse than the gun battles where you did not have to smell the breath of your enemy or feel the bristles on his chin against your skin as you wrestled and struggled to slice his throat. I had lost a third of my section by the time we came in sight of the Volga just as dusk began to fall.

If we had arrived even an hour earlier, I believe that the city would have fallen. The Soviets had been pushed back to a thin strip of earth on the bank of the river and the few men they had left were cowering in their foxholes under heavy fire from our infantry, our Panzers and the Stukas that dived down at them from the sky. The river behind them was filled with boats loaded with soldiers. It seemed that every last craft on the river had been pressed into service as there were gunboats, troop carriers, tugboats, fishing boats and even a handful of rowing boats. They were all so heavily laden that it was a wonder that they did not capsize in the waters that were being churned up by the artillery, machine gun and mortar fire that was being directed at them. One of our artillery crews scored a direct hit on a gunboat and it disappeared in a cloud of smoke leaving only splinters and burning fuel on the water along with floating corpses and men screaming as they burned. No man from the first boat to land took more than five paces before he was cut down due to the intensity of our fire. Those in the following boats fared a little better for a great number of them reached land at the same time and so divided our fire. Those few who made it as far as the first shell holes then returned fire and forced us to duck down and so provided some cover for more of their comrades to disembark. The empty boats immediately turned and made for the far bank to pick up more of the Russian soldiers who awaited them there. I do not understand how a single one of them stayed afloat or how a single crewman stayed alive when so many bullets were sent tearing through their hulls. Their luck and their courage held out long into the night and, by the time we had used the last of our ammunition, they had suffered thousands and thousands of casualties but had retained a small sliver of territory on the west bank. More than two thirds of the Soviets who occupied that meagre bridgehead were corpses. We dug in, sent runners for more ammunition and awaited the dawn.

It was not a Russian counterattack that forced us back but our own artillery. The shells were falling so close to our positions that we were choking on the thick dust thrown up by the explosions and had suffered a dozen casualties from falling masonry, flying shards of rock and white-hot shrapnel. We retreated only two hundred and fifty yards and I set my section up in what Manfred laughingly called our 'winter quarters'. The front wall of the barrel-maker's workshop had been blown out and the interior of the ground floor had been badly damaged, leaving only the upper floor intact. We knocked three holes in the thick walls, one for our machine gun and two for the lookouts who would watch for enemy activity while the rest of us tried to get some rest. The constant noise of artillery fire and explosions, the unceasing rifle fire, the shrieking of diving Stukas and the drone of heavy bombers made sleep impossible. We counted ourselves lucky in our exhaustion if we were able to doze for more than a few moments at a time before being jerked back into sudden consciousness. The Russians were intent on wearing us down by ensuring that we were never able to relax. We quickly learned never to stand anywhere near the window, for even the briefest glimpse of a German uniform was answered with a bullet. We spent our days straining our eyes to see where the Russian infantrymen had hidden themselves amongst the dirt, dust and rubble. There were a few full-frontal assaults during those early days but we repelled them easily and learned to disguise our firing points to avoid giving our positions away to the spotters who watched through their binoculars for the tell-tale puffs of smoke. Even the hours of darkness brought us no respite, for that is when their bombers took advantage of the absence of German fighter planes and swooped in to drop explosives down on us. The psychological impact of this outweighed the physical damage that it caused. It

214

ensured that we did not sleep but instead spent the hours of darkness listening for the sound of bomber engines being switched off and then waiting with bated breath for them to glide in silently to drop their deadly loads. The constant stress of this wore at our nerves and made us constantly jumpy and liable to discharge our rifles at the slightest sound or shadow.

I was staring out across the dark wasteland in the dead of the night when the sound of low voices beneath my feet made me tense and cock my head to one side. The silence dragged on for so long that I had almost persuaded myself that I had imagined it. I knew that I was not mistaken when the sound of a flint being struck was followed by the crackling of a fire. I locked eyes with Manfred and pointed towards the floor. He nodded slightly and then rubbed his hand in a circular motion over his belly. It was only then that I detected the faint aroma of frying meat. Manfred pointed towards the trap door in the middle of the floor and used his hands to mime two people crawling towards it and then one pulling it open so that the other could fire down into the ground floor. I shook my head and pressed my index finger hard against my lips. Manfred rubbed at his belly again, widened his eyes as far as they would go and pleaded with me silently by putting the palms of his hands together as if he was praying. The smell of cooking was now making my mouth water and I indicated that I would pull the trap door open so he could shoot.

The two Russians did not stand a chance. They looked up in fright as the ceiling suddenly opened up above their heads and Manfred had shot them both in the chest before they had even reached for their weapons. The pan contained four little sausages and we plucked them out while they still sizzled and gobbled them down greedily. It was our first decent food in a week and it left us feeling normal and restored once again. We searched the two Russians but found that they were in a worse state than us. Their tunics were worn and thin and their boots had seen better days. We snorted in disbelief when we discovered that they had only four bullets between them.

'How can we beat them when they will come forward to fight with so little ammunition?' Manfred demanded sourly. 'It defies all logic and sense.'

I ignored his question because my search had unearthed something of much greater importance. Manfred grinned as I shook the little tin and the tobacco inside rattled gently against the lid. I do not think that I had ever enjoyed a cigarette so much, even although the tobacco was dry and burned my throat each time that I inhaled.

I missed that little barrel-maker's workshop when we were ordered forward in the first of a hundred counterattacks. Its walls had protected us from the elements and had given us a false but comforting illusion of safety. I yearned to return to it during the days spent huddled out in the open with only the rubble and the shattered bricks to cower behind. It was gone by the time we were forced back once again. A huge, water-filled crater now stood in its place with a bloated corpse floating at its centre. I say this without certainty for the destruction of the city was now so complete that it was impossible to tell one street from another with any degree of accuracy. The hopelessness of our situation was such that we were homesick for a miserable, derelict building and did not even dare to dream of our homes back in Germany.

There is always chaos in battle but Stalingrad took this to unimaginable levels. It was often impossible to tell where the frontline lay as it changed from one hour to the next and it was not uncommon to find yourself being fired on from all sides simultaneously. The Russians would disguise the entrances to cellars and sewers with rubble so that their soldiers could hide there and emerge once our units had passed and then attack us from behind. We would use flamethrowers and grenades to clear any basements that we uncovered but could do little about those that we did not detect. There was also the great difficulty involved in telling friend from foe. When coated in the fine dust that hung in the air, a Russian looked very much like a German and I lost count of the number of times the more nervous of my men fired on their own comrades. The fluidity of the front and the lack of remaining landmarks meant that we were often in as much danger from our own planes and artillery as we were from those of the Soviets. We were advised to lay out swastika flags to direct our bombers away from our positions but they were often spotted by

Russian observers who would then direct their artillery fire at us.

We enjoyed a respite of sorts for several days when a massive offensive was launched from the south. Two Panzer divisions and six infantry division were committed to driving the Soviets from their narrow spit of land. It is beyond me how a single Russian survived the onslaught. The bombardment was so intense that we were forced to tie strips of cloth across our mouths and noses to stop us from choking on the dust and smoke. It is a wonder that those at its centre were not suffocated by it. Lammert likened the Soviets to cockroaches for their ability to come scuttling out of the blackened ruins the moment the bombers left and the artillery fell silent. It is no exaggeration to say that all hope died when that great offensive came to an end with no gains to show for all the thousands of men and the tonnes of materiel that had been expended upon it. We now knew that we were damned to spend the winter locked in the bitter struggle amongst the rubble.

It was the week before the first snows fell that Horse was killed. We had been sent forward to clear the snipers from the roof of a burnt-out warehouse, a perilous duty that we now performed several times a week. It was only when we had reached the safety of our shell-hole after an afternoon of fruitless searching that we noticed that he had not returned with us. We went back and found him on the warehouse floor just as the sun was sinking in the sky. They had stripped him bare and cut his genitals away to deny him any dignity in death. He had been beaten so badly that all his limbs were broken and his face was so mangled that we only knew it was him because of his missing tooth. That was the last time I cried in Stalingrad. I stood over my friend's broken corpse and let the tears roll down my cheeks. It was a release that I had denied myself when the ranks of my own squad had been horribly thinned and when so many of my officers had died that I had stopped learning their replacements' names. It was pointless to make the effort when they too would likely be dead within days. This latest loss, when piled upon all the others, left me numb and no longer able to feel.

The first time that we buried Horse, Julius said some comforting words about God and heaven and wished our old friend eternal rest. We laid him out in a shell hole and covered him in a thick layer of rocks and earth. We did not see him again until the next afternoon. The Russian bombardment had churned the ground and unearthed all of him apart from his legs. I could not look at his face when we dragged him into a fresh crater and threw dirt over him for the last time. It was another week before he surfaced again but he was headless now and rotten and the enemy fire was so heavy that we had to leave him. I was glad when we were forced back that evening for it meant that I would not have to look at him or bury him for a third time.

My already weak grip on sanity loosened considerably after poor Horse's death and his subsequent grotesque resurrections. I still functioned sufficiently well to discharge my duties but I now floated through the carnage, the din and the constant fear of death as if I was a disembodied observer watching myself go through the motions. I watched impassively when we came across a woman howling like a wounded beast as she cradled her dead daughter in her arms. The top of the girl's skull was missing and they were both soaked in her blood. I had once thought that the Russians were barbaric for failing to evacuate their civilians before the battle for the city commenced, but I now found that I no longer cared. The mother's bestial keening and the obvious depth of her misery and despair might have once moved me to tears, but I had become so benumbed and detached that I felt nothing at all. I did not even react when one of my men put a bullet into her head to bring an end to her suffering. We take our humanity for granted, but to lose it is a terrible thing and to do so without mourning the loss is worse still.

In spite of all that I endured, some small vestige of the civilised and decent man I had once been still clung on somewhere deep inside me. I saw this when Willy Maier, a young boy from our home village, was posted to my squad as part of a batch of replacements for the men lost at the front. I did not know Willy well as he was much younger than me, but I had seen him around and I knew his mother. The widow Maier had taken in laundry and sewing from my own mother to make ends meet and had often been at the schoolhouse to deliver or to collect our clothes. Two things about Willy Maier really bothered me. The first was that he was so young. He might have been seventeen years of age, but I saw him as a defenceless infant amongst the hardened and damaged men of my squad. The second thing that bothered me was the fact that he was an only child. The widow Maier had not had the best fortune in life. Her drunkard of a husband had condemned her to a life of poverty when he had fallen into the river and drowned when drunk on cheap schnapps. She had remained cheerful and pleasant in spite of being forced to clean other people's soiled underclothes in order to scrape together enough coins to bring up her beloved son. She doted on him and would be both devastated and impoverished in her old age if anything was to happen to him. Her precious boy had now been thrown into the mincing machine of Stalingrad and I knew that his life expectancy could now be counted in days rather than weeks. I watched silently as he tried to appear tough and unafraid in front of his comrades, but his trembling fingers, his clean, new uniform and his hairless chin marked him out as the frightened boy he was. It was as I observed him clumsily trying to smoke a cigarette that looked oversized in his fingers that I decided to shoot him.

I did it during a half-hearted Russian assault. I ordered him forward and then drew my pistol. I put the bullet into the back of his knee in the hope that the injury would leave him able to walk but with a limp that would disqualify him from frontline military service. He squealed like a little piglet as he went down and was still squealing when the medical orderlies loaded him onto a stretcher and carried him off towards the rear.

'Will you do me next?' Julius asked me as I tore my eyes away from Willy. He was grinning as he spoke, but I could not help but detect the desperation in his eyes.

I returned his smile and clapped him on the shoulder before turning back towards the fighting. I have replayed this scene in my mind a thousand times since then and each time I have asked myself why I did not draw my pistol and send my good friend home. I have yet to find an answer to that question that brings me any comfort.'

18

'It seemed to us that the whole world was intent on killing us and on torturing and tormenting us as we died. The Russians had taken to mounting assaults each morning and evening and seemed content to sacrifice huge numbers of their own men in order to gradually wear away at our ranks. The success of this tactic was evident from the fact that Russian prisoners of war were increasingly employed as stretcher bearers, labourers and food carriers to make up for the lack of German manpower. When they were not attacking or shelling us, we still had to stay alert and keep our heads down to avoid the eyes of the snipers who lurked constantly within range of our lines. The battlefield was strewn with rotting corpses and their putrid flesh brought disease along with the stench that even the stiffest breeze did not dissipate. My own men were lucky to avoid the typhoid and the cholera, but none escaped the dysentery and the stink of watery, infected shit hung about us like a fog. When we were not sick or in fear of our lives, we were plagued by the cold and by the legions of lice that infested every fold and crease of our uniforms. With no fires to warm us and no facilities to wash in, there were times when death seemed preferable to the endless misery and suffering.

Our one daily comfort was the hot food that was brought up to our positions from the rear. The Russians targeted these men more than any others apart from officers and artillery spotters. A few well-aimed shots could deprive us of food and water for a whole day and force us to drink the disease-ridden water from where it had collected on the ground. One of these men took a sniper's bullet in the centre of his forehead when he was in the middle of pouring hot chicken broth into my bowl. I caught the hot canister as he fell and filled my bowl to the brim before passing it on down the line. Manfred reached down and took the spoon from the man's top pocket, wiped the spots of blood from it on his sleeve and then began to shovel the soup into his mouth. We left him where he fell until we had finished our meal. It is hard to be decent when your belly is empty.

The descent into madness brought casualties of its own. Three men in my squad took their own lives in a single day. These were not weaklings or cowards but were strong and courageous men who had reached the end of their tether. The first man shot himself through the eye rather than face the morning assault. He had been well-liked and sociable and the manner of his passing affected us all. Despondency and dejection spread through the squad like an infection and two more men had followed his example before the sun had set. We kept a wary eye on one another during the hours of darkness and thought ourselves lucky that no-one else had followed them by the time the sun rose in the morning. I was called to the rear to explain myself to a captain whose clean uniform and healthy colouring told me that he had yet to experience the delights of the front.

'You must impose discipline.' He scolded me. 'Make your men aware that they will face serious disciplinary sanctions for even considering such a cowardly act.'

'You mean that they would be shot?' I replied with a straight face.

'Yes!' He responded briskly, seemingly oblivious to the irony and futility of threating suicidal men with execution. He then passed me a form and told me that I would have to fill it out before I returned to my unit.

It was then that I realised that the whole world had gone mad and that the insanity was not just confined to those of us at the front. The form was a requisition for Christmas supplies and I was expected to detail my requirement for musical instruments, decorations and candles. I could not help but laugh at the thought of how happy the Soviet snipers would be if we were to play music to give away our positions and then mark them out for them with candles and baubles. I must have laughed too hard and too hysterically for the young captain stared at me wide-mouthed as if I had lost my mind completely.

The temperature dropped as November progressed and we noticed subtle but ominous changes in the patterns of battle. The Luftwaffe did not dominate the heavy, grey skies as they once had. The bombers and fighters were there in smaller numbers and for fewer hours and we felt the effects of this immediately. The Russians grew stronger and bolder now that the threat from the air was reduced. There was also a change in the way they used their artillery. They shelled us less often and took to firing over our heads in order to wreak havoc in our rear. The dire effects of this change in strategy were also felt almost immediately as communications were disrupted and supplies of food and ammunition became much less reliable. I began to wonder if our Christmas candles would now arrive in time.

'At least it can't get any worse!' Lammert announced grimly as he rubbed his hands together furiously in a vain attempt to restore the circulation to his fingers.

The cold had now joined the ranks of the deadly enemies ranged against us. One of our machine gunners lost two of his fingers when they froze to the trigger guard while he was firing at a group of advancing Russians. He did not wince when we used a knife to prise them away from the frozen metal even although the effort stripped away most of the skin.

'When you reach the bottom, there is comfort in knowing that the only way is up.' Lammert told us sagely. We all nodded because we were desperate to be consoled, but we all knew in our hearts that he was wrong.

The rumours began just a few days later, but we dismissed them as being too fantastical. It was unthinkable that the divisions guarding our flanks outside the city would simply desert en masse and leave us to be encircled. Our doubts and fears began to grow when the first of the Russian propaganda leaflets blew into our trenches.

'Fucking Romanians!' Julius spat furiously. 'I would not be surprised if they had run at the first sight of the Soviets.'

The leaflet claimed that the Romanian Third Army Corps had been overrun by the heroic men of the First Guards Army, the Fifth Tank Army and the Twenty-First Army. It stated that the Sixth Army was now completely surrounded and would inevitably be destroyed. It called upon all Germans still in Stalingrad to surrender and gave a guarantee that all who gave themselves up would be well-treated, would receive medical treatment, would be allowed to keep their own possessions and would be released to their home countries once the war against fascism had been won.

'Maybe we should think about it.' Julius suggested tentatively as he held the leaflet up. 'There would be no sense in dying here if the battle is already lost.'

'Don't be a bloody fool!' Lammert snapped back at him. 'This is propaganda, nothing more. I would not be surprised if this was another of their tricks. I take their word on nothing! Anyway, do you think that they will keep their promises when they see the SS blood group tattoos on our arms? They will torture us until we betray our comrades and then shoot us in the head.'

'I am due at headquarters tomorrow to pick up replacements.' I replied. 'I will find out then if there is any truth to these rumours.'

I arrived early and sought out Arti Grewer, one of the radio operators at the Sixth Army Headquarters. He was a terrible gossip and could easily be induced to reveal all kinds of secrets. He would always protest at first and claim that he could not possibly divulge any information that was classified. A cigarette was all that was required to loosen his lips and cause him to abandon all discretion.

'We're fucked!' He told me as he glanced around to make sure that we could not be overheard. 'We are surrounded! Paulus wanted to attempt a breakout from the encirclement but the Fuhrer has forbidden it. He has promised the German people that we will not abandon Stalingrad and so we must fight to the last man and defend every square foot of soil with our lives! Goering has promised that the Luftwaffe can keep us supplied by air!'

My heart sank at this news. I had been involved in the destruction of several encircled Soviet armies and knew only too well what was in store for us. Even the most determined and best supplied soldiers cannot hold their ground when they are assailed from all sides. It was inevitable that we would be pushed back into an ever-decreasing pocket and that our ranks would be thinned until further resistance was both futile and suicidal.

The intensity, frequency and ferocity of the Soviets attacks increased immediately. They were reinvigorated by the reversal in fortunes and were no longer hampered by the necessity of landing supplies on a thin strip of land on the banks of the Volga. They were determined to press home their advantage and annihilate us. Our hatred and fear of the Russians kept us fighting and we held our ground in the face of this initial onslaught. They threw themselves at us in unprecedented numbers and we slaughtered them mercilessly. If it had been purely a matter of courage and skill we could have held them off for months. It was the lack of ammunition that forced us back in the end. The Luftwaffe's promised air corridor proved woefully inadequate and delivered only a fraction of what was required. We would nervously count our bullets before each Soviet attack and would desperately search the dead and the dying for their ammunition when our own was used up. The struggle grew increasingly desperate and their attacks often ended in brutal hand-to-hand combat that reduced us all to slavering savages.

I came close to death as the Soviet noose tightened around the Sixth Army's neck. If that big Soviet's badly-made rifle had not jammed, I would have died in my dugout on that frozen December morning. He actually paused on the lip of the trench and grinned down at me as he pointed his gun at my head and pulled the trigger. The loud, hollow click told him that his weapon was as useless as my own empty rifle. His grin turned into a snarl and he leapt at me even as he threw his gun aside. He was so heavy he knocked the breath from my lungs when he hit me and was so strong that I could not prise his hands away from my throat. I tried punching him with all my might but my blows had no effect on his thick, square head. Black dots danced before my eyes and I knew that I was dying. I stopped struggling as I floated between life and death and was surprised to realise that I no longer cared what became of me. I knew that I did not want to die but neither did I want to continue to suffer the grinding misery of life amongst the rubble of that damned city. I saw his head jerk to the side but was too far gone to really register it. It jerked violently to the left another four times before his grip weakened and he fell onto his side. I gulped in great lungfuls of air and gaped down at him not really understanding how the side of his skull had been caved in. Manfred then leaned down into my field of vision and asked me if I was alright. The butt of his rifle was thick with blood and torn fragments of flesh.

'You saved me!' I gasped gratefully. "I was almost dead.'

'Merry Christmas Wolffie!' Manfred replied with a half-smile on his lips. 'Let's see if this ox has any gifts for us.'

He did. He had a tin of tobacco in his pocket and we rolled it in paper torn from a Soviet leaflet intended to encourage us to surrender ourselves to their tender mercies. It was not the best Christmas I have ever had, but I was happy to be alive and to be enjoying a smoke with my greatest friend. I suppose it shows just how far we had fallen that we could find even a moment of pleasure whilst sitting in a frozen hole filled with corpses with the sounds of gunfire and the groaning of dying men all around us.

I watched Manfred as he smoked and marvelled at how his cheekbones had grown sharp against his flesh and how his cheeks had become hollow. I realised then that we were starving to death. Rations had been cut and cut again and there had been times when two days would pass without any sustenance reaching us. We, along with our Russian adversaries and the city's poor citizens, had eaten the last of the horses, dogs and cats long before. Apart from the occasional rat or pigeon, there was no game to be had and every shattered building had been thoroughly scoured for any discarded grains of wheat. There had been rumours of cannibalism amongst our ranks, but we had not yet reached that level of desperation.

Rumours and complaints were the only things that were not in short supply as we were forced back from the suburbs and into a tight pocket around the centre of the city. We were told that a new army group had been formed under the command of Field Marshall Manstein and that he was leading a force to relieve us. We pinned all of our hopes on his arrival and were crushed and despondent when Arti Grewer told us that the attempt had been abandoned. It made it worse to know that Manstein had fought his way to within thirty miles of the city but that Paulus had refused to order a breakout so the two forces could meet up. He did so because he would not disobey the Fuhrer's orders and because we only had enough fuel to take us half the way there. We cursed Hitler

231

Goering and Paulus more viciously as January progressed but still could not bring ourselves to believe that we had truly been abandoned. Hardly a single day passed without some story of imminent rescue being passed along the line. I knew that it was hopeless when our territory shrank so much that there was nowhere left for the Luftwaffe to land. They did attempt to drop supplies in by parachute but this benefitted our adversaries just as often as it did us. This left us without food or ammunition and robbed us of the ability to evacuate our wounded.

The end came when we were dug in to the west of the ruined department store where Paulus now had his headquarters. The Sixth Army in Stalingrad had been split into three isolated pockets and word had spread that the Fuhrer had promoted Paulus to Field Marshal, something that was understood to be a signal that he should not surrender but that he must fight to the last man. We were surprised when we were ordered to hold our fire and look on as our generals crawled out of their burrow and made their way into no man's land. The Russian officers emerged from the rubble on the far side and came out to meet them. A short conversation took place and the whole group turned and made for the department store.

'The bastard is surrendering!' Lammert exclaimed in shock and disbelief. 'Listen! The other pockets are still fighting for their lives and this rat is only concerned with saving his own miserable skin.'

We knew that he was right for the sound of gunfire in the distance told us that our comrades were continuing to resist. I did not rush to join in with the condemnation of Paulus though his actions filled me with disgust. He had sacrificed hundreds of thousands of men in order to obey the Fuhrer's orders and was only moved to disobey when his own life was in danger. I would have respected him more if he had shown the courage to take his own life and so avoid dishonouring himself, his men and Germany.

'Then we are all dead men already!' Julius snapped angrily. 'We saw what they did to captured SS men in Demyansk. They skinned them alive so that we would hear their screams as we tried to sleep! That is what they will do to us here.'

'Then we cannot stay!' Manfred announced matter-of-factly. 'We must break out!'

Lammert's laughter was genuine but it was tinged with bitterness. 'What? The four of us? We are surrounded by a million Ivans and have hundreds of miles of enemy territory behind us. We are starving and have neither food nor more than a few rounds of ammunition between us. Do you really believe that we could fight our way out of this cauldron?'

Manfred shook his head. 'No! I do not believe that we can fight our way out, but I believe that we have a small chance of escaping if we do what we do best. If we do what we have learned to do so well since we first entered this damned city. If we crawl and creep and scuttle through the rubble

233

and dirt we might just make it. If we don't!' Manfred left the sentence unfinished and shrugged his shoulders to communicate the fact that we were dead whether we made the attempt or not.

'I suppose that it would be better to die on our feet.' Lammert conceded reluctantly. 'I would rather not put myself into the hands of these subhuman apes.' He then paused and rubbed at the thick stubble on his chin as if he was in deep thought. 'Then we must go now, before these bastards order us to lay down our weapons. But we must collect whatever food and ammunition we can before we do so.'

I owe my life to Lammert's cheek. It was his bluff and bluster that carried us past the sentries and into the headquarters building. The place was abuzz with men gathered in groups chattering in hushed voices and casting glances towards the room where General Schmidt was negotiating with the Soviet officers. No-one paid the four of us any heed as we moved from one room to the next in search of contraband. It seemed that every clerk, general and radio operator had been issued with more ammunition than my whole squad had seen in the previous month. We shook our heads in disbelief that they should be so well-supplied when they were never likely to be required to fire a single shot. I filled my pockets until they bulged and my shoulders sagged under the weight of all the bullets. I also helped myself to a full packet of cigarettes and a silver lighter from an officer's desk. I did not consider it to be theft as they would have been taken by some Soviet officer if I had left them there.

Manfred's nose for food did not fail him and he met with us just inside the front entrance with a satchel on each shoulder. Our mouths watered and our stomachs grumbled painfully when he flicked the flaps back to give us a tantalising glimpse of their contents. I saw chocolate, crackers and a fruit cake amongst the many cans of meat. I felt light-headed at the sight of it all. It was only Lammert's strength of character that stopped us from falling to the ground and making a feast of it there and then.

'Do you think your bellies will stay filled for long once the Russians have us?' He demanded angrily. 'We must go now before these cowards sell us to save their own skins.'

19

We made use of the uneasy ceasefire to crawl forwards from the German lines until we reached a partially collapsed cellar beneath the ruins of a grain store. We were ravenous and helped ourselves to the food from Manfred's satchel while we waited for darkness to fall. I was surprised to find that I was unable to gorge myself as much as I had hoped because my stomach became full and bloated after only a few squares of chocolate, two dry crackers and a third of a tin of tasteless pork. Even Manfred could manage no more than half a tin. We started the long crawl towards the Russian lines as soon as it was fully dark. Our progress was helped by the Russian victory celebrations. They had gathered together in groups to toast to their success and their singing and loud chattering enabled us to navigate our way around them. The tension was unbearable as we inched forward and we were constantly forced to halt and freeze in the darkness when the voices drew near to us. One drunken Cossack stumbled out in front of us and took a piss so close to us that I could feel the spray on my face.

We took refuge in a sewer before the first light of dawn. Lammert insisted that we press on as he believed that the sewer would take us further into the suburbs and away from the heaviest concentrations of Russian troops. We made faster progress below ground than we would have done on the surface as there was less need for stealth. I was overwhelmed by claustrophobia as we felt our way forward in the impenetrable darkness and slithered through the slimy shit that coated the bottom of the sewer pipe. The vile stench caused me to gag and I feared that we would all be overcome by the fumes and be suffocated before we could regain the surface. I do not know how I managed to control my rising panic as I became increasingly convinced that I would be crushed by the tonnes of earth above my head. I was almost relieved when a bright light in the distance indicated that the sewer roof had fallen in and revealed that rubble now blocked our path. We slept fitfully until dusk and then slipped out into the devastated city to continue our way north-west. We moved much more quickly now as there were no lights or fires in the darkness and no sound of human activity to deter us from haste. The din of battle continued in the distance to our rear but we could tell that the fighting was on a much smaller scale than before. We gritted our teeth and pressed on with urgency, convinced that our salvation was dependent upon us putting a great distance between ourselves and Stalingrad as quickly as was possible.

I knew that we had abandoned caution too early when a magnesium flare hissed into the air above us and turned night into day. We were still fifty yards from the nearest cover when the machine gun started to fire. Julius was cut down by the first salvo, the bullet tearing a great hole in his chest and sending him crashing to the ground. He was already dead by the time I reached him and knelt at his side. He gazed up at me with sightless eyes but I still tried to rouse him while the bullets continued to thud into the ground around me and throw up little clouds of brick dust and fragments of mortar. I heard Manfred screaming at me to run but I could not tear my eyes away from Julius. I bent my head down to kiss his cheek and to say goodbye to him. Manfred would later tell me that I was mad and that it was a miracle that I had not been killed when bullets had filled the air around my head. I never regretted pausing to wish my friend adieu and Godspeed as the agony of failing to do so with other loved ones would haunt me until my dying day.

I threw myself down behind a great stone cistern beside Manfred and Lammert and saw immediately that Julius had not been the only casualty. Manfred was bleeding from his chest and left arm but waved my concerns away and dismissed his injuries as scratches. Lammert had not been so lucky. The bullet had struck him below the knee and his lower leg now sat at a sickeningly unnatural angle that caused a wave of nausea to wash over me.

'Let's get him up and out of here!' I instructed Manfred as I bent down to grasp Lammert's shoulder.

'No!' Lammert snapped as he slapped my hand away. 'My leg is almost completely severed. It is only skin and muscle that holds it on!'

'We will not leave you here!' I replied as I bent once again to lift him.

He caught my hand this time and held it as he gazed pleadingly into my eyes. 'You must!' He hissed, his voice tight and strained from the agony of his wound. 'I am finished anyway and you will be too if you try to carry me away! Leave me here and I will pin them down for as long as I can so that you might get away. Let me do this last thing for you. Let me die with honour so that all that I have suffered will not have been for nothing.'

More bullets hammered into the cistern as he spoke and Manfred shook his head at me to indicate that Lammert was finished just as he said he was. There were tears in my eyes as we bound his wound as best we could and dragged him to the corner of the cistern to give him a line of sight across the field of rubble. I embraced him and kissed him upon the cheek and told him that I hoped that we would meet again but in a better place.

He laughed at this and let the tears run down his cheeks. 'I doubt if it would be possible for us to meet in a worse place than this!' He then reached out and pushed a hard object into my hand. 'Promise me that you will get this to my father!' He insisted, squeezing my hand so tight that he hurt me.

I made the promise and he rolled onto his front in preparation for this last, hopeless battle. It almost broke me when I saw what he had entrusted to me. It was the Iron Cross that the Fuhrer had awarded to him at my side in the forest at Compiegne. That happy day was so far removed from our current circumstances that it was impossible to believe that it was us who had actually experienced it. I pushed it deep into my pocket, nodded to Manfred that I was ready and then ran out into the darkness. I like to think that Lammert took a few of the bastards with him for the gun battle was intense and lasted long enough for us to put at least a quarter of a mile between us and them. A single explosion brought the fight to an end and told us that one of the Ruskies had finally crawled close enough to toss a grenade over the cistern.

We ran on and stumbled through the debris until our legs turned to jelly and the first light of dawn began to show itself at the edge of the horizon. We filled our mouths with snow to quench our thirst and found a basement in which to hide during the hours of daylight. We reckoned that it must have been a coal cellar beneath a fine house owned by a rich merchant, or a doctor or a lawyer, for the workmanship was of a high standard and there was no sign of damp. Nothing of the house remained apart from broken bricks and blackened timbers. It was by far the finest accommodation we had enjoyed since leaving Kiev. We ate fruitcake, smoked a couple of General Schmidt's cigarettes and then collapsed in exhaustion upon the stone floor. It was late afternoon when we awakened and I insisted on tending to Manfred's wounds.

'I told you that it was just a scratch.' He insisted as I inspected him. 'The bullet grazed my ribs and carried on into the underside of my left arm. It will be fine if we can keep it clean.'

I nodded my agreement for his injuries did not look too bad. The bullet had entered his rib cage and exited cleanly from the other side before striking his arm. The wounds looked angry and red but were clean and had already congealed so that he had suffered only a minor loss of blood. With this worry extinguished for now, I turned my attention to our current predicament. We had escaped the immediate encirclement in Stalingrad and now needed to decide what to do next.

'All we can do is continue west.' I opined earnestly. 'If we travel only at night and stay away from roads and villages, we stand a chance of reaching our own lines.'

Manfred snorted fiercely and put his head in his hands. 'Christ, Wolffie! Do you not remember how many days we spent travelling across the plains in our trucks? It was hundreds and hundreds of miles of nothing. And who knows where our lines are now? We are more likely to freeze to death in that wilderness than to reach safety!'

'But what else can we do but try?' I replied with a shrug. 'I know that we cannot stay here.'

We stayed in a cellar for another night and another full day. We said that it was to give Manfred's wounds a chance to heal but it was really because we were exhausted after long months of fear and privation and because we were reluctant to leave our safe haven. It was a relief when we finally emerged from the city, but we were daunted by the sight of the plains stretching endlessly before us. We put our heads down, wrapped our arms around our torsos for warmth and focused on placing one foot in front of the other. We made good progress during that first week and counted ourselves lucky that we did not catch sight of a single other human being. I began to hope that we would make it, though the frosts and the bitter winds made the going difficult. It was on the eighth night that I first noticed that Manfred had slowed. I attributed it to exhaustion until my nose detected the stench coming from him as we huddled together for warmth in a shallow depression in the ground while the wind howled around us. He refused to let me examine his wounds on the grounds that he would freeze to death if he was forced to unwrap himself from all the layers of clothes he had piled on against the frigid Russian temperatures. I offered to light a fire for him but he just laughed and said that he would like to see me try to do so in a gale with only frozen grass to burn. We trudged on and my anxiety grew as quickly as his strength deserted him.

I thought I was hallucinating when I first caught sight of the little, square of light floating on the dark horizon. It was only when the sun began to rise that I saw that it was a modest, little farmhouse with a rickety old barn alongside it. I kept my eyes upon it as we laid up for the day in a shallow, dried-up stream bed. The old man was stooped with a bushy white beard and he emerged from the house only five times during the hours of daylight. Once to fetch water from his well, once to collect eggs from his henhouse, once to fill a bucket with firewood and twice to carry a full bucket into the barn before returning to the house once he had emptied it. We had given a wide berth to any settlements we had come across up until then but my concerns about Manfred persuaded me that it was now necessary for us to abandon this policy.

The old fellow barely looked up from his plate of dark bread when we crashed in through his door. He glanced at us and continued smacking his lips as he mashed at the dough with his toothless gums.

'The old bastard might have a gun!' Manfred warned me whilst keeping his rifle pointed at his bald head with its few remaining tufts of snowy white hair.

'He doesn't have a gun.' I retorted in exasperation. 'He barely has a pot to piss in. Let's warm ourselves at his fire and then I can see to your wounds.'

I saw immediately that it was dried dung and not wood that burned in the grate but I did not care. We had not dared to light a fire out on the steppes for fear of broadcasting our position to every Russian for twenty miles. I groaned in both pleasure and pain as the circulation slowly began to return to my extremities.

'Does that old fossil even know that we are here?' Manfred demanded as he warmed his backside over the burning turds. 'He just keeps on gnawing at his bread as if it was the most normal thing in the world for two filthy vagabonds to

243

break into his house and make themselves at home. My grandfather was like this before he died. He ate and slept as normal but his mind had completely gone. He could not even remember my grandmother and would ask her what she was doing in his house at least a hundred times a day.'

The old man did not utter a single word as we boiled water over his fire, cooked and ate his eggs, drank his tea and tore strips from his sheets to bind Manfred's wounds once I had cleaned and squeezed the pus from them. The only time he really reacted to us was when I cut a small square of the fruitcake and placed it on his plate. He examined it for a second before putting it into his mouth and chewing.

'The old bastard likes it!' Manfred announced happily. 'Look! I think he is smiling. Give him another piece, Wolffie!'

The old man's smile was not our only reward that night. We boiled eggs on the fire and stowed them in our satchels to replenish our supplies. We also helped ourselves to bags of oats and dried peas. The best of it came when I followed the old man out to the barn and found his ancient horse. I knew immediately that we would steal the beast along with everything else for Manfred was struggling and we would cover the ground more quickly if he could ride. I felt sufficiently guilty to offer him my rifle in return for all that we had stolen from him. Manfred scolded me for my stupidity when the old man gave no sign of understanding the bargain I was offering him.

244

'Have you lost your mind?' He ranted when I insisted on leaving the weapon. 'I will kick your arse if the old bastard picks the damned thing up and shoots us down when we try to leave.'

I waved away his protests but must admit that I did glance back towards the house several times just to make sure that he did not have us in his sights.

I will never know for sure how the Russians found us, but must sadly accept that it might have been the German rifle in the old man's possession that sent them after us. I first saw their campfire as we tramped through the snow two or three nights after we had left the old man and his fire of dried manure. I hoped that we had lost them in the blizzard that blew through most of that night but caught sight of their truck in the distance as we huddled down at the base of an old wall.

'Up, Mani!' I ordered him. 'They are still on our trail. We must lose them in the snow!'

'I cannot!' Manfred sobbed with a determination and a finality that broke my heart. 'I do not have the strength to stay on the fucking beast let alone to mount it.'

'I will lift you!' I replied, although I did not know if I would be able to.

'You?' He retorted dismissively. 'Have you seen yourself? There's nothing left of you but skin and bones. You hardly have the strength to lift yourself into the saddle. You go! I will stay and fight them so that you will have the chance to escape.'

'I will not leave you!' I insisted as tears flowed down my cheeks. 'I would rather die here by your side than abandon you. Let us fight together this one last time!'

He shook his head defiantly and wiped the tears from his eyes and the snot from his nose. 'No, Wolffie! It is just as Lammert said. If I can buy you enough time to keep you out of their hands, then all of this shit will have been for something! If we both die here, then it has all been for nothing! All that suffering and death will have been pointless.' He then gave me the grin that had preceded every joke he had told me since we were small boys. 'And if you don't go now, I will shoot you in the cock!' His hand was perfectly steady as he aimed his pistol at my groin.

'But I don't want to, Mani.' I sobbed. 'I don't want to leave you here.'

His faced creased with the pain of keeping himself from crying. 'But you must, Wolffie! You must do it for me. You are the only one who can tell my family that I did not surrender with those cowards at Stalingrad. It is my final wish in this life and, as my best friend, you cannot deny me it.'

We embraced for the longest time and I told him that I loved him before kissing him on the cheek. I was still sobbing as I led the old horse out into the blizzard and did not care that my tears were turning to icicles in the biting wind. I turned back after a few minutes but the snow was falling so thickly and was being blown so hard across the plain that I was unable to retrace my steps.'

20

David Strachan laid his grandfather's journal aside, wiped at his eyes with the backs of his hands and shook his head in disbelief. His eyes alighted on the framed photograph of the old boy's wedding anniversary.

'For Christ's sake, Grampy!' He chided that familiar, smiling face. 'How on earth did you keep all this to yourself for all these years?' His question was met by the hollow silence of the empty house.

He pulled another of his grandfather's cigarettes from its packet and went out to smoke it on the back step. He shivered a little in the cold night air and then berated himself internally for bemoaning the low temperature when his old Grampy had suffered through so much worse. He was still reeling from the revelation that his sweet, kind and unassuming old grandad had been a decorated member of the Waffen SS, but that initial shock had been tempered by what he had learned of the horrors that he and his friends had suffered when they were still so young.

It was already very late but he knew that he would read on through the night until he had finished the journal. He flicked the cigarette butt out into the garden and turned to fill the kettle for the coffee that would sustain him through the wee, small hours.

'I lost my mind in the snow and the wind and would have died if it had not been for that skinny, old horse. I had lost all sense of purpose and direction and did not care whether I lived or died. I clung onto his back for the little warmth that came from his skin and he carried me on for day after day. I gave him no guidance, but something deep in his animal brain, some unknowable instinct told him to carry on to the north-west. It was just as we came in sight of the hills that marked the end of the plain that he faltered. The first time he staggered I thought that he had missed his footing. When it happened again I realised that his ancient and emaciated body was failing him. I dismounted immediately and led him on, determined to find a ravine that would give him some small shelter from the biting wind. He lasted for two more days without my weight upon his back, but the distance to the hills had been deceptive and we were still in the open when he finally lurched to the side and crashed to the ground. I tried to pull him back to his feet but stopped when he let out a terrible groan to tell me that he was done.

I lay down on the frozen ground and put my arms around his neck and stroked him to comfort him as he died. A stronger man would have left him there but I had abandoned enough of my friends and could not bring myself to let him die alone. He went quietly with a last gentle snort and a kick of his feet. I like to think that my presence soothed him and eased his passage to the great plain in the sky. I knew that I was mad when I spent two days collecting rocks to pile on his corpse in order to protect it from predators. It seems pathetic now, but it was the most important thing in my life at that moment. It was only when he was completely covered in stones that I turned and made for the hills.

I was not alone in my insanity during the weeks and months I spent in the hills. My old friends came to me and we chattered away as we always had. Lammert would berate me for my unsuccessful attempts to pull fish from the river with my bare hands. Manfred was always on hand with a critical eye and would remind me of the lessons we had learned in the forest under the direction of the redoubtable Helmut Fischer, our old Hitler Youth leader. It was he who instructed me on the building of my shelter and advised me when it was safe to light a fire to drive the chill from my bones. It was Julius and Horse who insisted that I move on when the frosts and the snow gave way to the spring. I moved slowly with no destination in mind and was intent only on finding food and on avoiding all human contact. My hunting and snaring skills improved with each passing week and by the start of the summer I had begun to put on some of the weight I had lost over the winter. If the world had just left me alone, I might well have lived out my life as a madman roaming the hills and forests along with the ghosts of all my friends.

249

The thunder and lightning jerked me from my sleep. I knew immediately that a major artillery bombardment had commenced no more than five miles from my little shelter. I was shocked because I had seen no soldiers since leaving the plains and had assumed that the war was being fought somewhere far from me. The horrible feeling of dread that had been my constant companion during the long months in Stalingrad now returned with a vengeance. It felt as if a large stone had been inserted into my stomach and it now lay heavily there. I caught intermittent snatches of the buzzing of hundreds of aircraft engines whenever there was a gap between the ground-shaking explosions. It did not take long for the counter bombardment to begin and I could feel the earth tremble beneath my fingers.

I climbed a hill that I knew would give me a clear view over the next valley. The explosions still boomed and flashed and lit up the dark horizon as I ascended the slope. The first light of dawn was visible just as I reached the summit and the guns finally fell to silence. I heard the tanks before I caught sight of them in the half-light. There were hundreds, if not thousands of them, charging across the valley floor for as far as the eye could see. I could just make out the infantry regiments following on behind them. Columns of smoke and dirt erupted from the soil around them with the sound of the explosions only reaching my ears a few seconds later. I had once been one of the little specks running behind the advancing tanks and the thought of it now made me nauseous and caused my hands to tremble. I noticed then that the sight of the battle had frightened my friends away. I turned to the west and continued my journey alone.

I suppose that it must have been the fear of being forced back to the front that caused me to avoid my own countrymen during those long weeks. I do not think that I did so consciously, but was directed by only a vague intention to return to the safety of my parents' home. It was not hard to slip through the German lines. The long months of cowering to stay out of the sights of the Soviet snipers had honed the skills of creeping and skulking to a razor sharpness. The only real hardship was the inability to light a fire whilst navigating the German rear. It was this that caused me to sicken. I had hoped that I would have the opportunity to cook the rabbit I caught in my snare, but I failed to find a place where the firelight would not alert the troops to my presence. I succumbed to the hunger gnawing at my belly and ate the meat raw. I had vomited it all back up by the morning and I spent the whole of the next day spraying watery shit from my arse. I pushed on again when darkness had fallen but did so doubled over in pain. I managed less than a mile before I collapsed onto the ground. The agony was so bad that I thought I was dying and it was a blessing when I fell into unconsciousness.

It was then that my father came to me. His voice was curt and insistent, just as it had been when he tried to rouse me from my bed when I was fifteen years old.

'Kurt! Kurt!' He snapped, his voice restrained and controlled but not sufficiently to completely hide his anger and irritation. 'You must get up now!'

'I am tired Papa!' I replied groggily. 'And I am not well. Just let me sleep a little longer.'

'Kurt!' He snapped. 'You must get up this instant! You must get up now or you will die!'

I looked up at him then and saw that he had aged since I last saw him. His moustache and eyebrows were almost completely white and his eyes were watery and red. I smiled when I saw Stelle sitting obediently at his heel. I had loved that mongrel when I was a child but had never been able to steal her affections away from my father. She followed him wherever he went and howled in misery on the rare occasions she was separated from him. The only time I had ever seen my father cry was the day that he buried that dog. It was then that I noticed the deep cut above my father's eye. I opened my mouth to ask him how he had hurt himself but he spoke first.

'You must get up now, my little man. You must get up or you will die here!'

I awakened with a start on the damp earth to find that I had vomited over myself and that I was burning with fever. I forced my protesting body up just as my father had instructed me and stumbled further west. I did not have enough energy to hunt and was therefore reduced to stealing vegetables from the fields and fruit from gardens and orchards. I could keep nothing down for more than an hour but reasoned that my body might be able to extract some goodness from it before I spewed it back up again. I grew weaker with each passing day and soon felt so wretched that I abandoned all caution and took to the roads in daylight rather than suffering through more arduous cross-country marches during the hours of darkness. Even in my fevered state I saw how people looked at me with nervousness and hostility. They saw me for what I had become, a filthy, bearded and diseased vagrant dressed in clothes that were so tattered and engrained with dirt that they were no longer recognisable as a uniform. At least, that is what I had assumed.

I realised my mistake when a gruff voice called out after me as I stumbled down a country lane. He spoke in Polish and I recognised both the term he used and the contempt with which he employed it. I ignored him and continued to drag myself along. I gritted my teeth at the sound of feet running after me and was too weak to resist when a hand grabbed at my shoulder and spun me around to face them. There were four of them and they could have been mistaken for peasants from their dress, but the ancient rifles in their hands marked them out as partisans.

'Szkop?' The ringleader insisted, demanding to know if I was a German soldier. His eyes were set hard in hatred and were filled with murderous intent.

I denied the accusation in Polish but he just bared his teeth and shook his head to convey that he did not believe me. It was as his eyes bored into mine that I accepted I was about to die. I did not have the strength to pull my pistol from my coat let alone enough to defend myself from the beating I was about to receive. I stood there unsteadily and held my arms out wide in an invitation for them to be about their business. I could see that my action had taken the ugly, wide-necked peasant aback, but his hesitation was only momentary. His rifle-butt struck the side of my head with such force that it knocked me to the ground in the middle of the track. I remember thinking that the horse and cart that had just rounded the bend would now have to wait until the bastards had beaten me to death before it could pass. Their boots flew in and stamped down on me but they did not trouble me for long as I was soon hovering on the edge of unconsciousness.

I knew that I was dead or close to it when the angel appeared before my eyes. Her lips were moving but I could not hear a word she said. I smiled up at her because she was so beautiful and because she was the spit of my own long-lost Ania. I decided that dying was not all bad and closed my eyes to let the waves of dizziness carry me off. The angel then slapped me hard across the face and snarled into my ear.

'Get up, you stupid bastard! If you do not, these men will kill you here!'

She then turned and growled at the partisans in a dialect I found hard to follow. I grasped enough in my woozy state to know that she was telling them that I was her idiot cousin. They did not look convinced at first but laughed when she made a joke about me being dropped onto my head when

254

I was a baby. She then helped me to my feet and supported me while another woman brought the cart up. I was unconscious before I hit the wagon bed.

I remembered nothing of the wagon journey when I finally awakened. I was still weak but my fever had broken. I looked around the little attic room and tried to overcome my disorientation and work out where I was. The crisp linen bedsheets felt good against my skin but I felt odd somehow and could not quite put my finger on what was amiss. It took a few minutes for me to realise that the unfamiliar sensation was that of cleanliness. My long and matted hair had been washed and trimmed, my beard had been shaved, my fingernails had been clipped and the dirt scraped from underneath them and I had been scrubbed and bathed so that my skin was white again. The lack of itching was the best part as the lice that had infested my clothes had plagued me night and day for a year or more.

I tried to raise myself into a sitting position but even that small exertion brought waves of dizziness that sent the room into a spin and made me nauseous. I lay still and cast my glance towards the small window that was cut into the wall just below where it met the slope of the roof. There were shutters across it but the angle of the slats gave me a view of a farmyard and a windmill that sat on the bank of a small, round pond. That scene was all that I was to see of the outside world during the months that it took me to recover my strength.

'Good!' A harsh voice announced from the far end of the room. 'You are awake at last!'

I turned my head slowly to keep the giddiness at bay and saw that it was the woman who had brought up the cart when Ania saved me from the partisans. Her expression reminded me of that of their thick-necked leader, for the same hostility burned in her eyes and her top lip was curled in disgust. She stamped across the wooden floor towards me and bent down to retrieve something from beneath the bed. The chamber pot she extracted was white with a dark blue rim. She brandished it like a weapon and I briefly feared that she was about to put more dents in the tin and more cracks in the enamel by thumping it off my skull. I was relieved when she simply tossed into my lap.

'Use this from now on!' She instructed me. 'I am sick of wiping the shit from your arse!'

Her tone stung me and the thought of her cleaning my naked body when I had soiled myself caused my cheeks to burn crimson with embarrassment.

'How long have I been here?' I asked, for the strength of her antagonism suggested that she was heartily sick of performing a task that disgusted her.

'Two months!' She retorted acidly. 'We were sure that you would die more than once and it would be better for us if you had. If we are caught harbouring one of your kind they will string us up by our necks. You would have been left to die in the gutter if it was up to me! You have Ania to

256

thank for that. If you are grateful you will regain your strength as soon as you can and take yourself away.'

Ania brought me a stew of pork and cabbage and she sat on the bed as I slowly ate it with a spoon. The urge to vomit had not left me but I was able to keep the food down if I took my time. I had an irresistible urge to ask her why she had not responded to any of my letters but I resisted it out of fear of appearing ungrateful and of causing offense. I asked her about her sullen friend instead. She smiled before she replied and I did not think that I had ever set my eyes on anyone so beautiful. Even her small imperfections served to make her more exquisite.

'You must forgive Halina. She means no offence. It is just that she is a worrier and your presence here makes her anxious. She knows that it would not go well for us if it was discovered that we were harbouring you under our roof.'

'The partisans would punish you?' I asked, though I thought that the answer was obvious.

'Not just them.' She countered. 'Your own countrymen would not look kindly upon us if they found out that we had sheltered a deserter. I have no doubt that they would award us a bullet apiece. You can stay until you have regained your strength but then you must go. Until then you must stay out of sight or you will endanger us all.'

I hid in that attic room for another two months. I began some light exercise when my legs grew strong enough to support my weight and I increased my exertions each day. When I was able to walk unaided, I took advantage of the long winter nights and strolled around the farmyard under cover of darkness. It was a wonderful thing to escape that cramped little cell and feel the cold air on my skin. My decision to leave was less due to my improving health than it was to the heartbreak of realising that there was no hope of any romance between Ania and I. I had gathered my courage over several days and finally summoned enough to creep to her room in the dead of the night. I had nursed fantasies of us falling into each other's arms and of feeling her lips on mine just as I had on that station platform in France. My heart sank like a stone when I peered around the bedroom door. Her bed was bathed in the moonlight that streamed through the window and I saw them with cruel clarity. Ania and Halina were locked in an embrace even as they slept. I could not even deceive myself into believing that they enjoyed nothing more than a sisterly embrace for they were both naked and the room reeked of their musk. It made it worse to see that Ania's body was even more beautiful than I had dreamed it would be.

I tiptoed back to my room and climbed into bed along with my anger and hurt. The anger was short-lived when I had time to think about it all calmly and objectively. I could not accuse Ania of leading me on because she had offered me no encouragement. I recalled how often my friends had told me to forget her when I complained about here failure to respond to my letters. Only my own pig-headed infatuation had prevented me from accepting this as a clear sign of her lack of interest in me. I also concluded that I could not blame her for turning away from men given what she had endured at their hands. I was even able to laugh when I realised that Halina's animosity was likely driven by her well-founded fear that I intended to come between her and the woman she loved. My anger might have dissipated rapidly but the hurt did not. Just the sight of her was enough to send daggers into my heart and I was eager to end that pain at the earliest opportunity. I knew that I had made the right decision when she made no attempt to dissuade me when I told her of my plans. She did not suggest that I wait until the weather improved or until I reached a higher level of fitness. She just nodded and immediately set about making the arrangements. She laid out her dead brother's winter clothes and coat upon my bed, polished his boots for me to wear and packed a basket of food for our journey.

We jolted along in that little cart for six long days and I should have spent every minute of the journey thanking her for all she was doing for me. I am ashamed to admit that I did not, for I was so immersed in my own misery that I was blunt and uncommunicative. The nights were a time of unbearable agony as we bedded down together in the back of the cart with blankets wrapped around us and a tarpaulin over our heads to protect us from the weather. It drove me mad with frustration to have her in such close proximity without being able to reach out and touch her. I lay awake all night listening to her breathing, smelling her sweet fragrance and feeling the heat of her body radiate through the blankets. I was able to maintain an impassive façade but on the inside I was like a little boy throwing a tantrum when he discovers that life is not always good or fair.

She pulled up a few miles short of the border and told me that I just needed to continue along the dirt track in front of us. I nodded my agreement for I could already see the familiar shape of the wooded hill that lay a little to the south of my boyhood village. She then reached into the pocket of her coat and held a folded piece of card out towards me.

'These are my brother's identity papers. He has no use for them now and I thought that you might have need of them.'

I took them out of politeness but I doubted that they would be of much help to me. I had already decided that I would spend a little time with my parents and then go to face the music. I had already been rehearsing the story I would tell and had some hope that the army would be convinced by my tale of an epic journey and a near fatal illness as an explanation for my long absence. I did not know it then, but Ania had not only repaid her debt by saving my life but had also given me the gift of a new life that would bring me more happiness than I either deserved or dreamed of. I am glad that I was able to overcome my petulance and bruised feelings sufficiently to embrace her, kiss her upon the cheek and thank her for all that she had done for me. I would have hated myself if her last memory of me was one of bitterness and ingratitude. I waved her off, watched her little cart until it had disappeared into the distance and then turned my feet for home.'

21

'My mother's face was a picture when she opened the door and saw me standing before her on the step. She clasped at her chest in shock before bursting into tears of joy. It felt good to be in her tight embrace and I could not stop myself from crying with the relief of being home and safe. Those tears of happiness were turned to tears of grief when she led me inside the house to find old Pastor Bonhoff sitting in the front parlour. I remembered him as a strict and unforgiving man who had tormented me through countless long afternoons of Sunday school when I was younger. He looked older now and much less fierce and his face was filled with an expression of such sorrow and sympathy that I knew immediately that my father had died.

'What happened?' I asked, now registering the fact that my mother was dressed in black to mourn her husband.

'A seizure.' Pastor Bonhoff replied gently. 'He was teaching a class and just collapsed in front of the children. He hit the floor so hard that he split his brow. We brought him home to his own bed and he passed away two days later without ever fully regaining consciousness. He did not suffer, Kurt. You can take some comfort from that.'

I nodded to thank him for I sensed that he had been a great support to my mother. 'When did it happen?' I asked tentatively, my thoughts flitting involuntarily back to my father's imagined visitation when I lay deep in my delirium in the forest.

'The third of September.' My mother answered immediately, the speed of her response reflecting the fact that this black date was now one which would forever stand out in her calendar as an unwelcome and morbid anniversary.

I must have given some outward sign of my thoughts at that very moment for the Pastor immediately asked me if something was wrong. I looked at them both and studied them while I decided whether or not I should share my experience with them. I hesitated out of fear of upsetting my mother and of incurring the old man's scorn. It was only when my mother pressed me that I decided to be fully open and honest. I told them the whole tale and was careful to emphasise that I had been gravely ill and suffering from a fever at the time. They had both turned as pale as ghosts by the time I stopped speaking and they exchanged such a glance that I demanded to know what was amiss.

'My son!' The Pastor replied, the quaver in his voice revealing his distress. 'It does not signify anything, I am certain that it does not, but it is strange that your hallucination bears some uncanny relation to your father's last words.'

'Papa's last words?' I repeated. 'What were Papa's last words?'

My mother reached out and took my hand in hers. Her eyes were brimming with tears as she spoke. 'He called for his dog, Kurt. Just as he died he called for Stelle and said, 'Come Stelle! It is time for us to walk in the forest!'

I am glad that I overcame my fear of revealing my madness for my mother took great comfort from my story in the time that was left to her. She lasted only a year after my father's passing but she spent that time fully convinced that she would be reunited with him. I gave her hope when she was at her lowest point and I am proud of that when I am proud of few other things.

I had no pride in me when I crossed the village to call on Manfred's parents. I was honest with them about how he met his end, but felt such shame at abandoning him that I could not bring myself to look either of them in the eye. Their kindness and understanding only served to make me feel more wretched. When I asked for their forgiveness they refused to grant it on the basis that none was required. They embraced me and told me that Mani had loved me like a brother and that he would not have wanted me to spend a single second on regret or recrimination. Manfred's father was most concerned about the precarious nature of my status with the military authorities and advised me to do nothing whilst he investigated the best way to deal with my predicament. I had spent a month living with my mother as we supported each other in our grief when the telegram arrived from Berlin. Herr Wissler had obviously approached his brother for advice on my situation for the telegram came from Hauptsturmfuhrer Wissler and ordered me to report to him at his office on Prinz-Albrecht-Strasse the following week. I had further reason to be grateful to Herr Wissler for this because it gave me enough time to help my mother move to a small cottage by the river as she was required to leave the schoolmaster's house in order to make way for my father's replacement.

I found it strange to be returning to Berlin for a whole host of reasons. It made me sad to be walking its streets knowing that I would never do so again with Manfred, Julius and Horse at my side. Our old haunts no longer held any appeal for me and I just passed them by. I also found it odd to be back in the centre of the Reich with all of its symbols of power and triumphalism after seeing that power ripped to shreds and reduced to nothing in the rubble of Stalingrad. That façade of strength and invincibility was also somewhat eroded by the visible damage that had been caused by the British bombing raids and the firestorms that followed them. The foundations of my faith in the Reich had been badly shaken and there was little that could be done to repair the cracks. These thoughts and anxieties were all coloured by my nervousness at the prospect of my meeting with Hauptsturmfuhrer Wissler. I had not spoken with him since he refused to help us escape from the insanity of the Einsatzgruppe in Minsk and was unsure as to what kind of reception I should expect. I feared that I would be disciplined for my long absence and had heard enough tales of the SS punishment battalions to fill me with dread.

I need not have worried for he rose from his desk on seeing me and embraced me warmly. He then whisked me out for lunch and we spent the afternoon drinking schnapps, commiserating and reminiscing. I could see that Manfred's death and his estrangement from him had weighed heavily upon his shoulders and realised that he was looking to me for absolution. I decided to be kind and grant it to him and told the first of the lies I told to the close relatives of my dear, dead friends. The Hauptsturmfuhrer's eyes grew glassy with unshed tears when I described how much Mani had regretted falling out with him. He pressed his hands against his eyes when I revealed that Manfred had intended to seek a reconciliation the moment he had leave to return to Berlin. Manfred had said no such thing but I doubted that he would have wanted his uncle to suffer such guilt. I suppose that I wanted to give him the same comfort that Manfred's parents had given to me.

The first of the evening customers had started to arrive in the restaurant before he reciprocated in kind.

'And what are we to do with you, young Wolff?' He asked as he sat back in his chair and examined me. 'Are we to send you back to the Eastern Front to bring the Soviets to a halt? The Sixth Army has been reconstituted during your convalescence and are battling the Red Army as we speak. Or perhaps you would rather rejoin your SS brothers in the Totenkopf Division who are engaged in heavy defensive fighting to the east of the Dnieper?' He paused then and tapped his index finger against his lips as if he was engaged in the process of making a decision. 'But it may be that you have already given enough. You fought with distinction in France and were decorated by the Fuhrer himself for your courage. You then went on to distinguish yourself at Kiev, Kharkov and Stalingrad. It might be argued that your talents would be better employed elsewhere. It just so happens that I have an opportunity that would suit an experienced combat veteran with some engineering training under his belt. Of course, if you would prefer to return to the front I could arrange that very quickly indeed.'

I agreed to his proposal with undue haste and amused him greatly by signing up before he had even told me what the role entailed. He then provided a brief outline of a secret project to develop a force similar to the British commando units and indicated that he needed to find someone who could oversee all of the associated logistical and supply requirements. I did not care that the role was within the SS or that it carried the rank of Feldwebel or Staff Sergeant, it was enough for me to know that it would be far from the frontline. He asked me to give him two days to make the arrangements for me to rejoin the SS and for my new orders to be issued.

This provided me with the time to pay my respects to the families of Julius, Horse and Lammert. The only one I did not lie to was Lammert's father. I handed him the Iron Cross his son had pressed upon me as he lay wounded in the rubble of Stalingrad and told him truthfully how he had died holding the Soviets up so that we could break out of that damned city. I could see that it meant a lot to him to know that his son had not surrendered to the Russians like so many of his comrades but had fought on to the bitter end. There were no out-and-out lies for Horse's parents, although I did omit a great deal to spare them from the horror. I never mentioned that he had died alone or that the Russians had mutilated him and I did not even allude to the fact that the Russian shells had unearthed him each time that we buried him. They were distraught but seemed to take reassurance from hearing that their boy was a brave soldier, a true friend and a dutiful son. Julius' mother took my face in her hands and kissed both of my cheeks when I described how I had embraced her son and kissed his cheek after he had fallen on the battlefield. I did not think that it would have benefitted her to know that he had been shot in the back while we were running away. It cost me nothing to alter the facts a little and tell them that he had been fighting courageously when he was cut down. Sometimes the facts can obscure the truth and I wanted them to know that Julius was brave and the best of men. I was relieved when these obligations had been discharged and reported for duty feeling that a huge weight had been lifted from my shoulders.

If it had been Hauptsturmfuhrer Wissler's intention to spare me from any more suffering then it must be said that he surpassed himself. I reported directly to him, was based in a small training camp in the Rhineland and had almost complete freedom of action for the first six months while Himmler dithered over selecting a senior officer to command the whole project. I led the team responsible for procuring food, equipment, linen, uniforms, mortars, sub-machine guns, rifles, side arms, vehicles, motorcycles and everything else you can imagine from boot-laces to shoe polish. Even with no budgetary restrictions, it was difficult to lay our hands on any of these items given that we faced fierce competition for resources from every branch of the military as well as from both civilians and local government. In many ways, it was my experience of scavenging for food and ammunition in Stalingrad that had prepared me for this challenge. I found it easy to cajole, persuade, threaten, charm, and, when it was necessary, bribe suppliers, storemen and quartermasters to get what I needed. I was even forced to relive a chapter of my youth in the Totenkopf when I led my men on a mission to steal cars from a military supply depot just outside Hannover. One of the advantages of being involved in a top-secret project is that not even the military can track you down to punish you for your transgressions.

When I was not on the road in search of supplies, I spent my evenings drinking and playing cards with the training officers, several of whom had served on the Eastern Front. We told stories and got fat on the little extras that fell into my hands as I went about my business. The war seemed to be a million miles away from us, though we were only too aware that the tide was turning against us. The Russians continued to push our armies further west, the British bombed our cities with an alarming frequency and rumours of a joint American-British invasion swirled around and refused to die away. We learned to ignore the propaganda pushed out by Goebbels on the radio and in the press and relied instead on the grapevine as the gossip, speculation and miscommunication was almost always more accurate than the lies put out from the centre. It was a greengrocer from Monchengladbach who told us that the Americans had landed in Normandy in June and a profiteering fuel salesman with an inconstant limp who told us that all of northern France was under allied control before the end of August. We were cossetted and spared from the hardships that afflicted our countrymen but knew that this happy situation could not continue indefinitely. I was ordered to report to Berlin at the beginning of September to meet my new commander.

I disliked Obergruppenfuhrer Prutzmann at first sight. He had an air of cruelty about him and had these large, piercing eyes that seemed to bore into you in search of something to rouse him to anger. He did not endear himself to me during our first conversation when he examined my file and tried to find something that would bind me to him and turn me into a loyal, unquestioning lackey.

'Ah!' He exclaimed in delight, pointing his finger at something in my file that had caught his interest. 'I see that we are kindred spirits and have travelled a similar path. You were at Minsk with Nebe and Einsatzgruppe B while I was in Latvia working closely with Einsatzgruppe A. It was difficult work, yes?'

'I was not with Einsatzgruppe B for long, Herr Obergruppenfuhrer. I joined the Wehrmacht at the earliest opportunity because I was eager to fight those who actually threatened the Reich with arms.' My tone dripped with hostility as I resented this attempt to link me with an organisation I despised. I knew that I should have bitten my tongue, as this man had the power to have me on a transport to the Eastern Front before the day was out, but I could not help myself. It was fortunate that my barb went straight over the idiot's head and he continued as if I had not spoken.

'The Reichsfuhrer himself has entrusted me with a responsibility of the utmost importance and you, Feldwebel Wolff, are to play a critical part in its implementation. You should be aware that all of our activities must be carried out in complete secrecy.'

'Yes, Herr Obergruppenfuhrer.' I replied dutifully. 'I have become used to operating in such a manner over the past six months.'

He shook his head slowly and looked at me as if I was a babbling fool. 'It has all changed, Wolff. Operation Werewolf is no longer concerned with training commandos to undertake missions behind enemy lines. Werewolf is now about the survival

271

of the Reich and about ensuring that we will prevail in the long and bitter struggle that lies ahead. The Fuhrer will hear no talk of the possibility of defeat, but the Reichsfuhrer is not so squeamish and knows that we must prepare for all eventualities. We must accept that it is possible that our enemies will defeat our armies and breach our borders. I have been entrusted with creating a resistance movement that will make it impossible for the Russians and Americans to govern the Reich even if they succeed in occupying it. We will recruit, train and supply cells of loyal men who will hide themselves away and then leap out to sow destruction and disorder amongst our enemies. It is through such guerrilla warfare that National Socialism will rise from the ashes and ultimately prevail.'

The longer he spoke the more incredulous and horrified I became. I was shocked by the revelation that Himmler was plotting behind the Fuhrer's back and thought that such disloyalty and disunity amongst our most senior leaders must surely condemn us to defeat. I was also appalled by the sheer insanity of what was being proposed. Any man who had come up against the Soviets knew full well that no war of attrition could be ground out against an enemy that thought nothing of throwing millions of poorly armed men forward to defeat machine guns through sheer weight of numbers.

'I have had good reports of your performance so far, Wolff.' The Obergruppenfuhrer continued. 'But you will need to up your game in the weeks and months ahead. You will be responsible for constructing and equipping bunkers and dugouts across Germany so that our men can remain hidden until the enemy advance has passed over them. They must have enough food and drink to sustain them and the weaponry, explosives and transportation to enable them to engage in sniping, arson, sabotage, ambush and assassination. They must also have the funds necessary to allow them to continue operating for a protracted period if that proves to be necessary. You will find all of the detailed requirements in this file. You report only to me. Heil Hitler!'

It seems strange to say it now, but the next six months were amongst the most satisfying of my life. I worked from dawn until late into the night and travelled tens of thousands of miles across the country. I relished the challenges involved in finding locations for the bunkers and in constructing them in secret. These challenges increased when supplies of concrete, equipment and materials grew tighter as our enemies closed in on our borders from both east and west. I took great pride in my initiative and creativity as I made use of caves, cellars and even the crypt of a ruined church whenever it was impossible to build from scratch. I worked tirelessly to stock the bunkers with canned meat, biscuits, crackers, chocolate, tinned vegetables, rifles, mortars, ammunition and explosives. Each dugout was also fitted with a safe hidden in the floor which was intended to secure the gold bars and coins that the Werewolf cells were to use to keep themselves operational for an extended period following an invasion. The need for secrecy was such that I possessed the only map that detailed the exact locations of all the bunkers, dugouts, arms caches and the gold. The work required industry, ingenuity and guile and I threw myself into it so wholeheartedly that I was almost able to ignore the shadow of calamity that hung over the country. I was not deaf to the distant guns or to the enemy bombers flying overhead, but I was so engrossed in my work that I never dwelled on it for long.

That is not to say that this was a time free of worry or concerns. My misgivings about Himmler and Prutzmann's intention of fighting bitterly to the last man had increased rather than diminished as the months passed by. This was largely driven by the failure of the Obergruppenfuhrer's efforts to recruit the necessary manpower. This had proven to be extremely difficult because all able-bodied men were being posted to combat units to replace the tens of thousands who were being killed or wounded in the defence of the Fatherland. Prutzmann sought to overcome this obstacle by recruiting from the ranks of the Hitler Youth and by engaging men who were considered too old or unfit for frontline service. I watched these recruits being put through their paces at a training centre near the town of Erkelenz and was sickened by the spectacle. I knew that their loyalty and fanaticism would count for little when they were faced by battle-hardened Soviet troops. They would be scythed down like wheat and would achieve nothing more than adding to the already heavy toll of unnecessary and pointless deaths.

I had realised quite early on that I had it in my power to prevent the deaths of so many boys and old men by keeping the guns and explosives out of their hands. I believed that they would not resist if they were denied the means to do so. My plan was not without risk, but I convinced myself that a sudden enemy advance on either front would create sufficient chaos to bring it to fruition. I thought that success was almost within my reach in late March 1945 and was consequently distraught when Obergruppenfuhrer Prutzmann reached me on the telephone from Berlin.

'I have great news, Wolff!' He exclaimed, his excitement clear in spite of a loud crackling on the line that made it difficult to make out his words. 'The Reichsfuhrer SS has made the Fuhrer aware of Operation Werewolf and he has requested a full briefing. You will accompany me to the Reich Chancellery to answer any detailed technical questions he may have.'

22

'The Fieseler Storch was buffeted by the wind as it began its descent and I caught my first glimpse of Berlin through a thick haze of smoke. The devastation caused by the allied bombing raids was clear even from that height. A few fires still burned on and the blackened skeletons of hundreds of houses and factories stood as a testament to how much more intensive the attacks had become in the months since my last visit. The greater part of Berlin was still fully intact, but it was shocking to see how far it had deteriorated.

Manfred's uncle was waiting for me in his Mercedes when the little plane had taxied to a halt. He seemed genuinely pleased to see me and wrapped me in his embrace before ushering me into the car. We made straight for his home and just the sight of it was enough to make me smile at memories of my student days there with Manfred, Maus, Julius and Horse. I even laughed when I recalled how old Frau Winkler had rapped her cane against the floor whenever we dared to speak in anything louder than the softest of whispers. I asked after her as politely as I could, though I was certain that she must have died a long time before.

'My mother-in-law is as hale and hearty as ever.' Hauptsturmfuhrer Wissler replied with a roll of his eyes. 'She was at death's door when my dear wife persuaded me to take her in. Her subsequent recovery was quite miraculous and I do not doubt that she will outlive us all.' He then paused before breaking into a grin. 'Do not worry. I will not put you into the cellar tonight and subject you to her ill-natured hammering. You will have a guest-room on the second floor.'

I enjoyed a perfectly pleasant dinner with the whole Wissler family before retiring to the Hauptsturmfuhrer's study for cognac and cigars. He poured me a generous measure in a crystal glass and then ruefully shook his head.

'Enjoy this while you can, Kurt. I used to have it shipped in from a vineyard on the Charente river but it is the damned Americans who will be drinking it now that they have occupied all of France. It's such a damned shame.'

Our pleasant and civilised conversation was only interrupted when our ears picked up the unmistakable drone of bomber engines in the distance. The Hauptsturmfuhrer rapped his knuckles against the surface of the wooden table three times for luck.

'They have not dropped their bombs in this area for more than three weeks now.' He informed me with a shrug. 'The British are such animals. They think nothing of the civilian casualties when they destroy residential areas. At least we Germans take care to attack only legitimate military and industrial targets.'

I waited for the punchline or the wry grin that I expected to follow such a statement but it did not come. He busied himself with lighting his cigar until I had no choice but to accept that he was serious. I could not tell whether he was genuinely deluded or if he was feigning ignorance of the great damage our own troops deliberately inflicted on the civilian populations of the territories we invaded.

'This will be my first visit to the Reich Chancellery.' I said when I felt that the silence had stretched on for too long.

'Oh, you will not be meeting with the Fuhrer in the Chancellery.' Hauptsturmfuhrer Wissler informed me. 'He now conducts almost all of his business in that damned bunker of his. You will almost certainly meet him in the Situation Room. Remember to take a deep breath before you enter the Fuhrerbunker. It is very stuffy in there. The ventilation system just seems to recycle the same old farts, body odour and bad breath over and over again. I avoid the place whenever I can and cannot understand how anyone could stand to live in it.'

The Hauptsturmfuhrer's assessment was very accurate. The air in the Fuhrerbunker was not quite suffocating but neither was it entirely breathable. I did not know enough about the operation of the ventilation system to be sure of it, but it certainly seemed to recycle the same air several times as the smell of chicken broth from the kitchens disappeared and then returned in waves during the four hours that Prutzmann and I were kept waiting in the corridor. What made it worse was that Prutzmann ordered me to refrain from smoking as the Fuhrer did not approve of the habit and he did not want to offend him. The presence of numerous other men smoking heavily as they loitered in the corridor served to make me even more irritable.

I was on the verge of dozing when Prutzmann suddenly launched himself to his feet giving me such a start that I almost fell onto the floor. I stood immediately to attention the second I saw what had caused Prutzmann to jump up so abruptly. Reichsfuhrer SS Heinrich Himmler graced us with a lazy salute and peered along the corridor through his thick glasses.

'Why are they not out yet?' He enquired impatiently. 'Bormann called to say that they were finishing up. They should be out by now.'

Prutzmann seemed nervous in the presence of his superior and prattled away in order to fill the silence as we waited. Himmler grew increasingly agitated and began to repeatedly slap his hands against his thighs in agitation. Prutzmann tried to introduce me to the Reichsfuhrer and to tell him a little about my work and my background but he could only bring himself to favour me with the briefest and most dismissive of glances. I absorbed this insult by recalling how sick and faint the Reichsfuhrer had become when faced with the product of his own murderous work back in Minsk. I had no time to dwell on this for the door to the room at the far end of the corridor had burst open to release a torrent of generals, field marshals and a host of other officials. I recognised a few of them, such as Jodl, Keitel and Krebs, but most were strangers to me.

Himmler made straight for the conference room with Prutzmann and I following in his wake. The air in there was even thinner than that out in the corridor and it was heavy with the stench of body odour and the gases expelled from bellies too used to large quantities of the finest food and drink. The room was dominated by a long table with a large map of Germany spread across its surface. I did not immediately recognise the stooped figure sitting hunched over in a chair on the far side of the table. It was only when Himmler addressed him that I realised it was the Fuhrer himself. I was astounded by the change in him. He seemed to have aged twenty years in the four and a half years since I had last set my eyes upon him. His skin had turned grey and lifeless, his eyes were red and watery, he seemed incapable of sitting up straight and his hands trembled even although he had them clasped tightly together.

I stood back from my superiors and watched as the discussion unfolded. Martin Bormann stood at the Fuhrer's left shoulder and Albert Speer, the Minister of Armaments and War Production, stood on his right. I was relieved to see that Himmler was determined to do most of the talking and so take credit for all of the work that had been done. He turned to Prutzmann for additional details here and there but was mostly content to rely on his own limited knowledge. What he did not know he made up and he was not shy about employing exaggeration or invention when he deemed the facts to be insufficiently impressive. I was happy to stay silent because the

Hauptsturmfuhrer had warned me about Hitler's sudden furies and had advised me that discretion was the better part of valour in these situations.

I thought I was on the verge of escaping unscathed when Prutzmann turned to me with urgency and began clicking his fingers in a show of impatience. It took me a second to realise that the Fuhrer had asked where the Operation Werewolf arms dumps and bunkers were located and that Prutzmann had ordered me to lay my map out on the table. I had just begun to unfold it when the Fuhrer tapped his forefinger impatiently against the table and ordered me to stop.

'That map is much too small.' He growled irritably. 'Come and show me the locations on this map!'

I felt my cheeks redden now that I was the centre of attention and I made my way around to Hitler's side of the table. It seemed to take an age to detail what had been hidden where and for what purpose, but I was not interrupted or challenged and both the Fuhrer and the Reichsfuhrer murmured their approval on several occasions. It was as I was covering the last of the bunkers in the south that I became aware that the Fuhrer was staring at me intently. I did not dare to turn and look at him directly and found that his scrutiny discomfited me greatly. I had no choice but to turn and face him when I had completed my report. There was a frown on his face as he studied me closely. I prayed that it was a quizzical expression rather than anything aggressive or disapproving. I felt my cheeks burn hotter and beads of sweat run

281

down my forehead as his inspection and the long silence that accompanied it stretched out uncomfortably.

'We have met before?' He asked finally, his eyes screwed up with the effort of trying to recall where he had encountered me.

'Yes, mein Fuhrer!' I responded immediately, relieved that I had not done something wrong and elated that the Fuhrer had remembered me.

'Now! Where was it?' He asked. 'No! Do not tell me! It will come to me in a second!' He held his forefinger up to indicate that I should not blurt out the answer.

'It was on our tour of Paris, mein Fuhrer.' Albert Speer interjected from behind me. 'He and his comrades accompanied us as we toured the sights.'

I was astounded that Speer remembered me, for I had only ever spoken to him on that one occasion at Napoleon's tomb. Prutzmann seemed to share my astonishment but did not appear at all happy to discover that I had some small connection with both Speer and Hitler. It pleased me that it caused him such great annoyance.

'No! It was not Paris.' The Fuhrer replied with a shake of his head. He then tapped his finger against his temple. 'I have always had a great capacity for retaining facts. It is one of my greatest strengths.' An expression of triumph then crossed his face and he turned in his chair to wag his finger at Speer in admonishment. 'It was not in Paris, Speer! It was at Compiegne. Eicke was with me and I presented this man and three of his comrades with their Iron Crosses. Do you not remember? They were my wolf pack! They charged a French machine gun nest and so saved a column of SS troops from the Death's Head Division from ambush. Am I not right, Wolff?'

It is hard to describe or to explain what I felt in that moment. After all that I had seen and experienced, I should have detested Adolf Hitler. I had seen first-hand how his ambition, cruelty and single-mindedness had brought slaughter and destruction upon my country and its people. I had witnessed for myself the great suffering caused when cities were reduced to ruins and their inhabitants brutalised. I had seen the outrages carried out in his name and had suffered the loss of my dearest friends because of his military failures. And yet, I did not despise him. He was undeniably diminished but he still possessed that inexplicable aura of power and magnetism that hung about him. I found myself standing to attention with the same ramrod straightness I had displayed before him in France. I was elated to have been remembered and to have received some small sign of approval from him. Far from hating him and wishing him ill in that moment, I wanted nothing more than to die for him and to sacrifice my life for his greater glory. I have agonised long and hard over this in the years since then but have never come close to understanding it. It is shameful to admit to adoration of such a devil when all logic, sense and decency screams against it. It is more shameful still to be unable to offer a single explanation or excuse for such a grievous

283

sin. I will never understand why God would curse the world by investing such great power in one flawed man.

'What about your comrades?' The Fuhrer enquired. 'Are they also involved in this Operation Werewolf?'

'No, mein Fuhrer.' I replied. 'They are all dead. They died at Stalingrad.'

I knew immediately that I had made a mistake because Himmler rolled his eyes in annoyance and Prutzmann grimaced. Hitler launched into a long and furious tirade against his generals. He berated them for their caution, their cowardice and their treachery and blamed them for every failure and setback that had befallen the Reich. He listed all of the occasions when he had been successful only because he had overruled their objections and pushed on with his plans in spite of their opposition. I knew instinctively that Himmler, Prutzmann and Speer had suffered this tirade before and that they were not enjoying this repeat performance. I, on the other hand, took great pleasure from it because Hitler repeatedly held me up as an example of courage and said that we would not have lost a single battle if only his generals had possessed a fraction of my bravery. I could deny that this was my proudest moment but it would be a lie.

It was Bormann who skilfully interjected and brought the diatribe to a close by reminding the Fuhrer that there was an important telephone call he needed to make. Hitler shook me by the hand, thanked me for my work and saluted me. I exited the conference room behind Himmler and Prutzmann and felt as if I was floating on air. The palm of my hand seemed to tingle with some magical residue from the Fuhrer's own skin. It was just as I drew close enough to the bunker's entrance to detect the sweet fragrance of fresher air that Speer caught up with me.

'Would you join me for a drink, Feldwebel Wolff?' He enquired, his voice low and polite but also somehow insistent. 'We could continue the conversation we began at Napoleon's tomb.'

I was eager to be free of Prutzmann's company and so accepted the invitation immediately. Speer led me to an area containing two canteen tables and went off to fetch glasses and cognac. He poured me a generous measure and drank to my health. I watched him nervously as he drank because I feared that he was about to berate me for some of the methods I had employed to lay my hands upon the goods and materials required to build and equip the bunkers. I was only too aware that I had often defied and stepped on the toes of officials who were part of Speer's sphere of authority. He brooded beneath those great, bushy eyebrows of his for long minutes and seemed reluctant to meet my gaze. When he finally spoke, he did so in a whisper and what he said left me speechless.

'Do you understand what an abomination this Operation Werewolf is? Do you understand that Himmler and Prutzmann will happily condemn thousands of young men to their deaths when the war is already lost? They will use their devotion and loyalty to convince them to throw their lives away on an empty, futile gesture.'

I returned his gaze and fought to conceal how tense I had become. The Minister was criticising an operation that had just been endorsed by the Fuhrer himself and I felt that he was encouraging me to do the same. I suspected that my loyalty was being tested and so remained silent.

Speer held my gaze for a moment longer and then sighed. 'Of course, you do not trust me. We hardly know one another, but you must see that I am not one of these zealots who would see Germany reduced to ashes in defeat. Unlike them, I can admit what is obvious to any man who is not determined to delude himself. The war is lost. We are being forced to retreat in both the east and in the west and it is only a matter of time before we collapse. My only concern now is to spare the German people from as much unnecessary death and destruction as is possible. I have as much love for the Fuhrer as you, but I have been disobeying his orders to destroy our infrastructure for some weeks now. I ask only that you consider taking such measures yourself. Do not put these young men in danger when no good can come of it.'

I chose my words carefully when I replied as even his own admission of disobedience did not fully convince me of his good intentions. 'The cells can only resist if they have access to their weapons and explosives. Only I am aware of the locations of all of the bunkers and the weapons caches and they are marked only on the map that is in my possession.'

Speer nodded to show that he understood. 'But what if the map is taken from you?'

'It would depend upon how accurate the map is.' I replied. 'The slightest error in the recorded coordinates would make the weapons almost impossible to locate.'

Speer smiled at this and seemed to relax a little. 'I knew instinctively that you were a decent man and hoped that you would take the chance to spare others from unnecessary harm. I must now ask you to aid me in saving thousands of other men. It will be dangerous work but the end of this war is now so close that the risk is one worth taking. Besides, what I have in mind will take you and your map beyond the reach of Prutzmann and Himmler. They cannot extract information from you if they cannot find you.'

What Speer was asking me to do was dangerous and entailed a high likelihood of me being executed as a traitor. He wanted me to convey a message from him to General Niehoff, the military commander of the city of Breslau, imploring him to ignore Hitler's order to hold Fortress Breslau at all costs. He told me that he feared that this order would result in the complete destruction of the city and the slaughter of its ninety thousand defenders and the tens of thousands of civilians still trapped there by the encircling Soviet armies.

'The Luftwaffe air corridor into the city is still strong.' He persisted. 'You could fly in, deliver the message and fly out again or you could lose

287

yourself and your map there and surrender with the garrison.'

I had no intention of surrendering myself to the Russians and so agreed to fly in and then straight back out again. I also insisted that Speer provide me with a written message to deliver as I felt that this would enable me to claim that I had no knowledge of the treachery he was suggesting. He agreed reluctantly, saying that he would have the message typed but would leave it unsigned. We shook hands and he promised to send the message and details of my travel arrangements to Hauptsturmfuhrer Wissler's house.

The Hauptsturmfuhrer was most displeased when I told him that Reichsminister Speer had engaged my services as a courier. I did not share the nature of the message I had agreed to deliver, but it seemed that Himmler and his inner circle already had their suspicions about the loyalty of the Reichsminister. He advised me against proceeding in the strongest terms and then insisted that I accompany him to Plotzensee Prison. I knew that I had been brought there to witness an execution the moment I stepped out into the courtyard and joined the small group of men gathered there. It was not the meat hook in the wall that gave it away but the familiar atmosphere of sick anticipation, fear and morbid excitement. I did not recognise the condemned man at first because he was dirty and dishevelled and had bruising around his mouth and his left eye.

'See how even the mightiest amongst us can fall!' Hauptsturmfuhrer Wissler hissed into my ear. 'See your former commander pay the price for his treachery!'

It was only then that I recognised Arthur Nebe, the commander of Einsatzgruppe B. They strung him up with piano wire without ceremony and watched in silence as he kicked his last as punishment for plotting against the Fuhrer. I felt nothing as I watched his terminal struggle and was surprised to realise just how much of my humanity had been lost to me. The long months of brutality and slaughter had eroded it to such an extent that I could watch the violent death of another human being without experiencing a flicker of empathy. My only consolation was the extent to which my lack of reaction frustrated the Hauptsturmfuhrer, for he had hoped to teach me a lesson in the cost of treachery and so persuade me against flying into the siege at Breslau.'

23

I regretted my decision the moment Breslau came into sight. The devastated city was enveloped in a thick cloak of smoke and dust. It put me in mind of Stalingrad when our bombers and artillery were first engaged in reducing it to rubble. The thunder of the big guns assaulted our ears even at such a great height and I could feel my throat begin to burn in the acrid air. All of this was rendered insignificant the moment the anti-aircraft guns opened up on us. The explosions were deafening and the little Fieseler Storch lurched and dropped sickeningly when the shock-waves struck it. I clung on for dear life and was horrified to realise that my survival was entirely dependent upon some Soviet gunner's incompetence or lack of skill.

'Look!' The pilot exclaimed as he wrestled with his controls. 'Do you see how many of the bastards are down there? There's fucking millions of them! They will be at the gates of Berlin within a week!'

I could not challenge his assessment. The ground around the city was filled with all manner of Soviet troops and their supporting infrastructure. The roads were filled with trucks, jeeps, personnel carriers and tanks. Field after field of tents provided us with an indication of just how many soldiers had been conscripted, hastily trained and poorly supplied before being sent west to overwhelm us with the sheer weight of their flesh and blood. Artillery placements had been dug in around the city so that they could bombard it from all angles all through the day and all through the night. A thick network of defences had been dug to the west to ensure that no relieving force could break through and come to the aid of the beleaguered defenders. I recognised their intention immediately from my own experiences during the invasion of Russia. Their goal was to annihilate the ninety thousand or so German troops trapped within the encirclement.

'Now for the tricky part!' The pilot announced grimly. 'Hold on tight!'

He descended hard and fast through a hail of flak and gun fire and aimed for an area at the centre of the city where all the buildings had been demolished to create a bumpy and uneven makeshift airfield. The impact on landing was hard enough to jar my spine but I did not complain because I was so glad to have made it down unharmed. I clapped the pilot on the back in appreciation as I disembarked.

'Look at the state of it!' He exclaimed angrily as he pointed at the wings. 'I'll be stuck here all afternoon repairing the holes.'

I repressed a shiver when I caught sight of the dozens of bullet holes that peppered the wings and the fuselage. It was sobering to realise that nothing more than luck had prevented one of the bullets from hitting the engine or ripping through my body or that of the pilot. My fingers were still trembling a little by the time I had picked my way through the smoking ruins of the city and presented myself at the Garrison Commander's headquarters. They kept me waiting for more than two hours and my nervousness grew as messengers ran urgently to and fro though the corridor leaving me with time to dwell on the wisdom of my mission. It would be no exaggeration to say that I was in a state of high anxiety by the time I was ushered down a subterranean passage and into General Niehoff's presence.

The general was tall and slim with short hair that was slicked back against his skull. He looked exhausted and harassed and a vein throbbed constantly beneath his right eye in a way that reminded me of the nervous tic Paulus had developed whilst commanding the Sixth Army during the siege of Stalingrad. He appraised me silently while an orderly laid out his cutlery and placed a plate of pork and cabbage in front of him.

'Have you eaten?' He asked as I stood to attention before him.

'No, Herr General.' I replied, my stomach rumbling at the sight of food as I had not eaten since rising at 5 am for the drive to the airfield.

Niehoff pointed me to a chair and then made a circular motion with his finger to indicate that the orderly should bring a plate for me. He had devoured almost half his meal by the time a much smaller serving was placed before me.

292

'So! You bring a message from Speer?' He demanded as he wiped at his mouth with a napkin.

'Yes, Herr General.' I replied in confirmation as I reached for my satchel with the intention of retrieving the printed sheet and delivering it into his hands. He held up his hand to indicate that I should stop.

'Are you well acquainted with the Reichsminister, Feldwebel Wolff?'

'No, Herr General. I have met him only twice and both meetings lasted for only a few short minutes.'

'Then I shall give you the benefit of the doubt, Wolff. I will assume that you are unaware of just how manipulative, self-serving and sneaky the Reichsminister can be. I will assume that you do not know that he is already engaged in burnishing his own reputation in the hope that it will save him if our enemies prevail. I have no doubt that he has sent you here to ask me to surrender the city and so prevent unnecessary bloodshed. I am also certain that he has done so, not to save innocent lives, but to create a trail of evidence which will demonstrate just how far he was prepared to go to thwart the Fuhrer's orders. The question that you must consider is, how far you are prepared to go to assist Speer in saving his own skin? The moment you deliver his message to me, you will leave me with no choice but to have you shot for treachery. I am sure that Speer would not mourn this tragic turn of events, for such an execution would be recorded and so would provide documentary evidence of his great humanitarian

293

efforts. Think before you make your next move. Ask yourself why he did not bring the message personally. Was he too busy or was he unwilling to take the risk himself when he knew well that I would refuse to betray the Fuhrer? He could have flown in and out just as easily as you and his presence here would have carried far more weight and so increased the chances of success. Eat your food and have a think but remember that what is spoken cannot be unspoken.'

I nodded and chewed at the greasy pork but my stomach churned so much that I had lost my appetite. I realised that I had come perilously close to disaster and would have signed my own death warrant if the General had not decided to treat me fairly.

'Well! What is it to be, Feldwebel Wolff?' Niehoff demanded when I had almost cleared my plate. 'Do you have a message for me from that shifty bastard or not?'

I gulped and struggled to swallow an unchewed lump of pork in order to clear my mouth. 'No, Herr General.' I replied. 'I seem to have misplaced the message.'

'Such carelessness is unforgiveable, Wolff!' He snapped at me. 'See that it does not happen again.'

I apologised for my negligence, thanked the general for his kindness and took my leave of him. I lit a cigarette as soon as I was back out on the street. My hands were shaking and I sucked in great clouds of smoke in a vain bid to calm myself. I could not believe that I had come so close to

294

disaster and was furious that I had been so easily taken in by a man concerned only with himself. A bullet from a German firing squad would have killed me just as surely as one from a Soviet sniper's rifle. I counted this as the closest shave I had experienced in the whole of the war. I lit another cigarette and began to make my way back towards the airfield. I knew that the pilot would still be repairing his aircraft but hoped that he could complete the work more quickly with my help and so have us on our way without too long a delay.

I do not know what it was that caught my eye about the soldier who crossed my path, but it was enough to bring me to a halt and make me watch him walk away. I thought that he must have just come from the house-to-house fighting in the suburbs because he was hunched over and weary and his clothes and hands were filthy with dirt and soot. It must have been his stance or posture that triggered something in my memory and made me call out after him. He carried on as if he had not heard me and then stopped dead in his tracks.

'Maus?' I called out tentatively, for I was not certain and did not want to appear foolish in front of a stranger.

'Kurt?' He responded incredulously as he turned. 'What the hell are you doing here?'

I ran to him laughing joyfully and embraced him and slapped him on the back. I will also admit that the sight of my soot-smeared old friend brought tears to my eyes.

'What happened to studying medicine?' I asked him when we had found a table in a Wehrmacht canteen set up in the cellar of an old department store. 'I thought you would be a doctor by now.'

He shook his head as he tried to wipe the dirt and soot from his face with a damp handkerchief. 'We were all conscripted about fourteen months ago. The whole class was taken in one fell swoop. There are only four or five of us left now.'

He did not need to explain this to me. The Soviets had thrown millions of their men against us to push us back towards Germany and the casualty rate had been horrendously high. In the madness of the last days of the war, it made some sort of twisted sense to hear that medical students had been sacrificed a year or so ago when we were now reduced to enlisting little boys and old men in a desperate attempt to halt the inexorable advance of the Russian military machine.

I tried to persuade Maus to come with me when I flew out that evening and promised him that I could keep him safe by absorbing him into my unit or by hiding him away in a bunker for the few weeks that the war had left to run. He just thanked me with a rueful nod of his head and laughed at the suggestion.

'It is alright for you in your SS uniform, Wolffie. They will let you pass but they will shoot any Wehrmacht man on sight if he attempts to board a plane without the proper paperwork. Many have tried to escape this hell before but none have survived the attempt. Our commanders are as fanatical as our leaders and will have us die here just to prove that we had the strength to resist even when all hope was lost. They mean to make a graveyard here to stand as a monument to the strength of National Socialism.'

I knew that he was right and became desperate in my suggestions as to how I might get him aboard that plane. Maus took it in good part and laid his arm around my shoulders to comfort me. It was then that I realised that he had already made his peace with God and had achieved an acceptance of the inevitability of his impending demise. That made me feel as sad, hopeless and depressed as I had been when I wandered on the steppes after Manfred's death. I lacked my friend's fortitude and strength of character and could not accept the prospect of losing the last person that I had left on this earth. I decided to stay with him, persuading myself that the end would come quicker here than it would in Berlin and reasoning that I would rather face whatever fate had in store for me with my friend by my side.

I would have made the same decision even if I had known that more than six weeks of constant artillery bombardment, withering machine gun and sniper fire and the grinding brutality of house-to-house street fighting lay ahead of us. We fought side-by-side and repelled so many Soviet attacks that we lost count of them. Ultimately, it was a struggle that we could not win because the Russians would willingly sacrifice ten of their men to take down one of ours and count it as a victory. It was hard not to admire their soldiers' bravery and to feel fear and disgust for their mercenary leaders and their willingness to pay such a heavy cost in human life for every patch of blackened earth they won. While we stood our ground in spite of our encirclement, the rest of Germany teetered on the brink of defeat and then finally collapsed. We learned of Hitler's death and the fall of Berlin through the leaflets the Russians dropped on us to encourage us to surrender. We hoped that these events would lead to an end to the siege but they seemed to reinvigorate our enemy instead and made him more determined to bring us to defeat through force of arms.

The final bombardment was merciless and lasted from midnight until mid-afternoon the next day. I knew that we would not be able to hold the line the moment I saw the mass of troops charging towards us. I doubt that we had enough ammunition to kill more than half of them even if every last bullet hit its target. I emptied my rifle into their ranks and then picked up another from the hands of a fallen comrade. It made no difference. The raging tide of fire and fury surged on towards us relentlessly and I clasped Maus's shoulder as I drew my pistol. I waited until I could see the twisted, screeching faces of our attackers before I fired at them. I knew that my actions would only delay the inevitable by mere seconds, but an anger seared within me and it seemed only right and fair that a number of them should accompany us on our journey from this life to the next. I could clearly see that our whole line had been overwhelmed and was about to be

298

completely overrun. I counted my shots and stopped firing when I still had one bullet left. I had kept it for Maus and not for myself. I wanted to spare him from a painful death. It was to be my last gift to him.

It was just as I brought my arm up in an arc to deliver the shot that the earth heaved up from under my feet and pitched me into the air in a shower of earth and stones. There was a second in which all was peaceful as I hung suspended in the air and then it was as if the world had come to an end. The roar of the explosion was so loud that it deafened me, all of the oxygen seemed to have been sucked from the air and I was thrown violently to the ground. I fell into unconsciousness as dirt and earth rained down on me in such quantities that I expected to be buried alive.

My eyes flickered open moments later to reveal the nightmare that the world had become. The ground on which I had stood only a few moments before had been transformed into a hellish, smoking crater. There was no sign of Maus and the other men who had been by my side. The sheer force of the blast had turned them to vapour. I was stunned and so deep in shock that I was not certain that I was uninjured. I ran my hands shakily over myself and could find no holes and identify no parts that were missing. It was then that I saw the Russian horde charging hard at me. I did not yet have the strength to stand so turned to grope through the churned-up earth in search of my pistol. When my fists closed around nothing other than stones, I stood to face my assailants and waited for the end to come.

It was if I had become a ghost. They streamed around me in their hundreds but did not give me a second look. I flinched involuntarily when some thickset, black-toothed peasant came close to me but he neither fired at me nor pulled the knife from his belt to slit my throat. I began to laugh hysterically when I glanced down at myself and saw that the explosion had left me blackened from head to foot. The situation was so ridiculous that I could not help myself. The enemy had enveloped me but seemed to assume that I was one of them. A few now cast glances in my direction but none seemed tempted to engage with the smouldering madman cackling manically in their midst.

I had gathered myself a little by the time the second wave of Soviets arrived and began rushing past me as I swayed unsteadily on my feet. I then did what I always did when the horror of life had overwhelmed me. I turned to the west and I walked. I ignored all that was around me and just put one foot in front of the other. I passed the dead and the dying, the advancing and the retreating, the resisting and the surrendering, the Germans and the Russians and not one of them paid me any heed.'

24

I wandered aimlessly for three or four weeks. I saw Russian, American and British soldiers during this time, but it was easy to evade them on roads that were choked with the great flood of refugees thrown up by the death throes of the Reich. It was like an exodus of the damned as every face was bleak and filled with hopelessness due to the shock of the totality of our defeat. People seldom talked with one another as we shuffled along and when they did open their mouths it was to curse our former masters and the calamity they had brought crashing down upon us. It seemed that people were quick to forget their former enthusiasm for those who had ruled over us. There was now no mention of the cheering, flag-waving crowds and of the millions of citizens who had fallen over themselves in their haste to display their devotion to the cause. When they talked of Nazis now they did so with disdain and were at pains to show that they referred to others and not to themselves. Our enemies must have been amazed to find that there was not a single Nazi left in all of Germany now that our armies had been vanquished. I could not help but laugh bitterly when I heard an old man at his prayers while I tried to sleep at the side of a road outside Nordhausen.

'Lord! Spare us from strong and powerful leaders, for it is they who will lead us to ruin and damnation!' He intoned with his eyes screwed tight shut and his hands pressed together against his chin.

'It is a little too late for that!' I thought to myself, though I did not speak the words aloud for fear that it would lead to yet another pointless argument.

The British picked me up three days later when I was loitering in Gottingen in the hope of finding something to steal that would fill my belly. I was so tired and numb that I did not even attempt to escape.

'Any weapons, mate?' The smaller of the two soldiers asked me as he tapped his thumb against his rifle to illustrate his meaning.

'No!' I replied. 'I have lost my rifle and my pistol.'

'SS?' He asked, though the boredom in his expression suggested that he did not expect a positive response. 'Are you SS?'

'Yes. I am SS.' I admitted, as I knew that they would discover the truth soon enough due to the indelible evidence of the blood group tattoo on my arm.

'We've got another one, Georgie boy!' He called out to his comrade. 'Get them to bring the truck up!'

The British treated me well. They did not search me but accepted my word that I was unarmed. I was driven to a temporary camp near Dortmund where they fed me and provided me with a hard bunk to sleep upon and the facilities I required to wash the worst of the dirt and the soot from my body and my clothes. I was there for only two days when I was loaded into the back of a truck with the other SS prisoners and driven towards the coast. It was during a brief stop on that journey that I first learned that the British and the Americans intended to hold trials intended to determine whether or not individual Germans were guilty of war crimes.

'They'll likely end up shooting all these SS bastards.' A curly-haired, English lieutenant told his comrade as they guarded us. 'I suppose that's why we've been told to round them all up. Serves them right after all they've done.'

This revelation caused quite a stir amongst the other SS men when those who understood English had translated the lieutenant's words. The level of anxiety was heightened when we were ordered down from the truck at the coast and marched aboard a ship bound for England. Some spoke of escaping but most just shrugged their shoulders and said that it would be pointless when there was no place left for them to run to. After a short but choppy crossing, a long drive in the rain brought us to a prisoner of war camp in Wales. The facilities were very basic but I was glad to be fed, watered and able to bed down in a place that was warm and dry. Men gossip when they are bored and have nothing with which to occupy themselves and the talk was about nothing but the coming trials. I was not overly nervous about what was to come because I knew that I had committed none of the crimes that many of my fellow prisoners were guilty of.

'Then you are a fool!' One of my comrades exploded when I told him this. 'They will have no interest in justice! They do not care about what you did or did not do! They mean only to make an example of us! We will all be found guilty by association if there is no evidence of an actual crime.'

I dismissed his pessimism at first but then had good reason to reconsider when I was recognised by one of our guards.

'I know you!' He told me when I almost walked into him as I came out of the wash house. 'Do you remember me?'

My guts tied themselves into a painful knot as I tried to work out where I had seen him before. His features were familiar but I was unable to put my finger on where I had previously encountered him. I froze in horror and felt a wave of nausea wash over me when he held his hands up and mimed the actions of a man firing a heavy machine gun. That simple action transported me back to the woods just outside the hamlet of Le Paradis five years before. I pictured Manfred standing by my side as I told the captured British soldier to take his injured comrade to the west and away from the men of the Death's Head Division who had just massacred his countrymen.

'I remember you well, Private McLelland.' I said now that I recognised him, though my head was spinning with what this might mean for me. This man could place me at the scene of a foul and unforgiveable atrocity carried out by members of the SS. If my colleague's pessimism was well-founded, that fact alone might well condemn me to a noose.

'I am glad that you found your way back home. I hope that your wounded comrade was equally fortunate.' I continued, my voice wavering in spite of my best efforts to appear unfazed by McLelland's appearance in the camp.

'It's Corporal McLelland now.' He corrected me as he eyed me suspiciously. 'We both made it back to our lines and were evacuated before the fall of France. I suppose that we have you to thank for that.'

'It was nothing.' I replied, uncomfortably aware that his scrutiny had caused my face to turn a deep shade of red and beads of sweat to appear on my forehead and upper lip. 'You were my prisoners and so were under my protection. If I had taken you east you would have been killed, so I sent you west.'

'A lot of good men were murdered by your bastard countrymen that day!' He snarled at me, his eyes flashing with anger. 'You spared us but I cannot help but wonder how many other men might have fallen at your hands.'

'I murdered no prisoners and did no harm to any civilians.' I snapped back at him. 'I killed only those I met in combat. You saw how I conducted myself. I disobeyed my orders and put myself at risk to do what was right. I have done nothing that I am ashamed of and nothing that I could be condemned for.'

McLelland stared at me for a long moment before speaking. 'Then you are the only man here who can say that. These animals have been gathered here so that they can be held to account for their crimes. I expect that every last one of them will end their days with a noose around their necks.'

I must have turned pale at these words for McLelland suddenly looked at me with concern and asked me if I felt quite well. I told him that I was fine but I was actually close to fainting. I was thinking that I would have preferred a bullet or a shell to a rope tightening around my throat.

He then leaned in towards me and lowered his voice. 'You will die if you stay here just as surely as I would have died if you had followed your orders and delivered me to your headquarters. I will now repay my debt to you. If you go to the north west corner of the fence tonight you will find that a hole has been cut in the wire. You should be able to wriggle through it. Where you go after that is no concern of mine. I will owe you nothing once the fence is breached. If you are captured you will be sent back here and your fate will be sealed. Do not be recaptured!'

I think that the security around the camp was light because the British did not expect any of us to attempt to escape when we were so deep in enemy territory. I ventured out once darkness had fallen, found the hole immediately and slipped out into the countryside quite easily. I ran through the darkness until my lungs were burning and my leg muscles were cramping. I pushed on through the pain to put as much distance as possible between myself and the camp before the sun rose. I expected to hear sirens and barking dogs and to see lines of torches moving towards me in the night, but there had been no signs of pursuit by the time I crawled into an overgrown copse to hide myself away during the hours of daylight.

I found a dry spot beneath the heavy branches of an ancient pine tree and laid my head down on the soft layers of needles that had built up on the ground over many years. I soon fell into a deep sleep due to my state of exhaustion, the comfort offered by my sheltered hideaway and the aromatic fragrance that filled my nostrils. I slept soundly until early afternoon when I was awakened with a start by the unmistakable sound of human voices close to where I was hiding. I was immediately alert and ready to flee for my life. I crawled forward slowly until I reached the edge of the copse and was able to peer out without being seen. I groaned when I saw that I had missed the little farm cottage in the darkness and had made my den little more than twenty paces from its door. An old couple were busy loading a ramshackle hand-cart in front of the house. They posed no immediate threat to me but I was acutely aware that a single sound at such close quarters would be enough to give me away. I held my breath as they went about their work and chattered away to one another in a language I did not understand. I might not have been able to catch any of the words but the tone and flow of the exchange revealed that the couple were engaging

307

in a well-worn and somewhat affectionate form of bickering in which they gently cajoled and berated one another. It made me smile as I watched them, for it put me in mind of my own parents.

That happy remembrance did not stop me from kicking their door in the minute they disappeared over the brow of the hill pushing their little cart before them. My actions were driven by necessity but the thought of the two of them returning to find that they had been robbed did fill me with guilt. I treated their possessions respectfully, made no mess and took only what I considered to be essential. The old man's only suit was a little small and tight and was shiny from too many Sundays spent sitting on wooden church pews, but it did make me look more like a down-at-heel civilian and less like a fugitive SS prisoner. I left him my coat and trousers and, though they were too worn and dirty for church, I hoped that he would find them warm enough to protect him from the worst of the winter weather when he was pushing his cart through the wind and snow.

I then turned my attention to the pot that stood on the hearth with a cloth covering it. I did not bother to heat the stew but set about spooning the potatoes, turnip, onion and mutton into my mouth as quickly as I could. I should have left them a few morsels for their supper but was so ravenous that I scraped the pot clean. I tried to resist the tin of tobacco that I found in the drawer of the sideboard but I could not do it. I smoked a single cigarette in the old man's chair and then slid his tin into the pocket of his jacket. I tried to atone for this theft by taking the time to repair the door before I left. The wood of the door jamb had been old and dry and had splintered when I kicked my way inside. I found a basket of old and rusty tools in the kitchen and used them to fix what I had broken. I hope that the old couple appreciated my efforts because I did a good job and have no doubt that the repair would have lasted them for years.

I left the cottage with no plan other than to put some distance between myself and the scene of my crimes. I moved cautiously and only left the treeline to cover open ground when I was certain that there was no-one around to catch sight of me. I had covered no more than five or six miles when I heard the sound of a train in the distance. A rough strategy began to form in my mind and I moved forward in search of the railway line. It was dark before a goods train came rumbling by and I was able to run alongside it and scramble up into an empty carriage. That train carried me all the way north to Glasgow and the first light of dawn found me wandering that great city's streets in search of something to eat and something to keep me from being recaptured and executed. It was the sound of men shouting and the crash of crates on cobbles that took me towards the market place in the hope of finding something I could steal. It was there that I found my salvation and it came in the unlikeliest form.

Harry Moncur was not the biggest man you would ever meet but he stood out from all of the others who bustled around him. It was not his three-piece suit and his pocket watch that marked him out as a boss but the piercing, steel-grey eyes that could bore into a man from thirty feet.

'You looking for work?' He demanded of me as I approached him. 'I need a body tae hump boxes and crates.'

I nodded my agreement immediately and followed him when he turned and made for a truck parked on the far side of the square. He reached into the cab and brought out a notebook and a pencil. When he asked for my name and identification I told him that I was Piotr Stachura and provided him with the papers Ania had given me when we last parted.

'Polish?' He asked and then wrote my name in the book when I nodded to confirm the fact. 'I couldnae give two fucks where you're from. If you work hard I'll pay you and if you're a lazy bastard you'll get nothing but the toe of my boot up your arse. Understood?'

He was true to his word and gave me work as a day labourer for much of that summer. I found workman's lodgings close by and began to make a life for myself. It was not easy at times for there was a hostility towards all foreigners as a result of the war and many people were unable or unwilling to differentiate between Germans and other nationalities. I avoided people as much as I could but could not do so when I was working. Some of the other labourers resented the presence of a foreigner amongst their ranks and went out of their way to bully and provoke me. I kept out of trouble whenever I could and finished it hard and fast when I could not because I did not want to be arrested and have my identity scrutinised. I was surviving from one day to the next and I was happy with that. My intention was to lay low for a year or two before quietly returning to Germany when I felt that the dust had fully settled after the war. The onset of winter brought three events that tore my plans to ribbons.

The first of these was the start of the Nuremberg trials. The newspapers covered these tribunals endlessly and it was soon evident that the more pessimistic of my SS colleagues had been accurate in their belief that the allies intended to have their revenge now that they had triumphed. My heart would thump hard in my chest whenever I read the reports and my blood turned to ice as the extent of the slaughter of Jewish men, women and children became increasingly clear. I felt close to panic whenever I read one of those reports and saw the name of someone I knew or had met written there in black and white. I began to think that it would never be safe for me to return home for the crimes committed by the Nazi regime were so vile that they would never be forgotten. The second event that was to change the direction of my life was Harry Moncur offering me a job driving a lorry for his agricultural company. I accepted it the moment he made the offer because the job came with a tied house and the opportunity to build a new life for myself deep in the Perthshire countryside. I felt sure that I would be harder to track down there than in a big, industrial city. The third life-changing event came about as a result of nothing more than day-to-day living.

Your grandmother worked in the greengrocer's shop where I bought my vegetables and we went from exchanging pleasantries in the summer, to jokes in the autumn and to dancing just before Christmas. I married her in January and we moved into our cottage just outside New Alyth at the beginning of February.

You know the story from there on. We built a good life together, had our family and enjoyed so many years of peace and contentment. I knew that I did not really deserve them but I took them gratefully. It is only now that I am dying that past regrets have resurfaced. If I was strong enough I would have set about addressing them myself. I am now feeble and weak and therefore must ask if you will act on my behalf. You know my story now and are therefore aware of who I am most indebted to. They are all likely long dead by now but there may well be opportunities to repay what is owed to their children or grandchildren. It is a lot to ask, but I have no other close family left and I would not entrust this task to anyone other than you. You have both the brains and the heart to do what is right.

I have left some things for you in your special place. Do what you think is appropriate with them.

Love, Grampy.'

25

David Strachan closed the cover of the journal and gazed at it for a long moment. The grey light of dawn was already showing around the edges of the curtains and his sore eyes and aching back were telling him that he needed his bed. His curiosity drove him out into the frigid morning air with the last can of Coke and the last of his grandfather's cigarettes clasped in his hands in the hope that one or both of them would revive him and fill him with energy. He unlocked the door and flicked the light on before entering the shed. He felt along the wall behind the workbench until he found the secret panel his grandfather had constructed to hide treats for him when he was a boy. He found the panel and pressed it with his index finger. That action was rewarded with a satisfying click and the varnished wood swung out to reveal a hollow that was just about big enough to hold a house brick. He reached inside and smiled when his hand closed upon his usual treats. His grandad would always hide exactly the same items, a small bag of KP peanuts and a bar of Cadbury Fruit and Nut. He opened the chocolate, broke off a chunk and popped it into his mouth. He then reached back into the opening and extracted an A4 envelope that had been folded and forced into the space. He tore it open with his finger and shook it to empty its contents out onto the workbench.

He knew instantly what the three items were. He reached down and picked his grandfather's Iron Cross up from where it had landed. He sighed when he saw that it was the 1939 medal, the one awarded to him by Adolf Hitler in France alongside Manfred, Lammert, Horse and Julius. The object stirred contrasting emotions in David Strachan. It troubled him that his grandfather had treasured something that had been touched by a monster's hand but he could also understand why he would value something won with his friends at a time when the war had still seemed to be an honourable and relatively untainted endeavour. The second item was the identity document that Ania had given his grandfather when they parted on the Polish-German border. It seemed impossible that such a tattered and unremarkable scrap of paper held such significance in his family's history. He gently brushed his fingertips against the delicate paper and marvelled at the fact that he now touched something that Ania's own fingers had held so many years ago. He also felt a reverence for something that had given his grandfather a path that led him away from the victors' gallows and towards a whole new life.

The last item was the one which gave him the greatest cause for pause. He knew without opening it that it was the one that most threatened the life he had built for himself. He shook the last cigarette from the packet and lit it. He gazed at the tattered and faded document while he smoked. He tried to persuade himself to leave it unexamined for he knew that simply inspecting it carried the risk of rousing his insatiable curiosity. He struggled admirably to resist the urge to look but only lasted until half the cigarette had burned to ash before giving into it with a curse. He folded it out onto the workbench and studied it. It was just as he had anticipated. The map of Germany was not a detailed one but each of the hundreds of little crosses was accompanied by the co-ordinates of where Kurt Wolff and his team had constructed and equipped the Werewolf bunkers. A dozen of these crosses were larger than the others and six of them looked as if they had been underlined in ballpoint pen quite recently. He quickly folded it again and returned it to its envelope.

'Some things are best left in the past, Grampy!' He told the empty shed as he collected up the identity papers and the medal.

He went straight to bed, pausing only to shut the shed, lock the front door and to shove the envelope into his satchel. He slept until late in the afternoon and then set about clearing the house and shed. The only items he wanted to keep were his grandfather's tools and he packed these in boxes to be couriered out to Singapore. With the house emptied, the utilities cut off and the special refuse collection arranged, Strachan closed the door on the old place for the very last time. He paused at the side of the hire car and cast his eyes over the little house as if to fix it in his memory. He then nodded a silent goodbye and drove off in the direction of Alyth to take possession of the room he had booked at the Lands of Loyal Hotel.

The rest of the week passed by quickly. He spent a pleasant day in Irene's company in Perth and enjoyed her gentle teasing while they shopped, lunched and took in a movie. Their banter was light-hearted and fun and he was glad that he had decided to keep his grandfather's secret from her. She had always been fond of the old man and he saw no benefit in tainting that fondness with revelations that were eighty years old.

The funeral was not quite as grim as he had expected, though it did feel a little perfunctory and impersonal at times. This was not helped by the fact that it was painfully evident that the young minister had neither met the old man nor had the faintest idea who he was. Strachan found himself critiquing the cocky young cleric's technique and awarded him a failing grade for not preparing adequately before delivering his presentation. He would not last a day in Strachan's firm with such a slack attitude.

It was the wake that had been a revelation. He had expected only a handful of people to make their way to the function room in the Blackbird Inn on the Blairgowrie Road for an afternoon of remembrance over warm sausage rolls and egg and cress sandwiches with the crusts cut off. The room filled up so quickly that there was only standing room left by the time the food was brought to the tables.

'How many people are here?' He asked Irene as they surveyed the room.

'Ronnie reckons that there must be a hundred and fifty or more.' She replied as she pointed toward the bar where Ronnie was struggling to stay on top of the drinks orders.

'Who the hell are they?' Strachan retorted, raising his voice in order to be heard above the rising hubbub.

'A few of them are neighbours but I don't recognise most of them.' She replied with a shrug. 'I suppose we'll just have to circulate politely and ask them.'

Strachan was not really in the mood for making small talk with strangers but, as next of kin, he felt obliged to do so. He was glad that he had taken the trouble by the time people started to make their excuses and slip away. Each of them had a different story to tell about Grandad but all of the stories shared a common theme. Each of them had come to pay their respects to a man who had shown them kindness and had helped them in some small way. One old lady who could only walk with the aid of her stick told how Peter had mown her lawn each summer for more than ten years and had refused all rewards apart from a cup of tea and a chocolate digestive when he was done. Numerous others told of times when he had helped them with advice or hands-on labour when they were struggling with brickwork, decking, plumbing, papering, tiling or various aspects of motor mechanics. These people included lawyers, doctors, offshore workers, lorry drivers, delivery

317

men, a retired university lecturer, housewives, pensioners and at least three businessmen. Their stories of kindness stretched over more than four decades and they made Strachan see the old boy in a new light for the second time since his death. He doubted that his own funeral would attract such an audience and he knew for a fact that there would be no avalanche of tales of all the acts of kindness he had performed. He was both touched and humbled by the experience and was doubly glad that he had decided to keep the contents of the journal to himself. It was, he believed, better to let these people judge his grandfather on what he had done for them rather than on his actions all those years ago.

Stepping back onto the plane for the journey to Singapore was like entering a portal that would transport him back to his own life. He was glad to be leaving Scotland behind him and he set his mind on throwing himself back into his old life. He found his apartment just as he had left it. It was large, cold and empty and he thought that he could detect just a whiff of Liliya's perfume as he wheeled his suitcase across the hall's white marble floor and into his bedroom. Her absence caused him a moment of self-pity that was quickly banished when he powered up his laptop and got back to business. He was soon immersed in the financials of a small Indonesian payments company that had developed software to enable fast and secure processing of in-game purchases on both Apple and Android devices. The turnover was small but the potential was huge. A little capital injection for expansion and a little more for marketing would be all that was required to grow the business and raise its profile sufficiently to attract the interest of the major credit card companies. These giants had huge cash reserves and an insatiable appetite for the tech acquisitions that were required to convince the markets that they were future-proofed and moving with the times. Strachan booked his flight to Jakarta and prayed that the young tech entrepreneurs who owned the company were gullible enough to be induced to sell cheaply. If they could grab the attention of more than one of the credit card leviathans, there could be a fortune to be made from the bidding war that would ensue.

Strachan barely saw his apartment for the next three months and became a full-time resident of the Ritz-Carlton opposite the Jakarta stock exchange. He wined, dined, befriended and charmed Ibnu Sutanto for a whole month before he had the young CEO hooked. He then spent the next two months immersed in an exacting and painstakingly forensic due diligence process. It was only when the ink had dried on the share purchase agreement and the champagne corks had stopped popping that Strachan returned to his apartment alone and found his mind drifting back to his grandfather's journal and the envelope that was now stored safely at the back of the safe built into his walk-in wardrobe. It was an idle internet search whilst relaxing on his balcony with a beer and a cigarette that pulled him back into his grandfather's world. Ania's brother's identity papers included the address of the farm his grandfather had hidden in while he was nursed back to health. It took no more than a few seconds to bring a satellite image of it up on the screen. The sails of the windmill had rotted away long ago but there was no mistaking the original purpose of the tall, curved, almost triangular building. The small, round pond was also clearly visible in spite of the fact that it looked to be choked with weeds or algae. Looking upon the scene that his grandfather had seen through the slats in the shutters of his attic room caused the hairs on the back of Strachan's neck to stand up. It took only that one moment of idle curiosity for him to become as firmly hooked as Ibnu Sutanto had been.

He approached the research with the same energy and focus that he would devote to a multi-million-dollar merger and acquisition process. He worked tirelessly through the weekend, leaving the apartment only when he had finished the last of his cigarettes and was forced to drive to a 7-Eleven to replenish his supplies. Most of his lines of enquiry were ultimately frustrated by barriers of language and time. He unearthed numerous references to Manfred Wissler, Heinrich Mueller, Kurt Wolff, Julius Kammler, Rudolph Stamm and Karl Lammert but found it impossible to know for sure if they referred to the people mentioned in his grandfather's journal. He also unearthed a badly scanned newspaper article about an Ania Stachura but could not decipher the Polish report enough to ascertain anything other than the fact that the

320

woman in the photograph had received some kind of teaching award. He printed each article off and placed it in a folder for further scrutiny.

His grandfather's map had also proven to be a source of frustration. Hours spent peering at satellite maps of the areas where bunkers had supposedly been built produced nothing of any use. Several of the sets of coordinates were in the middle of lakes or rivers, some were in areas of forest and scrubland and a handful were in suburban or industrial districts. He might have given up late on Sunday afternoon if he had not stumbled upon an article concerning a peripheral character in his grandad's story. The piece was not even a proper article but merely a bullet point list entitled 'The 10 Most Notorious Nazis Still At Large!!' He would normally have paid no attention to the site because it was concerned with conspiracy theories of varying degrees of sensationalism and he was on the verge of navigating away from the page when he saw the name out of the corner of his eye. Oberscharfuhrer Hans Sauer was listed at number seven. He was accused of participating in a sickeningly long list of massacres, including the one at Minsk, and of involvement in various atrocities while part of Einsatzgruppe B. It was reported that he had escaped to Argentina at the end of the war and had lived there peacefully until Israeli investigators tracked him down in 1986. He had somehow managed to evade capture once again and his subsequent whereabouts were something of a mystery. The grainy black and white photograph that accompanied the article was enough to convince Strachan that this was the man his grandfather had mentioned. He was just as his grandfather had described him, the beady eyes, the thick lips and the mouth filled with brown, uneven teeth.

This minor discovery persuaded him to persist with his task and he soon had reason to be grateful for his tenacity. He had a local history group to thank for posting a copy of Kenneth McLelland's obituary online. The accompanying photograph was of an old man with his secateurs in his hand tending to his award-winning roses but the obituary itself was undoubtedly a tribute to the man who had set his grandfather free. His war-time service was praised and both his evacuation from Dunkirk and his service in Wales were mentioned. It reported that he had subsequently joined an Edinburgh housebuilding firm as their accountant in 1947 and had worked for them until his retirement in 1984. He had died peacefully in his sleep at eighty after a long and happy retirement during which he had been active in fundraising for the British Legion and the RSPB. He was survived by his wife, Mary, and his son, Ewan, a research fellow in oncology at the University of Edinburgh. Strachan examined the photograph with a smile on his face and felt glad that McLelland had gone on to live a good, long life after the war. He also smiled at the irony of discovering that his grandfather had been mistaken to think that the Perthshire countryside was the perfect place to hide himself in and so protect his identity. McLelland, one of few men who had known exactly who he was, had lived out his retirement in the village of Blackford less than an hour's drive from his Grandad's door. It seemed that the world was indeed a small place.

Strachan might had ended his search there if fate had not intervened a few days after his less than fruitful weekend of internet surfing. He was just draining the last of his Starbucks decaf latte when the firm's senior partner, Abhishek Khan, strode into his office with a bottle of Suntory Yamazaki Mizunara single malt whisky clutched in his hand.

'Good work in Jakarta, Mr Strachan.' He crooned in a voice that was deep and resonant. 'I wanted to congratulate you with some decent whisky and not that Scottish crap that you insist on poisoning yourself with.'

Strachan took the proffered bottle and returned Abhishek's grin. The debate over the relative merits of Scottish and Japanese whiskies had been part of their banter since the Indian had first approached him to persuade him to join the firm. Khan was unfailingly generous with his gifts and Strachan knew that the whisky would have cost him several thousand dollars. He waited patiently while the older man told his well-worn story about how the Japanese had visited Scotland to inspect their distilleries and had then returned home to refine the processes and eliminate any flaws before setting up distilleries of their own. He then concluded, as he always did, by claiming that this was why Japanese whisky was better. It was essentially a perfected version of Scotch whisky.

'But it's the water that makes it, my friend.' Strachan countered good-naturedly. 'And that's the one thing that the Japanese cannot replicate. Without pure Scottish water it will never be anything other than a poor imitation of the original.'

Khan nodded and raised his hands in defeat. 'Okay! If you will not let me win this argument then you must do something else for me. Let Andre take the lead on this Jakarta thing now that the deal is signed and sealed. He can handle the recruitment and marketing over the next few months and free you up for greater things.'

'What greater things?' Strachan asked, the prospect of a new deal causing his pulse to quicken. He had no desire to become bogged down in the day-to-day running of the business and would happily step aside for something more stimulating.

Abhishek tapped his index finger against the side of his nose. 'It is very hush-hush at the moment but I want to look at a family-owned, private bank in Frankfurt. Its business is mainly asset management, capital markets, corporate finance and wealth management. It is small, only eight hundred employees, but it would give us the licences we need to enter a potentially highly lucrative market. The Haas family have owned and run it since 1832 but the current Chief Executive and great-great-great-grandson of the founder has had some problems with gambling and drugs and might be persuaded to sell. I might have miscounted the number of 'greats' but this folder includes all the details you will need to get you started. What do you think?'

Strachan held his hand out for the folder. 'Let me have a look at it. If the initial numbers look good, then I'm in.'

'Excellent! Excellent!' Abhishek beamed in delight. 'There is a report in there from a private detective. Make sure that you read it first. Your toes will curl when you see what kind of lifestyle this young arsehole pursues. It is as if he is hell-bent on wasting the family fortune on hookers, cocaine and horse-racing. If he is half as stupid as he appears, we could have his bank off him for a very sweet price!'

Strachan spent the afternoon studying the contents of the folder and conducting his own research. He quickly reached the conclusion that this was a deal he wanted to deliver. The private detective's report impressed him greatly. It was thorough, meticulous and painted a compelling picture of the Chief Executive's lifestyle and character. He knew that the insight it provided would be invaluable when he finally engaged with the principal himself. He composed an e-mail to the private investigator asking a few supplemental questions and then, on a whim, briefly outlined his grandfather's story and asked if she would be interested in investigating some aspects of it on his behalf. It seemed likely that a German investigator would make much faster progress than he ever could. Her response dropped into his mailbox less than ten minutes later. She answered his questions to his satisfaction and said that she would be happy to take on his personal case. She asked that he send copies of the journal and the supporting documents to her so she could get started right away.

Strachan was impressed by her efficiency and immediately went off in search of the young intern who had recently been attached to his team. Valerie Lim did not know it yet, but she had a long evening of document scanning in front of her.

26

Strachan's flight touched down at Frankfurt Airport two hours later than scheduled. This forced him to go straight to the Carmelo Greco restaurant rather than first taking a taxi to the hotel to drop his luggage off, jump into the shower and change his clothes. He arrived twenty minutes ahead of his meeting, left his suitcase with the maître d' and ordered a strong, black coffee in the hope that it would revive him. A few unexpected complications with the Indonesian deal had kept him in Jakarta for three weeks longer than expected and he had flown straight to Frankfurt from there. His jet-lagged body yearned for sleep but he was determined to power on until late in the evening before falling into bed and succumbing to exhaustion.

His guest arrived just as he was draining the dregs from the bottom of his cup. Sabine Erhart defied all of his expectations. She was much younger, much more athletic and much more attractive than any of the gnarled and hard-bitten retired police officers he had dealt with during the course of his career. The dark business suit she wore was suitably conservative and reserved but was expertly tailored to subtly accentuate her slim waist and ample bosom. Her light brown hair was cut into a short bob with just enough blonde highlights to lift her natural colouring and emphasise her bronzed and flawless complexion. Strachan felt an illogical relief when he noted the absence of a wedding band on her ring finger. She exuded a solid professionalism, a quiet competence and a strong femininity that made him regret his decision not to shower or change out of his crumpled t-shirt. He felt suddenly scruffy, unshaven and unwashed under her scrutiny as she reached across the table to shake his hand.

'My flight was delayed.' He offered by way of explanation. 'I had to come straight here and did not have the time to change.'

'It does look as if you have slept in that shirt.' She replied with a directness that made the colour rise to his cheeks. 'Shall we order first so we are not interrupted when the waiter comes to take our order?' She then turned and beckoned a waiter over without waiting for Strachan to agree. She ordered a seafood linguine and Strachan, slightly overawed by the force of nature that had arrived at his table, followed her lead.

'Thank you for coming to me with this case.' She began, her eyes shining with enthusiasm. 'It is very interesting and is very different from what I normally do. Cheating wives and faithless husbands do help to pay the bills, but those cases are normally very dull. Your grandfather's story, on the other hand, is highly intriguing.'

'So, what have you been able to find out?' Strachan asked in a business-like tone that did not reflect the effect she was having on him. The

328

strength of his attraction to her discomfited him and left him determined to mask it as far as he could.

'As I explained in my e-mail, I always start by assessing the veracity of the original account and by searching for evidence to corroborate or disprove what has been claimed. My findings indicate that your grandfather's account of the war was essentially correct. I was able to get an abbreviated version of his military records through the Bundesarchiv and they confirm that he was trained where he said he was trained, he served where he said he had served, he was awarded the medals he said he was awarded and they were presented by those he claimed had presented them.' She held two thin pieces of paper out towards him and invited him to read them.

Their pasta arrived while he was still perusing the documents and Sabine started her meal without him.

'My God!' Strachan exclaimed when he reached the bottom of the second page. 'I had no reason to doubt his word but seeing it written down here somehow makes it more real, more official. I mean, it was Adolf Hitler who presented him with his first Iron Cross!' Strachan tapped at the place on the paper where the word 'Fuhrer' was typed.

'There is nothing after Breslau.' Sabine continued as she chewed. 'The only mention of him I could find after 1945 was when he was included in a list issued by the Jewish Historical Documentation Centre in 1967. His brief

329

membership of Einsatzgruppe B in Belarus must have come to the attention of the Nazi hunters at that time, but there was no further investigation carried out, most likely because he had disappeared without trace.'

'So, he was not completely paranoid to fear that they might come for him?'

'Not at all. Even today there are ninety-nine-year-old former concentration camp guards on trial here in Germany. I have no doubt that they would have been knocking on his door if only they had been able to find him.'

'Did you find anything else?' Strachan asked as he loaded his fork with pasta.

'Of course!' She replied in a matter-of-fact tone which suggested that it was ridiculous to suggest that weeks of investigation might have produced only a single set of records. 'I have service records for them all and each of them confirms your grandfather's version of events.' She paused to wipe sauce from her lips before leaning over to pull a folder from her bag. 'Look! Here is the record for Rudolph Stamm, or Horse, as they called him. Reported killed in action during the Battle of Stalingrad. See your grandfather's name there at the bottom. It was he who reported the death of his friend.'

Strachan felt tears jump to his eyes on seeing hard evidence of the horrors that his grandfather and his young friends had been subjected to. 'That poor boy!' He exclaimed. 'It is very hard to contemplate what they did to him.'

'Julius Kammler and Karl Lammert were reported as missing in action, presumed killed in the chaos following the Sixth Army's collapse and subsequent surrender. Even our famous German record-keeping did not survive the turmoil and slaughter of that defeat.' She grinned to show that she was making a joke at the expense of Germany's national character. Strachan returned her smile with interest, although he had missed the attempt at humour because he was thinking about how beautiful she looked when she smiled and showed her white, even teeth.

'I am sorry to say that I had less luck with the map of the bunkers.' She continued apologetically. 'I visited twelve of the sites but found nothing at any of them. I even borrowed a metal detector, but it was a waste of time. Three of the locations were under water, just as your internet search had indicated. I think that the bunkers, if they ever existed, were either found and destroyed after the war or that the map is inaccurate. I can examine the other locations if you wish, but I suspect that it would be a waste of my time and your money.'

Strachan shrugged and tried to hide his disappointment. He had harboured some boyish excitement at the prospect of unearthing secret dugouts filled with an Aladdin's cave of treasures hidden by his grandfather. 'I suppose that it was always a long-shot.' He sighed. 'I am just happy that you have been able to unearth as much as you have. These documents prove that my grandfather was no liar and I am grateful for that.'

331

Sabine pursed her lips and raised her left eyebrow in an expression that was both coy and coquettish and seemed to suggest that she was about to tease him. 'But that is not all that I discovered, Herr Strachan. I have saved the very best for last.'

Strachan could tell that her excitement was genuine and demanded to know what she had found.

'Eat your pasta!' She instructed him. 'Once we have eaten I will show you what I have uncovered.'

She was resolute in her refusal to reveal any more and resisted his begging and his attempts at bribery. Strachan emptied his plate without tasting the delicious sauce and called for the bill without ordering a desert even although his favourite crème brulee was featured on the menu. He begged her some more once they were on the road in Sabine's Mercedes but she just grinned and kept her eyes on the road ahead. It was almost forty minutes before she slowed and turned into the grounds of a large house. Strachan reckoned that it was an institution of some kind and that it had been built some time before the First World War.

'What is this place?' He asked when she had come to a halt in a parking space at the end of the long, tree-lined drive.

'It is a nursing home, David. You are here to meet someone very special indeed.'

Strachan followed her as she entered the building and waited while she spoke with a lady

332

behind a reception desk who was obviously already acquainted with her. The lady pointed towards a long corridor to their left. Sabine thanked her and then instructed Strachan to follow. David was far more used to giving instructions than he was to receiving them but found that he was happy to follow her lead.

'Ah! Here's Gerde now!' Sabine announced before calling out a greeting and striding towards a tall, slim and slightly grim looking woman in her mid to late seventies.

Strachan stood awkwardly as Sabine conversed with the woman in German. He heard his name mentioned several times but found that his long-neglected schoolboy German was not sufficient to enable him to follow their conversation. The respective tones of the two women told him that the older of the two was being somewhat hostile while Sabine was trying to soothe and placate her.

'She does not like the look of you.' Sabine informed him when she finally turned to him. 'She is very suspicious.'

'Who is she?' Strachan demanded, still feeling confused as to why they were in an old folks' home talking to this resident.

Sabine enveloped him in her smile and touched him on the arm. 'David, this is Gerde Wissler. This is Manfred Wissler's daughter.'

'Manfred's daughter?' Strachan retorted, his face creased in puzzlement. 'But Grandad did not mention a daughter. Manfred was not married when he died. How can this be his daughter?'

'Think about it, David.' She cajoled him, her tone teasing but not unkind. 'I am certain that you will get there eventually.'

It took a few seconds for the realisation to dawn. His jaw then dropped open in astonishment.

'You should close your mouth if you do not want to catch flies!' She admonished him gently, surprising herself by being moved by the tears that the revelation had brought to the Scotsman's eyes.

'Manfred did not die out on the steppes!' he exclaimed. 'He survived the war and had a daughter. My God! I cannot believe it.'

He went to Gerde and offered her his hand. She took it reluctantly and shook it without enthusiasm.

'But why is she so unhappy?' he asked the investigator. 'Have you offended her?'

'It is not me she is wary of.' Sabine replied with a shake of her head. 'She is worried that you might be a Jewish Nazi hunter or a journalist. You must convince her that you are neither.'

'And how am I to do that?' Strachan demanded incredulously. 'Does she want me to drop my pants so she can see that I am not circumcised.'

Sabine translated his question and elicited a wicked laugh from Gerde before she responded.

'She says that you should show it to me so I can inspect it. She will trust me to be honest about what I have seen.'

'Are you serious?' Strachan spluttered, suddenly uncomfortable in the face of the two grinning women.

'No!' She admitted wryly. 'But it was worth it to see that look on your face. Showing her your business card should persuade her that you are legitimate and not here to trouble her father like those who have hounded him in the past.'

'Her father?' Strachan asked, his hand already halfway to his wallet in search of his card. 'You mean that...?'

'Yes!' Sabine answered his unfinished question. 'Your grandfather's old friend, Manfred Wissler, is lying on a bed in the room behind Gerde. Isn't it wonderful? If she will let you pass you will lay your eyes upon him just a few seconds from now.'

Strachan reeled back in surprise and felt his eyes fill with tears. His grandfather's story had affected him more than he had realised and he had to breath heavily to gather himself. This display of emotion seemed to melt Gerde's reserve and she took him into her embrace, whispering soothing and comforting words as she rubbed the palms of her hands over his back. She then took his arm and guided him into the room.

Manfred Wissler lay on the hospital bed with an oxygen mask over his mouth and nose and with two intravenous lines attached to his right arm. His breathing was thin and ragged and could scarcely be heard above the gentle and persistent hiss of the oxygen. His body had wasted away to the point that it was little more than a husk with a layer of paper-thin, mottled skin covering his bones. Strachan would have thought him dead if it had not been for the slight rise and fall of his chest as his shrunken lungs were filled with air and then emptied again. Gerde seemed about to awaken her father until Strachan held up his hand to stop her.

'Let him sleep, Gerde.' He instructed her gently. 'Do not disturb his rest for me. It is enough for me just to see him.'

The old woman smiled and squeezed his arm in gratitude when Sabine had provided the translation.

'Sit with him and hold his hand!' Sabine ordered him in a hushed and reverential voice. 'Gerde says that he sleeps for most of the time now but he can be lucid when he awakens.'

Strachan nodded and took a seat at the side of the bed. It felt strange to hold Manfred's emaciated hand in his but he thought that the physical connection was important. It was almost as if it somehow completed the circle of friendship that had been broken for so long. His heart ached at the thought of all the years of guilt and loss his grandfather had suffered. He sat there lost in his thoughts for more than an hour and scarcely noticed when Sabine took Gerde to fetch coffee. He did not know how long the old man's eyes had been open when he became conscious of his gaze. The watery and bloodshot eyes seemed to look at him sightlessly for a moment before slowly opening wide in surprise and fright. Manfred feebly raised his painfully thin arm and clawed weakly at his oxygen mask. He succeeded in pulling it down onto his chin before gasping for breath.

'Wolffie?' He wheezed. 'Bist du wegen mir gekommen?'

Strachan did not understand all that he said but caught enough of the words to know that the old man had mistaken him for his grandfather and was asking if he had come for him. He strained his memory back to his days in Miss Fell's German class and tried to pick out the appropriate words.

'Nein. Nein, Herr. Ich bin der Enkel von Kurt Wolff.' He stuttered awkwardly, unsure as to whether he had selected the right words and the correct order in which to place them. 'Kurt Wolff was my grandfather. He escaped to Scotland after the war. He died quite recently.'

The red-rimmed eyes continued to stare at him blankly but his eyelids now blinked rapidly as if he was struggling to understand what he had just been told. When he finally spoke, his voice was so low that Strachan had to lean in close to hear him.

'Nein! It cannot be true. Kurt died in Breslau. He did not survive the war.' He spoke haltingly as if he was working hard to recall the correct words from the English lessons delivered by Kurt's father almost a century before.

'He did not die there, sir. He was knocked unconscious by an explosion but then walked west until he was taken prisoner by the British. They took him to England but he escaped and made a life for himself in Scotland. He raised a family, enjoyed a long and happy marriage and died only a few months ago. He left me a journal that told me about his experiences during the war and I came here in search of your family. He wanted me

337

to help them if I could. I did not expect to find you here. He thought you had died when he left you on the plain. My grandfather never forgot you.'

The old man's fingers now closed tightly around Strachan's own and tears welled up in his eyes. He then sobbed so hard that his whole frame shook and his breathing grew raspy and laboured. Strachan was strangely affected by the tears of a man of such a great age. It surprised him to see that grief's edge is not blunted by the passage of the years and that pain is felt as keenly by the old as it is by the young. He was conscious that Sabine and Gerde had returned at some point but that they were standing back so as to avoid interrupting the emotional exchange. He reached out with the intention of pushing the oxygen mask back in place but the old man raised his hand to stop him. When he spoke, he was breathless but he did so with a determination to convey the importance of what he had to say.

'I am glad to have lived long enough to see this moment. Not a single day has passed when I have not thought about my little Kurt. There has been no anniversary, achievement or celebration in my life that has not been diminished by his absence. It fills my heart with joy to know that he lived and lived well. I can die happy now that I know this. I can die happy now that I have seen his grandson and kissed the flesh that came from his flesh.'

Manfred then lifted Strachan's hand towards his lips and pressed it against them with his eyes tight shut.

'Thank you for coming. Thank you for seeking me out. You have filled a whole in my heart that I thought could never be filled.' The old man's smile then faltered and he seemed to wince with pain. 'If only Maus had lived long enough to see this day. I wish with all of my heart that he had.'

'Maus?' Strachan asked. 'My grandfather said that Maus died at the siege of Breslau. The Russian shell that knocked him unconscious was the same one that killed Maus.'

Manfred shook his head and smiled a smile that was equal parts happiness and grief. 'Maus did not die at Breslau. He died in Berlin just eight years ago after a long and distinguished medical career. He was wounded by the shellfire and taken prisoner by the Soviets. The last time he saw Kurt he was lying at the bottom of a smoking crater half-buried in earth. He thought him dead. We all thought him dead. Maus would have danced one of his jigs if he had heard that he lived.'

It was at this point that Gerde could no longer contain herself and she burst forward to fuss over her father. Water was offered to moisten his throat, his forehead was felt to ascertain its temperature and the oxygen mask was replaced to aid his breathing. Manfred kept tight hold of Strachan's hand through all of the fussing and the pillow plumping and only released his grip when he nodded off and fell asleep.

They thanked Gerde, hugged her and said that they would return the next day. Her hostility had evaporated completely and she thanked them profusely for bringing her father so much joy.

339

Strachan felt emotionally drained by the time they reached the carpark and was both surprised and delighted when Sabine threw her arms around him and embraced him tightly.

'Wow!' She sighed. 'That was pretty damned intense! Thank you for letting me be part of something so special. I am thinking that your grandfather must have been quite a man.'

'He was that.' Strachan replied. 'Now, let me take you for dinner. There is a lot for us to absorb.'

'Not a chance!' She shot back with a mischievous smile. 'I'm taking you for a drink! I need alcohol after what just happened in there.'

Strachan nodded his agreement and did his very best to conceal his delight.

27

Strachan spent much of the following week in meetings with advisors, lawyers and board members in relation to the Haas Bank acquisition but carved out time in his schedule to visit Manfred Wissler and to have dinner with Sabine afterwards. He enjoyed the conversations with Manfred and could not help but admire his negotiation skills because he steadfastly refused to satisfy Strachan's burning curiosity about events during the war until his own appetite for insights into his old friend's life had been at least partially fed. His interest was insatiable and he demanded to know all about his marriage, his career, his hobbies, his interests and all of the mundane details of his everyday life. When he grew tired he would lie back and Strachan would read to him from his grandfather's journal. The old man laughed and cried with the story as if he was reliving his youth all over again. He would delight David by providing additional information and corrections and the younger man ate these up voraciously.

He revealed that his uncle, the one-time SS Hauptsturmfuhrer, had returned to his career in law after the war and had prospered in spite of his close connections to Himmler. He had even enjoyed an extended spell as the mayor of his home city.

'He always said that it was best to hide in plain sight and he refused to cower away like a rat.' Manfred informed him one afternoon.

'Did they not come after him?' Strachan enquired. 'He must have been sought out by the allies immediately after the war and by Nazi hunters later on.'

Manfred sorted derisively. 'They came after us all. The prosecutors, the fame hunters and the journalists in search of a story. My uncle was their most frequent target for he was a slave to his vanity and never refused a photograph with any member of the leadership. Some little mole would unearth a photograph of him with Hitler or Himmler or Goebbels every few years and the whole circus would start all over again. If the government, police and prosecutors' offices had not been filled with former Nazis, he would have been in serious trouble.'

The greatest revelation came when Strachan was showing him photographs on his laptop screen. The old man pointed at the image of the little house in New Alyth with a puzzled expression on his face.

'But it is so modest!' He exclaimed. 'Why did he not use the gold to buy himself an enormous house? That is what I would have done.'

'What gold?' Strachan asked. 'Do you mean the Werewolf gold?'

'Of course. He told Maus all about it when they were in Breslau together. He even showed him a map. Maus and I would often talk about it in the years after the war. We thought that it was such a shame for it to go to waste when we could have done such wonderful things with it. It did not matter so much in the end. People always get sick and people always argue with one another so we made more than enough money of our own through medicine and the law. Still, it's a pity that Wolffie did not get to enjoy it.'

'I have the map.' Strachan informed him. 'But it is useless. Sabine has visited some of the sites but there was nothing at any of the locations. The bunkers were either discovered and destroyed or the map is inaccurate.'

Strachan feared that Manfred was having a seizure for he threw his head back and drew in a breath that seemed to have no end. He was only able to relax when the old man finally exhaled and bellowed with laughter.

'Of course the map is not accurate!' He roared breathlessly. 'He changed the coordinates to prevent the zealots from putting weapons into the hands of empty-headed young boys and frightened old men. He told Maus that the map would be useless to them if they tore it from his grasp or took it from his body.'

'How did he alter the coordinates?' Strachan demanded. 'Did he tell Maus?'

'He did!' The older man replied with a wink that put Strachan in mind of Manfred as the mischievous young man his grandfather had described him to be. 'But I will only tell you if you promise to put the money to good use. If you tell me that you will do the right thing and hand it in to the authorities, I will let the secret die with me. I could not bear to think of them wasting it on whatever politically correct nonsense happens to be flavour of the month at the moment. Use it to help real people!'

He nodded with satisfaction when both Strachan and Sabine agreed to his terms.

'It was quite simple. He added his lucky number to the last digit of both the latitude and the longitude. If you take three away from both numbers then you will have the coordinates necessary to come within ten metres of the spot.'

Strachan smiled because he knew instinctively that this was correct. Three had been Grampy's lucky number for as long as he could remember. Raffle tickets, lottery entries and pools coupons had always been completed with a focus on that number. He had stuck with it doggedly throughout the years in spite of it never bringing him a single win.

'So!' Sabine declared excitedly as they left the care home and made for her car. 'We go treasure hunting this weekend?'

'Not this weekend.' Strachan replied with a shrug of his shoulders. 'I have booked a flight to Lublin and hired a car to go in search of Ania Strachura's family. I think that my grandfather's greatest debt was the one he owed to her. I want to go and see if there is anything that can be done to repay it in some way.'

'You are right.' Sabine replied reluctantly, her shoulders slumping slightly in disappointment.

'Hers is an important part of the story and you should pursue it.'

Strachan left that thought hanging in the air for a few seconds while he gathered his courage. 'I thought that you might want to see how this side of the story unfolds. I bought two tickets in the hope that you would want to accompany me.'

'Just you try and stop me!' She beamed in delight. 'I might even consider giving you a slight reduction on my hourly rate. You know that I charge double on the weekends, right?'

They were standing in the farmyard in the shadow of the dilapidated windmill within six hours of leaving Frankfurt on the Saturday morning. The flight had departed and arrived on schedule and the rental car's sat-nav had guided them straight to the farmhouse door without a single hitch. The place was in an even worse state of repair than the online satellite images had suggested. The windmill roof had collapsed in on itself and its walls and crumbling mortar looked set to follow it in the not-too-distant future. The pond was so choked with weeds that it was impossible to tell whether or not it still contained any water. The farmhouse itself was boarded up and fragments of the many tiles that had slipped off its roof were scattered across the yard. Strachan looked up towards the window from which his grandfather had gazed out through the slats of the shutters. The wooden shutters had rotted away to nothing long ago, but there were rusty stains on the stonework to mark the positions of the mounting pins that had once supported them. It was a shame to see the farm in such a poor condition but he was glad that he had come and stood in a place that had been so familiar to his grandfather.

His reverie was broken by the sound of heavy feet stamping up the drive towards them. He cursed to himself when a heavyset, middle-aged man in a stained, off-white vest emerged from behind the hedge and approached them aggressively. He growled something in Polish that, although neither of them understood the words, was clearly not intended to welcome them to the neighbourhood.

'English?' Strachan asked as the man drew closer. 'Do you speak English?'

'This is private property!' He snarled. 'You should not be here. You go now!'

'We came to find the owner.' Strachan replied, holding his hands up to placate the man and calm him down.

'They do not want to sell the land. You should leave them alone.'

'I do not want to buy the land. My grandfather stayed here a long time ago. Ania Stachura was very kind to him. I came to find her family and to thank them for what she did for him.'

The man looked from Strachan to Sabine and back again but did not appear entirely convinced. 'You are not from the bank?'

'No! We're not from the bank.' Strachan insisted. 'We're friends of the family.'

346

'You look like a banker!' He retorted sourly, but his stance was less sure now and it seemed that he was softening.

'Where would we find the family?' Sabine asked, her tone gentle but firm. 'I can see that they don't live here. The place is falling apart.'

The neighbour sighed and nodded sadly as he cast his eyes over the farmhouse. 'It was once a wonderful farm but has long been in decline. Old Ania was a schoolteacher and neglected the farm to care for her pupils. What she earned was not enough to maintain the place and it grew worse when her daughter, Halina, followed her into teaching. They struggled along for a while on old Ania's pension and Halina's wages, but it has been a losing battle since the old girl passed away fifteen years ago. Halina is old now herself and is in a care home in the next village. Her son, Piotr, is working in England to try and earn enough money to save the farm. He has plans to restore it and turn it into a hotel.' He shrugged his shoulders and swept his hand around the farmyard. 'But you can see how bad it is. He would need a fortune to carry out his plans. He will have to give in to the banks and the developers eventually. I do not see any way around it. It is very sad. The Stachuras have farmed this land for more than eighty years.'

Once Viktor had opened up, it was hard to get him to stop and it took Strachan and Sabine more than half an hour to thank him for his help and make good their escape. They found the care home without too much trouble and were able to persuade the staff that they were distant relatives.

The care assistant escorted them to the room and pulled the door open so that they could see Halina Nowotarski, Ania Stachura's daughter. The frail, old woman was fast asleep on her bed with her bony arms on her chest on top of the coverlet.

'Alzheimer's.' The assistant stated sadly. 'She no longer recognises anyone now. She had periods of lucidity when she first came in but not anymore.'

Strachan and Sabine watched her for a few moments. She seemed so peaceful and the room was filled with evidence of a life well-lived. A cork-board at the side of the bed was pinned full of greetings cards and the three bouquets of flowers in the room were fresh and large enough to suggest that no expense had been spared. The cabinet by the window was covered in framed photographs of weddings, birthdays, picnics and holidays by the sea. A fresh, young version of the lined face before them smiled out at them on the arm of a handsome young man on her wedding day and beamed with happiness whilst holding her new-born son.

'Look!' Strachan exclaimed. 'That photograph there is the one I found of Ania on the internet. See! It was her who received the teaching award.'

'Both Ania and Halina are very well regarded around here.' The care assistant interjected helpfully. 'They both taught in the village school and did a great deal to look after the children in this area. She never wants for visitors or flowers and cards. Many people are very fond of her and her family.'

The assistant became awkward and hesitant when she showed them back to reception and haltingly raised the issue of Halina's fees. 'Her son has always paid them up until quite recently, but they are now several months in arrears. He is working in London now and I have not been able to reach him. I am sorry to raise such a sensitive issue, but I thought that I should, given that you are family.'

Strachan pulled out his wallet and gave her his personal credit card. 'I'll cover the arrears and pay for the next six months in advance.' He tried to appear nonchalant while the payment was processed but was secretly delighted to see that Sabine was impressed by the gesture and the generosity that underpinned it.

Strachan and Sabine were both quiet and thoughtful on the drive back to the airport. It was always sad to see a person diminished by age but there was great comfort to be had from knowing that they had achieved something worthwhile and had not wasted the precious years granted to them.

'Are you glad you came?' Strachan asked her when they were buckled into their seats on the plane.

'Of course!' She replied, squeezing his hand as she did so and then leaving it there long enough to signify a growing level of intimacy. 'It was an important part of the story. It is good that we know the fate of all of the key players. All that is left now...'

'Is to find those damned bunkers and whatever is inside them.' He interrupted, completing the sentence for her.

'We will go to my brother's house as soon as we land. He has every tool known to man and he will loan us whatever we need.'

'Just what will we need? You have the metal detector already. Surely all we will need is a couple of shovels.'

Sabine shook her head and frowned in concentration. 'Your grandfather talked about metal hatches and safes in the floor. We will need spades, crow bars, cutting gear, a cordless angle grinder, a car jack, hacksaws, chisels, torches and anything else that might be useful.'

Strachan could not help but laugh at how thoroughly she had thought this through. 'And have you decided where we will look first?'

'Yes.' She replied, either missing or ignoring the accusation in his question. 'I have selected a site in a location that is very remote and is heavily forested. It is one of the ones your grandfather underlined for you and so must be one of the most important. We will be able to do whatever we need to do there with little danger of being disturbed.'

He shook his head and rolled his eyes in mock exasperation. 'And what the hell is the car jack for?'

'You'll just have to wait and see!' She replied enigmatically' 'You will soon discover that I have a few tricks up my sleeve!'

Strachan really hoped that he would see her tricks before too long. In fact, he was counting on it!

He saw that she had not been exaggerating the moment her brother flipped the switch and the fluorescent tubes burst into life, flooding the triple garage with light. It reminded him of the scene in almost every Terminator movie where Arnold Schwarzenegger hits a button and a false wall slides away to reveal a cache of armaments sufficient to equip a whole army. The garage was decorated more like a laboratory than a utilitarian space for storing vehicles in. The walls had been painted white and were filled with custom-built shelving and display boards and the floor had been finished in some kind of white epoxy resin that shone as if it had been polished. Strachan gaped at the dizzying array of hand tools, power tools, clamps, saws, generators, transformers, spanners, drills, augers and hundreds of other items that he could not even put a name to.

'What do you do for a living again?' He asked sarcastically as he gazed around the garage.

'It is just as I said before.' Paul replied, unaware that he was being teased. 'I analyse data for retail organisations so that they can accurately target their marketing spend in order to optimise the return on their investment.'

Sabine was already hard at work pulling tools from their shelves and piling them at the centre of the garage floor.

351

'If you tell me what you need them for.' Paul offered. 'I could advise you on the best tools for the job.'

'Okay.' Sabine agreed, waving away Strachan's objections with her hand. 'But you will have to lie under oath and deny all knowledge of it if we are caught and charges are brought against us.'

Paul look horrified and shook his head vigorously. 'Okay. Just take what you need and bring it back in the same condition it was in when you took it.' He gave his younger sister a long, disapproving look. 'I liked it better when you worked for the police. This private detective thing does not seem entirely legitimate.'

Only half of the borrowed tools fitted into the boot of Sabine's car and the rest rattled and clattered on the back seat as they headed back towards the city centre and Strachan's hotel.

'We should hire a van in the morning.' Strachan announced when the din had started to play on his nerves after only a few minutes on the road. The site Sabine had chosen was a few miles outside of Duisburg and he did not think that he could stand nearly three hours of clanking and banging on the way there.

'There is a Hertz on Camberger Strasse. That is on the way to my apartment. We could stop there, hire a van and load it up all ready for the morning.' Sabine suggested as she glanced at Strachan in the passenger seat.

'Then you would have to double-back to drop me at my hotel.' Strachan replied. 'It is too late to

352

put you to all that trouble, Sabine. Let's pick the van up in the morning.'

'Or.' Sabine declared, before pausing to consider what she was about to say. 'Or you could stay at my apartment. I don't have a spare bedroom but there is a couch in my study that I am told is very comfortable.'

Strachan told her that he would like that very much and his smile was such that she felt moved to emphasise that he would be sleeping on the couch. He did sleep there but he did not do so alone. She came into his arms as they entered the apartment and he kissed her lips and felt the firmness and heat of her body against his. They made love twice and talked long into the night until Sabine drifted off to sleep in a state of happy and satisfied exhaustion. Thoughts of Nazis and bunkers were far from his mind as he watched her sleep in his arms and he could not recall a time when he had been happier.

28

She awakened him with more kisses and loved him with more vigour and less tenderness than she had the night before. He would have happily spent the whole day in bed but she would not allow it. She pulled the covers from him, slapped his bare arse quite hard and ordered him to shower while she prepared breakfast. She did not complain when he emerged from the shower in a towel and pressed himself against her as she worked the eggs with a wooden spatula. He slipped his hand under her t-shirt and rubbed his hand over her ample breast whilst stroking her hardening nipple with his thumb.

'Come on!' He begged as he nuzzled into the soft skin at the side of her neck. 'It won't take long!'

'I know that already!' She countered with a wicked grin. 'These eggs need another two minutes. Perhaps we could do it twice and still eat them while they're warm!'

'You're a wicked, wicked woman!' He moaned as he pressed himself hard against her.

'You love it!' She retorted, her hand already turning the cooker off.

He did love it. Once before breakfast and once in the shower. It was almost lunchtime by the time Strachan drove the van onto the A3.

They made rapid and unimpeded progress along the autobahn, arriving at the outskirts of Duisburg just before three in the afternoon. They pulled into a service area to buy ham baguettes and coffee for lunch and a detailed local map to help them to find the location of the bunker marked on Strachan's grandfather's map. They found the place on the map and marked it before the coffee was cold and the baguettes reduced to crumbs. They were in high spirits when they set off again and were optimistic that they would find what they were looking for before the afternoon was out. Two hours of trawling up and down the same country lanes served to turn their high spirits to frustration and to temper their optimism to the point of despair.

'The track should be here! Right here!' Strachan seethed as he tapped his finger hard against the screen of his iPhone.

'Park here!' Sabine instructed him. 'I swear I will shoot you if you drive along this road again. Let us look on foot. Perhaps we are missing something.'

Strachan saw it just before she did. The ancient and rotten gatepost had fallen onto its side and was so overgrown with ivy and moss that it was no wonder that they had not spotted it from the road. Another five minutes of searching revealed that the second gatepost was still standing but had been almost completely absorbed into the trunk of a tree that had grown up hard against it.

'Get the metal detector!' Strachan instructed her, his frustration now replaced by excitement.

'It should be just under two hundred meters north-west of here.'

The undergrowth grew thinner as they ascended the gentle slope ahead of them. They scanned the ground as they went but nature had reclaimed the land long ago and had erased any signs of human activity.

'It's like searching for a needle in a haystack!' Strachan puffed as he paused to catch his breath on the summit. 'If we are out by even a metre or two we could spend months digging here and never find it.'

Sabine used her hand to shield her eyes from the sun and slowly scanned the forest floor. 'There!' She announced suddenly. 'See that slight depression in the ground. That may have been caused by subsidence where a hole has been dug and then filled in again.'

Strachan saw it now that she had pointed it out but had completely overlooked it when he had examined the ground before. 'I missed it.' He admitted ruefully. 'I am impressed that you noticed it.'

Sabine grinned back at him in triumph as she began to fiddle with the controls of the metal detector. 'It is one of the advantages of a career with the police. This is not the first time I have searched for something that someone has tried to hide by burying it in the ground. At least there will be no bodies this time!'

Strachan watched her as she swept the clearing methodically from one side to the other. The device gave out a number of high-pitched squeals as she worked and she marked each of the locations with a stone. The loudest and most high-pitched of these came at the edge of the depression in the ground. She marked this as she had the rest and then continued until she had scanned the whole clearing.

'Do you see it?' She asked him when she had finished and switched the machine off.

'I think I do.' He replied. 'You found nothing on this side of the clearing but there would seem to be around ten small pieces of metal on the far side and one large piece of metal at the edge of the depression. If there is a structure buried here, it is likely that the larger signal is where we will find the entrance.'

'Not just a pretty face!' She declared happily as she leaned in to kiss him on the lips. 'Come! Let's go and grab the spades. If we are lucky we will find something before it grows dark.'

The ground was much harder than they had expected and the excavation proved to be both tortuous and slow. They grew tired, dirty and sweaty and might have lost heart if they had not unearthed evidence of the building work they believed had been carried out on that spot. Strachan held up the fragments of concrete in the fading light and Sabine nodded with determination before taking her turn with the shovel. It was almost completely dark when the clang of metal on metal caused them both to freeze. Strachan dropped to his knees and pulled his phone from his pocket. He flicked the torch on and scraped at the earth and the stones with his fingertips.

'You beauty!' He cried out in triumph. 'Look! It's a metal hatch!'

He beckoned her to kneel beside him and held the torch up so that she could see. She squealed in delight at the sight of the metal and threw her arms around him.

'My God! We have done it! We have really done it!' She gushed ecstatically. 'Let's keep digging!'

'It's almost dark.' Strachan replied. 'And I am almost out of battery. Let's find a hotel for the night and a hardware store where we can buy some more equipment. It'll take days to scrape this earth away with spades. A pick-axe will cut through it much faster.'

Sabine agreed reluctantly for darkness was closing in and they would soon be unable to see their own hands in front of their faces. Even in her present state of enthusiasm, she did not relish the prospect of being out in the forest with only a fading iPhone to provide them with light.

Strachan feared that the concierge at the Hotel Rheingarten was going to refuse to let them take a room such was the look of horror that passed across his face when they approached the front desk. He did not entirely blame him because they looked as if they had spent the day tunnelling out of a prison. Their hands and their clothes were filthy and sweat and dust coated their hair and faces. His expression changed from horror to mere distaste when he caught sight of the American Express Centurion Card in his hand.

'Our car broke down.' Sabine offered with a shrug by way of explanation, but the man did not seem persuaded by the vague excuse.

'Luggage?' He asked with disdain, obviously not yet convinced that they were legitimate guests.

'We drove in from Frankfurt.' Strachan replied. "We intended to return this evening but, with the breakdown and everything, we will have to stay the night here. I would be grateful if you could provide us with directions to the nearest shopping mall. We really would like to be able to change out of these dirty clothes.'

They found the retail park within a few minutes of leaving the hotel with their room card in their hands. They bought two sets of jeans and t-shirts, two sets of overalls, a powerful torch and batteries, a pick-axe, sandwiches and enough snacks and soft drinks to sustain them through the following day.

'We should carry this all in through the lobby.' Sabine said with an evil grin on her face as they pulled into the hotel carpark. 'I think the concierge would have a heart attack at the sight of us carrying a pick-axe up to our room.'

They showered the dirt from their bodies and dressed in the thick, fluffy bath robes provided by the hotel before ordering from the room-service menu. Their physical labour had left them ravenous so they both ordered burgers and fries, ice-cream, cheese and biscuits, Cokes and a bottle of red wine. Their room boasted a spectacular view over the Rhine and they drank it in as they ate.

'We should turn in early.' Strachan suggested as he drained his wine glass and patted at his satisfyingly full stomach with his hand. 'There's a lot more digging to be done tomorrow, so we should get as much rest as we can and make an early start in the morning.'

'You just want to get me into bed.' Sabine replied sleepily. The food and wine combined with the day's exertions had left her struggling to keep her eyes open.

Strachan could not deny the accusation and so just offered her his hand and pulled her towards the bed and its inviting, crisp, white sheets. They were fast asleep by eleven and were up, refreshed and raring to go by seven the next morning. The hotel's breakfast buffet was too tempting to resist and they filled themselves with coffee, croissants, toast, cereal and orange juice before checking out and heading back towards the bunker site. Sabine sighed when they reached the brow of the slope carrying the pick-axe, shovels, crow-bar, angle-grinder and their bag of snacks and drinks.

'Ach!' She moaned in disappointment. 'I thought we had made more progress than this. Look! We have hardly scraped the surface here. It will take us all day just to uncover the hatch!'

'The sooner we get started the sooner we'll get finished.' Strachan replied with an irritating level of cheerfulness.

The work was back-breaking and repetitive but they stuck at it doggedly throughout the morning.

Strachan wielded the pick-axe and hammered it into the ground hard enough to loosen the earth and stones for Sabine to scoop it away with her shovel. Their arms were aching and their bodies were hot and sweaty by the time they took a break just before eleven. They sat under a pine tree to slake their thirst with cans of the soft drinks purchased the night before.

'We might not finish it today!' Strachan announced as he surveyed the narrow trench. 'If that hatch is big enough for a man to walk through unbowed, say six feet, it could take us another full day to clear it.'

Sabine swore and drained her can. 'If I have to do this for another full day you'll have to bury me in that damned hole. All those long hours sitting in my car conducting surveillance has not prepared me for such physical work. It's not even noon and I'm exhausted.'

Strachan pulled her to her feet and they soon found their rhythm again. Their thoughts drifted as they laboured on mindlessly and the trench gradually deepened inch by muscle-sapping inch. He was running through the next steps in the Haas Bank acquisition process when her squeal ripped him from his contemplation. His heart jumped into his mouth out of fear that he had somehow hurt her with the pick-axe but her face was filled with delight rather than pain.

'Look!' She ordered him as she pointed into the trench. 'It's the bottom of the hatch! It's not a full-length door! It's just a small hatch for crawling through!'

Strachan wrapped one arm around her and shook his other fist in triumph and relief. The whole hatch was now exposed and their digging was at an end. All that was left to do was to prise it open before they could enter the bunker and discover its secrets. This was to prove to be easier said than done given that they had no key to insert into the lock. It took half an hour of hammering at the metal with the pick-axe to bend the thick steel enough to fit the end of the crow-bar between the hatch and its frame. Another hour of wrenching and straining succeeded in widening the gap by only another four or five inches.

'I wish we'd taken one of your brother's big petrol saws.' Strachan complained as he sat on the ground and ate his lunch of potato chips, still lemonade and a packaged egg mayonnaise sandwich. 'One of those beasts would have ripped through that hatch like it was cardboard.'

'I hate to see my big, strong boy so sad!' Sabine teased him. 'You must rest and have your lunch and then I will open that hatch for you just to see a smile upon that grumpy face.'

Strachan grinned back at her despite his frustration. He liked being the subject of her teasing. 'That I would like to see!' He retorted without bothering to even attempt to conceal his certainty that she would not be able to deliver her promise.

He remained unconvinced when she struggled to force the car jack between the hatch and its frame. She was so focused on her task that she did not even notice him laugh when her first efforts to

362

open the jack's jaws caused it to drop back out of the opening and fall to the bottom of the trench. She succeeded in jamming it between the hatch and its frame on her third attempt and started to slowly wind it so that it opened further. Strachan jumped to her side when the steel began to groan under the pressure and he used his strength to turn the jack further. It soon became so difficult to turn the lever that he was only able to shift it a degree or two at a time by wrenching at it with all of his might. He was on the verge of admitting defeat when the lock suddenly gave way with a loud, metallic snap that sent Strachan, the jack and the lever crashing backwards into the trench. He cursed angrily as he pushed himself back to his feet because he believed that the cheap car jack had buckled under the strain. He gaped in wonder at the black hole that now stood where the metal hatch had so stubbornly resisted him only seconds before.

Strachan's open-mouthed astonishment was reflected in Sabine's face. 'We did it!' She declared almost as if she did not believe the evidence of her eyes. 'We only bloody did it!'

'Get the torch!' Strachan instructed her. 'Let's see what we have here.'

Strachan pushed the powerful torch through the opening and beckoned Sabine to his side so that they could both see into the bunker's interior. The space was longer and narrower than they had expected and both walls were lined with shelving from floor to ceiling. The shelves to the right were stacked with canned food, sacks of flour, boxes of biscuits and crackers and cans of coffee. The quality of the bunker's construction was evidenced by the lack of damp or mildew and the fact that no insects or rodents had been able to enter it and feast upon the provisions stored within it. The shelves to the left were filled with wooden crates containing a wide array of military equipment. Even with his limited command of German, Strachan was able to scan the words stencilled onto the crates and deduce that they held large numbers of Luger and Mauser pistols, MP 40 machine guns, Gewehr rifles, hand grenades, mines, Panzerfaust anti-tank weapons, reels of wire and several hundred metal ammunition boxes.

'Jesus!' Strachan exclaimed. 'Just think how many men would have died if this equipment had fallen into the hands of Nazi zealots at the end of the war. They could have fought on for months. Look down the far end! See the radio equipment, boots, tools and clothing. There is enough here to equip a small army.'

'We have your grandfather to thank for that.' Sabine replied, still straining her eyes as she scanned the inside of the bunker. 'Can you imagine how much all of this is worth? Everything is in mint condition. There are collectors who would pay a fortune for this stuff.'

'I am more interested in what is stored behind that door.' Strachan replied as he swung the torch towards the metal hatch set in the wall at the far end of the bunker. 'Grab the angle-grinder! We'll need it to cut through that beast of a padlock.'

364

Strachan lowered Sabine through the hatch and then scrambled down behind her. They paused to examine the shelves as they went because the sheer volume of arms, equipment and provisions was even more evident when viewed from closer quarters. The hardened steel of the padlock resisted the destructive power of the angle-grinder for a creditable ten minutes before the shank was cut all the way through. This allowed Strachan to pull it away from the hasp and toss it onto the concrete floor. He hesitated and looked Sabine in the eye before grabbing her hand and pulling the door open with a metallic screech.

The torch beam illuminated a small concrete-lined room with shelving from floor to ceiling on all three walls. Small, wooden crates filled the lower shelves with larger metal boxes stacked on the upper shelves.

'Out!' Strachan ordered suddenly, grasping Sabine's arm and hustling her back towards the entrance as he rubbed at his eyes.

'What the hell is it?' Sabine coughed, grimacing at the fumes that now stung her eyes and irritated her throat.

'Shit!' Strachan cursed when they had squeezed through the hatch and emerged back into the sunshine and the fresh air. 'I think the fumes were a mixture of chlorine and ammonia. Did you see the boxes on the top shelves? Several of them were leaking and oozing and some of them had crystals forming along their bottoms. I think that they might contain explosives that have deteriorated over time. It may well be highly unstable, so we should not continue. We should alert the authorities and let them deal with it.'

Sabine sat down on the edge of the trench with a grunt and reached for a bottle of Apfel-Schorle. She drank deeply before wiping her mouth with the back of her hand and offering the bottle to Strachan.

'You are right.' She admitted after a long silence. 'We should not continue if it is dangerous.' She then leaned in towards him and locked her eyes on his. 'But what about the smaller crates? Are you not curious about what they might contain?'

29

Strachan had protested at first but he shared her burning curiosity and allowed himself to be persuaded that the smaller crates merited further examination. He insisted that only he should take the risk of entering the bunker again. He passed up three of the small but deceptively heavy crates before climbing back out into the open. They carried the crates away to a safe distance before opening the first of them with the crow-bar. The dry wood splintered as he attempted to lever it up and he had to use his fingers to brush the fragments away and reveal the contents.

'My God!' Sabine exclaimed in wonderment at the sight of the ten gold bars sitting in the remnants of the crate. Each bar was embossed with the Nazi Imperial Eagle with a swastika in its claws along with the words 'Deutsche Bank, 1 Kilo Feingold, 999.9' and a serial number.

Strachan picked one of the bars up and shook his head in disbelief. The second crate contained another ten bars of gold but the third was filled with gold coins. They examined them and found that there was a mixture of coins including 1855 and 1857 Napoleon III 50 Franc coins, Dutch 10 Guilder Willem III gold coins, Danish 20 Kroner Frederik VIII gold coins and a variety of coins bearing the images of the Kings of Saxony, Bavaria and Wurttemberg.

'My God!' Sabine exclaimed again. 'There must be a fortune here! How much is it worth, David? There must be hundreds of thousands of Euros here.'

Strachan was already running the numbers in his head. He had some of his own money invested in gold and was therefore roughly aware of the current market price. He turned pale as he realised the enormity of what they had unearthed.

'Just by weight alone it is worth over a million Euros, but that's without taking account of what value a collector might place upon the coins. Even if only a few of them are rare or collectible that could increase the value significantly.'

'My God!' Sabine ejaculated once again. 'Then we must bring it all out. We cannot leave it in there!'

'No! You do not understand. What we have here already is worth more than a million Euros. There are at least another sixty cases like this still in the bunker. If they all contain the same amount of gold, the total value would easily exceed twenty million Euros.'

Sabine leaned towards him and kissed him hard on the lips. 'Then we had better get to work. Both your grandfather and Herr Wissler said that we should do some good with this treasure. It will benefit no-one if we leave it in the ground.'

Neither of them could remember having ever toiled as hard as they did that afternoon. Strachan tied his t-shirt over his mouth and nose to protect him from the worst of the fumes and worked slowly and carefully to avoid causing any vibrations that might cause the leaking explosives to detonate. Just carrying the crates from the back of the bunker and handing them up to Sabine left him drained and with an aching back and strained muscles. They then had to carry them all the way down to the roadside to be ready for loading into the van once darkness fell. It was already dusk by the time they finished and they still had to face the task of refilling the trench so that no-one would stumble upon the bunker and either help themselves to the weapons and ammunition or risk blowing themselves to smithereens.

They were less than half a mile away from the bunker and were still debating the best way to inform the authorities of its location and contents when the explosion lit up the night and caused the van to shudder. Strachan pulled off the road immediately and they leapt out of the van to look back in the direction they had just come from. A bright orange glow illuminated the thick column of black smoke that rose ever higher into the night sky. They reached out for each other and embraced, their faces pale with the shock of realising that they both would have been dead if the unstable explosives had detonated even a few minutes earlier. They watched the fire until a fine dust began to rain down on them and sting their eyes. The sound of approaching sirens jolted them from their state of shock and bewilderment and they quickly returned to the van and set off in order to vacate the area before the police arrived

369

to investigate the explosion. They were largely silent on the drive back to Frankfurt as they could not help but dwell on close they had come to disaster.

Strachan did most of the talking when they went to see Manfred Wissler the next morning. The elation of finding the treasure had been well and truly tempered by the explosion and the shock of having avoided death by a mere matter of minutes. The old man's joy at hearing of the fortune that had been extracted from the bunker seemed to have been eroded by the younger man's pessimism.

'So!' he interrupted him irritably. 'You want to hand the gold to the authorities for them to waste on chauffeur-driven limousines and fat civil service expense accounts. I doubt if that was what your grandfather hoped for when he entrusted you with his legacy.'

'But there is the difficulty of processing so much gold, Herr Wissler.' Strachan protested. 'Any bank that I approach is legally bound to report any transaction of this size. I would be required to prove that it came from a legitimate source and would be found criminally liable when I was unable to do so. At the very least I would be guilty of failing to declare what was found and for attempting to launder the proceeds. I would go to jail. I can see no way around it.'

'Then you are even more short-sighted than I am!' Manfred snapped back at him. 'There is always a way around these things. All you would need is a lawyer with expertise in the European banking system and who has high-level contacts in Switzerland. How do you think billionaires are able to move their money around and avoid the tax authorities? There is a whole industry that does nothing but facilitate the covert movement of wealth.'

'I know of no such lawyer who I would trust in this matter.' Strachan replied, his cheeks reddening in the face of the old man's disapproval. 'I wouldn't know where to start looking.'

Manfred paused to take a few breaths of oxygen. 'You could start by looking towards the end of this bed.' He pointed a shaky finger towards his daughter. 'Gerde ran my legal firm for more than twenty years after my retirement. There is hardly a millionaire, senior banker or bullion dealer in all of Europe who does not owe her a favour or two. If you ask her nicely she will solve any problem that you put to her and she'll keep you out of jail.'

Gerde returned Strachan's gaze and shrugged her shoulders. 'I think you worry too much. There is no great crime here. The money was not stolen or gained fraudulently and, as long as you use none of it for yourself, there is no issue of personal gain. Money laundering triggers can be avoided if the money is spread across multiple trusts. It can all be done without you appearing on anyone's radar just so long as you are discrete and do not seek publicity.'

'Will you help us then?' Sabine asked hopefully. She had steeled herself against the disappointment of having to give the fortune up and hardly dared to hope that a more positive way forward was possible.

Gerde looked between Strachan and Sabine as if she was weighing up the best course of action. 'I will!' She declared finally. 'But there is a condition. I will arrange for the gold to be sold and for the proceeds to be distributed across a number of charitable trusts only if the two of you agree to administer them once they are established. I am too old to take on such responsibilities.'

They agreed immediately, hugged Manfred and Gerde and went off to eat, rest, celebrate, make love and plan for the future.

Gerde took her father's hand in hers and stroked it tenderly. 'You are sure about this, Papa?'

Manfred nodded and forced himself to smile even although the terse exchange with Strachan had left him weak and weary. 'I am sure, little Gerde. Put all of the documents in my name and I will sign them. If any of this comes to the attention of the authorities, then I will take the blame.' He paused to laugh and squeeze her hand. 'After all, what can they do to me? I will be dead long before a trial can be organised.'

She shushed him then, for such talk was forbidden even although they both knew that he spoke the truth.

Strachan watched her nervously as she read each document in turn. The last three months had been hectic but he had no doubt that they had been the happiest of his life. He had brought the Haas Bank deal to a successful conclusion and had exploited the goodwill it generated to persuade his partners to grant him a six-month sabbatical to deal with his personal matters. He had spent long hours with Gerde working out the structure of the charitable trusts and on determining who the initial beneficiaries would be. He had done all of this as a permanent fixture in Sabine's apartment and had yet to find himself banished to the sofa.

Sabine's eyes filled with tears when she turned the last of the documents over. 'Your grandfather was wise to entrust this task to you and he was right to say that only you had the brains and the heart to do what was right. You have honoured him and his friends and have ensured that their names will not be forgotten. Under-privileged students from all over Europe will speak the names of Maus, Julius, Horse, Manfred and Lammert and thank them for providing scholarships to fund them through the educations that they themselves were denied. It is most fitting.' Tears then flowed down her cheeks and Strachan went to take her in his arms. 'You even remembered the horses.' She sobbed. 'Those your grandfather mourned that died in the battle for Kharkov and the one that saved his life by carrying him across the frozen Russian steppes. I am sure that he would approve of the grants given to the horse refuge charities. He would be proud of you, Davey. Very proud.'

Strachan hugged her as tightly as he could and basked in her approval. He had read his grandfather's journal from cover to cover several times over to ensure that nothing was missed. He trusted Sabine's judgement more than any other person and was delighted that his choices had moved her.

'There are just a few outstanding awards from my grandfather's trusts.' He told her as he planted a kiss on the side of her neck. 'I am holding those back until the twenty-first of May so they arrive on Grandad's birthday.'

Epilogue

21st May

8.45 a.m. Perth Scotland

Irene Walker swore under her breath as she fumbled with her keys in her haste to unlock her car and get out of the rain that now poured down in a deluge. The short dash across the psychiatric hospital's car park had soaked her and left water dripping from her hair. Her morning had gone from bad to worse since the 6 a.m. call that had let her know that one of her most vulnerable clients had suffered a psychotic episode and had been sectioned and detained at Murray Royal Hospital. The poor woman had been heavily medicated by the time she arrived and she was not entirely certain that she had even been aware of her presence. Irene had made every effort to appear detached and professional in front of the medical staff but the sad turn of events had left her feeling low and thoroughly dejected. The client had been making great progress and was on the verge of being granted supervised access to her children after staying free of drugs for six months. Irene had supported her throughout this struggle and was dismayed by this major setback. She doubted that she would be able to recover from it.

'What now?' She snapped at the sound of her phone ringing in her bag. She grimaced when she saw her son's name on the caller ID screen. He seldom called her when she was working and only did so when some domestic emergency compelled him to do so. She wondered if the hot water heater was broken again as she answered the call.

'Morning Frazer.' She began, trying to keep her voice light. 'Is everything alright? It's not that bloody heater again is it? Have you tried switching it off at the wall?'

'Are you sitting down?' He asked, his voice tight and a little higher pitched than usual.

She cringed and prepared herself for the bad news. 'I'm sitting in the car, Frazer. Just tell me what it is? I didn't think my morning could get any worse.'

'I've got sponsorship to do my degree at Oxford!' He announced, the words tumbling out of his mouth in excitement. 'I can't believe it!'

'My God!' His mother exclaimed in delight and disbelief. 'So, they will pay your fees? That's fantastic! That's brilliant news! Is it just for the first year?'

'No, Mum!' He squealed. 'It's everything! Fees, accommodation, books and living costs for the full duration of my studies. I have the letter here from the Wolff Foundation. I still can't believe it, but it's here in black and white, Mum, I won't have to borrow a single penny!'

'Wow!' Irene replied, still reeling from the shock of it. 'I didn't think that any of the schemes you applied for covered everything. I thought that the best we could hope for was to have your fees paid and then take out a student loan to pay for everything else.'

'That's the funny part, Mum. I can't even remember applying for this one.'

'I'm not surprised! You were filling out so many application forms I was worried that it would affect your grades. Now, get back to the studying! This Wolff Foundation won't pay you anything if you don't get on the course in the first place. Well done! I'm very proud of you!'

The dismal, dreich Perth morning now seemed much brighter and Irene slicked her wet hair back from her face and prepared for the short drive to her office. The phone rang again just as she slid the key into the ignition.

'Irene Walker.' She answered, the lack of a caller ID causing her to assume that it was probably something work related.

'Good morning Mrs Walker!' A deep, cultured and lazy voice greeted her, the words delivered slowly and in the clipped and precise syllables unique to those educated in the more expensive and exclusive of Edinburgh's private schools. 'This is Cameron Mackenzie of Mackenzie, Myles and Black. I am calling with regard to the will of Mr. Peter Stachura. I did send a letter inviting you to the reading of the will at our office in Alyth, but you were obviously unable to attend.

I wonder if now would be a convenient time for us to discuss the matter.'

Oh, yes. I apologise for that. I have been very busy at work recently. My cousin, David Strachan, was dealing with all that. He was Mr. Stachura's grandson.'

'I'm very familiar with Mr. Strachan.' Mackenzie replied, his tone suggesting that he had not necessarily found the experience to be one that entirely met with his approval. 'He has been good enough to find the time to grace me with the occasional call from Germany whenever his work there has allowed him to do so. He has now completed his duties as executor of his grandfather's last will and testament and has instructed me to inform you of its contents.'

'I'm actually at work at the moment, Mr. Mackenzie. I don't really have the time for this right now.'

'Such a busy, busy family.' The solicitor drawled, the honey in his voice not quite masking his irritation. 'Perhaps I could just give you the overall gist over the telephone now and we can arrange an appointment to go through the details and complete the formalities at a time and date that is convenient for you.'

'Okay.' Irene sighed. 'Though it's David who is his heir. I'm not sure why it's so necessary to fill me in.'

'You're partially correct, Mrs Walker. Mr. Strachan was a beneficiary of the will in that his grandfather bequeathed all of his personal possessions to him. That included the contents of both the house and the shed on the property in New Alyth. The rest he left to you.'

'To me?' Irene exclaimed in shock. 'That can't be right!'

'Mr. Stachura was very specific. You are to receive the house along with his savings, a small number of Premium Bonds and are the named beneficiary of a modest life insurance policy. All in all, these amount to a sum of just over twelve thousand pounds.' Mackenzie paused to clear his throat. 'Then there is the matter of the cash found in the house at new Alyth.'

'Cash?' Irene asked, her head still spinning at the unexpected direction the call was taking. 'What cash?'

'Mr. Strachan apparently found a large sum of cash when he was clearing the house. Two hundred thousand pounds to be precise. He claims that it was stuffed into a shoe box secreted beneath Mr. Stachura's bed.'

'Bloody hell! Two hundred thousand pounds? That's a lot of money!'

'That's exactly what I said to your cousin. I said that it was a lot of money to fit into a single shoe box. In fact, I asked him if the box had once contained clown shoes because I did not see how so much money could be stuffed into such a small box.' The solicitor paused to chortle at his own joke. 'He just said that his grandfather had big feet and that the bills were of high denominations. In any case, I had no opportunity to investigate further because Mr. Strachan had already deposited the cash into a personal account before transferring it to us to be dealt with as part of the estate.'

'But Davey was his direct heir. All of this should have gone to him. There must be some mistake.'

'There's no mistake, Mrs Walker. Mr. Stachura was quite specific about his wishes and was of sound mind and good health when the will was drawn up. Mr. Strachan has made it quite clear that he will respect his grandfather's wishes and has waived all rights to challenge the will. The assets I have mentioned are both legally and morally yours. Please arrange to drop by the office so that the formalities can be concluded.'

Irene dropped her phone onto the passenger seat and shook her head in disbelief. The day had started badly but two short calls had transformed it very much for the better. It slowly began to dawn on her that her days of constant financial struggle were now behind her.

9.30 a.m. Edinburgh Scotland

'Professor McLelland!' The secretary persisted from her position just inside the frame of the office door.

Ewan McLelland blew his cheeks out in exasperation and abandoned his pretence of being oblivious to her presence. 'Good God, Jean!' He snapped in irritation. 'I said that I was not to be disturbed. I've got this damned speech still to write for tonight's fundraiser and I'm struggling to come up with any platitudes that I've not used a hundred times before!'

The sight of her pained expression peeping around the edge of the door caused him to regret his outburst immediately. His fearsome reputation was an asset in that it discouraged the many time wasters who were drawn to him in his role as the Clinical Director of Oncology at the University of Edinburgh Medical School, but he did not want his long-suffering assistant to be on the receiving end of his irascibility.

'Come on in, Jean.' He instructed her. 'I'm sorry for being so ratty, but I could well do without this Cancer Research UK function tonight. If we weren't in such desperate need of funds for the new clinical research centre, I'd cancel the bloody thing in a second! Now! What is it? It had better be good or I'll insist that you compensate me for the interruption by scooting across to Starbucks and treating me to a skinny decaff latte!'

'I thought you'd want to see this right away.' Jean replied as she held a sheet of paper out towards him.

Professor McLelland perched his spectacles half-way down his nose and peered down at the letter. Jean waited expectantly and watched as his eyes moved along each line in turn.

'Bugger me!' McLelland exclaimed as he collapsed back in his seat and removed his glasses as if he was in a daze. 'Two and a half million pounds a year every year for the next four years. If this pans out we'll have the clinical centre up and running years earlier than we had either planned or hoped for.'

'That's just the thing, Professor McLelland.' Jean replied with a shake of her head. 'It has panned out already. The funds were transferred into our account this morning.'

'What?' McLelland spluttered. 'The whole two and a half million?'

Jan nodded. 'Aye! All of it. But did you see the conditions to the donation. They're in the addendum on the back of the letter.'

McLelland turned the letter over and pushed his glasses back into place before reading the short paragraph aloud. 'There are two conditions attached to this donation and both are to be considered to be inviolable. 1) The donation is to be treated with the strictest anonymity. The Wolff Foundation should not be mentioned in any publicity documents, brochures, press releases or be otherwise communicated in any form or through any medium. 2) The clinical research centre is to be named 'The Corporal Kenneth McLelland Research Centre' in honour of the great services he performed during the Second World War.'

The professor stared at his secretary, his face paler than she had ever seen it before. 'That's my father's name, Jean. Why on earth would a German foundation donate such a huge amount of money in his memory?'

'He must have done something pretty amazing for him to be remembered after all this time.' Jean replied, her face breaking into a smile. 'Now, I'm thinking that it should be you who scoots over to Starbucks and treats me to a coffee. Seeing as you're paying, I'll have a large caramel cocoa cluster Frappuccino with hazelnut syrup.'

'Fair play!' McClelland replied cheerfully as he jumped up from his seat and reached for his blue herringbone tweed jacket. 'I'll even break the bank and throw in the whipped cream and some sprinkles!' He then froze with one arm hallway into its sleeve as if something had just occurred to him. 'Bugger it!' He declared after a few seconds. 'Get your coat Jean! I'm whisking you away to the Balmoral Hotel for a champagne breakfast. We should celebrate this and, God knows, I need a drink more now than I have ever done before.'

7.45 p.m. London England

Piotr Nowotarski kicked the door shut behind him and let his toolbox clatter onto the floor at the foot of his bed. He had kept himself to himself and stayed away from the communal kitchen after the theft of his tools the previous month. He knew that one of his housemates had stolen them but could not prove it. He emptied the carrier bag onto the crumpled duvet and sighed at the sight of the meagre meal he was to enjoy after a long, hard day on the building site in the wind and the rain. Four beers, a cold pork pie, a packet of Quavers and a Galaxy Ripple hardly represented an appropriate reward for all his toil and suffering.

His mood soured as he ate and reflected on the ill-fortune he had suffered over the past few months. In addition to the cost of replacing his tools, he had been forced to pay for a new van when the engine on his old one had seized and reduced the vehicle to scrap. Worst of all, he had been left out of pocket for a month's work when a developer went bust and disappeared without paying him for his labour and materials. If it had not been for some random foreigner paying his mother's care home fees, he would have been left totally destitute by this run of bad luck.

He let out a sigh, opened another beer and began to sort through his mail. The presence of several bills caused his heart to sink. He overcame the urge to ignore them and instead forced himself to find out just how far into debt he had now fallen. The electricity bill was not as steep as he had feared. This was probably because he had spent little time in his room due to the long hours he was working. He decided to pay it online there and then so he had one less bill to worry about. He put the Council Tax letter to one side to deal with later. He knew that the arrears had accumulated to the point that he would probably be forced to visit the council offices to agree a payment plan. He had sorted through several loan offers and a bank statement before he came to the stiff, white envelope with the Frankfurt Am Main postmark. He hesitated before opening it. The heavy paper was of a quality that, in his experience, was used only by lawyers. He supposed that the cost did not matter to them as they would simply charge it to their customers.

384

He noticed how ragged and dirty his thumbnail looked as he used it to tear the envelope open. He frowned when he saw that the letter was written in English and frowned harder still when he found that an identical letter written in Polish accompanied it. The lines on his forehead grew tighter and tighter the more of the letter he read. He threw it aside when he had gone over it three or four times and snatched up his phone. He scrolled through the menu until he found the number of Aleksy Balcerzak, the family solicitor from his home village who had been fending off the bank and the developers and frustrating their hopes of taking possession of his farm.

'Did you get a copy of this letter?' He demanded when the old man finally answered.

'Yes, Piotr. I received it this morning. Isn't it wonderful? All of our prayers have been answered.'

'Is it? I cannot make head nor tail of this legal shit. Do I own the land or not? It sounds as if I do not!'

'Okay, okay! Let me explain, Piotr. This charitable trust has paid off the mortgage on the farm in its entirety and now has ownership of the farm. However, the trust itself is controlled by you and will be transferred to your heirs in the event of your death. This effectively means that the farm will remain in your family in perpetuity. You will not be able to sell it or raise loans against it but no bank or developer will ever be able to seize it and take it from you. In addition, the trust will pay for all labour and materials required to restore the farmhouse, windmill and grounds and will pay you a salary of two hundred and fifty thousand Zloty a year until the renovations are complete and the farm is up and running as a hotel.'

'So, who is behind this?' Piotr interrupted, his voice full of suspicion. 'I have never heard of this Ania Stachura Trust.'

'I did make some enquiries this afternoon.' The lawyer replied. 'The trust is administered by a German legal firm. All they would tell me is that your grandmother did someone a great kindness at some point in the past and this person, whoever they are, decided to repay that kindness by securing the future of the farm. I knew your grandmother well, Piotr. She was a determined and courageous woman. She did a great deal for people in this area even when that involved taking risks with her own safety and well-being. It does not surprise me that someone has remembered this and wishes to honour it. Just accept it and thank God that your prayers have been answered. It's a miracle!'

'What's the catch?' Piotr demanded, not yet convinced. 'There must be a catch!'

'There are conditions attached, but they all favour you. The first is that the trust must remain within your or your family's control. The second is that all of the rooms must be reserved for teachers from under-privileged areas of Poland for the duration of the high season. You will be responsible for administering the scheme and for advertising the free breaks to qualifying teachers, but you will be reimbursed for this work and you will receive the full market rate for every room that is occupied as part of the scheme. This income alone should keep the hotel afloat financially. Anything else that you earn will be pure profit.'

Piotr lay back on his bed when the call was ended and reached for what was left of the pork pie. He lifted it to his mouth but stopped to examine the cold pastry and the pale meat covered in its layer of jelly.

'Screw it!' He announced to the empty room as he reached for his phone and searched for the number of the local Chinese take-away. He decided that he would pay the extra and have it delivered directly to his door.

Hamburger Morgenpost – November 6th

Hamburger Polizei have announced the discovery of a World War Two era bunker on the outskirts of the city following an anonymous tip-off. A spokeswoman confirmed that large quantities of weapons, ammunition and explosives have been made safe and recovered from the site. She declined to comment on unconfirmed reports that the bunker had recently been accessed and unknown items removed from its interior. This is the third World War Two era bunker to be discovered in Germany this year. Polizeidirektor Hans Schneider refused to rule out any link between the three bunkers and the explosion that devastated an area of forest close to Duisburg in September of last year.

Printed in Great Britain
by Amazon

26f02fba-5b4c-4714-abfd-2a3b9e2d9c2bR01